BETWEEN TWO REALMS

MAZRINE L. AMARIS

Between Two Realms. Copyright © 2022 by Mazrine L. Amaris. All rights reserved.

ISBN: 978-0-6457092-0-9

ISBN: 978-0-6457092-1-6

ISBN: 978-0-6457092-2-3

NOTE TO READER

I want you to feel safe and seen. The following book contains themes that may be triggering to you. This book includes but is not limited to themes such as drug use/impairment, detailed violence and gore, sexual violence, sexual content, coercion/manipulation, domestic abuse.

If there is a possibility that any of these themes trigger you, I urge you to reconsider reading this book.

CONTENTS

Between Two Realms

Official Playlist

In My Head – Ariana Grande

Merry-Go-Round of Life – Joe Hisashi

Moonlight Densetsu (From "Sailor Moon") – Harpsona

Great Fairy Fountain (From "The Legend of Zelda") – Streaming Music Studios

Simple and Clean – Hikaru Utada

Middle of the Night – Loveless

Gravity – Sara Bareilles

To all dreamers and readers that escape into the realms of fantasy.
I'm glad you're here.

PROLOGUE

2001. MELBOURNE, VICTORIA.

"You know they're going to find you, right?" he said, his voice low and strained with frustration.

Leaning back against the kitchen sink, he breathed a heavy sigh as he combed his worn fingers through the greying ringlets that spilled over his forehead. The cacophony of cicadas that carried on outside the Taliesin household hushed at his words, as if they were intrigued by the conversation.

"They haven't yet and that means we're still safe," she said, deep in thought as she picked at the remnants of rice left on her dinner plate. The air was thick with palpable worry.

Sophie pushed her cheeks against the small gap of the kitchen door as she spied on her parents. Having swelled out of shape from the dry Australian heat, it left the perfect-sized space for her to peek through.

"This leaves us in danger." He paused. "...Danna please. You know that right?"

He grunted off the edge of the kitchen sink as he walked purposefully over to Sophie's mother. Her mussed silver hair and golden eyes sagged with exhaustion as she sat engrossed in the rice grains that remained from dinner.

He lifted her chin swiftly, forcing her to look at him in the eyes. "Danna, we can't live like this. We can't keep looking over our shoulders waiting for them to take you or her. It's not a life I'm willing to live." His voice softened and hitched as tears began to well.

"I know, but she's my daughter. Our daughter. She's only six. Where else is she to go?" A single frustrated tear found its way down the peak of Danna's cheeks.

Sophie hated the sight of her mother crying.

"We can't have her here. She'll—"

Sophie pushed the door open, determined to stop her mother's tears from flowing. Her parents' heads turned swiftly as they stared at her small form standing by the kitchen door.

The conversation stopped entirely.

"Mummy, is Daddy trying to get rid of me?" Sophie stared pointedly at her father as tears threatened to spill. She clenched her tiny fists as the temperature of the room rose with her anger. She knew they were talking about her and the thought of that made her stomach plummet as if some creature had died in it and its soul was clawing its way out of her mouth.

Danna stood swiftly. Her chair screeched as it pushed across the floor. She hurried over to where Sophie stood and knelt with outstretched arms planning to calm her.

Sophie dodged her mother's touch, pulling her face out of the way as hot angry tears ran down her sweating cheeks. Why did her mother and father want to get rid of her?

"Oh honey, what are you doing up? It's way past your bedtime." Danna swept Sophie's tears away with the pads of her thumbs. "No one is trying to get rid of you, okay? Mummy and Daddy are just having an adult conversation. It's nothing you have to worry about."

Sophie fixed her eyes on the floor trying her best to avoid her mother's eyes as she ran her hands up and down Sophie's little upper arms. Her body eased at her mother's touch – a steady tranquil stream made solely for soothing the fires that burned inside her too often.

Danna peered over her shoulder to Sophie's father who remained by the dining table. She signalled for him to leave with a quick flick of her chin. He dipped his chin in acknowledgement and turned on his heels to exit through the back security door.

Sophie tracked every movement.

Waiting until the door clicked shut, Danna swiftly returned her eyes to Sophie's. "I would never ever get rid of you, Sophie. You are my one and only daughter. I love you with every single piece of my heart. They'll have to steal you from right under my nose." She flicked Sophie's little nose. "Plus who would ever want to take care of a bossy boots dressed in unicorn jammies?"

Sophie squirmed as her mother tickled her milk-filled belly. The palpable worry that once filled the room dissipated with Sophie's sweet giggle. Sophie smiled through unshed tears and uncrossed her arms as she gave her mum a tight hug around her neck. Her cherub cheeks squished against her mother's neck as she buried her nose in her long silver hair. Her mother always smelled of sweet fresh strawberries.

"You promise with all your heart right, Mummy?"

"Cross my heart and hope to die." Danna pulled back from the hug and pinched Sophie's still-wet cheeks. "C'mon, Miss Bossy Boots, back into bed you go." She grabbed Sophie's little hand as she stood. "Maybe I can tell you more about the princess with silver and purple hair. Would you like that?" She peered down lovingly as Sophie rested her head on the back of her mother's hand.

Sophie nodded quickly. She loved the princess with silver and purple hair because the princess's hair was just like hers.

That night, Sophie dreamt of a beautiful blue and green swirling night sky.

1

20 Years Later

S ophie's phone blared with the alarm that she'd hit snooze on for the tenth time. 7 am.

Fuck this.

Nothing pained her more than waking up thinking it was the weekend, only to realise that unfortunately it was a Friday. It was some sick joke the universe played on her every single week.

Slapping the phone quiet, Sophie pulled her phone off the charger. She peeled back her bedsheets and shifted out of bed. The frosty bite of Melbourne mornings threatened to freeze her black silk camisole right off her and the gruelling jiujitsu practise she had last night didn't make waking up any easier. Despite twelve years of practise and competing in tournaments, her arms and legs were unbearably tight and sore.

Jumping into her grey bunny slippers and clipping her black bob-length hair up, Sophie trudged her way to the bathroom, lightly stretching as much as she could, ready to take on a full day of work.

Brush teeth, check messages, SPF, make-up and coffee – that's the way mornings usually went.

Sophie unlocked her phone to find three messages from Grayson.

Grayson was a guy she had just met through a dating app. So far, he was ticking a whole lot of boxes in the 'Sophie's husband material' list – a list she'd devised in her head based on the various car-crash relationships she'd had over the years and the string of ick-inducing dates she's had this year to date.

Morning gorgeous, I'll meet you after work today. 7 pm at The Celtic Inn. I've booked a table for two.

Sorry, make that 7:30 pm, think it might be a late one in the office today.

Can't wait to see you x

Perfect. Something to look forward to after the absolute dumpster fire that is work.

Sophie smiled to herself. She had a good feeling about Grayson. He was a humble marketing executive, he was ambitious, had manners, he was devastatingly handsome and it seemed like they were on the same page – what could possibly go wrong?

Sophie had been playing the dating game for almost two years and she was hoping Grayson would be the answer to her most-likely-unheard dating prayers.

For Sophie, the dating game was tough. All she ever wanted was the kind of love that was strong enough to soar you through the skies and kind enough to keep you warm at night. The kind of love that was brave enough to hold you tenderly even if it was scared to lose or hurt you. The kind of love that was just right – without explanation or doubts – was just simply and truly right.

What pained Sophie the most was that she had felt that kind of love before. Perhaps it was a figment of her dreams but nothing, or more so no one, had ever managed to ignite that level of fire and familiarity within her. It was a feeling she constantly chased and no matter how hard she tried to see things through, she could never seem to grasp it.

Stopping mid brush to respond, Sophie wiped the dripping toothpaste off her silk cami.

Can't wait. See you soon x

Sophie quickly dusted on her make-up and took three deep breaths. She stared at herself in the mirror and started her day off the right way – with her morning mantra.

"You are a badass fae queen. These mortals don't know you and the power you hold. Make them think twice before messing with you." A smile made of unrelenting determination made its way across her face. She'd clearly read too many fantasy books but to Sophie, nothing compared to the fae queens she obsessively read about; their unwavering swagger, battle-winning wit, close-call decision-making skills and their ability to live life to the fullest with no fucks given. Perhaps it wasn't a dream that catapulted Sophie's relationship standards into an unrealistic, non-existent realm and maybe all the smutty books she'd been reading were to blame. Regardless, if acting like a badass fae queen got her through the day, then a badass fae queen she would be – figuratively anyway.

Popping on her high-waisted black culottes and black cropped tee, Sophie made her way out of the bathroom while shoving her classic first-date outfit into her work bag – her tight black high-waisted jeans that did wonders for her curves, her black lacey corset-style bodice and her trusty black strappy heels. Hesitating, she shoved in her oversized blazer for good measure. Unfortunately, Melbourne weather was unpredictable at the best of times.

Sophie headed downstairs to the best part of her morning routine – coffee. It was the sweet nectar of the gods that brought Sophie back to life, the only thing that got her through Hell on Earth itself – work.

Jumping off the tram on La Trobe Street with her coffee cup in hand, Sophie popped on her headphones and blasted the sounds of Ariana Grande. If the fae world were real, Ariana would undoubtedly be the gorgeous fae bard or pixie who entertained everyone amidst giant extravagant feasts.

Sophie loved gloomy Melbourne mornings. The smell of locally roasted coffee wafting through the air always seemed to find her. The dings and bells of rickety trams, the rush of people heading into work and the threat of rain hanging in the air was a steady morning rhythm she grew fond of. Nothing beat it.

Sophie had been to Sydney and found it a little too crowded for her liking. She'd been to Perth which was extremely beautiful but too sleepy. She'd been to Brisbane which she found gorgeous, but it was beyond humid. For Sophie,

Melbourne was the perfect in between in terms of weather, and its people were always welcoming.

Walking in time with the beat of Ariana's music, Sophie reached the steps of her office building and pulled out her key fob to scan for entry.

Here we go, ladies. Sophie sighed while craning her neck to look up the tall office building. 'Plaster on that big fake smile and pretend you love what you do' was the name of the game at Orsus – the powerhouse creative agency in Melbourne – and boy was Sophie good at it.

Smiling to the lovely receptionist on her way in, Sophie headed straight for the lifts, hoping that having her headphones in would ward off any morning people who wanted to start an awkward elevator conversation. Being the marketing lead for the entire agency had its perks but dealing with morning people wasn't one of them.

Sophie had always believed in doing what you loved as a job. A younger Sophie would have killed to be in this position, but as years went by and the notion of 'influencers' as opposed to 'people of influence' became the focus, she lost her passion for marketing and began to do the opposite of what she believed in. It felt like the world had put out her fire. She was stuck in this weird place in her career where she felt like she was too old to jump ship and start a totally different career. While her current job paid the bills and afforded her a lifestyle, she felt like she was destined to do more – like she had a higher purpose than sitting behind a computer screen all day. It was a feeling she couldn't shake.

Hopping out of the elevator, Sophie opened the double glass doors to Orsus and made a beeline towards her desk.

Thank the gods Lorien is here already.

Lorien was speed typing what was sure to be a passive aggressive email to one of her clients.

"Good morning, Lorrie, you're looking glam for a casual Friday. I like it!" Sophie wagged her eyebrows and beamed at Lorrie as she pulled off her headphones. Lorien was Sophie's best friend who happened to be the digital lead role at Orsus. It meant they sat next to each other every day for thirty-eight hours a week – a dream come true.

Lorien was the only person that kept Sophie sane and the major reason why Sophie hadn't rage quit the only thing financially fuelling her reading habits. It was safe to say, she kept Sophie grounded.

Lorien peered up from beneath her thick black frames and pushed aside her wavy red fringe. She was short and plump like a sugar plum fairy.

"Good morning to you too, Miss I-only-wear-black," Lorien smirked while furiously typing.

Gasping dramatically in feigned shock, Sophie crossed her hands over her chest. "Och, you wound me and also it's a classic Melbournite uniform, didn't you know?" Sophie pulled off her work bag from her shoulder and placed her headphones down by the computer.

"Ugh that blasted know it all! He keeps asking for amendments to a Word document which funnily enough he can actually edit himself. He's absolutely useless BUT," Lorrie paused slightly while a faint woosh signalled her email being sent off, "what's more important is have you read chapter fifty-five yet?" She sat right up, brimming with absolute excitement as she waited for Sophie's answer.

"Judging by my lack of excitement, I'm going to say no. I haven't. Is it that good? I've only chipped away at the first few chapters and I'm in love already!" Sophie swooned. "How on earth does she make us feel this deeply so quickly? Ugh. And don't you dare spoil anything!" Sophie pointed a finger from her desk, promising retribution if Lorien spilled a drop of information.

Lorien pinched her forefinger and thumb, motioned the zipping of her mouth and dramatically threw the figurative key away.

Together, Sophie and Lorien had read the same books since they were thirteen and had just started reading the newly released sequel by their favourite author. Fantasy was their favourite genre – from the fae, to hunters, gods, goddesses, supernatural beings and to all the raunchy things they got up to at night. It was impossible to not... get sucked in and immersed into the fantastical realms – once a Twihard, always a Twihard.

"I promise, hand on heart, that I won't spoil it for you, but you have to promise to live-tweet me your reaction. Please. I need a play by play from your point of view. I'm still reeling from reading it." Lorien dramatically swooned as she leaned back in her seat, no doubt replaying the scene in her head.

"Absolutely. You know I will, but not tonight. I've got a date with... drum roll please... Grayson!" Sophie managed to squeal from her seat while doing a little victory dance. This would be their first time meeting face to face after weeks of texting and late-night phone calls.

"You mean Mr Tall Dark and Handsome that you showed me the other day?"

"Yep. He's booked us a table for two at The Celtic Inn, 7.30 pm and your gal is excited." Sophie picked up the remainder of her coffee and sculled it.

"Oh my goodness, yes I love this for you! You have a good feeling about him, right? Could he be, dare I say it, the one?" Lorien seemed much more intrigued by Sophie's impending date than she just was with chapter fifty-five.

Sophie paused, unsure if she'd be jinxing herself if she let the universe in on her feelings. "You know what? I think he could be. I don't want to jinx it, but I think my two-year dry spell is coming to an end." Absolutely smitten, Sophie smiled to herself.

Sophie wondered if anyone else felt like time was punishingly warped after lunch. It felt as if there weren't four hours between one and five but in fact, there were eight.

Finally having the chance to sit down after her back-to-back meetings, she pulled out her phone to check for any messages.

Ah. One missed call from Mum. She hoped nothing was wrong.

Quickly ducking out into the foyer and dialling her mother back, Sophie chewed away at her lower lip, anxious that something had gone awry.

"Hi, honey!" a beautiful warm voice trilled from the other side of the phone. Danna was chirpy as always. Sophie blew out a silent breath of relief. Now that her mum lived by herself, Sophie had become one of those always-worried daughters.

"Hey, Mum, everything alright? You sound like you're outside. Are you gardening?" On the other side of the phone, birds chirped and the spray of a garden hose swaying back and forth rattled through. Sophie could see them already – the roses and lavender that her mum grew in her quaint front yard.

"Yes of course I'm alright, honey. And yes, I'm just watering the garden at the moment..." The sound of a garden hose twisting shut squeaked through the phone. "I just wanted to remind you that we're having brunch tomorrow in Brunswick. I know you're such a busy bee, so I'm calling to verbally confirm that you will be there in the flesh, preferably not hungover from whatever Friday-night shenanigans you've got planned." Danna chuckled as the last few words left her mouth.

Once upon a time, Sophie had rocked up to a family brunch absolutely fried while wearing the same clothes she'd donned the night before. Sophie was so hungover that she ordered fried eggs on toast and in return, the cafe got a plate full of scrambled eggs to clean up with a touch of gin. Her mum had never let her live it down since.

"Mum! It was ONE time. I assure you I will not be late nor hungover, nor will I throw up on my plate." Danna always had a way of making Sophie laugh, no matter the situation. Even if it was the shittiest day in the world, she'd always pull Sophie up from whatever hole she decided to bury herself in.

"Good. I haven't seen you in weeks and I miss you terribly. I think I'm getting another bout of adult acne from all the stress of missing you."

"Highly doubt that, but seriously, Mum, you've never had a pimple in all of my twenty-six years of life. Stop being dramatic."

Danna's warm laughter filled Sophie's ears, then paused. A short exhale followed. "Your dad asked about you."

Sophie and her dad rarely spoke, and when they did, it was extremely clinical. She found it hard being around him, ever since that balmy night he walked out their family home almost twenty years ago and abandoned them for reasons she didn't fully understand. It took several years for him to reach out to them again to make amends. Let's say he didn't receive a warm welcome; well, at least not from Sophie.

"Just the usual 'how's she going?' I presume?"

"He's trying, Sophie."

"Sure." Sophie paused to check the time on her watch. "What time should I meet you tomorrow?"

"Twelve thirty. Please don't be late, okay? I've been waiting for this big breakfast special for weeks and, Sophie darling, you will not rain on my parade." Danna's voice lifted with what Sophie knew was a smile.

"Yes, Mum, of course. I will be there twelve thirty sharp, ready to scoff a big breakky with you. I wouldn't miss it for anything." Sophie smiled right back. "Hey, Mum, I've got to get back to work, but let me know if you need anything between now and then, okay? Love you."

"Love you with every piece of my heart, darling. See you tomorrow. Bye, honey."

Pushing her phone in her back pant pocket, Sophie made her way back to her desk and glanced at the desktop clock. 4.57 pm. *Ugh. Finally.*

2

The Celtic Inn was a gorgeous former Irish pub turned high-end bar, hidden in the dead end of one of Chinatown's dark and questionable alleyways. It was an odd placement but one that drew in crowds.

Laden with lush velvet green chesterfield couches, checkerboard tiled flooring, intimate seating arrangements and a lavish oak bar with a smorgasbord of liquid courage to boot, The Celtic Inn was as fancy yet humble as bars got in Melbourne. The air was layered with trills of jazz music. It had the mood lighting and all – a perfect place for a first date.

Sophie waited by the large ceiling-to-floor green double doors, constantly checking the time on her phone. 7.34 pm.

Okay. Let's give him another five minutes. But no message, seriously?

By Sophie's books, if you weren't ten minutes early then technically you were late. While punctuality was important, what was even more important was communication – especially for a date. Perhaps he was struggling with his Uber, Sophie thought.

The night was starting to dip in temperature. Soft breezes danced through the alleyway and a light sprinkle of rain threatened to make an appearance. Sophie did a once-over on her outfit.

If this date turns into a pile of shit, at least this outfit is cute.

7.45 pm. No message. Sophie felt like she'd checked her phone at least ten times but gave it another two minutes before she'd head in and have a few cheeky beverages by herself.

In the distance, Sophie heard the flustered sounds of someone running full pelt towards the end of the alleyway where the green doors towered behind Sophie. The sharp sound of soles clacking against the cobblestones echoed back and forth.

The alleyway was dark but the vague outline of a six-foot-five man with broad shoulders became clearer as the clacking against cobblestones grew louder. Before she could even see him, her senses were hit with the hint of cedar wood and mint.

Grayson.

His profile photos certainly did not do him justice. Grayson was an absurdly tall, dark and handsome man – exactly how Lorrie described him. He stood a giant compared to Sophie's five-foot-two height even with heels on. His huge arms strained against the flannel shirt he rolled up to his forearms. Dark jeans and boots were the bow to wrap up his perfectly sharp features and dark chiselled beard. If the fae world were real, Grayson would be a noble knight and in his spare time, he chopped wood without a shirt on – that would be guaranteed.

And just like that, Sophie felt as nervous as a bag of cats at a greyhound meet. The nervousness lodged itself in her throat, waiting to make a fool of her as she tried to form some sort of greeting.

"Sophie, I'm so sorry. My phone died. We got lost, so I jumped out and sprinted my way here. I'm so sorry I'm late." He crouched down, catching a breath with his hands braced against his knees.

Grayson was even more stunning in person. Sophie stood there, her jaw ajar and her chest tightening ever so slightly.

Wow. Okay. Breathe, Sophie, you bloody idiot. You are a badass fae queen, so you can and will hold a valuable conversation without drooling all over yourself – preferably using your words.

A moment of silence went by as she tried to pick up her jaw from the floor. Sophie finally blurted, "Oh my goodness, no, no, all good. I wasn't even waiting for that long. It's so lovely to finally meet you." She stepped in closer towards him for a hug.

It felt easy with Grayson, natural even. Sophie's heart pattered, remembering the late-night phone calls they had bonded over during the last few weeks. Reaching to put her arms around his neck, Grayson slipped his arms around her waist as they shared an intimate hug that lingered past a greeting. They pulled apart reluctantly.

His dark eyes met hers of purple. "You are absolutely stunning, Sophie." His big hands lingered by the curve of her back. Grayson shook his head as if to shake himself out of a trance. Sophie tried her best not to avert her gaze – a habit that rarely manifested nowadays but occasionally surfaced when she was nervous. Her purple, pale eyes were an anomaly, as her mother had described. When she was born, doctors feared that she was blind. After several tests, her eyes were deemed functional – normal even – though that didn't stop the other kids at school from calling her an alien, among other things. People had a lot to say about her eyes, but Grayson didn't. His eyes lingered as he took her right hand in his left. "Shall we?" He gestured with his other arm towards the doors of The Celtic Inn.

Sophie smiled sweetly and nodded. A tiny little spark ignited in her gut.

Seated in the corner of the room, it felt like they were the only souls there. They'd flown through the basics; family, friends, interests and their plans for the future. They could have kept going all night.

Grayson was charming, with his chiselled face and quirky quips. They liked the same food – Greek – and his favourite movie franchise was Star Wars. Sophie was pinching herself with excitement.

He could really be the one.

A lone saxophone player rattled off the notes to Amy Winehouse's *There Is No Greater Love*, adding to the warmth that The Celtic Inn provided.

Grayson made his way back to their corner of the bar, where two single chesterfield accent chairs faced each other. He'd gone to grab them their second round of drinks. Grayson had a smug confidence about him as if he had something to prove. Sophie couldn't quite place her finger on it.

Grayson handed over her gin and tonic before sitting directly in front of her. Almost knee to knee with him, Sophie let her heart flutter at the promise of what they could be. If this date didn't turn out right, she would have to call it quits on the dating game, Sophie thought.

"Hey, I hope this doesn't come across weird, but I'd love to take a picture of you. You know, just to remember how amazing this night was and how beautiful you look. Is that okay?"

Sophie found it an odd request. Tilting her head slightly at the question, she inclined her head in permission, appreciating that he had even asked at all. "Umm... yeah sure. I guess?"

Considering how great this night was going, what harm could be done? It could be something they'd look back on fondly in the future.

Grayson pulled out his phone from his breast pocket. Sophie furrowed her brows at the sight of it. *Wasn't his phone drained of juice?* It was the reason he claimed he couldn't contact her. Perhaps he'd been charging it in his pocket, Sophie thought.

Trying not to think too much of it, Sophie took another sip of her drink and posed for the camera.

"One, two, three, cheese!" Grayson marvelled at the picture he took. "Wow, you are honestly the most stunning woman I've ever met. Honest to God." He placed his phone back in his shirt pocket.

Sophie paused at those words. She thought herself to be average – a solid six, maybe even a seven if she deigned to wash her hair. The compliments from Grayson made her feel unsettled. Unsure what to say in response, Sophie saluted him with her drink in hand and took a long sip.

"I've also been meaning to ask, actually, about that tattoo you've got on your forearm. It's so unique, where did you get it from?" He reached over to run his fingers across the tattoo on her left arm – a torturous touch leaving a trail of goosebumps in his wake.

Sophie cleared her throat. "It's a funny story. I don't remember how it all happened. It would've been my eighteenth birthday. I'd been drinking a LOT with my girlfriends, as you do at an eighteenth, and I woke up the next day with it." Sophie turned her arm, examining the ink. "Funny thing is that it didn't really hurt. You could say my mum took it well enough – well enough to not speak about it again I guess." Sophie chuckled, thinking back to the time she woke up with the intricate, Polynesian-Asian-fusion style tattoo of patterns and vines starting at the crook of her elbow, wrapping around her entire forearm and hand.

It looked like an ancient language or script that stopped halfway across the back of her hand and tapered all the way onto her forefinger, forming the shape of a key. That tattoo was inked in deep dark black and so detailed, as if it were laser-printed on. It was as if the artist had inhumanly stable hands. It was a masterpiece.

Sophie wanted to get more tattoos from the artist but couldn't remember for the life of her where or how she got it in the first place. And when it came to her mothers reaction, 'well enough' was putting it mildly. Her mother shat bricks when she discovered the inked artwork on Sophie, the day after her birthday. All she could do was stare, from Sophie's face to the tattooed forearm and back to her face. Not a word of reprimand left her mouth, just silence. Danna never spoke about it again.

"One day, I'll have to hear the full version from your mum." He let go of her forearm reluctantly and his eyes hitched at her lips as they travelled up, searching for something in her eyes. "Tell me more about yourself." He smiled while taking a sip of his drink.

"Well, Grayson, what else do you want to know?" A hint of a flirty side smile appeared across Sophie's face. She looked from underneath her long lashes, making sure her right dimple made itself known.

"Well, I'd like to know how a beautiful woman like yourself has managed to stay single for so long. As if no one has managed to nab you yet? What's the story there? Too many exes in the closet?" he teased, taking a longer sip of his drink, a bead of sweat appearing just by his temple.

Though it was a joke, Sophie felt a little stab of self-consciousness. Grayson was sort of right. While Sophie had a fair share of semi-serious relationships, she had the unshakable habit of tightly holding on to an idea of a person as opposed to seeing who they really were. Ultimately, she'd get her heart broken thinking she could fix someone with her love. Sophie learnt the hard way that you couldn't help people who didn't want to be helped.

"It's something I ask myself every day. I'd like to say I've a particular taste and what I'm after is not what everyone else wants." Her mind trailed back to the failed relationships she'd had. All things considered, she'd learnt a valuable lesson. She would never let herself get hurt again. Not that deeply. Never. Again.

"And what is it you're after?" Grayson tilted his head inquisitively while circling the rim of his cup with his forefinger. He glanced down at Sophie's plump glossed lips and leaned in closer.

Sophie watched the hypnotic circles his fingers made. She noticed that his hands were worn from work which was at odds with his job as a marketing executive.

Sophie leaned in closer and popped her drink down on the table. Her breasts peeked above the bodice she wore. Crossing her legs over, Sophie tucked her short black hair behind her ears. She knew exactly what she was doing. "I'm after love. I think that scares a lot of people." She glanced down at his lips this time. Her chest tightened with anticipation, as he slightly parted his lips in response. She wasn't just after any kind of love – she was after the proverbial 'one'. The kind of love that felt like the lightness of soaring through the skies or warm like the sunshine that covered your skin on a cold winter's day. With each failed date, she grew weary from the search and wondered if the other half of her soul was searching for her too. The little flame that burned in her heart for them told her to keep going. To keep searching. Sophie hoped that she'd find them soon.

Electricity flitted over both their bodies and both parties were all too aware of it. It was then she noticed a flicker in his eyes – like something had flipped inside him. A wicked excitement now gleamed in his eyes. Sophie's gut instinct, the force inside that guided her always, pushed her to take a closer look.

"It doesn't scare me." He stared into her piercing purple eyes.

The sweat the pooled across his brow didn't ease. It was cold in the bar. Her eyes darted down towards the slight tremble in his marred hands. Her mind hitched against that detail. He hadn't mentioned any labour-intensive hobbies that would warrant worn hands. Perhaps he was actually a lumberjack, Sophie thought. The guiding force inside her gut pulled at her again. It tried to tell her something, but she just wasn't sure what.

She shook her head to refocus on reality and stared back into his dark eyes. Where she saw a spark of excitement now lived determination – something entirely feral. Unease roiled inside Sophie's stomach.

"But you don't know me. Not yet, anyway. The love I'm after is hard to find..." Something Sophie couldn't quite grasp was that she'd felt that intense, burning love before.

In each relationship, her body constantly battled with her mind. It was instinctual. It was a force within herself that constantly pulled her into a different direction. It told her that the relationship she had wasn't right and that there was something else waiting for her.

The force felt like a tether, but as she moved along it, she couldn't find the other end. It felt as if it were frayed and worn or fell into another realm. Despite that empty feeling, the end of that tether was something that she'd never give up trying to find.

Sophie's eyes caught Grayson's trembling hands. His phone began to buzz with notifications. She cleared her throat as the distracting buzzes slowed her love-filled thoughts to a grinding halt.

Grayson looked as though he was about to jump out of his own skin as his phone kept pinging. Maintaining eye contact, he slowly reached for his phone. He fumbled. The phone almost dropped between his huge hands.

"Grayson, are you alright? You're sweating profusely."

"Yeah, sorry. I'm alright... Honestly, I'm just a little nervous. I can't help but feel like this is the start of something beautiful." He smiled, a little too intensely into her eyes. There was something sinister beneath that smile. His eyes grew ten shades darker, like a lion focused in on its prey. Locked and loaded. Ready to devour.

This didn't feel right at all.

Blinking to focus, Sophie's head spun. Pulsing and growing heavy, her head lulled. Her skin turned balmy and warm, even though it was still cold in the bar. A chill ran down her back. "Sorry, did you say you worked in an office as a...?" She was slurring.

Sophie pinched her fingers over the bridge of her nose, trying to straighten herself. The second gin and tonic had hit her fast. Maybe a bit too fast. *I should've eaten something for dinner*, Sophie thought.

"Oh, I'm a marketing exec at Clarity Creative actually..." he said calmly. His tone was a contrast to what the sweat pooling around his forehead indicated.

Clarity Creative... huh. She'd never heard of it, and it was her job to know who the big players in the industry were. Sophie struggled through the heaviness building in her head.

Grayson wiped his large hand across his brow, ridding the sweat that had accumulated there. His phone continued to ping. It was distracting and awfully loud.

The room was spinning. Sophie promised then and there that she'd stop drinking. Clearly she was getting too old to be doing this drinking thing.

"Hey, you know what, whatever it is, it sounds urgent. You should tend to it. I won't be going anywhere." Sophie smiled, slightly frustrated by the interruption and the blurriness that continued to build inside her head. Her mind felt foggy, she felt off balance. Kneading the tension in her neck, Sophie tried to blink the fog out of her eyes.

"Sorry, do you mind? Let me just duck outside and grab this. I won't be long. Sorry. Just stay put." Grayson jumped up a lot faster than Sophie anticipated. He glanced back at her with his charming smile. He pocketed his phone and skirted around their seated area towards the back door that led outside.

Sophie skulled the rest of her drink in his absence, looking down at the clear liquid courage that had... a thin white powdery residue sitting sinisterly at the bottom of it.

Jesus Christ in a 2002 Toyota Camry. Holy shit.

In all the gin and tonics Sophie had consumed in her lifetime, she was sure as hell that gin and tonics weren't meant to have a thin, awfully sketchy, white residue. Perhaps it was on the other side of the glass and not actually in it.

Eyes widening at the sight, Sophie hurriedly took the sleeve of her oversized blazer and wiped the bottom of the glass to make sure that the questionable white powder was on the other side of the glass and not infused with the liquid she'd just consumed.

Placing the glass down, Sophie examined the sleeve with both her hands. Nothing. Absolutely clean. *Fuck.*

She dipped her fingers into the bottom of the glass, hoping to the gods that her fingers did not meet some form of gritty substance.

She lifted her fingers. Between her thumb and finger lay a thin gritty film. Nervousness balled up in her throat and her stomach clenched in fear. This was no normal gin and tonic.

It explained why Sophie's head felt like it was about to fall off her neck and why everyone in the room was rugged up in jackets while she was basically sweating out of every single orifice.

Okay, Sophie. Breathe.

The bodice she was wearing was too hot, and tight. She had to take it off.

Stop. Wait. She couldn't take it off, she was in public. *Where is that son of a bitch Grayson?* She knew it was too good to be true. Why did she even agree to this? *Okay. Focus, Sophie.* She needed to get out of this situation. Stat.

Her arms were jelly wading through water, and she could no longer grasp her cup properly. Her glass was clearly made of melting ice and it was slipping through her fingers.

The room was so much darker than she remembered and the people in the bar now spoke much louder.

I've been drugged. Shit.

Sophie gawked at the realisation. Panic roiled deep in her gut. She felt like she was a freshly birthed baby deer who had never walked a day in her life. Through her blurred vision, she spotted the large outline of Grayson striding towards her.

Run, Sophie, run damn it. Move your fucking legs. She couldn't. This was the deadliest game of stuck in the mud she'd ever played. Her legs were leaden.

Grayson bent down on one knee, bracing Sophie's cold-to-the-touch arms, looking her dead in the eyes. All Sophie saw was darkness shrouding his figure and an unsaid promise for something terrible. She felt like vomiting. She hoped with all her might that her mind would somehow break through the effects of whatever drug she'd just ingested. She hoped that it would signal her poor stomach to violently projectile vomit, straight into the face of this absolute creep. Of course, that didn't happen at all.

"Hey, Sophie, you're not looking too good. Looks like you're ready to head on home. The boys will be so excited to see you." His sweet saccharine smile was made entirely of nightmares.

Sophie's stomach dropped.

His worried tone juxtaposed the words he uttered.

Her jaw went slack. Her lips buzzed with numbness. Her hearing was muffled, and her sight blurred viciously. Sophie knew that this was game over. She couldn't even function like a normal human being let alone alert anyone in the vicinity that she had been drugged. She was being fed to a pack of dogs and for no known reason.

"What... boys... why?" Sophie managed to push from her lips. Her eyes were hooded and heavy. The room spun on its head and her head started to bob. Lights glowed feverishly and seemed to dance around the room.

Grayson picked up the blazer from her side and draped it gracefully around her warm shoulders. The typically endearing act sent chills down Sophie's spine. Her mind imploded trying to wave giant red flags. It tried its best to communicate effectively with her own body – to back out of this situation immediately.

He gently lifted his hand, tucking her hair back off her face and lifted her chin so that she could look into his blackened eyes.

"I've just caught the sweetest treat and it was so much easier than I thought. You should be less trusting of strangers, Sophie. Especially when they hand you a drink." He winked while licking his lips.

Was this guy seriously giving her a pep talk about strangers, when he was the exact stranger mothers cautioned their too-naïve daughters about?

The audacity of this man. God. Wow. Hello lumberjack arms. Fuck. Damn it, Sophie. Focus. Okay. Breathe. What would a badass fae queen do in this situation? Hmmm. Sophie's thoughts muddied amid the chaos. She struggled to maintain a logical thread of thinking.

A badass fae queen would most likely fall back on her years of training in the battlefields as a warrior and assassinate the offender in front of everyone here – preferably with some sort of iron blade infused with the bones of her ancestors' enemies. Sophie giggled at the thought. Her head swayed as she did.

Option one was out of the question given that Sophie couldn't even string a sentence together, and the blaring fact that she lacked years of assassin training – note, that actually wasn't available anywhere in Australia. She'd jokingly tried doing a Google search which yielded nothing. Nada. Zilch.

Option two, Sophie. What's option two? C'mon.

Sophie wracked her muddled brain. A fae queen would make a scene. She'd make a scene and then she'd run for it. Slim chance it was going to work but she had to do *something*. Perhaps she could lull him into thinking she was more incapacitated than she was. Considering she was already quite fucked up, acting more drunk than she already wouldn't be too difficult of a task.

Grayson pulled Sophie up from the lounge by her two delicate hands and wrapped his arm around her shoulders. Going for the Oscar she knew she deserved, Sophie leaned into his side, barely reaching the height of his chest to lean on with her head.

Grayson guided her toward the main double-door exit, his phone still buzzing with who knows what kind of disgusting messages. To outsiders, they looked like a smitten couple who were ducking off for an intimate night after a very successful date. Sophie was screaming internally for help and couldn't control her face enough to even utter a word or plea of help.

Unfortunately for Sophie, the numbing effects of the drug were only building. Whatever Grayson had made her ingest was a strong tranquilliser of some sort to render her helpless like this.

Sophie's legs flip flopped underneath her, servant to whichever direction he was leading them to. Grayson dipped his chin, lips lowering closer to her ear. "You're burning through what I gave you oddly fast, my dear. Maybe it's because you're so tiny. All the more delicious to devour, I promise."

Bile rose in the back of her throat. Sophie pretended that her legs went from underneath her as she fumbled and grabbed a tighter grip on Grayson. She tried to delay the inevitable the only way she physically knew how.

Option two, here we go. If she could lull him into a false sense of security, she'd have the element of surprise up her sleeve.

"You weren't meant to get to this stage until about 1 am. It's only 11 pm. Well, it's as close to it at least. I'll have to top you up when we get there." He snickered. He actually snickered.

Grayson held Sophie tightly around the waist to keep her from falling. The scene unfolding before her eyes was bone chilling. Sophie needed to vomit. The thought of what awaited her beyond those double doors almost sobered her up. Almost.

They were so close to the exit. The dread that holed up inside her stomach continued to build.

Option two, come on, option two. She had to make a scene. She needed to make a scene.

It was then she could feel her head slowly start to clear as if a thick heavy veil was lifting – too slowly. Maybe she could pretend to pass out? And then the security guards would come to her rescue and seek some sort of medical attention. Oh god, but what if Grayson blamed it on how many drinks she's had, and the security guards simply handed her over peacefully to the devil himself to take her home? *Fuck. That couldn't happen.* But what if it was her only hope? Sophie mulled over her options.

There were people around and these people could help her. If she stepped foot outside of this bar, who knew what was going to happen? What if he topped her up like he promised? There were too many dark alleyways to navigate.

Sophie was sweating profusely, and the adrenalin lodged in her chest was fighting to take over whatever hold the drug had on her. The security guards were too busy admitting people into the venue and checking IDs to even notice the sweaty, messy dumpster fire of a situation she was in.

Perhaps it was the panic that roiled through her veins or a guardian angel deigning to intervene, but her vision became crisper. Her mind cleared through the muddiness of the drugs and, now, it was just a matter of opportunity. While she knew how to fight, the sheer mass of Grayson put her at a disadvantage. She had to time her escape. She had to time it right.

Grayson held her closer to his chest as they walked by the security guards, playing the part of a caring boyfriend all too well.

"Hey! Hold up!" someone shouted from behind them in the hallway. Grayson stopped dead in his tracks and tightened his grip possessively around her shoulders. "Bro, you didn't pay off your tab. Do you mind doing that before you leave?" The small male bartender shouted down the hall, not caring who heard... causing a scene.

Thank you. Whoever is watching over me tonight, thank you. Sophie almost whimpered with relief, but adrenalin told her this was her moment. She couldn't stop. Not yet.

Grayson sighed, clearly embarrassed that he was being pulled up in front of the group of people waiting to get inside The Celtic Inn. The patrons waiting in line stared on awkwardly at the outburst.

Gathering all the adrenalin and courage she could muster from every single facet of her body and mind, Sophie twisted out from underneath the blazer around her shoulders, hinged at the hips and kicked back as hard as she could, heels first, right into Grayson's balls.

She'd never heard a man being castrated before, but she imagined the sound that came out of Grayson's mouth then and there was the sound that the particular form of punishment induced.

Everything played out in slow motion.

Bullseye. Sophie felt her high heel puncture what would've been his pants. Using the momentum of the contact, Sophie ran into the dark alleyways of Melbourne's Chinatown.

From the corner of her eye, she saw Grayson's giant figure double over, cupping his jewels as if doing so would make him feel better.

Take that, Satan!

Running in heels on cobblestone was no easy feat. It felt like she had snapped her own ankles ten times over and she was unsure how far she'd even managed to run.

Leaning up against a graffitied wall that smelled awfully like urine, Sophie peeled off her heels and tied the loose straps to the belt loops of her black jeans. She had to keep moving.

The ground was cold, gritty and bits of god knows what clung to her feet. All she could hear were wolf-whistles from bystanders as she sprinted away. She didn't know where she was running to, but she knew she had to keep moving. Grayson could very well find her and take her to whatever end he had intended for her.

Picking up the pace, her breath loud in her ears, Sophie kept running.

In the distance, the faint crackle of trams clanged through the air. Bourke street.

Great. She was relatively far away from Chinatown – by foot anyway.

The city lights were bright, momentarily blinding Sophie. She slowed to a jog by all the shops, scrunching her eyes in attempts to adjust to the city's luminosity.

Finally, Sophie had the courage to turn around and check if she was being followed. Nothing. All clear. No trace. No hungry giant lumberjack giving chase.

She whimpered, letting her tears catch up with what was going on. She wiped underneath her eyes with the back of her hands. Locals were milling about as if nothing were out of place. People laughed, cheered and chattered away.

She couldn't believe what had just unfolded.

Sophie slowed her walking down to a crawling pace. The cold bite of Melbourne weather never felt more cruel. Her skin pebbled from the cold. She was no longer sweating from the drugs that Grayson had forced into her.

Crossing her bare arms over her chest to ward off the cold, Sophie couldn't have felt any smaller. She looked like a crazed woman but she didn't care. She was almost sold off into some sort of crazy human trafficking ring, or worse. Her organs could have been sold off to the highest bidder and she would've died without saying goodbye to her mum. She would've died not knowing who her true love was.

Her face was burned from the cold wind and wet. She was crying. Softly. She couldn't stop. Like a constant stream, her tears knew no end and her throat ached from the pain of it. She couldn't believe what had just happened.

Taking a left on Swanston Street, she headed on foot towards Flinders Street.

She racked her brain, thinking of reasons why it was her tonight. Did she seem weak? Like some sort of easy prey? Why her?

She knew he was too good to be true. Grayson was too charming. He seemed to have the right answer to every question she had, like a seasoned predator.

She should've known. She should've called him out. She should've but she was too desperate in her search for love, and he was clearly a seasoned professional. She couldn't begin to imagine what other women, or how many other women, fell victim to his Prince Charming act. She couldn't believe she'd fallen for it. She was smarter than that — or so she thought.

Beyond disappointed in herself and unable to stop sobbing, Sophie walked herself to the back steps of Saint Paul's Cathedral just on the corner of Swanston and Flinders Street. The tall, dark church loomed over her as if to say she should have known better. The oncoming crowd gave her a wide berth too, eyeing her oddly as she sobbed on.

She just needed to catch a break. She needed to digest what happened and perhaps cry until she couldn't anymore.

Sitting down on the quiet cold steps, Sophie let out a frustrated cry. Her throat burned from disappointment. The grit of the steps bit into her feet and through her jeans. She felt so raw and angry, her chest almost bursting from the frustration that welled there. Hot tears felt like acid as they swam down her frosted cheeks. It was so cold, and she was all alone.

Pulling out her phone from her back pocket, the screen brightness blinding her momentarily, Sophie propped up an arm to support her forehead. Tears that pooled in her eyes splashed onto the screen as she struggled to unlock it. Two messages from Lorrie.

> *How's the date going with Mr Handsome?*

> *You haven't responded so I can only assume you're having the best time of your life. I hope you've got some juicy goss to share with me come Monday. Stay safe sis x*

Sophie turned to the floral bush she sat by and vomited from all the adrenalin and the thought of Grayson that bubbled to the front of her mind.

The burn in her throat was a welcome distraction. If only Lorien knew. If only she knew how terrified and alone Sophie felt, and how sick to the stomach she was. She couldn't even bring herself to pick up the phone and dial Lorien. Sophie knew her best friend would force her to report what had happened to the police immediately, but Sophie was just so tired and too distraught to face it. She was not ready to deal with questions. What if she was grilled by a narrow-minded police officer, asking why she was wearing what she was wearing, as if she'd welcomed this kind of behaviour with her decision in clothing? There was no way she would be able to deal with that. She felt so broken at this very moment that all she wanted to do, to refrain from vomiting or crying, was to just sit and breathe.

Hours had passed and Sophie remained seated on the cold steps of Saint Paul's Cathedral. The streets had quietened to a happy hum of people. The trams had slowed in frequency and couples littered the streets, embracing each other in the cold weather.

Sophie was frozen in her bodice and jeans, but at least she'd stopped crying.

She ebbed and flowed between questionable whale-sounding sobs and soft sniffles, though her head was now much clearer. She could see properly and if she tried hard enough, she knew she could walk straight. She wasn't back to her normal self, but she was getting there.

Sophie pulled out her phone again to check the time. It was 1.53 am.

She'd spent the last two hours crying her face off. The last train back to West Footscray was scheduled to leave at 2.05 am from Flinders Street Station, which meant she had precisely twelve minutes to get her shit together, grab some water then haul ass to Platform 4 and head home.

Legs numb from having sat for two hours straight and the number of drinks and god knows what kind of drug she'd ingested, Sophie stood up.

Using the pads of her middle fingers to clear the running mascara from beneath her eyes, she combed her fingers through her short hair and took three deep breaths, peering up to the skies, hoping whatever god or angel up there looking after her tonight would give her a break and make her way home a safe one.

In the distance, a star burned brighter for only a millisecond.

3

Water bottle in hand, head hung low between her knees, seated on the steel seats at Flinders Street train station, Sophie looked like an outright mess. She gave zero fucks though. Her heels, still tied to the belt loops of her jeans, dug into her side as she sat.

"The next train to arrive on platform four arrives in three minutes." The tinny computer voice echoed across the empty platforms.

Perfect. She couldn't wait to get home to her bed. She couldn't wait to sink into her mattress and just disappear.

Pulling out earphones from her purse, she plugged them into her phone and popped on Joe Hisaishi's 'Merry-Go-Round of Life'. This was her happy place.

Sophie closed her eyes and breathed deeply, filling her chest to the brim with air. She imagined a beautiful blue-and-green swirling sky above lush green mountains – the place she ran to when things in this world got a bit too overwhelming.

Getting lost in the beautiful strings of the song, she pushed out the thoughts of Grayson and focused on getting home. Turning the volume up on full blast, all she wanted to do – in fact, all she could do – was get lost in the soundtrack.

The rumbles of approaching and departing trains vibrated through her feet. The strings of the song lulled her heart to calm. Finally, a second of relaxation.

Sophie looked up at the oncoming train and stood up while tucking her phone away into the front pocket of her jeans. The train docked itself by the platform. Mindlessly, she opened the train door and took a seat against the window along a three-person seat.

Trains in Melbourne had funky patterns covering all the seats and the carriages always smelled stale – even more so when it wasn't sardine packed with commuters.

The PA system blared with that tinny voice again. "The next train... here. Do... board. The next... will terminate..."

Sophie tried to catch the announcement, but she'd missed it entirely.

2.02 am. The train arrived earlier than she thought it would. Sophie thanked the gods it was entirely empty. It meant she could ugly cry in peace without the nosy stares of passers-by.

Faint shrills of train guards going about their last rounds of the night pierced the air.

What train guards were tasked to do at night when everyone had a few drinks, was to make sure all commuters boarded on the train safely. They made sure those who were onboard already weren't being harassed by the new passengers.

Blowing their whistles as they cleared each carriage, the guards seemed to be frantic. They waved their arms in the air, signalling each other with urgency. Sophie could just hear their panicked voices but was too exhausted from the events that unravelled earlier to even care.

Sophie lay down, kicked her feet up across the three-seater, placed her purse underneath her head as a makeshift pillow and closed her eyes.

Unshed tears slid their way down the sides of her face as the music peaked in her ears. She could hear an argument between train guards break out. The clamour of closing train doors rattled through her as they slammed shut. The train jerked into motion, almost knocking her off the seat.

The train sped off. Fast. Sophie struggled to straighten herself back on the seat.

Good. It means I can get home faster, curl up into bed and have a good cry. That's adulting, right?

It must have been the rippling effects of the concoction of drugs and alcohol, but Sophie felt as if the train was moving unnervingly fast. Bits of rubbish and empty cans rolled towards the back of the train, highlighting the alarming speed the train travelled.

Isn't there some sort of speed limit trains have to abide by? Geez.

Unable to balance herself while lying down, Sophie sat straight up wondering what on earth was going on. Wiping her tears with the back of her hands, she peered out the window and all she saw was darkness. No street lights. Perhaps she was in a tunnel, Sophie thought.

Bracing her tattooed hand on the windowsill, she looked around the carriage nervously. Nobody else was on the train. The realisation made her stomach drop in panic like the feeling of riding the Tower of Terror at Disneyland, except this time the tower was a tin-can train that was trying to beat a world record.

She willed herself to calm, reassuring herself that the train was travelling at a safe speed. She was fine, she tried to convince herself.

Leaning back against the covered seat, she readjusted her earphones, closed her eyes and practised deep breaths. She tried to escape to the blue-and-green swirling skies but couldn't quite get there. The train lurched forward, speeding up. Sophie braced against the windowsill, steadying herself. Her knuckles turned white as she gripped the ledge with force.

Breathe. Breathe.

As she opened her eyes again, the carriage lights began to violently flicker.

Oh, for fuck's sake. This is how I'm going to die, isn't it? Completely high off my tits, in a litter-filled speeding train. Great.

Sophie could see it now. The headlines 'Barely clad woman dies from an overdose on the Watergardens line'. Tragic. Truly tragic.

There was one thing Sophie learnt from trying weed for the first time when she was fifteen. Don't give into the paranoia.

While her situation wasn't weed-induced, she was sure she would more likely lose her mind entirely, given she had zero clue what that prick of a monster gave to her.

The lights in the train crackled and popped, completely frying. Darkness consumed the entire carriage, and, in a panic, Sophie searched for any sign of where she was headed. There, in the distance, city lights sparkled.

Wait... What?

She wringed her eyes with her hands to make sense of what she was seeing. The city lights were beautiful, like distant stars linking arms and dancing. The tall buildings seemed lively and moving, bobbing up and down. Wait, no. The city was submerged in water, Sophie realised, the very top levels of its skyscrapers were just peeking out of water that lapped up against its structures. Sophie blinked quickly again, trying to focus on the lively lights of the city but still, she couldn't make sense of it. It was mesmerising.

The train jerked forward, catapulting Sophie out of her daze.

And just as they suddenly appeared, the distant city lights disappeared. In their place was a thick wall of darkness slightly lit by moonlight. The sudden whoosh of entering a tunnel felt like a punch to her ears. It scared the daylights out of her, so much she let out a little yelp.

Sophie's blood pumped through her ears.

A slight tingle washed over her entire body as if she'd just passed through a wall of electricity. A tether inside her snapped awake. Awed by the feeling, Sophie focused on the feel and flex of her hands. Her skin was alive and thrumming with energy. She was definitely too high.

It was at that moment she could no longer hear the clangs and repeated screeching of the train against the train tracks. The silence of the train drew her attention away from her hands. It was the equivalent of driving a car on a bumpy highway for a long drive, then suddenly hitting smooth, newly laid asphalt. The difference was stark.

Did this train just fly into the air or something?

Throwing caution to the wind, Sophie tucked her headphones hurriedly into the front of her jeans and peered outside the window, feverishly searching for any sign of those pretty city lights or anything to indicate where she was. She needed to know what was going on.

"Please don't let something scary pop up. Please don't let something scary pop up," she whispered repeatedly.

Then it started.

The sound of scratching reverberated along the sides of the train as if it were pushing past trees. Trees. The train was passing through trees. She could hear the melodic bending of branches and the trickle of leaves caressing the sides of the train.

Trees?

This was a different level of high than she'd ever experienced in her life. It felt so real. It sounded so real. There wasn't a haze or heavy veil shrouding her vision. Everything was crystal clear.

Sophie stuck her face closer to the window. She tried to see through the darkness and strained her eyes to focus. She could see the leaves of redwood trees. Its bristles brushing up against the sides of the train, scraping by the window she now stood by as if greeting her – saying welcome.

She placed her fingertips delicately against the glass trying to reach for the beautiful, dark green leaves that sped by. It looked like the leaves and branches were trying to reach back. They were unlike any tree she'd seen in Melbourne. Too thick. Too grand. Too old. Perhaps they existed in regional Victoria but not in metropolitan Melbourne.

The train was gliding now. Slowly. Not in a rush as it was before. Moonlight seeped through the thicket of trees as the train pushed its way through what one would assume was some sort of forest.

The moonlight danced across the window in welcome. Sophie felt warm again despite not having her blazer. She placed both hands up against the window, intrigued by the way the moonlight flitted across her tan skin. It seemed ten times brighter than your average moonlight. It was gorgeous. It felt alive as if it were playing a duet with the Joe Hisaishi song she had on repeat earlier.

The train banked left.

Bracing herself against the window, Sophie spotted the city she saw not too long ago. It was still quite distant, but the lights were closer. She could differentiate the colours; blue, white, pink and green. All different shades reflected and submerged in what looked like water. It was a beautiful painting against a dark blue night sky.

She pressed her cheeks against the cold window again, trying to see where the train tracks led. As much as she tried, she couldn't quite see below the train. It was too dark.

With the thick trees out of the way, she could see the night sky again, though it was different. It swirled with royal blue rays of luminescent light and underneath were mountains, like the ones she'd always escaped to in her mind.

They were beautiful, laden with thick trees across three peaks. The tallest in the middle, the shortest to the left and on the right was one that was just in between. The beautiful city lights lay just at their base, painting the perfect foreground for the breathtaking mountains.

The lights of the city danced with the swirling blue sky and the waters that met the city danced too. A strange feeling sat in Sophie's heart. She'd been to this place before. It felt familiar, like having left a city for several years and coming back to it changing. The feeling of home was still there, but nothing else was the same.

Oh fuck.

Sophie eyes widened as she caught sight of where the train tracks led, or rather disappeared into. Her jaw dropped from its hinge. She braced herself against the window. The train was heading straight for the city... through the water.

It was then she felt the dip of the train. It was a roller-coaster she didn't remember getting on. The train was heading straight for the city. Downwards. Down. Into the water.

It was then, Sophie decided, that this was the craziest yet most beautiful high she'd ever had in her life and boy was she was terrified. It felt like her heart had back flipped up her throat, beating so fast that her eyes were going to explode.

Breathe Sophie.

It could've been worse. She could be lying in a dark alleyway, but instead she was seeing the most magnificent hallucination she didn't know she could even hallucinate.

Sophie's breath stalled as she watched the first few carriages of the train splash into the water – completely submerging. She'd watched *Titanic* the other night, which clearly explained what was happening here in her head. Where was the damn string quartet and a love-struck Jack Dawson to come and tell her that everything was going to be okay?

"C'mon, Sophie. The drugs are making you see things. Get your head straight. Just ride it out. You'll be fine," Sophie muttered frantically.

The faint flicker of the carriage lights struggling to turn back on buzzed through the carriage. Sophie's eyes widened in wonder at the sight before her.

Water splashed, sloshed and danced around the windows. The stark hum of diving deep into water amplified throughout the train. The water didn't come busting through the carriage like she imagined it would, unlike the flooding sequence in *Titanic*.

The train was gliding through the water, not sinking. Just gliding. Completely unfazed. She imagined this was what being in a submarine was like.

The water rushed past. Bubbles danced across the windows. The sound of the train gliding through water, now that she was fully submerged, was soothing. And the water... the water started to glow. From dark black waters, the water turned a lighter turquoise as if changing from night-time to day-time.

Entranced, Sophie placed both hands up against the window. She found calmness in the water as it sparkled by the windows, turning turquoise to clear and glittering as she whooshed by.

Sea creatures, big, small and colourful stopped in their tracks to look her way. And like the trees, it looked like they were welcoming her – acknowledging her presence.

The water was captivating.

Squishing her cheek against the window, daring to get another look at where the train headed, Sophie gasped. What she saw made her eyes well up. She smiled. Laughed.

Sophie moved to cover her mouth with both hands.

The sight she beheld left her in a state of shock.

A quiver of excitement quelled any feelings of fear she'd experienced earlier.

A single tear of overwhelming joy found its way down her cheek. She couldn't tear her eyes away.

She knew exactly where she was right then and there. It was exactly as she had imagined it to be – beautiful, vibrant, bustling, magical and enchanting.

She was in Faery.

4

The city Sophie saw earlier, half submerged in water, was exactly that.

She could see the shapes of the buildings. They were made of grey and blue stone, covered in various vines of various heights. The lights in the windows showed faint silhouettes of families and couples, cheering, feasting and happy. Mer-people swam by the windows and littered the waterways, arms linked and laughing. Various sea creatures and fae with breathing devices were busy going out their daily business, delivering mail and setting up underwater market stalls. She was in an underwater court of some kind.

Sophie let out a little squeal.

The train glided right through the town centre, bubbling its way through.

All the books she'd read did such a fantastic job at describing Faery. Although, there were a few notable differences. The colours were so much more vibrant, not flat like how you'd see it in the human world but dancing, moving like they were sentient beings.

Deep down in her gut, she willed herself to calm down. This wasn't real at all and she needed to not lose her mind, she had to keep reminding herself just that.

The train slowed its pace as if to dock at a station. Sophie pressed her cheek onto the windows again, daring to look ahead, though not really wanting to tear her eyes away from her first taste of Faery.

The train whooshed again, lights guttered out, drenching her in darkness. They'd just entered a tunnel. A few seconds went by, and the lights flickered back on. Sophie gasped.

Peering down the length of the train, the interior now looked like the innards of an old steam. In place of strange patterns were ornate, warm designs. The seating in the carriage was lush – regal even.

Through the smaller windows, the station ahead looked like a typical old English style train station. Giant swirling purple portals that lead to gods knows where, took the place of train tunnel entrances.

Looking around, she could see that there was only one set of train tracks – the one the train was currently on.

Grinding to a soft halt, the train dinged happily, signalling its arrival.

Like clockwork, various Faery beings left their posts to commence their carriage clearances. A shot of panic sliced through Sophie. They were going to find her. Or worse, they were going to find her *and* grill her.

It's fine, Sophie, this isn't real. You're fine.

She reminded herself that this was all a hallucination. Perhaps they wouldn't even see her? This was her hallucination after all, right?

Struck out of her awe-induced stupor with fear of being caught, she did what any sane, normal person would do when given the opportunity to meet mythical creatures – she sat still. If this was her fever dream or trip, then it meant that she was safe. You never get hurt in your own dreams.

The train guards approached the now docked train – one that looked like a tree spirit and another that looked like human-shaped racoon. Systematically, they made their way through the carriages. They scanned the exterior of the train then hopped inside the carriage to clear each seated section as they combed through.

The fae before her were beautifully strange creatures. Even more strangely though, they had human mannerisms.

The sound of the carriage doors clanging open pulled Sophie from her trance. The two guards let out an audible gasp. She willed herself to not make eye contact. Maybe, MAYBE if she pretended that she didn't see them, they wouldn't see her.

Judging by their audible gasp and the stares pointed in her direction, Sophie had an inkling that it was a little too late.

The tree-like fae prowled toward Sophie's end of the carriage, snickering. "Well look what we have here Rafeen, it seems like we've caught ourselves a human mousey, a very cute mousey at that." His voice was low, scratchy, like bark. He wore purple breeches, grey-ish silver armour and black scruffy boots. In his hand he fashioned a short spear bejewelled at the hilt with small purple gems the size of peas.

The racoon-like fae, Rafeen, scurried his way to his partner. He was dressed in the same uniform and donned the same short spear. "Gee, how did the humans let this little treat slip? It's not often they let any pass through... they must have been in a hurry. Thanks to the humans, it looks like we're getting a little human feast tonight!" He started crowing, rubbing his hands together in utter delight.

Now THAT pissed Sophie off.

How was it that she crossed into a completely different realm and still, this type of disgusting vermin deigned to exist? The type that would go out of their way to make snide, dirty comments and objectify women. Where were the gentlemen? Someone please find them because there was one damsel in distress waiting to be saved right now.

Utterly disgruntled by their predatory looks and uncouth comments, Sophie scrunched her nose, furrowed her brows, crossed her arms and did what she'd always dreamt of doing in moments like these – she started a fight.

"Excuse me? There will be no meals had with this human, thank you very much. I'm sure you understand the simple concept of consent, even if you are a sentient rat and you, a sentient tree. It's a big fucking NO from me." She stood, a fist clenched by her side and her other hand pointing directly into the beady eyes of the two fae guards that happened upon her.

In a huff, she pushed past them, purposely knocking into their shoulders to demonstrate how truly pissed off she was. This was her dream, and in her dream there was a zero-tolerance policy on dirtbags.

Sophie huffed her way off the train and turned around ready and willing to give them a big old flip of the bird. They were standing like stunned mullets, frozen in time.

She heard Rafeen whisper to his partner, "She talks a lot for a human. She's not cowering in fear like the other humans either. Maybe she's one of the crazy ones...?"

Standing just outside the carriage, arm part way through flipping them off. "What? Never had a woman with big enough lady-balls to put you in your place?

Doesn't mean you have to whip out the 'oh let's just make her feel crazy' card to sweep your nonsense behaviour under the rug," Sophie shouted.

Make a scene why don't you, Sophie?

"You go left, and I go right. We can't let this human get away." Rafeen sneered, baring his sharp claws as he made a move for her. His tree-like friend used that moment to his advantage and lunged towards Sophie.

Oh no they won't.

"Not in MY dream, boys! You've just opened a giant can of whoop-ass." Sophie quickly hit the deck, sweeping her leg out like how she learned to in her jiujitsu lessons – the motion itself like second nature.

As the tree-fae made his merry way face first into concrete, she hooked her leg around his and tightened her leg-lock as hard and fast as she could. Screaming in agony, his racoon-mate made a move to drag her off.

As he ran closer, Sophie only tightened her grip on his friend – a threat. His screams echoed throughout the station.

Rafeen stepped back, stood tall, placed his short spear between his hands and posed in prayer. He whispered under his breath a spell or a prayer, Sophie couldn't quite make it out.

Through his gritted teeth, the tree-like fae shouted urgently, "Do it quick!"

Whipping her head between the two beings, Sophie loosened her grip, distracted. It was a mistake.

The tree-fae swerved his free leg over and kicked Sophie just above her shoulder. The kick connected, leaving her shoulder throbbing, the sudden pain travelling through her body. She shouldn't have felt that. You don't get hurt in dreams which meant... this was real. It had to be. There was no other explanation. Her senses were clear and crisp. A haze no longer coated her mind. She could smell the musty train station, the sweat that coated both guards but, more strongly, she could feel the thrum of magic and energy that filled the air. Faery was real and had been real this whole time. And she'd just stumbled into it.

The realisation left a mixture of panic, excitement and confusion swelling in Sophie's stomach.

The tree-fae tried to kick her again, bringing her back to her newfound reality. She swung her head back knowing full well he was aiming for her face.

Rafeen, still uttering his prayer or spell, began to glow red. Red meant danger, at least it did in Sophie's head.

"What the fuck is he doing?" Still reeling from the gnarly kick she got to the shoulder, Sophie panicked.

"He's sending you to the Sha—" The tree-fae was cut short by the presence of a black misty figure. An angry black misty figure at that.

"Shadow Realm. Try to finish your damn sentence at least, scum." From the black mist the figure of a tall lithe woman started to form. She wore a dark forest-green cloak that hit just above her knees. Her red hair jutted through the edges of her green hood. Her armour was a dulled gold that moulded her body like a second skin. She was built strong and she meant business.

Using her rather grand entrance to distract the two guards, she popped both of them a righteous left hook, then right. They were flat on their faces in an instant.

"You. Human. Put this on." She unclasped her green hood, lifted Sophie up by her shoulders too easily and wrapped the cloak around them, covering Sophie's head with the hood. Sophie was nowhere near as tall as her. The woman warrior stood about six foot. The cloak landed just by Sophie's lower calf.

"Thanks," Sophie muttered. This was her new reality. She didn't know if it was an appropriate time to laugh.

"No need to thank me yet. You don't even know where we're going. Follow me." She turned quickly, not even checking to see if Sophie followed. She ducked her head and jumped into the black mist from which she came.

Gulping, looking around nervously, Sophie hesitated. Could she trust this female? Her gut told her yes, but the biggest rule in Faery lore was that you couldn't trust anyone or anything in Faery. This female could very well try to kill her, but the fact was that Sophie had just landed in a once-fictional realm of which she knew a fair amount about but never would have thought she'd actually be able apply her knowledge to traverse. She was a fish out water and out of sorts. The female warrior before her was her only lifeline.

Throwing caution to the wind, Sophie held her breath and jumped into the portal.

"Look straight ahead, human. We don't want you to get lost now do we?" The red-headed woman chuckled. Sophie couldn't see her, but she could hear her. The portal was how it looked on the outside – black and misty – but inside, it seemed a bit more glittery, sparkling even. It was as if they were moving through time and space.

"It's just a short jump, so be prepared to run your little human legs off," the warrior-woman shouted, the end of her sentence curling into a smile.

"My what? Where are we going? Wait, what is happening?" Sophie shouted towards the general direction of the female.

They ran their way through the glittery mist until light started to peer through on the other side. Running full speed towards the light, Sophie picked up her legs as much as she could in attempt to catch up with the female.

Bright light blinded Sophie as she felt her entire body being sucked into what felt like a vacuum. The force made her knees wobble. She'd just found the other end of the portal and the magic that skittered across her skin left a slight smile across Sophie's face. This was real alright.

Steadying Sophie with two firm hands on her shoulders, the warrior-woman motioned Sophie to look behind herself with a flick of her chin. The black glittery portal they'd just jumped through dissipated into a fine mist, revealing the train station platforms they were just on about fifty metres away. They stood at the precipice of a dark, wide tunnel with walls coated in a dark metal.

"We've reached the end of the station. My magic will be muted from here." She pointed to the ground where gravel transitioned into hard-packed dirt. The start of the metal-covered tunnel. "If you look behind you, you'll see the fools that tried to banish you still struggling." She was right. Rafeen was crouched over his friend, consoling him.

Sophie finally let out a laugh.

"Now I hate to stop your enjoyment, but we've got to run, girl."

"What are we even running from?" Sophie's eyes widened with concern.

"The guards, dummy. The ones that tried to banish you. They've most likely sent word to the queen that there's a human on the loose."

Sophie's eyes widened even further.

"I'd get used to it if I were you, human. The queen's been banishing you lot for almost twenty years now." Finally understanding that Sophie had zero clue what she was talking about, the warrior-woman shook her head swiftly. "My name is Elowan. You can call me Ellie. And right now, we need to tuck tail and get you to the other humans." She darted off into the wide, dark tunnel ahead.

Sophie swallowed in nervousness but did as the warrior-woman asked and hauled ass into the tunnel ahead.

The ground was gritty, like fine dirt had been spread haphazardly across it. Unlike the misty portal they'd used to jump from the guards, this tunnel had definitive structure. Dark hallways, twists and turns. The only light source being a low purple glow in the distance, like a neon sign about to sputter out.

The only way Sophie could make out Elowan was her build and the slight shine of her armour.

"Where are we going?" Sophie managed between heavy breaths. She struggled to keep up with Elowan mostly because one, she was clearly a fae warrior given her pointed ears of tan skin jutting out behind the billowing of her fire-red hair and two, because Sophie was half her size.

"To safety. Run now. Questions later." Elowan bit out, focused entirely on their route to an unknown destination.

Keeping her best pace, Sophie started to feel the burn in her chest and the ache in her throat from running what must have been a few hundred metres. *And to think I was fit.* Sophie started to slow, her humanness becoming clear. Elowan kept her preternatural pace.

Grinding to a halt in front of a small circular crawl space, Elowan crouched and inspected the hole in the wall with a short spear she had pulled from her belt. It was the same as the guards Sophie had encountered except with red stones lodged in the hilt. Sophie let out a tiny gasp and stepped back from Elowan. Perhaps she wasn't as good as she seemed?

Elowan motioned for Sophie to crawl into the small entrance to gods knew where.

Wary, Sophie took another slight step back.

Elowan watched Sophie's movements while still crouched in front of the hole. It looked as if she were about to continue speaking, but she stopped herself, recognising the distrust plastered across Sophie's face.

"How do I know you're not of the same ilk as those guards that tried to kill me? You've got the same spear."

"You've got no other choice but to trust me, don't you?" A smug grin appeared across her face. She was stunning, Sophie thought. Her dark brown skin and soft features reminded Sophie of South-East Asia with a mix of other-worldliness. She had high cheekbones, cat-like eyes, pointed fae ears and plump lips.

Sophie caught the humour that lay underneath Elowan's guardedness. It was as if she'd done this a hundred times – supposedly saving humans from the guards. Sophie wondered what she'd gotten herself into.

Something inside her, that gut feeling that told her to run away from Grayson now told her to trust this woman. Inclined to trust the feeling again, Sophie nodded in silent surrender.

"Righteo. Off we go into the questionable dark hole in Faery then. This day couldn't get any worse." Sophie knelt and crawled forward all the while gritting her teeth and rolling her eyes underneath closed lids.

Exasperated and clearly frustrated with herself, she huffed. Sophie gave up the 'I don't think I can trust you' act within milliseconds.

Gods, I'm an idiot. This could be an elaborate trap and there wasn't even any arm twisting involved.

Elowan crouched and crawled into the dark hole in the wall, chuckling as she followed behind Sophie.

Sophie could faintly see a glow rising behind her. Slowly she turned her head back towards Elowan only to find the fae female holding her spear between her palms – posed in prayer just like Rafeen had, whispering a short prayer.

Sophie stopped crawling. "What did you just do?" Sophie waited for an answer.

The last time someone did a voodoo spell thing they were trying to cast me to the Shadow Realm, and if you watched the non-PG version of Yu-Gi-Oh, that blatantly meant to death. There isn't an actual realm. You just die. Painfully.

"All these questions." Elowan tsked. "You're the chattiest human I've met. It's rather endearing. Normally you humans are all silence and fear and..." She paused, shifting her tone. "It's a spell, to cloak our trail."

"Oh cool. Love that." Sophie brushed her off. She was well versed in all things otherworld thanks to her reading habits, but she wasn't about to tell that to Elowan.

Elowan held her breath for another moment before she scoffed, nudging Sophie farther into the crawl space with a soft nudge to her foot.

The two crawled their way through the small tunnel for a few more metres in utter silence. The slight purple glow in the distance was the only light for their journey.

Elowan's shuffling paused as she patted around the walls. "It should be just... about..." she said slowly, feeling for something.

"Should be just abou— AHHHHHHHH!"

Sophie's heart lodged in her throat as she plummeted. Her insides almost found their way out – which end, they hadn't decided yet.

The gritty ground the two had been crawling on had been ripped from right underneath them. Sophie felt like Alice in Wonderland, free falling into the unknown.

With a thump, Sophie landed knees first on something firm yet warm. Her eyes bolted shut from the free fall. She clutched onto what felt like a thin cloth for her dearest life. Sophie had one too many surprises for today and she didn't want to open her eyes to find any more.

"Elowan you fucking twat, why didn't you warn me we were going to FALL from the damn roof? I'm going to projectile vomit any second now and it's all because of your LACK of communication! Is that some sort of fae trait? Oh god, my fuck—" Sophie was cut short by two firm hands sitting her upright from behind.

Elowan dipped as she whispered in Sophie's ear. "I suggest you don't projectile vomit on the only male who can get your human ass out of this mess."

Sophie's eyes flew open at that.

Underneath her was a vision she'd remember for the rest of her measly human existence. Remember Grayson? Murderous traits aside, he was now a flat negative two out of ten and the fae male Sophie so comfortably straddled, albeit in anger and fear, was a straight twelve out of ten.

This was a specimen she could only dream up. Her favourite authors weren't wrong when it came to fae good looks. They weren't wrong.

5

By the time Sophie gathered her wits and her jaw from the ground, the stranger she so delightfully straddled had cleared his throat in silent prayer to get her off him.

Grabbing her firmly by the waist, the stranger lifted her effortlessly off his own hips and plopped Sophie down on her knees by his side. His hands were big and weathered with hard work. It was no wonder how he lifted her as if she weighed a single feather. He wore several rings but the one that stood out the most to Sophie was a signet on his wedding finger – bright gold with a green gemstone. Not emerald but a glowing jade. It seemed to pulse with life as he let her go.

Still flabbergasted, Sophie lifted her eyes to his. Turquoise, a bright shade of sea that complemented the ring he wore. The colour was piercing. His midnight black hair was neatly pulled back into a bun. Sophie was not normally one for man-buns but this was the epitome of a perfect man bun. It felt like she'd seen his sinful eyes before, but she couldn't quite put her finger on it.

Tilting her head, Sophie flipped through all the possible memories and books she'd read to pinpoint where she'd seen eyes like this before. The voice in her gut told her to keep searching. To dig deeper.

"Why is this human tilting her head like that?" The male chuckled at Sophie's mannerisms. His deep raspy voice wrapped around Sophie like a warm blanket.

His smile was heaven. And the two dimples that appeared? They lined up perfectly with the two points of his fae fangs.

"Don't get me started boss, she's got loads of questions and I tell you what, she isn't afraid to ask them." Elowan laughed.

Sophie was still on the floor. The specimen of a male slowly stood up, dusting the dirt and debris off his plain shirt. He moved to pick up his chest plate that had been knocked out of his hands. He wore garb similar to Elowan's, except he had a red gemstone stuck right in the middle of his chest plate. They were like the ones Elowan had fashioned to her short spear. It must have signified his importance.

Noting that detail, Sophie pulled her attention to the matter at present. She hadn't realised she was surrounded by four other fae who, from what she could gather based on their outfits, were a part of a group of merry males and females with a vendetta. Whatever that vendetta was she was yet to figure out. None of them were of the animal kind. They were the typical, strangely handsome and beautiful, potential wing-having band of fae.

Peering just behind where they stood, Sophie noticed a few humans – judging by their lack of pointed ears. They huddled in a group by a small fire, eating and chatting away. They seemed happy. They seemed safe.

"That's good to know. I'm taking the crew out now to search the ground. Stay here. Protect them," the fae male said as if someone hadn't just fallen from the ceiling right on top of him.

"Good luck, boss. May the gods guide you," Elowan said firmly.

"To where we're destined to be," he responded.

With that, he spun on his heel – the entire six foot four of him. Despite his size and build, he moved with ease. A hypnotic grace. His pointed ears accented with gold rings and his tanned skin suited him perfectly. Although, it looked like he'd suffered a few days at war – hard war. If he were human, he'd be roughly twenty-eight years old. Just a touch older than Sophie but since they were in Faery, and judging by his scarred hands, Sophie assumed he was a lot older than he appeared to be.

The crew flanking the fae male followed suit down the hallway, past the humans and up a steel ladder.

Before disappearing, the fae male Sophie graciously landed on stopped in his tracks. He snapped his head toward Sophie and opened his mouth slightly to say something. He seemed to fight against his words but decided against saying anything. He shook his head and continued to climb up the steel ladder behind his crew.

"Try not to drool, human. Us fae have been created to lure you in and ensnare you. Keep that in mind," Elowan said, amused by Sophie's lack of decorum around what she assumed was the leader of this group. Elowan let a little giggle slip through.

Dusting off the dirt coating her jeans and the green cloak, Sophie stood and stretched out the pain of the impact she'd just been dealt.

Nervously kneading the back of her neck, Sophie had to ask "So... um who was that?" She rocked back and forth on her heels trying her best not to be so overt. It didn't work.

"That was Kaine Dormarth Aaryn. We call him Kaine. He's been helping the humans, like yourself, who somehow slip through the realms."

Right, fearless leader leading the fearless men in saving all humans. Cute. We love a strong hero type. But what is he saving us from?

"Right so, what d—"

"Okay. Before you ask your incessant human questions, let's get some supper into our bellies. That way I can answer your questions angrily as opposed to hangrily."

"You know, for a fae, you're actually quite funny. I'm surprised you even know what hangry means. I feel like we're on the same wavelength here." Sophie crossed her arms, smirking at her newfound fae friend. The adrenaline rush from the train station through to scrambling their way through portals and tunnels left her famished. Still, she was unsure of how much she could really trust this Elowan character. She seemed too nice and almost too human.

"You know, for a human, you're actually quite entertaining. I don't say that to just anyone." A wide grin appeared across her face. With both hands on Sophie's shoulders she shuffled her towards a table where the rest of the humans sat, enjoying their meals. Sophie wondered if they stumbled into Faery the same way she did, or if they were freaking out internally as much as she was. If they were, they were doing a good job of hiding it.

Elowan picked up two brown wooden bowls, two spoons and ladled what could only be described as stew, generously into each bowl. She popped two slices of bread into each and shoved one of the bowls into Sophie's cold hands.

"This one's for you. Try not to get entranced and all that nonsense that you humans think you'll get from eating Faery food. Capiche?" Elowan said as she guided Sophie towards a vacant log by the fireplace.

"I can't tell if you're being serious. Should I be worried?"

And I've had enough shit to deal with today. She was hungry. She was ready for food. She did not need to become further incapacitated by Faery food. The stew smelled divine but if she could potentially lose her mind, more than she already had, she wouldn't even entertain the idea.

"I'm kidding. Please eat, otherwise you'll wither away and die. Funnily enough, it's the opposite of what we're trying to achieve here." Elowan waved her hand around the room as she perched herself upon a log closest to the fire. Without an ounce of hesitation, Elowan gulped down the entire bowl of stew, placed the bowl on the floor and began picking apart the bread, piece by piece. There was something so fluid and magical about the way fae beings moved. It was like a trance. A trance, to ensnare humans. Sophie finally understood what those authors, myths and legends had so thoroughly warned humans about.

Perching herself on the log, full bowl of stew in her lap, Sophie began dipping her bread. Letting the bread soak up the stew, she closed her eyes silently praying that Elowan was indeed joking and bit down on a piece of stew-soaked bread. Her eyes widened, and then narrowed in satisfaction.

What in the world? This is the most rich, flavourful food I've ever tasted in my entire life. And it's just plain freaking stew.

"Huh, weird. When a human eats Faery food for the first time, they usually start frothing at the mouth and become uncontrollable. Normally we'd have to enchant the food a little. Dull down the flavours a bit so you don't implode. You seem to be taking it very well though," Elowan said with a devilish grin. She looked at Sophie's face, to the stew then back to her face.

Sophie dropped her stew-soaked bread instantly. "You're saying, you gave me this food knowing full well that my brain could potentially implode, for what... entertainment? You're sick!" Sophie readied her hand to swat Elowan but thought better of it, considering she was a fae warrior.

"Obviously. It's as much entertainment as we're going to get around here. Try not to take it personally, human. I would've just enchanted you so you could sleep it off." Elowan smirked as she popped another piece of bread into her mouth. Her fangs made a quick appearance. "If it helps, you're my favourite human yet. It was quite impressive what you did back there at the station. You also kept up with my running. Normally it's a human over the shoulder kind of affair." She nodded, looking off into the distance with exaggerated gratitude.

This female was dramatic, sarcastic and badass. Sophie was trying her hardest to not to like her for her own safety, but she couldn't help but gravitate towards her.

"Well in that case, thanks for not killing me? You can call me Sophie." She smiled wide. She continued to dip the remainder of her bread into the stew and savoured the taste as it melted effortlessly into her mouth. Sophie decided if she were ever on death row, this would be her last meal of choice without a doubt. Dusting the crumbs off her fingers, she lifted her tattooed arm to shake Elowan's hand.

Elowan blinked at the markings that covered Sophie's arm. Her nose flared slightly as she shook her head, as if trying to clear it. Elowan's larger hand, her skin of dark porcelain, reached out to Sophie's in return. She squeezed. "Nice to meet you, Sophie. Welcome to Faery. I promise we don't bite unless you ask."

6

"Before I let go of all my trade secrets, I need you, my favourite human thus far, to answer some questions." Elowan grinned, grabbing Sophie's empty bowl and placing it on top of hers.

"You don't need to persuade me. The faster we burn through your questions, the faster we get to mine – of which you know I have many." Sophie wrapped her cloak tightly around herself and leaned in.

"First of all, you're suspiciously calm for a human who's just crossed the human-fae border. Should I be worried?" Elowan narrowed her eyes.

Sophie gulped but had no real reason to. "Woah, woah, woah, who says I'm not freaking out?" Panic began to rise in Sophie's throat. She was off to a good start.

Elowan held Sophie's stare. It was then and there that Sophie knew Elowan could skin someone alive without batting an eyelash. A small, cool, vibrating sensation wrapped around Sophie's skin, starting from her hands. The feeling of it engulfed her, working its way up her neck and constricting her airways until it dissipated and vanished on whisper of wind. Sophie's shook her head to clear the feeling. Was that Elowan's magic she felt?

And is if she snapped back into reality, Elowan roared into knee-slapping laughter. "You get riled up so easily. The next few days are going to be hilarious!"

"The next few *days?!*" Sophie whispered harshly, wary of the people that surrounded her.

"Yep. Kaine, myself and a few others will take turns in leading you back from whence you came."

Sophie's heart skipped in excitement at the mention of Kaine. *Calm down, Sophie, you've seen this guy for about two seconds and he seemed thoroughly unimpressed by you.*

Before Sophie could even open her mouth, Elowan continued, "You didn't even set off a trigger by the border. Humans normally do, alerting our crew. I'll have to clarify THAT with the boss. Maybe the borders are weakening again..." Elowan trailed off, shrugging her shoulders as she did.

When Elowan didn't continue, Sophie started. "Is there anything else... you need to ask me?" Sophie searched Elowan's emerald eyes for an answer.

"For once, I'm stumped. It's the first time the borders didn't trigger a pulse our way. Consider yourself special. For now." Elowan shook her head, clearing the puzzle that presented itself before her. She smiled slightly, as if to bring herself back to the present. "Alright, ask me. All your questions."

"Okay this should be simple enough. One, why the fuck am I here, and two, what the fuck is happening?"

Elowan cackled. "Simply put, there are a multitude of realms that exist in the universe but only two of them intersect. Faery and the place you call home, Sotera. The human world. Do you understand what I'm trying to explain?"

"Yep, I'm picking up what you're putting down." Sophie laughed at the casualness that spilled out of her mouth, so out of place with where she was right now. She wondered if they were in the human world, if they would be best buddies. Elowan reminded her so much of Lorrie with her red, enchanting hair. At the thought, a pang of sadness hit Sophie's chest. She wondered if her friend even knew where she was right now.

Sophie motioned Ellie to go on with a wave of her hand.

"Sometimes, humans, like yourself and those humans over there, slip through. Twenty years ago, it would be very rare for someone to cross. We'd have maybe one slip every two years. But in recent years, it seems as though the boundaries separating our two worlds have thinned or weakened. We don't know why. More and more humans are starting to slip through the cracks. The majority will be killed on sight by the Royal Guards but Kaine and others like me, put a stop to it. Us fae create and protect life, not take it away." She paused and swallowed deeply as if reflecting on past trauma. As if she were replaying something she wanted no part in.

"But you're wearing the same uniform as them, you even carry the same weapons."

"Ah you have a very keen eye. It's a ruse. We're not part of the Royal Guards. We're part of the Elite. Same, same, but different. It keeps the queen looking amongst her ranks in the palace for traitors as opposed to us – her gifted warriors." Something like sadness and regret washed over Ellie's face. "We work for the queen like the Royal Guards do, so we have access to the money and resources required to support our activities. It allows us to do what we do. It's a means to an end, nothing more."

Sophie wasn't sure how to interpret that. They worked for the queen, who controlled the Royal Guards, who were killing humans – banishing them to the Shadow Realm. How could they sleep at night knowing that? Sophie shook her head at the thought.

"You mentioned slipping through. How does that happen? Are there cracks in the boundary?" Sophie was eager to hear how she ended up in another realm.

With her finger, Elowan drew two overlapping circles on the ground. "This is Faery, where we are right now." She pointed to the circle on the left. "And this is Sotera. Earth. Where you just came from." She pointed to the circle on the right.

Inside each circle, Elowan began drawing several lines that fanned out from where the two circles overlapped. "Ley lines," Elowan said, staring right into Sophie's eyes. "They're natural sources of magic buried deep in earth. Since our realms are interconnected, these ley lines run across both realms." Elowan drew tiny dots in the area which the circles intersected. "To keep the borders strong and impenetrable between worlds, humans and fae must provide what we call mana. What you humans call magic. This magic fuels the ley lines." She drew a thick line down the centre of intersecting circles.

"Aeons ago, humans and fae would gather at points along the border either on foot or horse, to offer their mana by touching what they call syphons." She pointed at the tiny dots that ran on both sides of the intersecting line. "These syphons gather and combine fae and human mana. The magic is pumped back into the land to bolster the borders." She thickened the bisecting line for emphasis. "As means of travel evolved and Faery's intent on keeping separate from the humans grew, Faery created train lines and a carriage made of syphon material. They placed the tracks on top ley lines across both realms. An effective solution for what would be days and months of journeying on foot." Elowan rubbed out the syphons along the border and began drawing a latticework of train lines. Across the circle on the right, the lines converged into one before crossing the borders between realms. In the circle on the left, the train line formed a giant loop. "The syphon train travels across both realms and unless it's cleared properly by specialist guards on the human side, some humans tend to slip through to the Faery realm." She ran her finger across a train line and marked an X in the one place where it intersected the border.

Sophie marvelled at the map Elowan drew. She hadn't read any books that explained the convergence of realms. It was also the first time she'd heard of mana in the context of Faery.

Elowan smiled at Sophie's wide eyes.

"Okay so, if you're looking here"—Sophie pointed at the intertwining train lines on the circle that represented Sotera—"there are thousands of train lines. Are there thousands of trains to manage?"

"There's only one train," Elowan said plainly.

"What do you mean there's only one?"

"There is only one train that is Faery-made. It travels across all the major cities of the world, through portals, collecting mana." Elowan pointed at various points across the globe. "The last stop before reaching Faery is Melbourne, Victoria. Any humans that unknowingly slip through, typically come from Australia. The other humans from different parts of the world are quickly dealt with by the human authorities – mostly shipped back to their home country with a slew of drugs to help them forget that they accidentally jumped countries on a train." She shrugged her shoulders.

Gee jumping countries and seas via train would be an experience.

"...In that case, I can just hop on the train tonight and be on my merry way. Better yet, you could just open a cute portal for all of us to walk through, right?"

"Well, no. First of all, the train from whence you came runs through all stations in Faery. Did you want to get caught, killed or tortured?" Elowan raised an eyebrow.

Sophie sat in appropriate silence.

"Didn't think so. It takes a full week to reach the departure portal that'll lead you back to Melbourne. Unlucky for you, that portal sits not so conveniently on the other side of Faery."

"You mean I'm going to be stuck in Faery for a full week?!" Sophie tried her best not to panic, but her heart rate spiked, and a sweat started to break. Her mother would be worried sick, and Lorrie would help her launch a search party. She couldn't miss an *entire* week without letting someone know her whereabouts.

"Time moves differently in Faery. A day in Sotera is a week in Faery. Your friends and family shouldn't be too worried." Elowan waved a hand carelessly. "All it means is that we'll have to wait a full week here in Faery before we can smuggle you on a train. A full week of hiding and not getting caught or killed," Ellie said, leaning farther into the space between them. "And as for the matter of creating portals, there are too many of you. One human, sure. Twelve? We'd drain our power in an instant." She clicked her fingers for emphasis. "It's why we must stick to the underground tunnels of Faery. Whilst the tunnels are wrought from iron that mutes our powers, it offers a safe passage for you. A double-edged sword we're willing to live with," Elowan said as she pointed above.

"Wait, I though the fae were deathly allergic to iron – why would you have a system of underground tunnels made of iron? That makes no sense."

"Ah. So you do know something about the fae. Explains why you're relatively calm compared to those folk." Elowan pointed to the group of humans sitting not too far away. She leaned in closer to Sophie and whispered. "I had to spell them to calm them down." Elowan scoffed in amusement. "Yes, you're right. We're deathly allergic to iron if the metal makes its way into our bloodstream. If we are in the presence of the metal, say in the form of the tunnels we just walked through, it dulls our powers and senses significantly. One instance we'll die, the other, we'll be significantly weakened." Elowan shrugged her shoulders as if it didn't bother her at all. "And as to why we'd cover our own underground tunnel systems with iron, the queen's approved answer would be to keep Faery safe from the deadliest of fae that wish to escape the dungeons and harm the fair citizens of Faery. I say it's for her own benefit. To keep the citizens of Faery with no way to escape whatever plan she has been spindling for all the years. Who knows really?" Elowan idly picked at the loose threads of her pants, contemplating on the words she'd just spoken.

Sophie took a moment to digest that. "I'm going to guess the reason why the Royal Guards are killing humans is because of their duty and loyalty to this queen?" Sophie tried not to laugh. The evil queen trope was something Sophie was very well versed in.

Elowan blinked in surprise but continued. "It's not really their fault. They're obeying orders of the queen who has grown more wicked with every year of her reign. Her violence started the moment the king left to build New Terrin, across the Fallen Seas. About twenty years ago, she decreed that any human caught in Faery was to be killed on sight." Ellie shook her head as her face screwed in disgust. "She believes the reason why Faery dies is because of humans. According to her, their presence in this realm throws off the magical equilibrium in the land. As every year of her reign passes, the number of humans slipping through continues to grow and Faery continues to suffer..." she said, staring at the floor. Enraged.

"Faery... is dying?" Sophie fought the urge to lay a comforting hand on Elowan's arm. She could see the hurt and worry that flashed across the fae warrior's eyes.

"Each year our crops are less bountiful, the colours of the leaves and flowers dim, fewer and fewer children are born and, slowly, the earth rots beneath our feet. There is a plague that rots our lands, a plague we cannot find the source of. The queen blames the humans, yet no reprieve comes from the deaths." Her words were clipped, filled with emotion.

Sophie tried to lighten the mood. "Sounds like you've got yourselves in a bit of a pickle."

"Some of the Faery folk believe it's just a ruse. That she's trying to kill off the prophesied true heir of the throne." Elowan picked at the seams of her pants with more fervour.

Sophie couldn't have rolled her eyes farther back into her head. *There's always a damn prophecy.* "And what, pray tell, is the prophecy?"

"It was prophesied that Faery's true heir would return. And with their return, the full power and might of Faery would return too."

"Is the queen not the true heir?"

"No. At least not according to the whispers of crazed oracles and the rare few that lived to see the king depart for New Terrin. Rumours have claimed that the king had found his true mate... after his marriage to Queen Calliea. And from the bond that trumps all, they bore a child. The true heir to Faery. There is no evidence whether these rumours are true."

"And what about the true heir. Where are they returning from?"

"I don't know." Her words were clipped.

Sophie paused her line of questioning. "Do you believe the rumours? The prophecy?"

Elowan sighed. "I don't know. We don't know." She gestured to the general space around her. "All we can hope is if there is an heir out there, that they return from wherever they've been hiding for all the years. That they take their rightful place on the throne and that Faery stops dying. That's all we can ask for." She paused, staring blankly into the distance. "Though most of us have lost all hope. It's been twenty years since Faery has started its decline. The entire Winter Court has sundered and become uninhabitable. It is only a matter of time until other courts are taken by the plague. Surely, if there was a true heir, they'd make themselves known by now. What true heir would leave their rightful duty and let their people suffer?" she said solemnly, idly brushing off the dust off her armour.

An heir that doesn't know who they really are. The words whispered and danced through Sophie's mind. The thought quickened her beating heart, pushing a string of excitement through her chest.

Elowan's distant eyes and the sadness etched across her brows pulled Sophie back down to earth. Sophie had run out of quirky remarks to lighten the mood. Their land was dying. They were under rule of some malicious queen and innocent people were being slaughtered. There was nothing funny about that. "For what it's worth, I'm sorry that you and your people are experiencing this. I'm only human but I will do what I can to help." Sophie reached out to comfort her with a firm squeeze of her arm.

"Thanks, Sophie." Elowan sniffled and peered into the fire just behind her. She wiped a tear from her face. Even crying she was beautiful. Elowan let out an exasperated breath. "I think it's time I introduce you to a few people you'd like to meet. Come with me." She grabbed Sophie's two hands and dragged her to the group of humans that sat by the fire. Their tired eyes peered up to Sophie. Assessing at first, but soon, they washed with warmth and welcome. Another human, just like them. Sophie knew they'd make quick friends. Friends stuck in the same, strange situation. "Everyone, there's someone I'd like you to meet." Elowan smiled, nudging Sophie closer to the group.

"Hi." Sophie shyly waved to the group in front of her. "My name is Sophie."

7

"**M**y name is Brone." An old man, about seventy years old with mid-length hair, neatly tied back was the first to introduce himself. For a man of his age, he moved with sure steps and his shoulders were broad with confidence. His back curved with use but the smile on his face was warm and wise. He stood up from where he sat, the group surrounding him as if he were part way through telling a story. He held out a hand for Sophie.

"Lovely to meet you." Sophie took his warm hand and shook it. He held hers still and guided her to take a seat among them.

A slew of greetings flung themselves at Sophie. She couldn't quite catch all of them but there were a few she remembered. Dolores was a young girl, about eight or so. Her brown, chestnut coloured hair matched that of her mother's, Mallory.

Sophie would get to know them all eventually. The week's journey ahead of them all would make sure of it.

"When you're ready, I'll show you where you can all rest for the night," Elowan chimed in. Sophie had almost forgotten the fae warrior was there, too engrossed in learning the human faces – the only sense of familiarity in the unknown of Faery.

Elowan led the group of them down a musty stone-covered hallway. There was barely any light.

The smell of stale dirt and wood that hadn't quite dried hit Sophie like a train. She lightly jogged on the spot to keep herself warm. The bodice and jeans she still had on underneath her cloak didn't do her any favours. Her sore and dirty feet didn't help either.

She scanned the small room left to right. It was lit by two dim sconces. The warm yellow light cast neat little shadows of the humans who had laid out their mats, ready to rest for the night. There were about twelve humans altogether, including Sophie.

"Here, take this horse blanket. Choose a mat. It'll be cold tonight. I'll be just outside in the hall where we had dinner. You'll be safe," Elowan assured her, passing her a thick heavy blanket as she did. Sophie softly took it off her hands, still not quite believing how she got here, in Faery, a realm she thought had existed only in the beloved books she read over and over again.

Noticing Sophie's introspection, Elowan placed a firm hand on her shoulder and peered under her lashes. "We'll clean you up tomorrow and we'll get you some weather-appropriate clothes. Can't let you freeze to death, can I?" She smiled. Sophie could tell she was trying to shine this shithole of a mess.

The adrenaline that had kept Sophie going sputtered to a stop and all the questions she'd been dying to get answered were relentlessly firing and clanging through her head. This was real. She was in Faery. What if they couldn't make it back to the portal? How would her family know that she was okay? That she was just stuck in another realm that they've most likely never even heard of? How would she even get out of here? Could she trust Elowan, Kaine and their band of merry fae to get all the humans out safely? She needed to guarantee her safety and the safety of the other humans before anything.

The questions ran rampant in her mind. They didn't stop. They couldn't stop.

Sophie picked the mat closest to the door should she need to make a quick escape. The mat was a little thicker than a yoga mat and didn't do anything for warmth. She wrapped herself tightly with the horse blanket Elowan had handed to her and laid down. It wasn't the most comfortable. Dirt puffed up under her weight.

Assuming a fetal position, she tried her best to close her eyes and relax her body, limb by limb. She was exhausted and her eyes were operating under enormous pressure. Her feet were throbbing now that they weren't being used, and so were her knees from all that crawling. It was then and only then, in the dark dim cavity, that Sophie let herself cry. Hot tears streamed slowly down her cheeks, dampening the mat and blanket underneath her. The questions she longed to be answered would have to wait until tomorrow.

Turquoise, smoky-silver eyes bore straight into Sophie's; washed with worry or fear, she couldn't quite place it. The long devastating scar that danced through his left brow to the outer corner of his left eye, though brutal, brought her fondness. And she knew it did the same for him too. A secret only they knew. His eyes welled and she felt hers do the same. Sophie's lips quivered. She could tell this would be the last time that she'd see his beautiful soul again.

They stood in front of a grand castle, covered in thick vines and white and violet orchids. Barefoot, they both stood on the grass, knowing full well they would stand here together for as long as they could. She peered down to where their hands were interlocked, joined. Her best friend. Her world.

In the distance, a figure rushed from the castle garden grounds, across to where they both stood. It looked like he was part of the Royal Guard, fae. He was shouting, although Sophie couldn't hear him at all. It was like a silent movie, but still, she felt a terror deep down in her chest.

From behind, she felt someone pick her up with a strong arm wrapped around her waist. With a gasp of surprise, her little feet were swept off the floor entirely. She snapped her head up, not wanting to be taken away from her one and only best friend. The guard with his silver hair, who had come running with fear in his piercing purple eyes, held the boy with turquoise eyes and black hair back.

Her best friend screamed. Tears ran rampant down his cherub cheeks. She couldn't hear what he was saying but unlike before she could feel her heart tear and crumble. She felt true pain. He wanted to go with her, he wanted to keep her safe forever.

She shrieked and struggled, clawing at the arms that had torn her away from the other half of her soul. She didn't want to leave. She needed to stay. She needed to let him know that she'd do whatever it took to find him again. She opened her mouth to make that promise. Though she felt her mouth open, no words or sounds came out – only silence.

She felt her throat wretch under the pressure of her screaming, but still she couldn't hear a thing. The world around her started to tilt, then it started to shake wildly. Her best friend, blurred with her vision. She'd never see him again.

"Mother of Faery, wake up, you blasted human!"

Sophie heard yelling right in her ear. Fluttering her eyes open, she noticed Elowan had her hands tight around her shoulders, shaking her.

Elowan's eyes were wide with worry. A bead of sweat peeked through her hairline. "Oh Faery, you're alive!" she said, relieved. She let go of Sophie's shoulders.

Still thick with sleep, Sophie rubbed her eyes with the palm of her hands and stretched.

"Is it common practise to wake up people up by shaking them violently?" Sophie yawned, stretching her hands high above her.

Elowan gaped, incredulous. "Sophie, you've been shouting in your sleep for the past HOUR. A WHOLE HOUR. I thought the Faery food had finally imploded your brain. I couldn't wake you up!" Elowan shouted defensively. Raking her hands through her hair, she stood up and reached out a calloused hand for Sophie to grasp. "Come on, we need to get moving if we want to get you humans to Northern Helm on time."

Northern Helm. The station that housed the portal back to Sotera. A week's journey away.

Wringing the sleep out of her eyes, Sophie grabbed hold of Elowan's firm hand. She hoisted herself from mat that stuck to her sweat-slicked back.

"Um, you've got..." Elowan stopped, reaching towards the sleeping mat that had awkwardly clung to Sophie.

"Oh yeah, don't worry about it, it happens to me all the time. I tend to overheat when I sleep, especially if I have nightmares. It's embarrassing really..."

"What do you me—"

"Overheating. The human body repairs itself during sleep... human stuff. I guess you wouldn't understand." Still sleepy, numb from her night terror, throat aching, Sophie noticed the mat that had mottled from the heat she'd radiated in her slumber.

"Yeah, sure. I get it."

Sophie wasn't convinced. Elowan turned to Sophie, picking up a pair of plain breeches, a blouse and knee-high boots and handing them to her. "Get changed. The other humans are already outside, waiting. We move in five minutes," Elowan said, a wary smile splaying across her face.

Nodding thanks, Sophie quickly stripped herself bare and popped on the breeches, blouse and boots that, to her surprise, fit her perfectly. She scoffed, knowing full well she looked like she'd come straight out of a renaissance festival or was a cast member at Kryal Castle.

Before turning on her heel, making tracks for the main cavern where they'd had supper last night, Sophie whispered to herself, "You are a badass fae queen. These mortals don't know you and the power you hold. Make them think twice before messing with you." Except she wasn't dealing with mortals anymore. She was in Faery.

She shook her head, still not believing this was entirely real.

8

20 Years Ago

"I don't care what you think, you imbecile. I decree it, so it shall happen. Question my motives one more time and I'll make sure that you have no tongue to speak," Queen Calliea drawled, examining her long, blood-red, claw-like fingernails. Her chilling, twangy voice trilled through the throne room. Her dark blood-red hair pulled into a crown, paid compliments to her blood-stained lips. Her skin, like delicate porcelain, was leached of colour. Queen Calliea was striking, mad surely, but striking.

"Yes, Your Majesty. It will be known." Alston Taliesin bowed deeply by the dais to the blood-red queen who sat content with the killing order she'd just decreed. The lush, red velvet throne atop the dark stone dais was menacing. He didn't know what to make of her and the decree she had just ordered. He knew Faery was starting to wither. For a long time now, it'd been struggling to absorb the mana that the humans and fae created through their alliance, but he wasn't happy with this solution either. Queen Calliea had ordered that any humans who slipped through the fabric between worlds was to be killed on sight, no longer allowed refuge until the train departed at Northern Helm station. She said their very presence tainted the already struggling land. He lifted his head from his bow, turned on his heel, ready to task the palace messengers with the queen's decree for every court to read.

"Oh, and before you leave, Alston, it's the king. I've been informed that he has just reached New Terrin. He's requested that every family send a child to his stronghold, to be taught how to nurture and cultivate the lands there. A true honour, for the children of Faery, don't you think?" Her cold saccharine smile made Alston think otherwise.

"Yes, Your Majesty. The lands of New Terrin will prosper and, hopefully, Faery with it." He turned again, facing the dais. Hand on his heart, Alston hoped with all his might that Faery would indeed prosper again.

"See to it that it happens, Alston." She paused, boring into his bright purple eyes. "Now go." With the flick of her spindly fingers, Alston bowed at the waist and turned quickly before she could stop him again. Padding across the plush red carpet, the royal guards opened the floor-to-ceiling heavy oak doors for him. As he moved into the hallway, his mana spoke to him then, not with words, but the guiding feeling it always spoke with. A force. It told him that what the queen wanted was wrong. That it would be the beginning of Faery's end, not its journey to prosperity.

As the heavy doors of the throne room clicked shut, Queen Calliea waved her hands across the space that Alston had just occupied. Dark shimmering matter manifested from her fingers. Before her appeared a hooded and hunched being, kneeling before the dais, arms restricted by iron chains.

"What have you done, you fool! You defy the Fates. Faery will sunder!" The being rasped, its blackened skin stretching and straining against the shackles it bore.

"What did you think was going to happen, my silly little oracle?" Unimpressed by the creature's accusations, Queen Calliea gripped the arms of her throne. She lifted herself from where she sat and made her way down the dais to tower over the kneeling being in front of her. She bent low, face to face with the wrinkled oracle. She wrapped her fingers around the oracle's fragile throat. Her white porcelain skin was a stark contrast against the blackened skin of the oracle. She seethed, "My reign will never end. I shall see to that." Locking her yellow-gold eyes into the pale green eyes of the oracle, she willed the air with her mana, stealing it from the oracle's lungs. Sputtering, choking and clawing at the talons lodged at its throat, the oracle struggled against Queen Calliea's grasp. Then it stilled. The light in its eyes dissipated, fading into a milky white.

Queen Calliea let the figure slump before the dais. Chuckling softly. Damn the Fates, she thought. Her reign was to never end, not if she had any say in it.

Turning back to her throne, she snapped her fingers. The slumped form disappeared into thin air. She sat, crossed her legs, leaned back and began humming a haunting tune. A slow, cold smile made its way across her face. Underneath the smugness though, she couldn't help but pause at the words that carried on a phantom wind, in the voice of an old and aged oracle...

The return of the strongest warrior that Faery will ever come to know, will bring the full might of Faery, but only with the love they sow.

Together with their fated, the blood reign will end. A life of peace and prosperity, more than one can comprehend.

She'd do everything in her power to stop that from happening. This was her throne, and she'd fight tooth and nail to see that it remained that way.

9

Present Day

"The queen has doubled security. It'll be harder for us to travel through the tunnels, so stay focused, keep your wits about you," Elowan announced to the twelve humans in front of her. They lined up in two neat files – backs donning packs that held water, a small portion of food and medical supplies for their march towards Northern Helm station.

Brone, together with the help of a middle-aged man named Tristan, went around the group of humans, securing the packs that everyone wore – making sure they were as comfortable as possible for the journey ahead. They both served in the Australian Army when they were younger, Sophie had learned, and used their experience on the battlefield to quell the unease that roiled the humans. Most had never hiked long distances before. And most certainly, none of them had traversed another realm. They'd need all the help they could get.

Sophie jumped in place, testing the weight and comfort of the pack she wore. Happy with how it fit her body, she secured the clips across her chest. Beside her, she noticed someone's stare. It was Dolores. At eight years old, she was small for her age. Her brown eyes shone brightly. She was excited for the adventure ahead, Sophie overhead her proclaiming to her mother. She didn't understand the dangers that potentially awaited them.

Dolores stood there, wide eyed, staring at Sophie.

Sophie met her eyes and smiled. "Good morning, Dolores, did you sleep well?"

Dolores blinked but did not answer. She clasped the edge of her blouse, wringing it between her hands. She was shy.

"Dolores." Her mother Mallory whispered harshly, pulling at her arm with a jarring tug. "Sorry about that. We're quite tired." Mallory laughed shyly, pulling her daughter closer to her. Dolores continued to stare from behind her mother.

"Oh, it's fine." Sophie crouched down so that she was at Dolores's eye level. "I sometimes lose my words when I'm tired too. Even the most confident of people lose their words. It's what makes us human."

Dolores smiled shyly.

Sophie looked up at Mallory who mouthed the words 'thank you'. Sophie smiled knowingly. She was once a shy girl, unsure of the world and the people around her.

Earlier that morning, Elowan had gathered the humans after breakfast and detailed their week-long journey. They needed to march through the underground network of tunnels surrounding Southern Helm station, reach the underground gates signifying where Fyllera – the Autumn Court – ended, climb back on mainland to cross the river and head back down underground into the tunnels of Wrenntia – the Winter Court. The crossing would be the most difficult part, especially with twelve humans. From there, they'd traverse the underground tunnels of Wrenntia, making a beeline for Northern Helm station, where they would take a memory-erasing potion before embarking on the train back to Sotera. Sophie was unsure how she felt about that last part. She didn't want to forget, but she understood the reason why.

Timings were key. They needed to reach Northern Helm before the syphon train departed. If they missed it, they'd have to risk another week of being in Faery, with a bigger group of humans to smuggle.

"Alright, let's move. Freedom awaits!" Elowan ordered her second-in-command, Camrine, to lead the humans into the network of dark tunnels ahead. Camrine was almost the twin of Elowan. They had the same skin tone and bright red fiery hair. But where hers was long, his was short. And his eyes, while green like Elowan's, were much lighter. He stood taller than her though, at six foot five.

Staying back to guard the back of the humans, Elowan quickly turned around to ensure that she truly was the last person.

Sophie turned back with her as the humans began their march. Sophie had decided to stick to the back of the group so she could ask Elowan more questions.

Happy with her final check, Elowan started forward. Noticing Sophie's attention, she grabbed Sophie's shoulder, guiding her forward as they spoke.

"Are you feeling better, human?"

"I am, thanks again for waking me." Sophie smiled to herself, shucking her backpack into a more comfortable position. It dug awkwardly into her hips. It was clearly made for a large fae warrior and not a petite human woman, but it would do.

"That's alright. Now stop with the flattery, what do you want to know? Unless you purposely chose the worst position in the group so you could indulge in the wafting farts of the humans ahead."

"Ugh. Well, shit..." Sophie thought about it. Cringing at the small tidbit Elowan had just revealed. Clearly, she had done this journey enough to experience it. She sighed. "You mentioned the queen had doubled her security. Why?"

Falling in step beside Sophie, Elowan said, "We don't know yet. Kaine sent word this morning. He'll let us know if he finds anything out." She kicked a few rocks out of her path. The humans ahead spoke low enough, trying not to make too much noise. "And before you ask, he's to join us tonight. He'll take over while I go and fulfil my duties as part of the Elite." Elowan smiled mischievously, nudging Sophie in the arm. "The pitter-patter of your human heart betrays you, Sophie." Sophie turned red. Her eyes widened and looked at anything but Elowan. She muttered to herself in embarrassment. A vision of his beautiful turquoise eyes faded before her.

"Alright. You caught me."

"Come on, we've got a long walk ahead of us, save your energy and questions for tonight." Elowan smiled sweetly at Sophie and nudged her on the back so she fell in line with the other humans.

Sophie was about to start but thought better of poking at a fae warrior's patience. Fine, her questions would have to wait, but she would get her answers.

Hours had passed. They'd stopped every now and then to allow for the humans to drink and nibble at the sustenance they packed in their bags – fruits and nuts. The low conversation that hummed through the group earlier grown to a silence. Joints and muscles began to ache. The group had taken turns piggy-backing Dolores. Her young legs could barely keep up. Tristan had helped Brone with his pack. Sophie had to give the old man credit for keeping pace with the rest of the humans, though with a bit of hobbling.

Ahead of the group, Camrine signalled with a fist in the air for the group to halt. Elowan jogged to the front of the group, pack clanking against her back as she did.

"We'll rest here tonight. We're approximately a third of the way across Fyllera. The pace is gruelling for humans, we understand this. So please rest as much as you can tonight. We've still a while to go until we reach Northern Helm." With that, the group dispersed, lining up their packs against the left wall of the tunnel as they were instructed to before they stepped off on their journey towards Northern Helm.

Elowan padded up to Sophie as she was laying out her sleeping mat for the night, beside Mallory and Dolores's.

"I'm to head on land to gather more supplies for you all and then I'll leave for my posting tonight. If you need anything, Camrine will be able to help you." Elowan placed a comforting hand on Sophie's shoulder.

With that, she jogged back ahead to where Camrine stood watch over the humans. Sophie couldn't help but watch as her friend moved with that unnerving fae grace. She'd never seen anything like it. Every muscle was sure in its placement, swift and flowing like silk in the wind. Elowan and Camrine exchanged whispered words, both taking a quick look back at Sophie as they did. Waving a hand in goodbye, Elowan turned on her heel, heading towards a discreet steel ladder, shining in the distance up to land. Up to Fyllera.

What was up there? Sophie needed to know. Was it how she imagined Faery to be? Would everything try to kill her or poison her? What were the dangers that awaited them? Faery was dying, was there anything she could do to help? Was there any way she could contact her family? When would the killing of humans end? The questions balled themselves into a never-ending bundle.

Sighing from the tiredness that lay heavy in her eyes, Sophie plonked on the sleeping mat she'd rolled out and began to massage her tight calves. Sure, the authors in her favourite books detailed tiring treks, but she didn't realise how badly her calves would hurt from the constant walking. She looked around the camp at the others, even more worn and tired than she was. Dolores had fallen sleep on her mother's lap. Tristan, though tired from carrying both his own and Brone's packs, walked around the group, making sure that everyone was okay.

Lying back on the mat, Sophie took in a few deep breaths. Throughout the day, she hadn't had the chance to question where she was. She only allowed herself to wonder what her mum was doing and if she'd noticed Sophie was gone. If her friend Lorrie was doing okay. Tears threatened to spill.

She didn't hear but felt a presence approaching the group. Her gut told her to sit up, look, listen. Find. Sitting up slowly so that stars didn't dance in her eyes, she stared down to where Camrine had stood watch. Low and behold, there stood Kaine, grasping his brethren by the hand in greeting. Her heart clenched. Raced. Her breath hitched. He looked as beautiful as he did the night she'd landed on him. He wore his full kit; gold brushed armour with a big red stone in the centre, dark purple breeches, red-stone-embellished short spear like Elowan's, dangling by his hip. His dark hair pulled into a tight bun at the back of his head. His earrings sparkled in the distance. Sophie realised she was staring. She cleared her throat and stood up.

Sensing her approach, Kaine trailed off on his handover with Camrine. His fae brethren turned to acknowledge Sophie's approach as well.

"Hello... Sir... Kaine." Sophie could've died from embarrassment.

Hello, Sir Kaine? Really, Sophie? She spent the ten metres from her mat to where they stood trying to come up with an appropriate greeting and landed on 'Hello, Sir Kaine'? Good one, Sophie. Gods above, with your divinity please intervene and assist this poor human soul, because any chance of getting to know the gorgeous fae warrior was squelched by her damned, embarrassing turn of phrase.

Sophie shifted nervously on her feet. Camrine, red hair and green eyes, turned away swiftly, trying his hardest not to laugh. Clearly, he wasn't trying hard enough as a small choking sound escaped his lips. Sophie turned.

"Hello, human." Kaine looked toward Camrine, then back to Sophie, clearly amused by the greeting. Saving her from embarrassment, he dipped his head in greeting.

"I hear you're staying the night. I'd like to book an appointment with you ahead of time as I know you're most likely going to be running around the realm being the main character to whatever storyline is playing out here. I want to know more about what's happening up there"—Sophie pointed to what lay above the tunnel; Faery—"and Elowan mentioned you'd have the answers."

Kaine stared at Sophie clearly puzzled. He tilted his head and Sophie swore that her world tilted with it.

Blinking out of his stupor and clearing his throat, he said, "Of course, lady. Find me by the fire. Though unfortunately we did not carry any books with us. Apologies." Kaine's brows furrowed with confusion, it seemed.

"Oh, booking an appointment doesn't actually require a book. I was just..." She trailed off. Trying to explain a very human concept to a fae warrior made her laugh. "I'll find you by the fire. Tonight." She turned, nervous, still thrumming from the energy that raced in her heart. She made her way back to her sleeping mat, almost dead from embarrassment but celebrated the small win. She'd scored an audience with the leader of the seemingly rebellious movement. She'd get some answers then.

As she prepared her sleeping mat, she couldn't help but feel his eyes on her.

10

"The queen has tasked the Royal Guard to locate the source of mana that caused the surge we felt the other night. That's why she's doubled security," Kaine said quietly to Camrine. The mana surge was like a gust of wind that had blown across the Faery lands. Something powerful had entered their realm and everyone who was awake felt it prickle against their skin. He wondered if Sophie had something to do with it or if it was something else completely, perhaps the gods wreaking havoc for no reason at all.

Sophie, that was the name of the human with piercing purple eyes. He couldn't shake the sight of them. How a human had landed the unique fae colouring he did not know.

"But what does that mean for the Elite? Why hasn't she tasked us in finding the source?" Camrine asked, his features scrunching in confusion.

"I don't know. Like all the scheming these last few years, she hasn't made her plans known to me. My mana tells me that whatever it is, it is not right." And Kaine trusted his mana with all his heart. It had guided him through every decision he'd made. He grew strong and climbed the ranks of the Elite and was awarded the rank of captain because of it.

"My mana is telling me the same. We need to find out what she's hiding and get to the power source before she does..." Camrine trailed as Sophie approached them sitting by the small makeshift fire they'd pulled together by the other wall of the tunnel, opposite their packs. "I'll leave you to it, brother," Camrine said, gripping his brethren's shoulder tightly as he rose from the ground. He nodded at Sophie before he made his way to watch over the humans that sat by their packs, deep in conversation.

"Come, sit." Kaine, in all his otherworldliness, felt nervous. How could this be? Over a human? He patted the ground beside him as he sat, legs outstretched before the fire.

"Thanks." Sophie plopped down beside him. She brought over a small roll of bread and chunks of cheese to nibble on for supper.

"So, what questions do you have for me?"

"How do I know you and your crew can be trusted? Your loyalty doesn't lie with the queen, that much I know. Swear an oath that you will protect us all and deliver us to safety in Sotera. All of us."

Her directness came at a surprise. She was smart. Confident. She knew something about the fae, more so than the other humans. She demanded an oath – a promise – a currency more valuable than any gold or riches. A promise could not be broken or misfortune, perhaps even death would ensue on the oath breaker. It was a guarantee. And she was cementing her livelihood and the livelihood of her companions with it.

Kaine blinked. He was expecting more existential questions like how Sotera and Faery were connected. If there were another way around the one-week trip to Northern Helm. Anything but this. It intrigued him. She intrigued him.

Kaine peeled his eyes from the fire and found those piercing purple eyes staring straight at him. The tendrils of her short black hair, neatly tucked behind her round human ears. She sat cross-legged, picking at the bread and cheese she'd brought with her. The light of the fire reflected in her eyes and made them dance. Made them come alive. It was hypnotic and a pang of desire hit low in his gut. He'd never seen such a beautiful human before. It took all his fae might to not reach out and trace her lips in awe.

"Hey, hot shot, you're staring." Sophie smiled, clicking her fingers in front of him to pull him back to reality. Her small laughter and the motion of her arms loosened a few tendrils of hair from behind her round human ear. She was not afraid of him, unlike the other humans who hushed or made themselves look busy in his presence.

He cleared his throat. "That is something I cannot offer." Panic washed over Sophie's face. "But what I can promise is that I will do my very best to keep you all safe and deliver you all to Sotera. It is my will and I promise this." His words seemed to wash her panic away.

"Consider it an oath." Sophie nodded with a confidence that Kaine again, did not expect. She held out her hand for him to shake.

"An oath." He gripped her much smaller hand. He noticed then how much larger he was than her.

She smiled, no doubt happy with the small win for herself and her companions, Kaine thought. She took another bite of her bread roll.

"Did you want me to toast the bread for you? It's much nicer than eating it cold, trust me. I've been on enough missions to know," Kaine offered. Sophie nodded, slowly. Sweetly. His broad hands reached out, softly taking the bread and cheese from her hands, purposefully brushing his calloused fingers against her soft skin. He had to know what she felt like. Electricity flitted across his skin, almost as if his mana acknowledged her. Acknowledged her presence. A blush rose from her cheeks at that electricity he most certainly knew she'd just felt too.

Mana in the Faery realm was different to the magic that existed in other realms. It was like a pit of power that existed in their souls. They were born with it. It was alive and it guided them through life. The stronger you were, the more control you had over your mana. Once you harnessed your mana and learned to control it, you'd be able to control various elements. You could use it in conjunction with spells, or you could help hasten natural processes like healing. Despite being born with it, it took enormous effort and practise to will the elements. It is why only one element could be mastered. Some fae, despite being born with mana, couldn't even surpass the basic parts of mana wielding like healing, let alone master an element.

But Kaine was born strong. It was why he could still use a portion of his powers even in the iron tunnels. All the Elite were. For Kaine, his mana spoke to the air. It's why he could manipulate it, create drafts or float items across to him should he have the need. For Elowan, her mana spoke to the element of fire. There were four elements that existed – water, fire, earth and air. It was rare for fae to master one completely. It was why the queen loved the Elite. They were the strongest in Faery and the most talented. And they all could wield one element.

Clearing her throat, Sophie tucked the stray tendrils of her hair behind her ears again, adjusting herself as she sat cross-legged. Kaine placed the cheese atop the small bread roll, and with a small swirl of his hand, he harnessed the air around the fire with his mana, and suspended the roll in the air, just above the fire so that that cheese started to melt, and the roll started to warm.

Sophie gasped at the sight of his magic. Her fingers reached out to touch Kaine's mana that manifested as a glittery mist, taking shape based on what he willed.

Kaine, amused by the delighted reaction to his magic, made a show of it and lifted the warmed cheesy roll back into her slender hands. To which she smiled, eyes beaming up to him to show off the roll that had just landed in her hands on a magical glittery wind. She bit into the warm roll, closing her eyes, savouring the taste and started a small dance of celebration that made Kaine laugh deeply. He was completely entranced by the human.

Swallowing, Sophie noticed his attention. "And what of the queen? She's doubled her security. Do you know why?" she asked.

"She's after some source of power, we don't know what exactly."

"Yeah, I assumed as much. They're always seeking to destroy whatever threatens their throne and power. Stopping at nothing to keep their throne yada yada."

"Why do you speak as if you've experienced the wrath of a thousand fae queens?" He asked, cocking his head. Leaning back onto his arms, he tried his best to decipher the human before him.

"Because I have."

"Blasphemy. You look to be twenty-six, meaning only one queen – Queen Calliea – has ruled. Secondly, judging by how out of place and delightfully human you are, that couldn't be farther from the truth."

"Ah, so she has a name…" Sophie paused momentarily, taking a deep breath as if remembering a long distant memory. "Books. We have them in my world. There are hundreds of them. Tall tales, detailing the reign of various Faery queens and kings, their downfall, true heirs, and all…" As the words left her mouth, she tilted her head in question. "…Where's the king? Why hasn't he stopped the queen from killing all these humans?"

"The king is at his stronghold, across the Fallen Seas. To make the treacherous journey back to Terrin would be too risky for the king. He has a lot of people depending on him. As I'm sure you've been told, Faery is dying. In light of that, the king gathered his closest men and established a stronghold on a more prosperous land which he named New Terrin. With him, the young children of Faery live, learning how to cultivate the land."

"You realise that sounds extremely suspicious, don't you?"

It was Kaine's turn to look puzzled. "It isn't really. He's found a different land for us to prosper in. It's the queen we shouldn't be trusting." The truth of those words ran through his veins. He was right. The queen was a character to be questioned. For so long she has ruled and yet Faery continued to wither.

"Okay, you keep telling yourself that, oh strong warrior," she mocked, wriggling her fingers in the air for emphasis. She smiled. Kaine unwittingly, did the same.

Her eyes landed at his hips.

Kaine held his breath.

She blurted, "Can I touch it?"

Kaine stuttered, making to cover himself up. "I... I didn't realise humans could be so forward." He sat up abruptly, blushing.

"The short spear, you dirtbag. The short spear, NOT your member." Sophie burst out into laughter, her hands slapping against her legs as she shook. It was the most beautiful music he'd ever heard in his life.

At the realisation that Sophie was indeed referring to the short spear by his hip and not his member, he laughed with her, hands bracing his stomach in a fit of laughter.

He hadn't laughed like this in a long time.

11

Two days had gone by and they'd only reached the end of the Fylleran tunnel network. It meant that they needed to make the treacherous trip over land, across the river and back into the tunnel systems of Wrenntia.

Elowan had come back from her posting and took lead of the escape group while Kaine went ahead to scout the route. With her she brought Zala, Camrine's replacement while he went to fulfil his shifts with the Elite.

Zala was a warrior who seemed to have been born from the shadows itself. With her raven black hair, dark brown skin, piercing blue eyes and tattooed face, Zala was one of the fiercest warriors to join the ranks of the Elite. According to Elowan, she was a female of little words, who preferred her skilled swordsmanship to do the talking. Crossed behind her back were two rapiers, in place of the short spear the other fae warriors donned. She was the shortest of the fae warriors Sophie had met, standing at five foot six, but no doubt the deadliest.

"We move swiftly. We move quietly. Do not look around. Do not dilly dally. Stay focused," Elowan said at the front of the group. The humans were instructed to leave their packs behind at the end of Fyllera. There would be new packs waiting on the other side in the Wrenntian tunnels.

They were to climb out of the tunnel works, crawl along the grassy bank and cross the fifty-metre-wide river into chest-high water, using the cover of the night sky and the river bridge. From there, they needed to climb onto the grassy bank on the other side and back down into the tunnel works in Wrenntia. Easy.

Sophie was brimming with excitement. This would be her second time seeing Faery and its breathtaking lands. She thought of what the Autumn Court would look like. Would it be dusted with orange falling leaves? And what of the Winter Court, would it be snowing? Or would it be an Australian winter, wet and cold? She jumped in line at the back of the file the humans formed, so she could marvel at the wonders of Faery for as long as humanly possible. Though Elowan warned them about looking around and being distracted, surely a little look wouldn't hurt.

"Excited, are you?" Tristan, the former Australian soldier turned to Sophie. A few humans had stayed up last night, trading stories. Naturally, everyone was drawn to Tristan. He'd served on a few operations in the Middle East and had plenty of 'warries' – war stories, he explained – that he was more than willing to share. Sophie learned that he had a wife and three kids waiting for him at home in Melbourne. He joked that this was his first operation in a different realm. They all laughed with him.

"Absolutely. Aren't you?" Sophie smiled.

"As long as whatever's up there won't eat me. I think I'll be fine." Tristan laughed.

Sophie laughed too, though a little nervously.

Elowan had gone ahead of the group to guide the humans across the river while Zala remained behind, covering the flank and rear of the group.

Brone was the first to climb out of the tunnels. He turned to help Dolores and Mallory up. Then followed the four young men from Carlton, who claimed they were heading back from a night out when they somehow landed in Faery. They kept to themselves for the most part, which was fair. They were scared. Following them was Sloane, a middle-aged woman and her husband Campbell. They were a couple from the northern beaches of Sydney who owned several beach houses. Much like the boys from Carlton, they kept to themselves – not wanting to get too close to the others. Sophie knew they were scared too.

Lilith was next. A forty-year-old librarian from the eastern suburbs of Melbourne. She was a woman of few words, hiding behind her thickly framed glasses and often surprised the fae in company with her level of fitness. When Sophie shared what she knew of Faery, its myths and legends to the group, Lilith gave her a knowing smile. No doubt, the woman was a wealth of knowledge when it came to such subjects, but she did not let much on. She cowered in the presence of Elowan, Camrine and Zala. But most of all she feared Kaine. Sophie watched the woman in times where they rested their feet. Lilith would dart her eyes to Kaine, eyeing him suspiciously as she pulled her belongings closer to her, moving as far away as she could. But when Sophie deigned to ask what the issue was, Lilith brushed her off. Sophie gave up getting to know the woman altogether.

Tristan, with the ease of a supple leopard, pulled himself onto the Faery lands above. Sophie climbed the steel rungs leading outside into the world she'd only dreamt of. Her heart pattered in anticipation, palms sweating from excitement. She peered above her, greeted by the beautiful dark blue sky, the stars of all colours dancing across it. It was a reprieve from the dark dirty tunnels they'd been travelling through the past few days. Grabbing a hold of the lip of the tunnel entrance, she hoisted herself up and out, onto the grass of Fyllera. Dusting her hands off, she dared to look up and around. Her breath caught, though she didn't make a sound. Her hand lifted to her throat in utter awe of the lands that lay before her.

The Autumn Court was wondrous. A few hundred metres to her right, were scattered wooden cottages, with stone chimneys billowing smoke from woodfire. Each cottage was lit with warm yellow light. Some had beautifully manicured gardens while others had wide patios made for relaxing or enjoying tea. Large, dense maple trees surrounded the cottages, offering privacy for each. The ground was littered with orange and yellow leaves signifying that they were in the thick of fall. Faint laughter could be heard, of children giggling and families enjoying their dinner. The colours of the Autumn Court were vibrant, warm. The smell of cinnamon wafted through the air. It was beautiful. No signs of the plague marred this court at least.

A soft nudge on her shoulder was the only thing that alerted Sophie that Zala still stood behind her. Sophie nodded in silent acknowledgement, moving swiftly to catch up with the rest of the humans who had already slipped into the steadily moving water.

Bracing her hands against the edge of the grassy bank, Sophie slowly lowered herself into the water, making a conscious effort to not make any sloshing sounds as she did. Zala, like the wraith she was, jumped in without a single sound. How the fae female did that was a wonder.

Sophie's teeth chattered as she lowered herself farther into the water, until it covered her shoulders. Zala followed closely behind. They moved swiftly, keeping up with the rest of the pack Elowan was leading. Though instructed to maintain focus, Sophie couldn't help but marvel at the Faery night sky. It was a bright, yet dark blue. The moon was a ring of bright light as opposed to a circle or crescent. The stars indeed looked like they were dancing with each other, holding hands and running circles in delight.

It was then she slipped.

Trying her best not to make a sound she dug in her left foot to steady herself and looked up to the bridge above them, hoping no one had heard the out of place sloshing of water. She whipped her head towards Zala who stood behind her, a lot closer than she expected. The surprise threw her even farther off balance.

Zala braced two hands on Sophie's shoulders to balance her and with a gentle nudge, urged her to keep moving. But she couldn't. Her foot was wedged between rocks from the force she applied to steady herself. Her eyes widened at the realisation. Zala registered the panic in Sophie's eyes. Elowan and the few humans trailing closely behind her were halfway across the river already.

As calm as ever, Zala ducked underneath the water, looking to loosen the rocks that had a death grip around Sophie's left ankle.

At that moment, a small squeal from Dolores flitted across the water, echoing painfully upon its surface. Perhaps Mallory had slipped as she held her daughter, causing them to lose balance. Sophie couldn't quite tell. Mallory flung a hand across her daughter's mouth to silence the small yelp. But it was too late.

"Who goes there?" shouted a male voice from the bridge above.

On the other side of the river, Sophie could see Elowan pushing herself up on the banks of Wrenntia, lending Brone a helping hand. Sophie and Zala were still stuck in the middle of the river.

Mallory and Dolores, struck by fear, stood still in the water, just a few steps from the grassy bank.

The male voice edged closer to the other side of the bridge. "I said who goe— HUMANS!"

It was at that moment Sophie felt the release of the death grip holding her in place. Zala came up from the water, whipping her head between the bridge, the humans rushing to the other side of the river, then back to Sophie struggling to find her balance from the pain that lanced across her ankle.

The pitter-patter of feet echoed across the bridge.

"Halt where you are, humans!" another male voice shouted.

Elowan rushed to the edge the bank to help everyone up. Hauling Dolores into her arms, she bolted for the tunnel entrance, and dropped the young girl inside. Quickly, she turned to help Brone down the entrance. Mallory and the four young men sprinted up the small hill, leaving Tristan to help Lilith up on the bank. Sopping wet, it made the climb and sprint more difficult. They struggled.

Zala turned to Sophie again.

"Go. Help them. I'll distract." Sophie breathed heavily.

With a curt nod, Zala swam across the river with alarming speed. She looked like a shark, propping herself up on the grassy bank swiftly while Elowan guarded the entrance of the tunnels for the remaining humans to run into.

Grinding her teeth at the ankle that throbbed, Sophie took a deep breath and stepped out from underneath the cover of the bridge and stood up from her crouched position.

"HEY BUTTHEAD!" Sophie started waving her arms "Over here!" Sophie twirled in the water. Along the bridge stood four royal guards, lesser fae, torn between the humans who swiftly disappeared underneath to the tunnels and the single human making a scene in the middle of the river.

Zala remained with Tristan and Lilith guiding them up the bank as fast as she could. It looked like Lilith had been injured.

Sophie tried for a bigger distraction, shouting at the top of her lungs, "Oi, looky here. I'm escaping this way! Back into the Autumn Court! Not that way!" Her arms swung and her hips gyrated. She started dancing the Electric Slide. In a river. In Faery. Nothing could be more blasphemous.

One tree-like royal guard nocked the bow he had in his hands, aiming straight for Tristan and Lilith who Zala ushered up the small hill. Elowan covered for them with a short spear in her left hand.

The sound of another bow being nocked was the only thing that snapped Sophie's attention from where Elowan and Zala stood. The arrow was aimed straight at her.

"Oh tits." Sophie nose dived underneath the water and forgot how shallow it really was. She hit her lip on the edge of a rock. Her hands flew up to cup her face, trying to ease the pain that sliced through her face. The motion cost her seconds.

She kicked and swam as hard as she could towards the banks for Wrenntia, but the water of the river only grew more violent, adding resistance to her swim to shore. Sophie paddled underneath the bridge, hoping to use it as cover. Arrows whizzed by her as she did. Ten more metres. Just ten more metres until she was out of the water and onto Winter Court soil. An arrow shot through the water just in front of her. Grinding to a halt, she started swimming in zigzags to avoid the flying arrows.

Come on, Sophie. Just keep kicking. Keep going.

Her ankle was swollen and throbbing from the vice grip it was in earlier. Her lip throbbed too. She looked up for a moment to regain her bearings. And that cost her.

An arrow whizzed through the night sky and almost shot true if Sophie hadn't twirled in the water at the very last second. The edges of the arrow grazed the left side of her ribs, leaving a mist of red blood in its wake.

Sophie yelped, bracing a hand against the wound, accidentally breathing in water as she did. Sputtering and coughing, Sophie gritted her teeth and began kicking. She couldn't go out like this.

Kicking with all her might, she zigzagged to shore. Elowan was busy fighting the three fae guards that tried to reach the entrance of the tunnel, while Zala lowered Tristan down. The moment that he let go, Zala shot her head up, beelining for Sophie who struggled to get herself atop the grassy bank. The wound in her side screamed.

Grabbing Sophie by the back of her blouse, Zala hauled Sophie to her feet, forcing her into a sprint. Sophie pumped her legs and Zala did the same, aiming for the tunnel entrance like their lives depended on it. Because they did. Zala nose dived into the tunnel first, Sophie did the same, tucking and rolling at the last minute so she'd land on her feet. Behind her, Elowan jumped in, feet first, holding on the latch of the entrance, slamming it shut as she flew down. Hand glowing with a red glittery aura, she muttered a few words Sophie couldn't quite hear.

"I've just locked it." Elowan breathed heavily.

Zala ran ahead, lifting the wooden gate, motioning Elowan and Sophie to get underneath. They were all sopping wet, their boots squelching under their weight. Sophie rolled sideways underneath the gate. Elowan followed, though much more gracefully. Zala climbed in behind, silent as ever, standing again to lower the gate. As soon as she did, Elowan turned, held her short spear between her palms, and muttered another spell. Dim red light pulsed from her hand and the gate groaned in place, like something heavy had leaned against it. Trapping it.

"We should be safe now." Elowan turned around swiftly only to stop dead in her tracks. Zala dusting off the dirt on her clothes, did the same. They both stared at Sophie like she had suddenly grown a third head.

"What?" Sophie stared back unsure what they were looking at.

It was Elowan who started. "First of all, that was the worst dancing I've ever seen in my entire existence. And second of all, you're bleeding. Your shirt is entirely red, and it was white the last time I saw you."

"Oh you mean this..." Sophie twisted to look at the wound the arrow had left behind "...it's not so—"

The last thing she heard was the sound of Elowan and Zala rushing to catch her as she dropped to the floor like a wet noodle.

12

Sophie groaned. Her throat felt like she'd ingested a bag of sand. Her eyes felt like they were glued shut. There was a sharp pain by her left ribs and her left ankle throbbed with its own heartbeat. Sophie flung her eyes open and sat up sharply, posed for a fight, remembering exactly where she was – in the Wrenntian tunnels.

"Good. You're awake." A small, relieved smile played across Elowan's face. She knelt by Sophie who had been lying on the ground, dirt and all. Her palm rested gently on Sophie's leg.

"Why do I feel like I've been punched in the head by several ogres? Gods." Sophie lifted her sore arms to brace the low thud in her head. "How long was I out for?" She turned, blinking the sleep out of her eyes, towards Elowan who sat with fae stillness.

"Not that long, ten minutes I'd say. Though given how bad that wound by your rib is... I'm amazed you're even awake," Elowan said, frowning slightly. "Thanks for covering us. We would've lost a few of you if it weren't for your... disastrous dancing." Her hand flew to her mouth, covering it, trying her best not to laugh.

"Well, if that wasn't the best backhanded thank you I've ever received..." Sophie stared pointedly, narrowing her eyes at Elowan. But she smiled.

Elowan reached out, softly punching Sophie in the arm. "Dance moves aside, thank you." She grabbed Sophie's hands. "A debt is owed." A bright light glowed and flowed from Elowan's hands to Sophie's. Warmth followed along until it sputtered out. Sophie peered down, entranced by the mana that had left Elowan's hands. She noticed a tiny new tattoo on her right wrist. It was the size of a coin and shaped like a square, with a side missing. Inside the square lay two rings – the Faery moon, Sophie realised. Gasping at the sight, Sophie lifted her gaze to Elowan, silently asking what it meant.

"It's a blessing. A thank you. A kernel of my power now lives in you. You have my favour." Elowan smiled softly. Sophie didn't know what to make of it. Her heart felt full. She'd found a friend in this realm and her friend had valued her enough to give her a kernel of power. She realised that then that she wanted more time in Faery to get to know the fae she'd spent the last few days with. A week was not enough time to learn who they truly were.

"Thank you," Sophie said breathlessly. "You really shouldn't have." She brushed her fingers across the tattoo. It was smooth. She opened her arms intending to give Elowan a hug, but pain lanced in her side, the bandage applied crinkling and moving with the movement. Sophie looked down to her ribs with confusion.

"Sorry, I hope you don't mind. I thought it'd be easier to patch you up while you were out cold. Less painful." Elowan pointed to the bandages that wrapped firmly around Sophie's torso. "And with the favour, it is my pleasure. Our pleasure." Elowan waved to the room around them. Everyone was sitting by their new packs, resting from the crossing they'd just made. In the distance, Kaine and Zala were tending to those who had sustained injuries.

Elowan stood quietly. "Kaine will be over soon to heal your wounds, I'll go grab you some water." Elowan padded off. Sophie looked around the tunnel. It was much brighter than the tunnels in Fyllera. Sconces with eternal flames were spaced out evenly across the walls, lighting the way. It felt colder. Sophie's hot breath smoked out her mouth as she breathed. Her torn blouse and thin breaches didn't do much to warm the cold she suddenly felt in her gut.

"May I?" Kaine asked softly in his low warm voice.

Sophie nodded, meekly, from where she lay on the ground.

Kaine's large tan hands gently lifted her blouse, scrunching it up by her chest to expose the bandage Elowan had quickly applied earlier. Blotches of blood had already started to form on the bandage.

Breathing shallow, anticipating the touch, Sophie lay quiet, eyeing his broad hands.

"Can you sit up?" Kaine leaned over Sophie.

She pursed her lips, not only from the pain that ebbed through her but from Kaine's proximity. She made to move, slowly lifting her hands to support her weight. She lifted her eyes to his, this time taking hold of his turquoise eyes with her own. She knew her mortal heart gave her away again.

Kaine grabbed her hand gently, as if she were about to break, and slowly propped her up so she was sitting comfortably.

"I'll need to take the bandage off. It might sting," Kaine said grimly, noting the blood that had already seeped through the bandages.

Sophie dipped her chin — silent permission, focusing entirely on the huge fae male who sat before her, treating her with utmost care, as if she were a delicate porcelain doll.

Kaine moved, making swift work of the bandage, rolling it back around her, slowly revealing the wound. Where his fingers trailed, her body reacted with a flood of goosebumps. The gash was about twenty centimetres long. It was deep, exposing bone.

"I now understand why you passed out." He grinned. A flash of the fae fangs and the two dimples almost blinded Sophie. "Very brave human indeed." He admired as he set down the rolled soiled bandage by her side.

"You know this human has a name, right?"

"I know," he teased. A cheeky grin spread across his face. Sophie was lucky she wasn't standing. Her knees wobbled and her stomach fluttered.

Hovering his hands just above the wound, he closed his eyes, breathed in slowly and willed his mana. A bright white glow with glittery speckles roamed around his fingertips and across the wound by Sophie's ribs. Skin and flesh slowly knitted together. Then faster, as he pulsed more of his mana into it.

Sophie's lips, still not used to the sight of mana, parted in delightful surprise. She watched as her skin knitted together, fully healing. When the light from his palms dimmed, all that was left was new, shiny pink skin.

"It'll scar I'm afraid," Kaine said, lowering his hands. Without a word, he moved to her left ankle. "May I?"

Sophie nodded slowly. With her permission, he moved before her booted feet. He pulled off her left boot gently to avoid agitating her raw ankle. Setting her boot aside quietly, he grabbed her leg by the calf and propped her heel gently on his lap. Her ankle was red and raw, twice the size of what it was supposed to be. In reverent silence, he willed that same healing power. A faint glow appeared as he held his hands across her ankle. She knew she was staring. He was a warrior. That was certain. But he held her so delicately. Sophie's heart clenched at that.

As the glowing dissipated, he lifted her foot and gently tested its mobility. "Does that hurt?" He peered up at her.

She shook her head, smiling at him and the feeling of her newly healed ankle.

Placing her foot down softly to rest on the boot he had taken off, he smiled softly. "Well, it looks like my job here is done."

Sophie didn't want it to be. She wanted to feel his hands all over her. She wanted to know what it was like to straddle him again. She wanted to taste him.

She shook her head to clear her spiralling thoughts. "How can I repay you?"

"Survive." A wicked smile splayed across his face. He picked up the soiled bandages and strode back to the main group.

Sophie wasn't sure if she'd made up that entire encounter. The heated looks. The touching. Surely he smelled her desire from a mile away? Her heart slowed from its racing. When she arrived in Faery, she felt a tether inside her heart snap awake. A feeling that she could not articulate. A feeling that rose from her chest that lay dormant for a long time. A connection. A strong one. It was like she'd gone her whole life seeing through a haze and suddenly, she could see clearly. Was that awakening feeling a connection to Kaine?

Wrapped tightly in a thick blanket, Sophie lay as still as possible. Willing herself to become smaller. To become unseen. The woman in front of her rowed the boat hurriedly, keeping a low profile. She had long silver hair, gold shimmering eyes and delicately pointed ears. She looked kind and warm, though worry was etched deeply on her face as she methodically rowed.

Row. Row.

Sophie reached up to wipe her wet cheeks, trying her best to focus on something happy. Her little body felt tired. So tired. And her heart, her little heart ached. The connection she shared with her best friend withered the farther away they rowed. The tether that connected their two souls together faded. The connection they'd come to feel comfort in. The connection that allowed them to understand each other without whispering a word. The connection that plucked two souls from millions and joined them in unyielding unity. Fated.

She looked to the stars then. A welcome distraction from her heartache. She tried her hardest not to blink. She forged them into her memory. Forcing her mind to remember them, the way they shined for her. She wouldn't forget. Wherever she went. No matter how far.

The stars danced and sang, content, happy. The blue-and-green swirling sky danced with them.

As they rowed farther and farther, the stars and sky stopped. Just for a moment. Pausing their merriment to wave goodbye.

13

"We're to make our last stop tonight. Tomorrow, you'll board the train home to Sotera. So, please rest well. The journey will be tiring," Kaine announced from the front of the two neat files the humans had made.

They'd been marching for hours now. After Sophie had been healed following their eventful river crossing, Elowan and Zala had left for their shifts with the Elite. Camrine, the red-haired fae, had come back to replace them.

Sophie hadn't had much opportunity to learn about each member of the group in detail, but she was sure Camrine had made it his life mission to annoy Sophie ever since her blunder of an introduction with Kaine. At least that's what Sophie assumed. Every waking moment that it was his turn to lead the group, he'd refer to Sophie, strictly as Madame Sophie. "An ode to Sophie's blunder" he called it. He was the annoying brother that Sophie never asked for.

The group stopped for a short break, lugging off their packs to ease the pain that ebbed across everyone's backs.

Camrine no doubt thought this was the perfect opportunity to annoy her. Lo and behold, with his wildfire hair and light-green eyes of mischief, he sauntered over to Sophie, lazily swinging his short spear.

Sophie couldn't have rolled her eyes farther back into her head, even if she wanted to.

"Madame Sophie, heard you took a bit of a slip?" Camrine teased, nudging Sophie on the upper arm as everyone rummaged through their packs for water and fruit.

"I wouldn't call taking one for the team a mere *slip.*" Sophie narrowed her eyes at him, but a small smile started at the corner of her mouth. It was hard not to like Camrine. Not only was he the jokester of the group, but he was also resourceful, having served in several high-stake Elite missions. Naturally, he was drawn to Tristan and Brone who shared their fair share of war stories. They bonded over a range of military subjects from what materials would be best used to create fires or the best weapon systems they'd ever used, as Sophie and a few others listened by the fire. Despite being from different worlds, the combat tactics used were similar.

Camrine leaned up against the tunnel wall, a leg propped up for support as he flipped his short spear in his hands. "Heard you got bandaged up too. I wonder who heal—"

"I'm going to stop you right there," Sophie whisper-shouted, pointing a finger at him.

"Oh, whatever do you mean?" Camrine drawled dramatically with a huge grin plastered across his face.

"What I mean is that if another word comes out of your silly fae mouth, I'm going to—"

"Cam! I need you here," Kaine, with his deep voice called from the other side of the tunnel. Sophie turned to see Kaine, hovering over Brone who seemed to have an ache in his shoulder.

"Duty calls." Camrine winked, pushing himself off the wall with a bit of pep in his step.

Sophie shook her head. She was glad to have his sunshine warming the group. Things would've been duller over the past few days if Camrine hadn't been cracking jokes... trying to make everyone forget about the dangers that lurked above and beyond.

After a few moments of rest, Camrine resumed his position at the front, leading the section while Kaine hung back, just behind Sophie to guard the back of the group. All twelve humans were still here, though some were battered and bruised. Kaine was doing well in keeping his oath to her.

The group kept a steady pace. Quiet. Tristan, Brone, Dolores and Mallory were excited to finally return home. The others remained scared though less tense as they neared the end of their week-long journey through Faery.

Sophie was torn. She missed her mum sorely. She missed her best friend, Lorrie. She missed the comfort of her own bed and the taste of coffee. But equally, she knew she'd miss the beauty of Faery. She'd miss Camrine who teased her about the handsome fae warrior leading the pack. She'd miss Elowan. She'd miss seeing mana being used, even if it were the muted variant. She'd miss Faery. Sure, she'd visit it in the books she'd read, but it simply wasn't the same.

Sophie was pulled from her thoughts by a strong hand, firmly gripping her shoulder, pulling her to a stop. She whipped her head back, meeting Kaine's turquoise eyes. He was calm but focused ahead with a finger across his lips, signalling her to stay quiet.

With eyes wide, Sophie pulled her focus back to where Camrine stood, fist in the air, signalling all to halt. They'd made it to another intersection of tunnels. Tunnels that were unnervingly quiet now.

With fae grace, Camrine then signalled the group to form a line, hard up against the left wall of the tunnel, as they were instructed, in case they came across a patrol or someone unexpectedly combing through the tunnels.

On silent feet, Sophie pushed herself up against the wall. Kaine stood by her, keeping watch of the humans. With a curt nod towards Kaine, Camrine unsheathed his short spear and slowly advanced, scanning right to left as he made his way into the intersection, short red hair shifting slightly from the draft.

Sophie felt Kaine tense beside her.

His nose flared. He unsheathed his short spear too. His eyes narrowed, focusing on something. Perhaps he smelled something she could not.

Sophie watched as Kaine pushed off the wall and circled around, facing the intersection of tunnels they'd just left. Sconces with eternal fire flickered.

The hairs on the back of Sophie's neck rose. She gulped. This didn't feel right at all.

Kaine snapped his head back to the group. "RUN!"

The group scattered like cockroaches, scrambling to get to where Camrine had been at the front. The red-headed fae sprinted back to help Dolores and Brone whose limp had grown more devasting over time. They ran forwards while Kaine protected their backs. Sophie pumped her legs as hard as she could. Lilith fell, screeching as she ripped open her knees on the rocky ground. Sophie swung back to heave the librarian off the floor, forcing her into a run again.

"Come on, you've got to keep going!" Sophie panted, hand on the back of a crying Lilith who started running, but not fast enough.

Behind her, Sophie could hear Kaine running, doing his best to keep security from the back. In the front, Camrine sprinted with the Dolores in his arms toward a wooden gate in the distance. Sophie dared to look back at what chased them. And she regretted it.

Charging for them were hundreds of lion-sized spiders. Sophie almost vomited, mid sprint, at the sight of them.

They were obsidian with at least eighty eyes each. Covered in sparse, matted black fur, their pincers struck together violently as if they knew they were in for a succulent, human meal.

"Move! Move! Move!" Camrine was at the front, almost at the wooden gates that would offer them a sort of refuge.

Kaine with his short spear sliced and diced any spiders that'd dare cross his threshold. A warrior in his element. He flipped, kicked out, punched out and sliced his way through them. With his real power muted in the tunnels, he had to take them out the old-fashioned way. Sophie feared that it wouldn't be too long before they'd mow him down. He was clearly outnumbered and the humans were struggling to move quickly.

Hanging back, Sophie helped Lilith move, panting. One of the four young men had fainted after laying eyes on giant spiders that gave them chase. Two of his friends helped, while the other ran ahead.

"I'll take her from here." It was Tristan.

"Thanks." Sophie breathed as she let go of Lilith's middle, handing her over to Tristan who threw the forty-year-old over his back like a bag of rice.

A burn started in Sophie's throat. She was so tired. So sore. But she kept pushing. They were almost home. They couldn't give up now.

As Sophie ran, she could faintly hear Kaine's grunts as he surely twisted and turned, slashing out, trying his best to keep the spiders at bay. Between the fray, the sound of glass shattering chimed through the tunnel, and it wasn't long before—

BOOM.

Sophie hit the ground brutally. Her knees scraped, her ears rung and her mouth became gritty. The tunnel seemed to twist and turn in front of her, as smoke and dust billowed from the ground.

The screeches started then. Sophie turned to the source of the force that struck her down. The spiders had caught on fire. Fire that was green. Hellfire. She recognised the magical flames rumoured to kill the mightiest of beasts.

The spiders surged forwards, towards the group. Some melted, screeching as they did. Some disintegrated entirely into dust. They scurried, trying to claw themselves away from the hellfire.

Fuck. Sophie scrambled to find her feet. She had finally made it to the intersection of tunnels when the wind went out from her lungs and her feet left the ground entirely. Then she felt it. Pincers tried to tear her apart. A group of spiders had intercepted them. She couldn't breathe.

She kicked, thrashed and punched her way through the darkness. All she could hear were the screams of the friends she'd made over the past few days. They were screaming. Some were crying. Then another boom sounded. The ground vibrated.

Bits of debris, or spider, flew in the air and fell, coating Sophie's face with slime and dust. She finally had the chance to open her eyes but was met with a gaping grey mouth with thousands of razor-sharp teeth. She screamed, horrified. She scurried back as fast as she could, narrowly missing the chomp of the teeth that aimed for her legs. She'd been knocked into the tunnel that ran perpendicular to the one they were meant to journey.

She kicked out, dodging as pincers tried to pin her flesh. Pincers made for pinning prey. Pincers that promised a slow, tortuous death.

Another explosion reverberated through the group again. The screaming of humans was now joined with screeches of the spiders. Sophie could barely breathe. Hearing its brethren shriek in pain, the spider that held her down paused.

Sophie used that to her advantage.

She jumped up onto her feet, kicked up the dirt and rock she had just been lying on, into the spider's eyes. It shrieked, using its many limbs to clear its eyes. Sophie palmed the sharp rock she'd found in her scurrying, and lunged, bringing it down as hard as she could between the spider's eyes. She pushed and pushed as it screamed, pincers flailing, trying to dislodge Sophie from where she stabbed it.

Push, push, push.

The spider went still. With a grunt Sophie let go of the rock, panting, covered in slime. She jumped off the spider and sprinted for the group she'd been dragged away from, dodging the spiders felled by the hellfire. Dodging the other spiders that feasted on... someone. Sophie stopped in her tracks. She didn't want to look but she had to. She knew who it was. She recognised his weathered hands. Brone. Once full of energy and wisdom he now lay lifeless, wide-eyed and empty.

No. no. no. Sophie tried to get near to him, but a loud roar sounded beside her that almost knocked her off her feet. A giant spider basked in glory as it feasted on... Mallory. Her chestnut hair spilled across her grey, blood-splattered face, her hand reaching for the gate.

"Mallory..." Sophie freely sobbed now.

Shrieks and screams blended into one in the tunnel. It felt like a fever dream. She had to keep going. If not for them, then who?

Sophie picked up her pace. She was about to round the corner for the gate where Camrine was running to, when something sharp caught hold of her legs. Flipping around to free herself, Sophie was met with large black pincers coated in bright red blood. Sophie whimpered. Screamed. Kicked. But nothing worked. She was being dragged back into the direction she just came. She clawed the floor trying to get a hold of anything.

Rocks skittered by. They dug into her back, legs and arms as the spider pulled and pulled. She was crying. Screaming. She was so close to home. So close. She would be home tomorrow if she willed it.

The thought of home being so close, fired up newfound energy and determination inside her. She crunched up, grabbing a hold of one of the spider's legs, placed it into a lock in her arms and squeezed. The spider shrieked. Sophie squeezed and squeezed, gritting her teeth, screaming as she did. Then, *CRACK.* The spider stopped its forward movement and turned on Sophie, outraged. She could barely move her legs. The spider lunged.

Sophie was greeted with a mouth full of razor-sharp teeth, inching closer and closer. She shut her eyes and screamed, the only thing she could do. Her arms were pinned to the ground by its pincers. Her legs, pinned by its other legs. The world around her quietened. Darkened. Only for a hum of metal to pass through air. A silver short spear found its mark at the centre of all its eyes. The spider crumpled on top of Sophie. It was so heavy Sophie could barely breathe. She tried to topple it over using her knees when strong arms hooked underneath hers and dragged her out from underneath.

His sweet and spicy scent hit her.

Whimpering, Sophie braced herself against Kaine as she tried to stand.

"I've got you." In one swift motion, he lifted her off her feet and cradled her.

"I can run. I just..."

"We don't have a moment. It'll be faster this way," Kaine said firmly.

He sprinted past the fallen spiders. The live ones feasted away on more people they'd managed to capture, but Sophie could not see who they were. Her throat ached from the pain she felt on their behalf. They'd never see home again.

Rounding the corner, Kaine sprinted with unearthly fae speed. As they neared the gate, he set Sophie down on her feet so they could roll swiftly underneath it. As they did, Kaine freed small vial of green liquid from his belt and let it roll to the other side of the gate where the spiders were. Slamming the gate shut behind him, Kaine rushed to his feet, short spear between his palms just like how Elowan had. He muttered a few words. A huge groan fortified the gate in place.

"That should do it," he panted.

As if on cue, the hellfire he released exploded, obliterating any spiders that were left on the other side.

Sophie turned on her feet to find Camrine standing, facing the gate. Dolores clutching for dear life onto his leg. He looked down at her, then back at the gate. Her mother would not be coming home with her.

Sophie counted then. One. Two. Three. And then she counted herself. Four. There were only four people left. Dolores. Tristan. Lilith. And Sophie. The rest, gone. On the other side of the damned gate. Just like that.

Sophie clasped her hands around her mouth. Her hands were torn to shreds. And she whimpered. Then the tears came. For the people that didn't make it, and for the people that did. Her throat ached tremendously.

Kaine stepped forward and wrapped his arms around her. Cradling her head. Resting his cheek on top of it. Sophie leaned in, clutching his chest, the only thing grounding her in this moment.

Words, as if whispered on a wind, wrapped around Sophie's heart. "You're okay. You're safe now. I've got you, Sophie." Kaine's deep voice was a song of soothing.

Sophie cried like she had never cried before.

14

Elowan and Zala had been gathering intelligence for the queen all night. The Wrenntian mountain winds were crisp, cold, biting into Elowan's back. They were both huddled, making themselves small in a makeshift observation post they'd created between various trees and logs that had fallen.

There were reports of civil unrest in the city of Terrin. Whispers of a rebellion against the crown found their way through the town and the queen had caught wind of it. She would not have it. Not in her realm. So she tasked her Elite to do what they did best. Her strongest of warriors who gathered intel, strategised and executed on her behalf. What this usually meant were long observation shifts throughout the night, more than likely in the depressing cold.

"I swear if I have to do another observation shift, I'm going to blow it," Elowan muttered, tapping her pencil against the leather-bound logbook in front of her. Everything that Zala observed with her binoculars, Elowan had the responsibility of jotting down. From vehicles to the comings and goings of royal guards. Even the change in weather that could stir with the use of mana. Everything and anything could be vital to the queen's mission – to destroy all of Faery's enemies. Her enemies.

Elowan was met with silence.

Zala continued her methodical scanning under the cover of darkness, without a word of response.

They sat on the side of a mountain face on the edge of the Wrenntia. Their vantage point overlooked the main supply route between Castle Terrin, the town centre, and the rivers beyond. The mountain they chose was thick with wintery vegetation that served as the perfect concealment for their observation post.

"Thanks for the great chat tonight, Z," Elowan said sarcastically, shaking her head and rolling her eyes. She was so close to calling it quits tonight. It was freezing in Wrenntia, and barely anything moved along the main supply route.

"Five hundred metres," Zala said, pointing. "Castle Terrin Southern Gate. Wagon approaching gate, moving right to left. Heavy load given deep tracks left behind. One horseman. Two black horses leading the wagon." Zala's voice was barely a whisper and her words spilled out in rapid fire.

Elowan's cold-bitten hands could barely keep up.

"Logged." Elowan quickly flipped out the files she'd pinched from Castle Terrin's administration office. She scanned the log of vehicles that were approved to leave and enter within the hour. Nothing. Nothing was scheduled.

"Wagon has turned. Heading in direction of stables. It's the same wagon and horsemen who delivered the children to port for New Terrin earlier this afternoon. I recognise the brooch he's wearing," Zala said calmly. She was by far the best observer of their Elite team.

Elowan quickly wrote the notes down. "Logged. He's probably just left early or maybe he's forgotten something." She scoffed. Typical good-for-nothing royal guards.

Zala pulled down the binoculars from her face. Her bright blue eyes narrowed with suspicion. "It's odd."

"What's odd? That he's come back early because he's forgotten something, or he left the Port Ceremony because he was bored out of his brains?"

Silence.

Zala pulled up the binoculars to her face again. Searching harder. Scanning rhythmically. There was something askew. Elowan could feel it. And she knew Zala could feel it too.

"They normally don't come back this way."

"Logged."

"The tracks are the same depth from when he left."

"Logged."

"We need to get closer."

"Roger."

With a small wave of her arm, Zala opened a dark glittery portal before them. And like two ghosts in the night, they slid in.

Landing softly on the grass just outside the castle stables, Zala and Elowan visually cleared the area around them. Their cloaks added an extra layer of concealment to their bodies. They were nothing but shadows moving with the wind.

Together, they approached the wagon that had been left unattended and empty just inside the stable gates. Zala lifted the back flap silently and climbed in. Elowan stood watch.

Zala's hand softly tapped Elowan's shoulder. If she were any other person, she would have jumped with fright. After spending years training together, she'd grown accustomed to the way the wraith moved with deadly stealth.

"All clear. The scent of children is there, but faint."

Something was off. Elowan could tell. The all-knowing mana that lived inside her told her so. "Let's clear the stables. The driver couldn't have gotten far that quickly."

Zala gave a curt nod and led the way.

They hopped into the main stables, clearing each bay as they moved through the building. Hay was disturbed where stable hands ran back and forth throughout the day. Horses lay quietly while others grazed. Deafening silence hung in the air. Elowan held her breath as they neared the last stall. Her mana kicked about in fear as they closed in. The stall itself was dimly lit by a sconce and hay was strewn across the floor but nothing was inside.

"Is your mana freaking out as much as mine?"

"Yes."

"There's something wrong here but I can't see anything out of place." She moved closer to the stall, assessing the floor, the walls, the hay – all of it. Nothing. So instead of looking, she listened. There was a tiny hum, like static power that Elowan could just hear and a slight creak of a rope that sounded like it was holding substantial weight. Then she smelled. A slight tang hit the back of her nostrils but dissipated quickly.

"There's a glamour," Zala whispered. She'd come to the same conclusion as Elowan had.

A glamour was a fae trick of the mind. Passers-by would see what the trickster wanted them to see – in this case an empty stall – but to the trained eye, they could be spotted and with a bit of work, broken.

Luckily for Elowan, the being who'd pulled together this glamour was sloppy. In a rush, even. Bits of sound and smell seeped through, a sure sign that there was a crack in the mirage.

Zala was on it immediately. With deft flicks of the wrist, the wraith drew an unlocking spell over the wall of glamour. The symbol glowed bright but guttered.

"Here." They didn't have to use many words. Lifting her sleeve, Elowan took the tip of her short spear, piercing her skin just enough for a few droplets of blood to fall.

Zala quickly covered her fingers in Elowan's blood and drew the symbols against the wooden gate of the stall. The ancient fae symbol burned to life.

And like a dying beast, the glamour let out its last sputtering breath of magic and dissipated into a fine mist to reveal a scene Elowan wished, with every microscopic fibre of her soul and being, that she could unsee.

Several meat hooks hung on the ceiling beams.

On the large metal hooks hung... children.

Children.

Tied up by their feet in a whirlwind of knots.

They hung limp, greyed. Their veins had turned a deathly black.

Blood dripped carelessly down their arms and wrists into wooden buckets.

Their lifeless little bodies swayed.

There were four of them. Of all ages.

Bile rose in Elowan's throat. She couldn't make a sound. She couldn't even move. Her eyes watered with pain, anger, anguish and confusion.

Small, dying breaths sounded in the corner of the stall.

Three smaller bodies were piled together. Their veins turning a deep, dark black as the essence of life left their bodies.

Nightlock.

A poison that would kill a fae adult in a few minutes, but a fae child... a few seconds at most. A poison that was forbidden by the queen, for it changed the essence of the victim's blood, keeping it warm long beyond their death. For eternity, the legends said.

And there was only one use for that type of blood.

This type of blood.

The blood that dripped and dripped down their arms.

It was a sacrifice.

An offering made in dark blood magic that could grant access to unimaginable powers, strength.

An offering made to devils and demons that lurked in the Shadow Realm.

It was forbidden.

A bowl of the dark purple Nightlock berries sat sinisterly on a stool beside the children.

Someone had forced the children to eat the berries. That someone had to have taken the time to tie the children up then... bleed them. Hanging them carelessly above the buckets. How could they? For what purpose? They were kids. Faery children. The most blessed and protected beings of the realm.

A fire started in Elowan's heart. Then wrath came in on a blinding wave of rage. Whoever did this was going to pay. And she would see to it.

Zala gripped Elowan's wrist before she could make a move. "Elowan. Don't."

"Don't what? Don't give these kids the proper burial they deserve? Do they not deserve to live in the Elysian Fields as their ancestors have?" Elowan raged. Hot tears found their way down her cheeks. Her throat ached with a harshness she'd be willing to feel every day of her life if it meant the perpetrator of this vile act would suffer for all eternity.

Zala's grip only tightened.

"They do, but I fear this is much bigger than we are. It smells of a dark blood magic. We weren't meant to see this."

"No fucking shit, Z. Of course we weren't meant to see this. This is abhorrent."

"We need to go. Now," Zala said firmly.

"Let me go."

"No. Be a fool if you wish." The wraith's piercing-blue eyes burned with a fury. "But you know there is more to this."

Elowan yanked her wrist back to herself with frustration. She knew. She knew that there was someone out there orchestrating this. Someone cruel and vile. Someone who was desperate, though for power or revenge, it was unclear. This was a rare hole in their story that the Elite could capitalise on if they played their cards right. But who was it? Was the queen aware of what was happening in her very realm? She'd be devastated. And Kaine, did he know? He'd been on multiple supply route posts. He had to have known or at least tracked the other wagons coming back from the Port Ceremony. He was all-seeing. The captain of the Elite. There was no way he didn't know if something was awry in Faery. But there was a chance he was keeping it from her. He'd been known to do just that on a few of their missions. Which meant... she had a bone to pick.

With a quick pull of her mana, Elowan opened a portal before her.

"Where are you going?" the wraith asked firmly.

"To see our dear captain." Elowan grunted before jumping into the portal. She didn't wait to see if Zala followed.

15

The fire was smaller tonight. Kaine, Camrine and the four humans that had survived, sat around it. They mourned the friends that hadn't made the journey. They sat quietly, watching the fire crackle.

Sophie cleared her throat. "I don't know about you guys, but I think I can finally tick 'fight for my life against giant rabid spiders' off my bucket list." She laughed nervously but Kaine could see through it. Her throat bobbed and her smile didn't quite meet her eyes. She was hurting.

She was met with silence.

But slowly, the other humans started to laugh. Then they outright roared, bellies full of laughter. For if they didn't laugh, they'd surely start crying.

They were prepped and ready for the last leg of their journey, back home to Sotera. They had two hours left before they needed to make a move. They needed to make it past the last gate that indicated the end of the Wrenntian tunnels, onto the train tracks at Northern Helm station, then into the engine room of the train. Once the train exited Faery, then, and only then, could they head back out into the main carriages.

Kaine was disappointed in himself. Of all the journeys he'd made with humans from Southern Helm to Northern Helm, he hadn't experienced this many casualties. And while he chose his words wisely, he couldn't help but feel as if he hadn't tried his best to keep them all safe. He felt like he'd broken his promise to Sophie, and the feeling left him feeling wrong and unworthy. It seemed the efforts of the queen to rid Faery of human presence had doubled down and succeeded. His immortal heart ached. He mowed down enemies without a single bat of an eyelash, but it was the needless killing of innocent lives that kept him up at night. He could've done more. He *should've* done more.

Needing to breathe, to calm his mana and the anger that sat tight in his chest, he stood from where he sat next to Sophie.

"Where are you going?" She peered up with those glistening purple eyes.

"I... I need to think. Breathe."

"Up there?" She pointed above.

Kaine didn't know why it slipped out of his mouth. Maybe it was the need for comfort. Maybe it was because it was the last night he'd be able to see her. "Would you like to come?" He hoped she would say yes.

She nodded and swiftly moved to her feet. She was fast. Even for a human. She stood by him, motioning him to lead the way with a delicate wave of her hand.

They reached the steel rungs that lead outside into Wrenntia. Popping the latch, Kaine headed above onto land and cleared the immediate area before signalling to Sophie that it was okay to come out.

Sophie grabbed the lip of the ledge and hauled herself onto damp grass. Her boots made squeaky noises as her knees pushed against the ground. In an instant, Kaine was there, hand out in an offer to help her to her feet. Where they touched, electricity built and he swore his hands instantly warmed.

Together, they stood near the entrance of the forest surrounding Wrenntia. Thick pine trees towered over them, providing sufficient cover. The forest floor was cold and damp.

They carefully made their way to the edge of the trees. Kaine held her hand, leading her over rocks and divots in the ground. Then he stopped.

Sophie gasped. A sound that Kaine wanted to hear over and over again.

"It's exactly as I imagined." Kaine watched as pure joy radiated from her, her eyes wide open with wonder.

Wrenntia. The Winter Court, despite its weather, warmed his immortal soul. Below in the valley ahead, he could see it for all its beauty and he hoped Sophie could too. The cobblestone streets were lined with warm yellow lights and colourful, multi-storey houses, packed up against each other, as if the houses themselves were cold. A small steady river ran through the town centre, reflecting the colourful houses, making a vivid artwork. But where Fyllera bustled with activity and laughter, Wrenntia did not. The streets were empty, and a few houses even had their windows boarded up.

Kaine knew that Sophie had caught the same details as he did. She frowned.

"It hit Wrenntia first. The blight, if you will. The lands here cannot be cultivated. Many fae folk moved to other courts. Very few stayed," Kaine said slowly, looking over the lands with sadness in his eyes. "You'll see that darkness has consumed the outskirts of the court. A ghost of what it once was." Kaine pointed to the outer rim of the court where vegetation had turned black and dull. The Faery moon above cast ghastly shadows across ramshackle buildings, painting Wrenntia as an old, forgotten town.

"Still, it is beautiful."

"Without its people, Wrenntia is but a few pretty buildings."

"I knew Faery was dying, but I didn't understand the gravity of what you and Elowan had been telling me," Sophie said solemnly, the remaining wonders of Wrenntia reflecting in her eyes.

The entire Winter Court had been wiped out, pushed out of their homes as the lands did not give them what they needed. Couldn't give them what they needed.

Slowly, Kaine walked ahead and perched himself on the grass overlooking the winter town that once was. Sophie followed. She sat, arms wrapping around her knees and scooted close enough to Kaine that their thighs were touching. He could stay like this for a while, he thought.

"Can you tell me more about you... about Faery? Did you grow up in Wrenntia?" Something like reservation clung to her voice. He understood why. They'd have to take the potion to erase all memories of Faery before they boarded the train. It was the only way Kaine and his crew would permit them to leave. It was that or stay in Faery and risk getting killed.

Kaine, despite knowing she was to leave, wanted to open his heart to this human. He decided exactly that when he heard her screams as the spiders pinned and snapped for her. A moment where he thought it was too late. A moment where his heart sank at the thought of never knowing the feel of her soft lips against his. A moment where he realised he would never know how she became who she was – a strong woman who'd jump in the face of danger to save others.

"I spent most of my time growing up in Terrin, in the surroundings of the main castle where the queen lives. Though my mother was from Summeira, the

Summer Court." He had a natural tan that wouldn't shake even in the colder seasons. Afterall, he was from the court of sunshine and heat.

"Was?"

Kaine paused. "My mother passed away when I was very young."

"I'm so sorry." Sophie reached her hand out, resting it on his forearm in comfort.

"It was a long time ago. You need not worry." He stopped himself from placing his hand atop hers. Picking nervously at the grass underneath him instead, he continued, "I don't remember much before she passed, or much about her. I only have this." He pulled out a shiny pendant necklace in the shape of a sun that he wore every single day without fail. He leaned closer to Sophie so she could have a look at his most prized possession.

Sophie held it between her fingers. It was beautiful in her hands; half the size of her palm, still warm from where it sat on his chest underneath his armour. Gold gemstones decorated its rays, with one single sharp ray protruding at the top and in the middle, the face of a sleeping sun.

She peered up to him, and by the grace of the gods, Kaine could not stop himself from leaning farther into her.

"What... happened?" She chewed at her bottom lip.

"She was eaten alive by hellhounds almost twenty years ago now." In fact, many strange things happened twenty years ago. His mother's death was just one of them. "Again, it was all such a blur, but I remember that we were running from them. My mother tripped as we were running through the Redwood Forest just behind Summeira. They mauled her, right in front of me. I was helpless. I remember praying so hard to the Tienthan, but they never came." He scoffed. "They never helped. The hellhounds didn't make a move for me. I don't understand why. They just sniffed at me and ran in the other direction. A few days later, there was no trace of the Hellhounds. No lead I could follow. Like they just appeared on this plane and then disappeared." He shook his head slightly at the fateful night he watched his mother get eaten alive.

"Who knew bloodthirsty hellhounds had boundaries?"

"You've heard of such beasts before?"

"Of course. A thing of nightmares. Demons taking the shape of dogs." Sophie shook her entire body, chills no doubt running rampant at the thought of such nightmarish beasts. She was rightfully terrified. Most hellhounds had dark fur, blood-red eyes and flames for a tail. They were nasty, bloodthirsty creatures and they only obeyed one person – Terr, King of the Shadow Realm, or the Underworld as some referred to it. "For what it's worth, I'm sure your mother would be so proud of the handsome warrior you are today. Look at you, captain of the queen's chosen warriors AND the revolution against her." She nudged him with her knees, lightening the mood.

"Yes, I'm not sure what she'd have to say about that." He laughed with her. Though he couldn't quite shake the vision of his mother's silver swirling eyes dimming, her dark black hair matted with blood and her hands reaching out for him.

They watched the town in front of them for a moment longer. Quiet. Silent. Still, with no life.

"What's the Tienthan?" Sophie cleared her throat.

"Who, is the question. They're what some would call guardian angels of this realm. I've never seen them, but I've met a few Faery folk who have. They sing praises, but I'm yet to see them help us, help our people, or the blight of Faery for starters. For all I know, they're righteous, pig-headed warriors that only deign to frolic the Godlands, not help those in need. They didn't help my mother when she needed it, that is certain." Kaine pulled out the grass beneath him, annoyed at the thought of the warriors intervening when they wanted to, not when it was needed. Sounded a lot like virtue signalling, Kaine thought.

Sophie blurted, "Do they have wings?"

"Of course they have wings, they're angels."

"Do you have wings?"

"No I do not. That is preposterous."

"Hmm... well that's disappointing." Sophie smirked at that.

"What is that smirk for?"

"Well in the books I've read, there's this wondrous, holy thing called wingspan." Sophie emphasised it with the sway of her hands and wagged her eyebrows as she did. She let out a laugh. "Legends have it that the span of an immortal's wings, be it angel or fae, would be a good indication of the size of a particular male part. The bigger the wingspan... the bigger the—"

"I've got the picture." Kaine gaped, cutting her short, and then shook his head, utterly amused by the woman sitting beside him. "Humans and their forwardness. I'll never get used to it."

She looked at him, with pause and reflection. Scanning his face as if... she didn't want to leave. He didn't want her to leave either.

Leaning her head on her knees, she smiled softly and with a sadness in her eyes, she said less joyfully, "Well you won't have to deal with me much longer." She nudged him with her elbow in jest. "We should probably head back..." Sophie uncrossed her legs, making to get up from the floor but Kaine stopped her. His large hand wrapping around her wrist.

He felt it then. A rush. An urgency that shot through his chest.

Kaine pulled her back down.

Her eyes met his of deep dark desire. Their hot breaths mingled. Kaine could feel her breath on his lips. And it felt like in this world, only they existed. They inched closer and closer. Kaine knew he was damning himself, but he couldn't let her go. Not without tasting her. Not without feeling his lips on hers. Slowly. Timidly. Their lips brushed against each other.

A snap of a twig sounded behind them.

In an instant, Kaine was up on his feet, braced for an attack and shielding Sophie who still sat on the damp grass.

It was Elowan.

His second, tall and dark skinned, stood underneath the cover of the pine trees. She too, was posed ready for a fight, short spear gripped tightly in her hand. He sensed a feral rage emanating from her. Her brows scrunched. Her teeth bared. She wasn't going to back down. What had gotten into her?

Zala stood behind Elowan, a face full of worry and her two rapiers crossed at her back.

Elowan lifted a damning finger at Kaine. "Did. You. Know?" Elowan bit out. Her voice filled with emotion. Anger. Rage.

Zala stepped out from behind her, motioning Sophie to get behind her, to safety. Kaine watched the exchange with a careful eye. He watched as Sophie shook her head swiftly. Sophie did not obey, instead she looked back to Kaine. She trusted him.

Noticing her concern, Kaine lifted Sophie gently up from the grass by her two hands. He flicked his chin, silently signalling her to stand by Zala.

She obeyed.

As soon as Sophie was out of the fray, Kaine stalked up to Elowan.

"Put your spear down. Now," he commanded. He only used this tone when he needed to. The tone that would send enemies turning and tucking tail.

Elowan hesitated but obeyed.

"Did I know what?" he clipped out. He squared his shoulders, standing tall. His arms crossed, asserting his dominance.

"The children. The DAMNED CHILDREN, KAINE," Elowan shouted as tears threatened to make their way out.

"Spit it out, Elowan." Impatience grew in him.

"The children who are sent to the king." She sobbed. "They never reach New Terrin, do they? They don't even reach the Fallen Seas, do they?!" She wiped the back of her arm across her face, clearing the tears.

"I don't understand."

"I saw them, Kaine. I saw them. In the afternoon when they were gathered on the wagon, departing for the Fallen Seas. For New Terrin. Then again hung up in the castle's stables like useless pieces of meat. They were slaughtered, Kaine. DRAINED OF THEIR BLOOD!" Elowan gasped and sobbed as she fell to her knees.

Kaine rushed for her, holding her by the shoulders to steady her as she cried. He didn't know what to think of it.

Twenty years ago, when the king ordered that the children be sent to him, he also ordered families to say goodbye at their homes, not at the pier. He forbade anyone from approaching the pier within a hundred metres. He stated that it was for the safety of the children. So that they would not weep or worry about the families they had left behind. Perhaps it was all a lie, a diversion for what was truly happening. The thought of young children being slaughtered spoiled in Kaine's stomach. He felt sick.

"Please tell me you did not know?" Elowan cried.

"I did not know, Elowan. We will figure it out. You have my word." Kaine rubbed her back, trying his best to silence the tears of his second-in-command.

Looking back to where Zala and Sophie stood, he signalled for them to head back to the group with a flick of his chin. Sophie and Zala softly turned on their heels. Elowan's hunched form wept against his.

Kaine whispered, "We'll send these humans home first. Then we'll get to the bottom of it. I promise you that."

16

This was the last leg. All they had to do was make it past the last gate, crawl onto the tracks and climb into the engine room of the train. They had made it at last. A week-long journey of making new friends, losing new friends and experiencing, feeling and breathing in the realm of Faery – something Sophie thought she would never be able to say. Before this, she thought it wasn't real. That she'd only be able to visit Faery in the books she'd read. She never knew it actually existed. She never knew it was real. But now she did and deep down, she was heartbroken to have to let it go.

Together, Tristan with Dolores in his arms, Lilith and Sophie walked in two lines. Quiet. Contemplating. Sad even.

Elowan led the front though Sophie was certain it was to avoid Kaine. Zala protected their right, Camrine at the back and Kaine to their left, closest to Sophie.

It was an hour's walk before they'd reach the gates. From there, they'd take the memory-erasing potion then sneak onto the train already waiting at Northern Helm station – ready for departure. The effects of the potion would take an hour to kick in. After that, Faery would be nothing more than a bad fever dream. Gone. Just like that.

"I still can't believe it." Sophie smiled to herself. "Faery is real. It's real. It's been real this whole time. It was at my very doorstep and..."

Sophie let out a soft chuckle, shaking her head ever so slightly.

"Perhaps it was fate. Crossing realms is no easy feat." Kaine turned, facing Sophie as the group walked on.

"I'm not sure if I'm ready to face what's left back in Sotera."

"What do you mean by that?"

"Well, before I stumbled here I..." Sophie fell silent. She hadn't had the opportunity to properly process what had happened to her that night with Grayson. She understood it wasn't her fault, but the betrayal still stung like a bitch.

"Did someone hurt you?" Kaine asked softly, eyes washing over with worry. He waited for her to respond. Patiently.

Sophie's eyes flew up to meet him, surprised by the accuracy. "How can you tell?"

"Your eyes. They tell a story every time I look at them."

"Oh." She didn't know what to make of it. After a moment of silence, she continued, "I was drugged. I went on a date and..." A sort of sadness and disappointment hollowed out her chest. "I went on a date, and he took advantage of me. He spiked my drink. He sought to take me somewhere, I have no idea where, to do with me what he willed. I turned the situation around, just in time. I barely scraped through. I fled. I ran. I cried. And in my drunk and drugged-up stupor I ended up on a train. Little did I know it was heading here... I guess everything happens for a reason, right?" She scoffed, shaking her head.

"If it is any consolation, I'd kill anyone who tried to hurt you. All you've to do is ask." Kaine laughed, tapping the short spear that hung by his belt.

"You promise?" Sophie laughed at that. What a typical, territorial fae male.

"You have my word."

Sophie savoured those words.

Sighing, Sophie wished she had more time to know this fae warrior; what his favourite food was, what he did in his spare time. But she knew they were star-crossed lovers, destined to not see each other again. There was a bittersweet feeling that started in her chest.

"I'm glad to have met you." She smiled at him this time, lingering just a bit longer on his handsome, rugged face. Those turquoise eyes. The stubble that grew across his jaw and chin. The lines of his face. The divots of his dimples and the fangs that peeked through when he smiled.

"And I, you." Kaine reached his hand out for her tattooed one.

And with a certainty that had long been brewing, Sophie intertwined her fingers with his.

They walked the remainder of the way in silence.

"Here is where we depart, friends. It was a journey and I commend you for your bravery," Elowan stated before the gate.

Sophie moved to Dolores who was, despite all things, awake and aware. After what had transpired in the tunnels, she was distraught, constantly asking for Mallory. It broke everyone's heart. "You are the bravest girl we know. Please take care." Sophie embraced the young girl. Dolores was going to be escorted home by Faery's contacts in Sotera.

She turned to Tristan, the soldier who made them feel safe. A fighter who was on their side. "Thank you. For being you. For taking care of Dolores. I might see you on the other side." Sophie smiled.

With his muscled arms, Tristan embraced Sophie, clasping her on the back. He held her by the shoulders. "You've got a bravery in you that many soldiers would envy. Good luck on the other side, Soph."

Sophie embraced him again.

She then turned to Lilith, who stood quietly, empty from their journey. "Lilith. Good luck on the other side." Despite not really knowing the librarian, Sophie embraced her anyway. She looked like she needed it.

Finally, Sophie turned to the fae folk. Her protectors who guided them this past week.

Sophie's heart was heavy. She didn't want to leave but she was so excited to get home. To see her family. To see her friends.

Sophie padded up to Elowan and gave her the biggest hug she could possibly give. Elowan this past week was the sister Sophie never knew she needed. They laughed by the fire a fair few nights and kept each other sane. Sophie couldn't thank her enough.

"Stop your blubbering, silly girl." Elowan laughed into Sophie's shoulders.

"It's in my nature. Leave me alone." Sophie was now sobbing.

Elowan stepped out of her hold and took both of Sophie's hands in hers.

"It pains me knowing that I'll never get to return the favour." She looked down, brushing her thumbs across Sophie's wrist where the small tattoo appeared – a symbol of Elowan's power. Her favour.

"Maybe in another lifetime."

"Maybe in another lifetime," Elowan echoed, pulling Sophie into a tight embrace again.

From behind, Camrine cleared his throat. "I'd like a moment to say goodbye to the fiery little human who slayed Dakin spiders with a blunt rock and sheer will."

Sophie turned around and leaped into his arms, almost strangling him given how tight she was hugging. "Correction, the human who strangled a two-hundred-year-old fae warrior to death with her bare hands." Camrine pretended to cough. It only made Sophie laugh. She'd miss his teasing.

"I'll miss you, friend."

"I'll miss you too." Camrine smiled, setting her gently down on her feet.

Zala appeared from behind Camrine and held a firm hand on Sophie's shoulder. A soft smile appeared on her face. She nodded, saying goodbye in her own special way. Sophie nodded back, placing a firm hand on Zala's shoulder in return.

Elowan and Camrine gave her one last hug and turned to say farewell to Tristan, Dolores and Lilith. Zala followed.

Sophie turned to see Kaine waiting. She was avoiding this. She didn't want to say goodbye to him at all. He slowly stepped up to her, towering over her. He embraced her in silence. She was taken aback. Slowly, she wrapped her arms around his waist, savouring his scent and the feel of his muscled back underneath her hands.

"I guess this is goodbye," she muffled against his chest.

"That it is." He rested his head atop hers.

"Even if I won't remember this. I want you to. I want you to remember me."

"Your wish is my command, Sophie." He pulled out of the embrace to kiss her softly on the forehead. Sophie closed her eyes, savouring the feel. Committing it to memory, as pointless as it was. They breathed each other in. Just for a moment, they allowed themselves to have it and embrace it, just for a moment.

With a clap of her hands, Elowan pulled everyone's attention her way and began handing out small vials of potion to each human. It fit right in Sophie's palm. Purple glittering liquid sloshed inside the glass.

Together, the humans uncorked the vials and lifted them in the air, raising a toast. To the friends they'd lost on the way. To the daring Faery folk who risked their lives to get them home. To each other. To Faery.

"May the gods guide you..." the four fae said in unison.

"To wherever we're destined to be," the four humans responded, downing the purple glittery contents of the vial.

They were huddled low by the tracks, dressed in the clothes they came to Faery in. Sophie couldn't have felt more exposed or embarrassed.

The train, already set up for departure, sat idly by the platform. With a quick swish of his hand, Kaine signalled the humans to move. And so they did.

Dropping onto their guts, the humans leopard-crawled across the tracks, one behind the other. Tristan was first. He was the strongest so he could help haul all of them into the carriage. Behind him crawled Dolores and behind her was Sophie.

Moving swiftly on her elbows and knees, Sophie climbed onto the small steel ladder located at the back of the train. She lay flat on her belly and crawled past Tristan who reached out an arm for Lilith to latch onto. The last human.

As she cleared the ladder, they both lay as close to the ground as they could.

Reaching up to the door handle from the ground, Sophie silently opened the engine-room door, motioning the humans to crawl inside. As soon as they did, Sophie followed, silently shutting the door behind her. They all sat in silence, pressed up against the walls. They couldn't make a sound. Not a peep. Not until they left Faery.

The train blasted its horn then, signalling its departure. They'd made it. They'd finally get to go home.

But Sophie didn't want to let Faery go. She didn't want to forget. She didn't want to forget the humans who'd be forgotten as soon as they crossed into Sotera. She didn't want to forget Elowan and her wittiness, Camrine and his jokes, Zala and her badassery or Kaine... his heart and soul. The train jerked into motion, the horn blasting one more time. The wheels of the train groaned awake, and the whistles of the train guards shrilled ahead.

Sophie, doing the exact opposite of what she was told, dared to peek her eyes out the window above. One more time. One more look at Faery before she'd forget she'd even visited this magical world. She peered back to where they departed the fae. Elowan, Camrine and Zala had already turned their backs, though Kaine... Kaine lingered. He watched as the train rolled into motion. Moving faster and faster. Kaine blinked with surprise. Sophie knew he'd caught her peeking. She held her hand up against the glass. Their last goodbye. Tears welled up in her eyes.

Kaine nodded, then bowed his head, with a hand over his heart.

Sophie's throat ached. She bade Kaine, the beautiful fae warrior, one last goodbye.

She left her hand pressed up against the window until he was but a small speck standing in the dark.

A whoosh echoed through the carriage, indicating that they'd made it through the portal travelling back to Melbourne but still, Sophie did not move her hand. She did not look away from where Kaine most likely stood in a distant realm. She did not look away from Faery. Her dream came true. Her wildest dreams really came true.

A single tear slid down her face.

17

Kaine had made a promise to Elowan. Since Sophie's departure from Faery, he'd been head down, trying to understand why the children promised for New Terrin had been killed, and who the sadistic bastard behind it all was.

He'd gone back to the stables behind the queen's castle in Terrin. The castle which the queen resided in was a monstrosity. Its bricks were soot covered, and the two spires that sat close to the front were covered in black, dead vines. Between the spires stood a large steel gate. During the day it lay open for courtesans to freely roam through, but at night, the menacing dark steel gate stood tall, like a towering monster, warding off those who dared near it.

The stables were secluded with only one way in, and one way out... so the children could not escape, Kaine noticed. He quietly unlocked the main entrance latch, closing it swiftly, silent as an assassin despite his size. Keeping a low profile he made it to the back stall where Elowan had detailed the grim end of several children.

They were given Nightlock, a poison that stopped the fae heart and turned their blood into something else entirely. In fae adults, effects would take several minutes to kick in, but in fae children, the effects would be instant. The dark blue berries were extremely rare to find in Faery – they only grew in the Shadow Realm, a place that lay underneath Faery, where demons, nightmares and monsters prowled. A place that had been long forbidden for the fae. A place where Terr, King of the Shadow Realm ruled.

Kaine's heart clenched at the thought of the children being forced to ingest such a poison. They must have been so scared. To have been removed from their parents and then be given no other choice but to take Nightlock.

A shiver ran down Kaine's back as he assessed the newly laid out hay where Elowan said the children had lain lifeless. They were tied up and hung by hooks in the storeroom, their throats slit and their wee bodies drained of all blood. For what reason, Kaine did not know, but he was going to find out. In fact, he already knew who would have the answer – Felipina, head of staff at Castle Terrin. She was an old grey-haired fae female who knew all the ingoings and outgoings of the castle. There was barely anything Felipina did not know. She'd have the answer, Kaine was sure of it.

18

Since Sophie's leaving, Elowan hadn't seen much of Kaine. She'd been focusing on her role as second-in-command with the Elite, training with Zala and her shadows or having a few beers at the Lazy Tavern with Camrine – anything to distract her from thinking of those children. She couldn't. It made her sick to her stomach and made her question everything she'd ever known. The king and queen of Faery would had to have known about it. Their powers were too great to not feel such a tip in the equilibrium of Faery. That much she understood, but who was desperate enough to make a deal with the proverbial devil? And why children? The questions gnawed at her.

It was just before dawn as she started to roll out of bed, careful not to disturb Regin from where he softly slept. The bed moved under Elowan's weight and Regin's muscled, tanned arm caught her waist, not wanting her to leave.

"Are you okay, my sweet?" he said softly, croakily, sleep still having a small hold on him.

"It's just what I saw the other day. The promised children. I don't know what to make of it. I don't know how to make sense of it," Elowan admitted. If anyone were to understand it would be Regin, her fated. The soul born to find hers.

She sat on the edge of the bed, candlelight dancing across the walls. She hung her head in her hands and her brows furrowed at the thought. Why were they slaughtered? Why were they drained of blood? Did the queen know? What was the king trying to achieve? The questions ran circles in her head, and she was growing dizzier with each day that those questions were left unanswered. Kaine promised to look into the occurrence, only sharing with her the information on a need-to-know basis. He'd been investigating the matter for a few days, she knew that much, but still, he had not provided her any update.

The feel of two strong hands grasping her shoulders, trailing down her back, eased her out of the endless cycle she'd unknowingly dipped into. Soft kisses planted themselves down her spine.

"Come back to bed, my love. I can keep your mind off it," Regin whispered in her ear from behind. His hands still roamed her back, across her stomach, then up to cup her breasts. Squeezing. She moaned at the distracting feeling.

"You, sir, are very convincing." She breathed and turned quickly.

Regin paused, drinking her in entirely.

She swallowed, heating rising under his gaze. His long blond braided hair fell over his shoulder, reaching down to his navel. It led to a happy trail of blond curls, all the way to his pride and joy.

She and Regin crossed paths many times. He was the queen's favoured blacksmith and often made armour and weapons for the Elite. She found him sweet and always cordial when she came by to pick up anything from his shop. She finally had the gall to ask him out on a date. They'd been together ever since.

Elowan crawled slowly over to his form, lifting her hand into the blond curls splayed across his chest. She pushed him down onto the bed, so he was lying on his back. Slowly, making sure every curve of her body caught in the candlelight, she straddled him. His hands slowly guided her knees over him. He was everything she wanted in a male – strong, loyal and kind. She lifted her hips ever so slightly, so her centre teased his swollen head. He hissed, grabbing her thighs tighter and tighter. She slowly lowered herself all the way to his hilt. She moaned at the feeling of being filled up and allowed her body time to adjust. Just as she was about to grind her way into oblivion, an angry fist slammed on the front door of her cottage in Fyllera.

Elowan stilled, titling her head towards the door. Waiting.

Again, the door shook against the frame with a few more impatient knocks.

Regin held her still, eyes glancing quickly at the door. "Ssh, don't get it," he whispered. She wasn't going to, but she found it odd that someone would be looking for her at this time of day. She sat quietly for a moment longer, still seated on Regin. Her pointed ears peaked towards the front door, trying to decipher who it could be. She could smell two fae males.

"Ma'am, we know you are in there. The queen wishes an audience with you." One of the males shouted from the front door. Elowan whipped her attention back to Regin who knew better than to get in the way of the queen's business. He sat up, moving Elowan to the side as he did. She watched him the entire time. She loved the way he moved. He placed a chaste kiss on her stomach then rolled out of bed, making to dress himself.

Elowan hopped out of bed, donned a robe then made her way to the front door.

She busted the front door open. "How dare you wake me at this ungodly hour?" She bellowed. The two royal guards that stood before her shrivelled in fear.

One inclined his head. "Apologies, ma'am. Queen Calliea has said that the matter is urgent."

"Did she now? Well, I can't keep Her Majesty waiting, can I?" Elowan smiled, then swiftly lunged for them, baring her fangs. The two guards flinched. "Now skedaddle." They yelped and swiftly turned on their heels, their armour making all the noise as they scrambled to get away from Elowan.

She had that effect on royal guards. They were all scared of her and for good reason. One of their brethren had the audacity to make a snide comment about females and how they had no business being in command. She made a show of his uneducated comments by setting his tongue on fire with her mana. The royal guards hadn't fucked with her since.

Elowan turned on her heel, shutting the door behind her.

"That is why I love you so. You make ordinary males scream." Regin laughed.

"Are you forgetting that I make you scream too?" She smiled back at him.

"That you do, though we can both agree it's much more pleasurable." He smiled while padding over to her. He held her tightly around the waist, lifting her slightly so that their lips met. "I shall see you later, my love."

"You shall." Kissing him one more time, she let him go and waved goodbye as he left her cottage through the front door.

She leaned against the doorframe. What could Queen Calliea possibly want? She wasn't due to report to the castle until the end of week. Nervousness and anxiety roiled around in her stomach. Whatever it was, Elowan's mana had decided that it wasn't going to be good.

19

"Oh my! Captain Kaine Aaryn, it has been a long while since you've come to visit. How I have missed seeing your handsome face!" Felipina exclaimed from her desk. She was a plump older fae female. She was always chirpy and always happy to see a familiar face. She slowly made her way to Kaine, placing sloppy wet kisses on both his cheeks.

Kaine chuckled. "It's good to see you, Felipina." He embraced her small, wrinkled body. Felipina had been alive for centuries but never had she let her age bend her into cruelty or jadedness. Every time Kaine needed help or information, he could always depend on Felipina. She was kind, extremely knowledgeable and conveniently managed the day-to-day operations of the castle.

"Judging by those pretty flowers, it seems like you want something from me." She huffed, circling around Kaine on her shuffling feet to grab the small bouquet of flowers that Kaine had indeed brought for her. She snatched the pretty blue hydrangeas from Kaine's hands and chuckled. "At least they are my favourite, boy. You do not forget, do you?" She smiled, making her way back to her desk, sniffing the flowers as she did.

"Forget, I do not, Felipina." He bowed at the waist jokingly. Felipina always had a keen eye. Despite her age, she was always bursting with energy.

"Well, go on, spit it out then. I'm not getting any younger." She laughed, setting the little bouquet into a vase by her desk.

Kaine stood in front of her desk, hands clasped behind his back. Felipina's office may have been littered with books, records and scrolls but it was the epitome of cleanliness. Not a single speck of dust deigned to rest on the age-old desk or the scrolls scattered beside it.

"I've need to see the list of staff who've access to the royal stables," he said, quietly in case any unwanted ears were listening.

"Of course, dear, may I ask why?" She slowly shuffled to a large cabinet that held an unnerving number of folders and records. She ran her fingers across the files, back now turned to Kaine. "You answer your elders when they ask you a question, Captain Aaryn, or did you forget your manners?" She tsked as she searched for the file Kaine asked for.

"It's a need-to-know basis," Kaine stated flatly. He didn't want to compromise his investigation by leaving bits of information lying around. He was already risking her life by asking for this, though he didn't want to disrespect her by infiltrating her office to glean the file.

"Ah. Got it." She hummed happily as she pulled out a folder. It was thin. Grabbing her reading glass, she held it against her eye, pulling out the piece of paper enclosed in the file. "It looks to be up to date. Not many names. I hope this shall suffice?" She looked up from her reading glass, handing the file to Kaine.

"It will. Thank you." He bowed deeply, taking the file from her small old hands as he did.

"Whatever it is you're up to, boy, don't drag me into it." Her eyes narrowed on Kaine in warning, assessing him. Then softening them, she moved swiftly on her old feet and grabbed Kaine's cheeks between her hands. "Are you going to hold out on an old friend like that?" she smiled, eyes mischievous.

"How do you mean, Felipina?" Kaine asked, his face still firmly held between Felipina's small hands.

"Oh don't be daft. You're in love. I can smell it." She let go of his face and poked his strong chest.

Kaine was silent. He gulped once. Twice.

She cackled.

"You can continue your gulping outside. I've got work to do. Now shoo!" She rushed him outside of her office with the swing of her arms.

Kaine obliged, nodded his thanks one more time and padded off down the hallway. He shook his head and smiled slightly at the thought of Sophie. She'd left Faery two weeks ago now. Not that he was counting. At least that's what he told himself.

20

"Come in, Elowan!" she shrilled.

Elowan walked swiftly across the red carpet, all the way to the dais where Queen Calliea sat tall on her throne in a shimmering red gown, examining her red talons.

Elowan bowed deeply at the waist. "Your Majesty," she said, loud and clear for the queen to hear. Elowan could fault the queen on so many fronts, but at least the female stayed on brand – red everything. Like blood.

The throne room had remained the same over the past twenty years. Red tapestries lined every wall. Intertwined within them were pictures of a prospering Faery, of a red queen – Queen Calliea – and her husband, King Gydeon Taranis, ruling over it. Elowan almost scoffed. Faery was no longer prosperous, it was dying.

"You needed to see me, Your Majesty?"

"Yes, of course." She motioned the royal guards who stood watch around the throne room to leave with a quick flick of her finger. Silently, they filed out of the room leaving Elowan behind, alone with the queen. Elowan's hand twitched at the room's sudden emptiness. It almost flew to the short spear that hung by her hip, but she thought better of it. She had to stay calm.

When the door finally clicked shut, the queen sighed a breath of relief, uncrossing her legs, sagged in her throne and picked at the beads that lined her dress.

"Sometimes it is hard being the queen of Faery. Many people believe me to be a tyrant, but there are so many things I shield the citizens from. Things they cannot know of, for it would only break their world." She sat, peering into the distance, consumed with worry.

Odd, Elowan thought. The queen was not her normal cold self. She seemed more human today, like a cover or shield had been dropped.

"Heavy is the head that wears the crown, Your Majesty." Elowan nodded. Unsure of what to say, she stayed alert, not wanting to fall into a potential trap laid out by the queen.

Queen Calliea snapped her attention to where Elowan stood. "Come. Sit." She placed her pale slender hand on the stool that sat next to her right, dwarfed by the giant, extravagant blood-red throne. Elowan hesitated. It wasn't often anyone was allowed on the dais. Only select members of the council or the king or queen themselves. "It is okay, we are alone."

Elowan obeyed. Slowly, she walked up the dais and gingerly perched herself on the stool right beside the queen, feeling very much out of her element.

Queen Calliea turned to face Elowan. She was devastatingly beautiful, Elowan thought. She seemed to not have aged at all during her reign. When fae reached the age of twenty-three, the were referred to as settled fae – reaching adulthood. While aging was slow for settled fae, the queen looked to only be in her mid-thirties. Elowan knew she was much older; centuries, rumours claimed.

Elowan gasped as the queen held both her hands. Her hands were freezing cold, as if she'd just dunked them in buckets of ice. Elowan tried her hardest not to yank her hands away. She peered to the queen's yellow-gold eyes. They seemed to pierce through her soul.

"I'm told that you have stumbled across something. Something not for the faint-hearted." Elowan's heart dropped. How did the queen's spies see her? How did she know? Elowan tried her best to school her face into neutrality. "It is quite alright, my dear. You can tell me." The queen nodded, urging her to spill what she knew.

Still, the queen held Elowan's hands firmly, instilling in her the confidence to speak. Elowan hoped with her dear immortal life that the queen would be on her side. It was a gamble. She tried to reach down into her mana, to help her assess the situation, but her mana did not say a word. She swallowed. Nervous. She started shaking.

"I... I... saw the promised children." Elowan could've passed out on the spot. Her voice stuck in her throat. She continued, "They were murdered." Elowan prayed to the gods the queen was on her side. She prayed that she wasn't about to be called out for treason against the king and his whims. Despite her orders to kill humans, the queen would surely protect the children of Faery, wouldn't she? After all, that was the driving force behind her reign – protect Faery at all costs.

"I'm sorry you had to see that. I truly am. You've to understand that I needed to hear that come from you and not my spies. I had to make sure you saw what you saw. Do you understand that?" Queen Calliea squeezed Elowan's hands again, reassuring her. The queen paused for a moment.

Elowan had no idea what to think. The fact that the queen allowed her to sit by her side, even touch her hands, still shook Elowan to the core.

The queen peered down at where their hands joined and cleared her throat. "It's the king." She paused, waiting for Elowan to respond. And when she didn't, the queen continued, "I've known for quite some time that he had been sacrificing the children. I've been trying my hardest to collect information, evidence... evidence to overthrow him. I've been doing so for years now while trying to keep Faery alive." The queen's voice caught, tears threatening to spill. But still, she held firmly onto Elowan's hands and her eyes never strayed. "I am very close, Elowan. Very close."

"Your Majesty, I'm unsure what to say..." And that was true. Elowan had no idea how to interpret this. Was the queen just a caged female, threatened by and scared of her powerful husband? Did she put on a cold and cruel front to hide her scheming? For what purpose and to what end?

"If you will not say, then do. I've need of you Elowan. Faery dies with each waking day. The king has murdered thousands of children in efforts to make a deal with Terr himself."

Elowan's face drained of colour at the mention of the cruel Shadow Realm king. Shivers ran down her spine. "But how can that be? What would Terr even gain from King Gydeon?"

"He wants to rule Faery."

Fear struck Elowan right in the gut. Stunned, she couldn't even utter another word. Her hands stiffened in the queen's grasp.

"That is why I have need of you. We need help, Elowan. We are in grave danger. We need to ally with the human realm again. We need to make an alliance. The human realm is favoured by the Godlands, and if we are to ally with them, we will be safe, untouchable and out of Terr's reach." Tears spilled down the queen's porcelain face, though her hands were still cold to the touch. "I know that you help the humans, Elowan."

Elowan didn't know whether to run or hide. The queen knew. She'd known this whole time, and yet she hadn't done anything to stop them. She looked into the queen's eyes again. Questioning.

"I only allow it because I know in the long run it benefits Faery, and the human-fae alliance if we were to establish one."

"But you decreed the on-sight killing of humans almost twenty years ago. I don't understand." Elowan's face scrunched in question.

"It was... the king. He forced me. And so I played into it. A loyal queen to a brute king. The less he questioned my loyalty to him, the greater impact I'd have when I'd eventually overthrow him." She nodded. Queen Calliea let go of Elowan, turning her hands into her lap where she balled them into fists. "He has caged me for many decades. And caged, I wish to no longer be." She sniffled. "Please, Elowan." She looked up at Elowan again.

Elowan was torn. On one hand, she felt for this female. Caged by a brute king. Forced to be the face of his ruthless campaign. On the other hand, she was cruel and cunning – or at least Elowan thought. She knew what that feeling was like. Being caged. Treated like nothing more than just a plaything.

Elowan looked back up at the queen, assessing. "But how can I trust you? Your actions over the past few years have painted humans as the enemy, yet you're telling me they are not. That they are the answer to Faery's blight. Which one do I trust?"

The queen's eyes continued to spill with tears.

"I understand your distrust. I truly do. But if you do not trust my words, then trust this." The queen moved to pull out a golden ring. On top of the warm golden band sat a small garnet carved into the shape of a leaf – the Autumn Court stone. Elowan's throat constricted. Her heart ached. It was her mother's ring. It was meant to be her ring. When Elowan had learned that her mother was mauled to death by hellhounds, she searched high and low for the ring. The coroners had stated that no ring was found. She turned their entire house upside down to try and find it, but to no avail.

Elowan's hands flung to her throat. "How can this be?"

"Your mother bestowed it upon me, before her passing. A token of our friendship, Essenya said," the queen said lovingly. The delicacy at which her mother's name left the queen's mouth made Elowan feel like they were once good friends.

The queen reached over to place the ring inside Elowan's outstretched palms.

"I don't know what to say," Elowan breathed.

"Then do not. Act, Elowan. Find me a worthy human emissary. One to represent the human realm. So, together, we may find peace and happiness at last. For Faery, Elowan." The queen sniffled, pulling Elowan into a soft embrace.

Elowan leaned into it. She hadn't seen this ring for twenty years. It felt like the missing part to her heart. A piece of the mother she loved dearly and missed wholly.

"Yes, Your Majesty, I will." She nodded into the crook of the queen's neck. She sobbed.

"It is our secret, okay?" the queen asked.

"Of course, Your Majesty. Thank you. Truly. Thank you."

"It is my pleasure. Now go. Gather the resources you need."

Pulling out of the embrace, Elowan moved to descend the dais. She turned back to the queen who sat on the throne, leaning forward with tears in her eyes. No longer caged. Elowan bowed deeply at the waist, her hand with her mother's ring inside, clutched against her heart. For Faery she would do this. For her mother, she would help overturn the king and restore Faery. She padded out the throne room doors in silence, invigorated by a new sense of purpose.

When the throne room doors clicked shut, Queen Calliea leaned back in her blood-red throne and let out a bored sigh. With a wave of her hand, a plume of black glitter manifested beside her on her throne. A hooded figure appeared, chained.

"You could've fooled me with that performance." The oracle croaked from where it sat on the floor.

"And so it begins." The queen smirked. "Who knew prying that piece of junk off that bitch's still-warm corpse would work to my advantage? Pathetic." She scoffed.

The picture of the trapped weeping queen had been wiped away, and in her place was the cold, cunning queen everyone knew so well. She tapped her fingers rhythmically on the arms of her throne and began the haunting tune she so loved to hum.

21

The list of names was a dead end. Kaine had tracked and stalked all six names over the past several days. It yielded nothing. They were all humble, old stable masters with kind families. There was nothing sinister about them at all. He'd even gone back to Felipina to a fetch a list of horsemen who manned the carriages for the Port Ceremony. Nothing. Not a speck out of place.

Maybe he needed to start at the very beginning. Maybe he needed to go back twenty years to when the decree was made. Back to when the king announced that he was to travel the Fallen Seas in search of new land and with him a handful of children – the next generation of Terrin.

The thought brought him to the palace archives, below the palace library which held all the royal decrees made by the royal family, the family trees of Terrin and more. It held the history of Terrin in its intricate labyrinth of shelves.

Kaine donned his black hood and brought with him a small lamp, not daring to use his powers in the archives in case a protection spell was triggered.

He reached the shelf he was searching for. The shelf was dusty and held several scrolls outlining all the decrees made that year, twenty years ago.

New Terrin Decree ran across one of the scrolls. He slid it off the shelf as quietly as he could. Placing his lamp on to a hook built into the bookcase, he unrolled the scroll.

On this day, King Gydeon Taranis has decreed what will be called the New Terrin decree. Every family in Faery, from now until otherwise stated, is hereby ordered to nominate a single child to follow the king in his journey to seek and sow new territory. Failure to comply is an act of treason and not conducive to Faery's purpose – to nurture and protect life – of which an appropriate punishment will be delivered. You have been warned.

Below sat the king's signature, with the royal stamp, certifying that the signature was truly his. Kaine felt disappointed, mainly in himself. He wasn't even close to getting to the bottom of it all. In fact, he couldn't be farther from the truth. The thought of the children hanging, bloodied and lifeless, struck him. He had to keep digging. He'd promised Elowan. He had to get to the bottom of it, even if it meant questioning the king himself.

22

The palace training ring was a buzz in Faery's afternoon light. Dust kicked up with swift movements from a few fae who sparred in the distance. The sun warmed Elowan, Camrine and Zala who sat by the sidelines, stretching their sore muscles from a few hours of much-needed sparring.

"Queen's business." Elowan smirked.

"Oh, come on, Ellie, that's like dangling a carrot in front of us except we don't even know what kind of damned carrot it is. Is it an organic one or a genetically modified one? I don't know. All I know is that I want it!" Camrine laughed, sighing, hands clasped together in silent plea.

Elowan had almost blurted everything out after their session in the palace training grounds. She couldn't whisper a word of the queen's errand, not yet. Not only were they not alone, but she was worried they would convince her to assess the situation more. Make more plans. Back-ups even. It's what they were trained to do. Plan for every possible situation and more. But all she wanted to do right now was act.

Zala stood beside the exasperated Camrine, arms folded, lips pouted and unimpressed.

"You will find out when it is time. Until then, I suggest preparing your pack. We ride at dawn."

"Luckily, time is all I have, baby, 'tis the whole point of immortality." Camrine shot to his feet from where he rested on the ground.

"Call me that one more time and I'll make sure to never ever tell you why."

Camrine shot his hands up in surrender. Dramatic as always. He held out the crook of his elbow for Elowan to hook her arm through. She turned back to where Zala stood and held her elbow out for her friend. The silent wraith of shadows obliged.

Smiling, arm in arm, the three left the training grounds to prepare for their long journey. The journey to find the key to peace and prosperity in Faery.

23

"It seems the king has requested your presence in New Terrin. He's asked for one of the Elite to train his guards in combat. Considering you're the best, I don't see why I should be sending anyone else," the queen said matter-of-factly, peering down her nose at the white rose bush before her. Queen Calliea had requested Kaine to escort her through her rose garden. Her hand was impossibly white against the petals of the white roses she caressed. Her bright red nails drawing a sharp contrast.

Kaine kept a respectful distance beside her, arms casually behind his back.

The queen leaned into the rose bush, inhaling the scent.

"Felipina has organised a small boat for your travels across the Fallen Seas. It leaves in two hours. Ensure you prepare the Elite for your absence," she said, distracted, back still turned to Kaine who stood patiently. This couldn't have played out any better, he thought. He needed answers, and it looked like he was going to get them right from the horse's mouth. He silently thanked the gods that watched over him today.

The queen let out a hushed hiss. She'd pricked one of her fingers against a thorn. Blood, dark and thick, ran down her finger. She stared blankly at the cut as if hypnotised.

"Do not disappoint me, Kaine."

"I will not, Your Majesty. You have my word." He bowed his head, hand splayed across his chest.

"Now, leave," she said coldly.

Kaine didn't hesitate. He turned quickly, wanting to escape from the rose garden he hated so much. It was cold and smelled sickly there. Like death. The smell always stuck in his nose. He turned his head over his shoulder, back to the queen who still stood there entranced by the blood that ran dark down to her finger.

He ran to the barracks as quickly as he could in search of Elowan, wanting to provide an update. He found her pack gone, as with Zala's and Camrine's. She'd left a note on her bunk with his name written on it.

We've been tasked on a mission for the queen. I hope you're still trying to find the answers. We will be back. Don't wait up for us.

It didn't sit right with Kaine at all. He did not trust the queen. He knew that she had a hand in the treachery, but to what degree he did not know. All he knew was that he didn't want his friends involved, not yet anyway. It was better to keep them safe.

What also didn't sit well with Kaine was that he didn't know the nature of Elowan's mission. She'd normally detail what she was up to, but here she left zero clues except that the queen had tasked her with a mission. He scrunched up the note, threw it in the air then ripped it into tiny shreds with a small tug of mana. He swiftly prepared his pack, filled his canteens and set off for the pier.

The Fallen Seas were rough. They had earned their name centuries ago. The most tumultuous of storms permanently converged over the Fallen Seas. Never did the sun dare shine over them, as if it too were scared. The waters were black and below lurked the deadliest of creatures; giant squids and hungry water draekins – behemoth dragons that long lived in the deep dark seas. Some of the waves were hundreds of metres tall, and only a few experienced sailors were able to conquer them. The Fallen Seas had taken the lives of many. It was why the king dared not sail back to the mainland. If he died, there'd be no one left to rule Faery. He had no heirs.

Though the seas roared, and the boat struggled to stay upright, Kaine wasn't afraid. Nothing scared him these days. And to top that, he was determined. Determined to question the king and do what was right for Faery.

The small boat, with the help of the crew's mana, set sail from the royal pier not long ago. With him were four skilled sailors and four royal guards to keep him company on the several days travel. The queen had insisted, Felipina said.

Kaine stood at the stern, watching the water lap up against the boat. Forearms leaning against the edge, he breathed in the saltwater spray. He was a deadly vision with his dark black hair pulled back in a tight bun and his mighty fighting leathers.

The four royal guards remained below deck, not wanting to drench themselves in rainwater. Kaine scoffed at that. Weak. The rain brought him comfort and the cold kept him focused on his true mission. Once he landed in New Terrin, he'd oblige the king and he'd train whoever the king needed him to train but under that guise, he'd continue his investigation.

He'd never met King Gydeon before. No one had, except for those who dared make the journey for New Terrin. Older fae folk rumoured him to be kind and brave. He'd left for New Terrin when Kaine was very young. Kaine decided he'd have to win the favour of the king, make him trust Kaine so that he could then glean the information he needed to uncover the truth behind the promised children.

Tonight was a particularly rough night. The seas were angry, and lightning constantly rattled through the air above the ship.

"Captain! Come have a drink with us!" a male voice shouted. It was one of the fae guards, dressed in his Royal Guard garb – purple breeches and silver armour. "Come on, Captain. We won't get to New Terrin for a few days. Let's relax!" he shouted through the rain, beckoning Kaine to head below deck with a wave of his furry arm. Of the fae that travelled to the Fallen Seas, he was the only lesser fae; a racoon variant.

Kaine peered back over his shoulder, still leaning against the edge of the ship. The guard, Rafeen, was right. They wouldn't reach New Terrin for a few more days and perhaps a few drinks with the males wouldn't hurt.

Shifting his weight from the edge, Kaine stalked his way through the rain, to the door leading below deck. He jumped in, landing firmly on his two feet. With just a thought, he willed his mana to manipulate the air, drying him instantly.

"He's finally decided to pause his brooding to join us!" One of the other fae guards laughed, smacking the small wooden table the four fae guards sat around. He was clearly intoxicated. The quarters were small, wooden, with minimal supplies and minimal lighting. It smelled of dirty clothes and musk.

Rafeen, the racoon guard, smacked the intoxicated fae on the shoulder, signalling him to keep quiet.

"What?" the intoxicated fae slurred.

Kaine stood, arms crossed in front of the four royal guards packed into the small booth.

"Careful how you speak to the captain of the Elite," Rafeen whispered harshly, widening his eyes in warning. "Apologies, Captain, he's just excited about meeting the king is all," Rafeen said apologetically, clasping his paws tightly together, a small apologetic smile smeared across his furry face.

"No need to be so cordial," Kaine offered.

Rafeen quickly scrambled to find a spare glass, pouring the amber liquid from a flask. He offered it to Kaine who took it swiftly in one hand and nodded his thanks. He took a quick sip and sat down next to the four royal guards.

They were stunned by his presence. He was much larger than they were. Much stronger too.

Rafeen looked at his four comrades nervously.

Kaine took note of the nervous glance.

"Captain, tell us some of the tales of the Elite," Rafeen offered.

"Well, what do you want to know?"

"What about the time the Elite stormed the Wastes in search of those traitorous oracles? Nasty creatures that they are." Rafeen sneered.

Kaine shivered at the thought. An oracle was an ancient, powerful creature with obsidian skin and pale green eyes. It could tell the future and look into the past which truly meant meddling with the present. They lived in the Western Wastes and were highly sought after.

"Pillaging and having your way with the women, am I right?" the intoxicated fae shouted. The amber liquid sloshed about in his cup as he waved it around. Rafeen smacked his friend across the shoulder again.

"Apologies, it seems like Cardin has had a lot to drink tonight."

Kaine sat in silence. The mission he'd been ordered to undertake in the Western Wastes was the most difficult he and his Elite had been tasked to complete. The queen had ordered the capture of several oracles who were found working against the throne of Faery. The villagers residing in the Wastes, the dry lands sitting along the western border of Faery, did not want to give up the oracles without a fight.

Fires broke out, few villagers were injured but the oracles were successfully captured. It wasn't something he revelled in or was proud of. The oracles were helpless creatures, they didn't know how to defend themselves.

"No need to apologise. He's welcome to blame it on the alcohol if that makes him feel any better," Kaine said as he sipped more of his drink.

Cardin blanched, clearly embarrassed. The other three fae guards focused solely on their drinks then.

The most silent of the fae guards, with his alabaster skin and slender arms, scoffed from where he sat across from Kaine. "The Elite can't be that great."

Silence.

Rafeen looked away, anywhere but where the conversation was headed. Even Cardin seemed to not want to be there.

"Do you have something to say?" Kaine leaned in, placing his glass down, ready for a fight. He knew the Elite were the best of the best. The queen's chosen warriors. In fact, everyone in Faery knew it.

"I do." The quiet fae leaned in to meet Kaine's stern face. He was not afraid, Kaine realised.

"Then say it," Kaine gritted, clenching his jaw.

"Queen Calliea sends her regards." The silent but lightning-fast fae kicked the table out from where they sat, short spear already in hand. He landed on Kaine immediately, his weapon rammed up a hair's width away from Kaine's jugular. Despite his small frame the fae was strong, Kaine had to give him that. But Kaine was stronger. He made to push the slender fae off him, but he found his hands were starting to tingle and his face slackening. Enervo, Kaine realised. A liquid potion that would temporarily paralyse whoever ingested it. And boy the realisation of it made his anger swell. Kaine bucked as hard as he could with his depleting strength. He kicked his feet up, flipping to a crouch and dug deep into his mana. Oh, these males were going to learn today. They were going to learn that no one can mess with the Elite, least of all their captain. Pushing through the effects of the potion making its way through his system, he willed the air with his mana and stole it right out of the four fae standing around him.

Choking, Rafeen crawled his way to the door, attempting to escape. The others knelt, hands grasping at their necks. Choking. Dying.

The slender male's short spear clanked to the floor. His lifeless body followed with a dramatic thump. Cardin slumped in the chair, wheezing, his eyes turning milky white as life left him. His dark-skinned friend collapsed on the floor by the overturned table, taking small shallow breaths, going in and out of consciousness. Kaine, the dark warrior that he was, stalked his way to Rafeen who sat up by the door, pawing at his neck, straining for air.

"I, I wanted no part in it. I swear," Rafeen begged. His legs kicked out, trying to get away from Kaine, but the closed door stopped him.

Kaine knelt by Rafeen's struggling form. His fighting leathers creaked with the movement. He bent low, facing the racoon fae right in his beady eyes.

"Tell me why I shouldn't kill you right now." Kaine was angry. More than angry, he was infuriated. He was betrayed.

"I... I have children. A wife. Please. The queen..." Rafeen rasped. Kaine pulled his mana back for a moment.

Rafeen gulped in the air around him. Paws braced on the floor while he tried his best to catch his breath. "The queen found out you were snooping. You flew too close to the sun and for that, she said you needed to burn. You needed to be killed, she said."

Kaine blinked. The only sign of his surprise. How did the queen find out? He covered his tracks everywhere he went. He left no trace, or so he thought.

Rafeen cowered by the door, still panting. He looked up at Kaine with his pleading beady eyes.

"And what of the king?" Kaine asked.

Rafeen hesitated. "There is no king." He blanched.

Kaine's world began to crumble all around him. The queen had attempted an assassination on her captain of the Elite. And according to Rafeen, the king was no longer. That meant... Faery was dying because it was missing its true heir. It had long been tradition that when a king or queen died, the heir and their chosen partner would ascend the throne, bringing balance back to the power that ran deep in Faery's land. And to Kaine's knowledge, the king had no heir, not a legitimate one anyway. The piece of information Rafeen offered had answered so many questions, but in its wake left more yet to be answered. Kaine's eyes widened at the revelation.

"What do you mean?"

"The king died twenty years ago. The queen has had her claws latched in the throne ever since. She's very powerful you see. You must understand, it was to serve her or squander in the slums of Faery. I wanted more for my children. My wife. Me. Please." Rafeen begged, tears welling up in his eyes. His paws were clasped together. Pleading. Begging.

Kaine was shocked. Twenty years ago. The same year his mother died. The same year when the first signs of Faery dying showed. The information hit him like a train. All he'd worked for had been for nought. He trained, he went on missions, he killed all in the name of a queen he thought would bring peace and prosperity to Faery. Why hide this from the Elite? What was the purpose? His values, his morals – he questioned it all. He was a fool, a damned fool. Kaine shook his head, trying to shake out the rage and betrayal he felt in his chest.

Rafeen sat by the door begging for his life. Kaine towered over him. He wouldn't let the queen win. Not anymore. His blinding rage overtook him. He no longer had a firm grasp on his mind. His mana surged, stealing the air right out of Rafeen's lungs. The racoon fae thrashed and thrashed. Then stilled, his eyes turning milky and blank. His paws lay limp beside him, propped up against the door.

Kaine panted from the show of mana. His power was stunted significantly from the Enervo, but that did nothing to stop him from raging. From splintering all the furniture below the deck with a push of his mana. He was pissed. And he'd show the queen how truly pissed off he was. Her reign would end now, and her deadliest weapon would make sure of it.

24

BACK IN MORTAL LANDS

*B*EEP. *BEEP. BEEP.*

Sophie slapped her phone quiet, snoozing the alarm that blared awfully loud in her ears. Gods. Her head throbbed with a vengeance. It felt foggy. Her eyes felt crusty, swollen and heavy. She was still dressed in her jeans and the lace top that she'd worn last night on her disastrous date. How she managed to get home in one piece was beyond her.

Sophie stretched; her short black hair all messed up from her sleep. Why did it feel like she had run a marathon with no food or water to fuel her? Her feet throbbed, her knees ached and her ribs itched. Then she remembered that the bastard Grayson had drugged her, and she just managed to escape his grasp. Just.

"Ugh. Why me?" She groaned to no one in particular, burying her face farther into her sheets. "You're a fucking idiot, Sophie." She grumbled and kicked her legs like a child in frustration.

Peeling herself from her bed, she undressed and made her way to the shower, needing to wash away all the dirt, grime and the touch of Grayson. It made her want to vomit. She sat on the cold tiles underneath the shower head, arms wrapped around her knees and practised slow breaths. *It's not your fault*, she repeated in her head. Over and over. And as much as she repeated it, it didn't make her feel any better. The bottom line was that she somehow fell for the good-guy act, she'd been preyed on and swept up into the idea of love. She bowed her head in defeat, promising herself that it would never happen again.

Standing, she shut the water off, grabbed a towel, wrapped it around herself and padded for the mirror. She leaned on the marble countertop and breathed in deeply. Her morning mantra still stood true, defeated as she felt in that moment. She was a fae queen, and no mortal would stand in the way.

A burning itch launched through her side. She pulled her towel down to scratch whatever it was. She gasped. A huge shiny scar ran down the side of her ribs about twenty centimetres long. She couldn't remember for the life of her how she got it or when she got it. She furrowed her brows, racking her brain, trying her hardest to remember but she was met with cloudiness. Nothing tangible. Nothing she could grasp. It all felt so distant. It was like the day she woke up with her tattoos. She'd definitely need to get herself checked out if these blackouts persisted, who knew what could be wrong?

She looked at the scar in the mirror. It ran along the top of her breast, down to the bottom of her rib cage as if she had run past something sharp, and it sliced her open. She traced it with her middle finger. Smooth then... *ZAP*.

"Ow! What the fuck..." Sophie hissed. Her hand went numb as if it were shocked with electricity. She shook her hand, trying to free herself of the numbness. It was then her head started swimming. Her scar itched with madness. Her right wrist throbbed. A sharp pain shot through her temple and she fell to her knees, still damp from her shower.

Her hands clung on to her head trying to ease the pain. Her eyes were scrunched shut. She knelt on the floor, screaming. She screamed and screamed as visions flashed before her; eyes of a beautiful red-haired woman with pointed ears laughing by a fire. Of a male, twin to the red-haired woman, who punched her shoulder in jest. Of a dark-skinned woman balancing two rapiers in her hands. Of a man with turquoise eyes, dark hair and a smile that made her knees quake. She gasped as the visions relented. Her hands shook violently. She panted. Eyes still closed, she practised deep breaths, thankful for the momentary relief. Without notice, the visions flashed through her mind again; of spiders, of limp bodies being eaten alive, of sputtering water, of an empty town... of a vivid sky with stars that danced across it. Not visions, memories. Her memories that should have been squandered and deemed obsolete because of the potion she ingested. Sophie tried to catch her breath as her memories surged their way through her brain. She felt nauseous and dizzy. Darkness consumed her whole, and she collapsed all alone, on her tiled bathroom floor.

25

Sophie gasped awake, sprawled out on her bathroom floor, her towel scrunched up beneath her. She groaned, rubbed her eyes and eased herself into a seated position. She looked around. This was her bathroom. They were definitely her skincare bottles strewn over the countertop as if she'd knocked them over as she collapsed. Judging by her position on the floor, she most definitely had. She'd made it back home to Sotera... with all her memories. How was that even possible?

Slowly easing herself off the ground, she looked to the scar that ran across her ribs and scoffed. A vision of her dancing in the waters of Faery as a distraction played in her head. She quickly examined her wrist and what she sought was there. It was real. The favour, the debt owed by Elowan. The small tattoo shined in response to her acknowledgment. She smiled softly to herself. Tears welled up in her eyes. She was safe in Sotera and Faery was real. It was real. And oh, how she missed it. How she missed the dear friends she had made on her travels. And she remembered how much she missed her mum.

Her mum.

The thought pulled her out of the sappy moment. She ran to her phone. It was Sunday afternoon. Twenty missed calls and thirty messages from her mum. Oh, Sophie was in deep shit, she realised. She quickly scrolled through all the messages.

Honey, where are you?

> I am worried sick. Please call when you have the chance.

> I'm going to hold off on calling the police as I'm sure you're recovering from a few drinks. Please call when you can x

> Honey I just called Lorrie. She says you are ok and that you've been vomiting your guts up. Feel better soon. And call me, will you x

Sophie's heart wrenched. Her mother was worried sick while she was off in Faery fighting spiders and kissing hulking fae warriors. She felt so bad. Quickly dressing, she could deal with the revelation and existence of Faery later. She had to go see her mum.

Sophie flew down the stairs, pulling on a grey jumper as she did. By the front door, she quickly slipped on her Birkenstocks, grabbed her car keys and yanked the door open.

"AHHH! HOLY SHIT, MUM!" Sophie jumped back as her mother smiled brightly at the front door. In one hand was a Tupperware container full of hot soup and a tube full of electrolyte tablets in the other.

"Surprise?" Danna beamed. Her long silver hair was plaited back. She wore a beautiful sundress with various carnations printed all over it.

"Oh, Mum, it's so good to see you." Sophie pulled her mum into the tightest hug she could muster and breathed in her strawberry scent. She missed her mum so much it hurt. In the tunnels, after the Dakin spiders, after hearing about the promised children, there was no one else she wanted to see more. No one else she wanted to speak to but her mum.

"Remind me to always bring you soup and electrolytes if it means getting one of these hugs." Danna grunted lightly from the sheer force of her daughter's embrace.

Sophie laughed. "Come. Come inside." She grabbed the Tupperware container brimming with delicious chicken soup and pocketed the tube of electrolytes, kicking the front door shut behind her as her mum walked in, heading for the kitchen.

Danna went to the cabinets and pulled out a small bowl so she could ladle in the soup for her daughter. Sophie pulled out a stool by the kitchen bench and plonked in it. She beamed, beyond happy to see her mum alive and well.

"Why are you smiling as if you thought you were never going to see me again?" Danna raised a suspicious eyebrow, swirling the soup before her and grabbing a spoon from one of the drawers.

"Just cause." Sophie shrugged. She obviously skirted around the real answer to that because her mum was right. There were moments when her fear wrapped itself around her heart. There were times when she thought she would never see her mother again. Her family. Her friends.

"Gee, that bad, huh? Maybe it's time you stopped drinking, Sophie. It's not good for your liver for starters..." she trailed off. "Oh, for goodness sakes, don't tell me you got another tattoo?" Sophie almost yanked her wrist under the counter in a poor attempt to hide it. But she didn't. She needed to act as if nothing were out of place. She needed to act as if she hadn't crossed realms, saved lives, killed spiders... and that was going to be hard. Really hard.

Danna lay out her hand expectantly. Sophie obliged and rested her wrist in her mother's hand. Danna leaned in, examining the small tattoo a little closer. She choked. Coughed.

"Sorry, it's my allergies. They creep up on me all the time." She let go of Sophie's wrist. Clearing her throat, she said, "It's nice honey, where'd you get it?" She pushed the bowl of soup closer to Sophie so she could dig in.

"Oh um, this tattoo shop just on Flinders Street. Cute right?" Sophie hoped to the gods that her performance was convincing.

"Kind of matches your other ones, too." Danna smiled lovingly.

Sophie sculled the soup, trying to avoid the topic of tattoos entirely. She hadn't had normal, hearty food in over a week and her mum's chicken soup was the best. Placing the bowl down softly, she dissolved an electrolyte tablet in a cup of water her mum had prepped and quickly downed it.

Danna turned to her brown purse, lying on the countertop. Reaching in, she pulled something out. "I was meant to give you this yesterday at brunch, but you decided to stand me up," Danna said softly, leaning over the counter to place an exquisite gold locket necklace into Sophie's palms. The locket was beautiful, about the size of a fifty-cent piece. It was a golden heart engulfed in flames. On top sat a small, jewelled crown with turquoise and purple stones. In the centre of the heart was a keyhole in the shape of diamond. It was stunning. Sophie's jaw dropped in awe. She remembered this necklace. Her mum used to wear it all the time when Sophie was younger. "It was a gift from your father, from when we first courted. I want you to have it. I found it while I was sorting through boxes. Think of it as a family heirloom." Danna smiled, watching her daughter examine the beautiful piece of jewellery. "You can make up for bailing on me by wearing it. It'll protect you as it did me."

"Mum, it's beautiful. Thank you. My birthday isn't for another few days." Sophie placed the necklace over her head and laid the ornate amulet on her chest. It felt heavy. Warm. It felt familiar.

"I know. I couldn't keep it from you any longer. Don't take it off, okay? Promise me that." Danna pointed a finger at Sophie in warning.

"Of course, Mum. Thank you." Sophie pushed back her stool and ran to hug her mum tightly. The necklace was perfect. It reminded Sophie of her mother so much, her heart of gold and the warmth she brought into everyone's life. She started tearing up.

"Okay, now that I have confirmed that you're alive, I've got things to do. The plants at Bunnings won't buy themselves and the snags certainly won't eat themselves either. I'll call you later, honey." Danna pulled out of their embrace, kissing her daughter on each cheek. She grabbed her purse and made for the front door.

"Love you, Mum!" Sophie shouted towards her mother as the front door clicked shut. Sophie stood there in the kitchen examining the charming locket her mother had just gifted her. It was already warm from her skin.

A gift from her mother. She felt like she didn't deserve it. She was lying through her teeth, straight to her mother's face and that didn't sit well with her at all. She knew she had to keep Faery a secret. Her mother would think her crazy otherwise, but it didn't make her feel any better.

She wondered then what Kaine was doing, if he was safe, and if he remembered her like she asked him to. The scar he healed seemed to flare in response.

26

"Thank the gods you are here today!" Lorrie practically jumped from her desk and embraced her tightly.

Sophie had called in sick for the past two days, reeling from her accidental trip to another realm, still feeling the loss of the friends she'd made. She watched all nine Star Wars films in chronological order with a tub of chocolate ice cream in hand, just to fill the void.

"Lorrie!" Sophie hugged her best friend tight. Not wanting to let go.

"How are you feeling?"

"Much better. Not one hundred per cent, but much better." Sophie let go of her best friend.

"You know what would make you feel better?" Lorrie paused. "Coffee. C'mon, let's go downstairs and grab you a cup. You look like you need one." She pushed Sophie towards the front doors of the office.

"Ah, you know me too well." Though Sophie softly laughed, the laughter didn't quite reach her eyes.

Lorien and Sophie sat on the office balcony, sipping at the hot coffee they'd just ordered. Sophie breathed in deeply, struggling to come to terms with her reality.

"There's something not quite right. I can feel it. You're giving me the 'inner turmoil' kind of vibe today and I'm not vibing it." Lorrie pushed her thick frames off her face as they fogged from the coffee steam. "Spill."

Sophie sighed. Taking another sip of her coffee. "Would you lie to someone for their safety?"

"Well, it depends. Will it *actually* harm them if they knew the truth, or are you just withholding information to protect yourself from their reaction?" Lorrie sipped away at her coffee.

"That's a solid question. One I'm afraid I'm not ready to answer." Sophie slumped her shoulders. Defeated.

"Whatever it is, whoever it is, deserves the truth. It's what any human deserves. It's up to them how they react to it. And it's up to you how you react to that reaction."

Lorrie had a point and Sophie struggled with that. She knew it would be the right thing to do by her mother to tell her of her accidental crossing of realms, she had the scars and tattoos to prove it. Her mum had told her stories of Faery all the time as a child, of a princess with silver and purple hair. Her mum would probably be ecstatic, if anything, knowing that Faery existed. That it was real. But what if her mum thought her delusional and in need of psychological evaluation and help? The thought gnawed at her. A risk she wasn't willing to take. Not yet anyway. And the need to tell someone only escalated. She had to tell someone. She wanted it to be her mum, but anyone would do, at this point. Her discovery was eating away at her soul. And so she told Lorrie. Sort of, anyway.

She told her best friend of a dream she had; that Faery was indeed real, of the train network that ran across the world and realms, of the friend she'd made there with red hair, of how they travelled through the tunnels dodging killer spiders and evading the evil queen. She described the handsome Fae warrior that guided her and leaned on her.

"You should *totally* write a book about it. Honestly. The Aussie girls will EAT IT UP!" Lorrie exclaimed from where she sat.

"You think?" Sophie laughed.

"I'd bloody read it. Can you imagine? Faery. Right at our doorsteps. Not some random place in Europe or America but here in Melbourne! Outrageous," she marvelled, laughing at the impossibility. If only she knew.

27

Sophie gasped awake in the middle of the night. She dreamt of being stuck in a giant spider web; a Dakin spider slowly eating her legs away, its body shrieking in laughter as it did. Sophie's entire bed warmed with heat. Her sheets were mussed up from her nightmare fit. She sat up straight, trying to calm herself with several deep breaths. She held onto the necklace her mother gave her, grounding herself.

Bump. Scuffle.

Sophie tilted her head at the small noises that echoed from downstairs. She ignored it, thinking it was a branch brushing up against a window. She pulled up her sheets and nestled back into bed.

Bump. Scuffle. Sshh.

Now that definitely wasn't a branch. That was definitely an intruder, two by the sounds of scuffling and shushing.

Sophie's eyes widened, now completely alert. She grabbed the steel baseball bat she hid underneath her bed for this very purpose. She never knew she would have to use it. It was a 'just in case' purchase.

Sshh. Bump. Scuffle.

She slowly stalked her way to her bedroom door, bat held high ready to whack-a-mole the intruders that dared raid her house. She silently turned the knob. The bumps and shuffles continued. They came from her dining area, just by the back sliding door. She slowly walked down the carpeted steps; eyes having adjusted to the darkness completely.

Step. Step. Step.

She reached the bottom of the steps. Her hand blindly felt for the light switch, her right arm ready to swing. The intruders' movements stopped entirely. She took that moment to switch on the lights and rushed for them without warning.

She screamed at the sight of them.

And the intruders, frozen in place, screamed right back at the sight of her bat-wielding form.

Camrine had his arms braced on the kitchen table while Elowan was trying and failing, to yank off the small robot vacuum that had latched itself onto Camrine's dark blue cloak.

They all paused.

Sophie burst out into laughter, keeling over, hand bracing her stomach. She couldn't have laughed harder if she tried.

She felt a sudden shadowy presence behind her. Before she could turn around, two cold fingertips touched her temple. Darkness consumed her immediately.

Sophie's eyes fluttered open. She was on a train, she could tell by the stingy smell, the awfully bright lights and the sound of metal gliding on metal – the train tracks. She sat up, immediately remembering the sight of Camrine and Elowan in her kitchen. She blinked, trying her best to adjust to the bright lights. Before her sat Elowan, her bright green eyes, worried, reserved. Without a word Sophie stood up and embraced Elowan with all her might.

"How is it that you remember?" Elowan gasped.

"I don't really know, but I touched the scar the arrow had left behind, the one that Kaine healed, and it felt like a veil lifted. My memories of Faery came flooding back." Sophie pulled her friend in for another tight hug.

"We thought we'd have to steal you in the night, hence the cloak and dagger approach but as soon as you cackled, we knew you'd at least gained some of your memory back." Elowan released herself from the embrace.

Sophie turned to Camrine who sat on a two-seater. In his lap sat her poor robot vacuum. Sophie burst into laughter again and so did Elowan and Zala who stood by the window.

Camrine rubbed his forehead in annoyance. He sighed. "The more I move, the more it wants to eat up my cloak. This is my favourite cloak too," he pouted.

Sophie, still laughing, approached him and landed an endearing kiss on his cheek. "It's so good to see you again, my friend." She swooped down to the robot vacuum he held still in his hands, pressing the off button. It buzzed to a stop, releasing Camrine's now creased cloak from its clutches.

Camrine peered down at this cloak, breathing in a sigh of relief. He smoothed out the wrinkles, glaring at the little machine as he did. "Get that blasted creature away from me."

"It's a machine. Not a creature. It will do you no harm." Sophie picked up the machine and placed it on another seat.

She looked out the window. They'd just left Flinders Station, she could tell. They were headed for Faery. "So." Sophie clasped her hands together. "Anyone care to explain to me what the fuck is going on or do I have to torture it out of you immortal lot?" She surveyed the group. Oh, how she'd missed them. And judging by their grins, they'd missed her too.

And so Elowan did. She explained how the queen had been caged by the king who was the puppet master orchestrating the killings of innocent fae children as a sacrifice to the Shadow Realm king, Terr. And she explained that Queen Calliea had been collecting evidence to overturn the king and was building alliances where she could. Which is why they were here, tracking down Sophie through Elowan's favour, to be the human emissary representing Sotera in the Faery-Sotera alliance. Elowan showed everyone her mother's ring too.

Camrine eyed the ring suspiciously.

Zala was consumed in the moving world outside.

It was the first time the two had heard the explanation. If they had opinions about it, they didn't voice it.

"You know you could have just asked me, and I would've gone with you willingly?"

"I couldn't risk it," Elowan argued.

"Look, I'm not mad. Seeing Camrine fight for his life against my vacuum definitely makes up for the less-than-savoury approach." Sophie wagged her eyebrows at the red-headed male. Camrine just shook his head and scoffed, focusing on the moving world outside. "So, what happens next?" Sophie continued.

"We get to Faery. We take a boat to Castle Terrin. You'll meet Queen Calliea and discuss terms of the alliance," Elowan said matter-of-factly.

"I'm flattered, honestly I am, but this is way above my pay-grade." Sophie scoffed, shaking her head. Inside, she baulked at the idea. She was nowhere near qualified to represent a country, let alone an entire realm of living and breathing beings.

"There is no one more worthy, Sophie. Please know that." Elowan reassured her with a firm grip on her shoulder.

They wooshed past the trees that lay on the other side of the large portal leaving Sotera to enter Faery.

Sophie stood and walked towards the large windows of the carriage. She looked out towards what she knew now was Faery in all its light-filled beauty.

Her flaming-heart locket warmed at the sight.

She felt like she was home again.

28

"Alright, hop in," Elowan ordered the group.

"Are you sure I'm not meant to be like, I don't know, in disguise or something?" Sophie tried her best to maintain her balance as she stepped into the rowboat. She was still wearing her black flannelette pyjamas.

"We're on queen's business. No one will hurt you. Plus, I've got some clothes prepared for you." Elowan threw a bag of supplies Sophie's way.

"Ah, you are just so resourceful. Thank you. Remind me to keep you forever." Sophie laughed, plopping down towards the front of the rowboat while Camrine and Zala climbed down.

"Don't thank me just yet. You haven't met the queen. She can be very... interesting." Elowan chuckled, grabbing hold of a pair of oars.

"Oh I certainly won't be holding my breath. These cruel-queen arc types just never really do it for me." Sophie laughed, pulling on the brown breeches, blouse and boots Elowan had sourced for her.

Zala silently unlatched the boat from where it was tied off on the pier, and softly pushed the rowboat northwards, towards Castle Terrin. The trip would take about three days. They'd need to take the river straight down to Castle Terrin, past Soxis – the Spring Court – and Fyllera – the Autumn Court – and alternate rowers to avoid stopping.

"Alright, lady and Faery folk, rule number one, keep your hands inside the boat. Rule number two, keep your hands inside the damned boat." Elowan grunted as she propelled them forward.

"I think you're forgetting that we literally swam in it the other day... or week, or whatever ago," Sophie pointed out.

"Well, that's because we crossed the Eastern River. This is the Southern River. It's twice the size and..." Elowan grunted, pulling them all into a steady pace. "...things dwell in it."

"Things?" Sophie raised her eyebrows, unsure if she wanted to know what these "things" were.

"Things. So, trust me when I say, keep your damn hands in the damn boat." Sophie gulped.

Camrine and Zala just laughed.

They had rowed for hours, and it was Camrine's turn to row. Sophie kept him company while Zala watched the rear and Elowan rested, picking at the fruits she'd packed for the group.

To the right, Sophie could see the outlines of Fylleran cottages, spaced out between large maple trees. To her left, she could see the beautiful stone cottages of Soxis, the Spring Court of Faery. The blight hadn't yet reached the flora-filled town. Vibrant flowers and grass-covered hills dotted all through the village. It reminded Sophie of Hobbiton, except for fae-sized beings. People danced and laughed. They seemed happy. Wholesome. If Sophie could choose, she'd live in Soxis, she thought to herself. It spoke to her the most. She sighed. "If you could live in any court, which would it be?"

"Well, that's easy, Fyllera." Camrine scoffed, grinning as he did.

"Why did you say that as if I was supposed to know?"

"Because that's where I told you I was from. Unless someone wasn't listening and just staring at Kaine when we were in the tunnels?" Camrine accused. Sophie paused, narrowing her eyes at Camrine. "What? I get lost in his turquoise eyes too. Don't pretend like you're above it." Camrine laughed, though something like sadness washed over his face. "It also reminds me of my mother and father."

Sophie knew that tone too well. She didn't respond, allowing him to continue.

"You may have noticed all the Elite have something in common. Our parents have all expired. The same way."

"Hellhounds?"

"Indeed. All around the same time."

"Twenty years ago?"

"Did you want me to tell the story, or did you want to?" Camrine raised a challenging eyebrow.

"Sorry. Go on."

"You're right, twenty years ago. Strange things happened that year. Many died and the blight on Faery began. The queen, despite her very questionable approach over the last few years, has given us"—he motioned to Zala and Elowan resting towards the back of the boat—"a place to belong. And we're grateful for that."

"You trust the queen then?"

"Not necessarily. To think all our parents died and we all coincidentally ended up in the same place, fighting under the same banner? There must be some sort of reason behind it. Who is orchestrating it all and for what purpose, I'm unsure. Though Ellie seems to think the queen is completely innocent." He laughed, motioning his chin towards Ellie.

"She's our best bet so far," Elowan shouted from where she lay.

Camrine lowered his voice further so only Sophie could hear. "What I'm trying to say, Sophie, is to keep your wits about you. Trust your own gut. We know who the players are now, but we don't know where they stand or who they stand for." Camrine warned. "I'm a realist, Sophie. I understand that this is a system that we cannot escape. This is all we get and all we can do is survive."

Sophie mulled over that. She tried her best to decipher what was up and what was down. On one hand her friend believed the queen to be innocent. Her other friend seemed to not trust either side. But what was her own gut saying? Sophie took a moment to reflect.

Despite Elowan campaigning for the queen's innocence, it didn't change the fact that Sophie's gut, that power inside her, told her to not trust the queen at all. It told her that Queen Calliea was playing a dangerous game.

"You could be the key to change, Sophie. We've never had a human emissary, for the entirety of Faery history. It's just the next level in whatever game is being played," Camrine said softly.

Sophie agreed. This was the next level in a dangerous game, and they'd need to play it carefully to find out what happened next and who was responsible for what.

Sophie looked ahead, squinting past Camrine who propelled them towards Castle Terrin. In the distance, a small figure flapped furiously towards them. It grew larger and larger. A raven. With a message.

Sophie stood up tall on the boat, reaching for the bird as it dipped. Sophie opened her palm to catch the small scroll just in time. It plunked in her hands. The raven shot upwards and, cawing, circled back into the direction in which it came.

"Who is it from?" Elowan sat up from where she lay, climbing towards Sophie. Sophie unfurled the small tea-stained parchment.

"The queen." Sophie gulped.

Elowan huddled close to Sophie, shoulder to shoulder, so they could read it together.

"It's a message for the Elite," Elowan explained.

An attempt on the queen's life has been made. For treason of the highest order, Kaine Dormarth Aaryn, former captain of the Elite, if sighted, is to be killed.

"I don't believe it. It doesn't make sense." Elowan shook her head.

"Are you sure it's from the queen?" Camrine asked from where he rowed.

Zala floated towards Sophie, snatching the parchment from her hands, and read the scroll. Over and over. Her face washed with concern.

"That is definitely her handwriting. Maybe he's gotten his wires crossed. Kaine must still think the queen is behind it all," Elowan suggested.

"But to make an attempt on her life? That's not like him. He's smarter than that and you know it," Camrine rebutted.

"Kaine can be unpredictable. We all know that. We need to get to him before anyone else does. And if this parchment speaks true, we need to stop him before he ruins Faery's only chance."

Zala moved over to Camrine with a wraith-like silence, handing him the scroll and taking over the oars. Camrine read the scroll. Over and over. And paled.

"How can you be certain we can trust the queen?" Camrine argued.

"Because." Ellie unfurled her hand, her mother's ring glinting in her palm.

Camrine paused, staring at the ring, then back up at Ellie. "Are you forgetting all that we've been through? He's our friend. Our brother." Camrine shook his head.

"But if this scroll is true, he also stands in the way of peace and prosperity. We can't risk that either. We need to stick to protocol or at least bring him in to the queen for questioning."

"You can't be serious?"

"Think about it." Elowan raised.

"Think about what, Ellie? He is our brother. We cannot risk it!"

"Listen. The queen has the power to make an alliance to protect us from the hands of Terr. She has the ability to bring Faery back."

"It's been more than twenty years since the start of her reign and look at where we are, Elowan. You can't just blindly trust her because she gave you your mother's ring!"

"But..."

"Did you ever think about how she obtained it in the first place and why she chose this very specific moment to give it to you?"

"I haven't—"

"Use your head for once, Ellie, and stop projecting. I get it. You miss your parents. We all do. But you can't let that control you," Camrine said, wringing his hands through his short red hair. "You should have told us about the ring BEFORE we stepped off to Sotera. We may as well have killed Sophie ourselves."

Zala, silent as ever, continued to row, not wanting to get between the two.

Ellie and Camrine now stood face to face.

Sophie moved between the two towering fae. "Look. Let's take a breather. It's clear we're all working through our own struggles. Let's not kill each other while we're trying to figure it out, okay?"

Ellie snarled, baring her teeth at Camrine, her green eyes dancing with fire.

"It's not even worth it. Arguing with a fool makes two..." Camrine muttered as he turned, moving towards the front of the boat, past Zala.

Sophie frowned and turned to Elowan who was visibly shaken from the heated argument. She gave her friend a consoling rub on her shoulders and guided her to the back of the boat where they both sat, leaning back to watch the sky. The Faery night sky was its marvellous self tonight.

"Are you okay?" Sophie asked quietly.

"I... should have questioned her motives more. Cam does have a point." Elowan fidgeted with her mother's ring around her finger.

"Don't be so hard on yourself, Ellie."

"I know. I just... wanted to believe the queen so badly. It felt like I had a connection to my mother again."

"I don't blame you. You never got to say goodbye to your mother. What the queen offered was the closest thing to closure you could get. Heck, it's what I would've done if I were you," Sophie said, hands clasped across her abdomen as they both stared up into the sky.

"I guess we'll find out soon enough where the truth lies." Elowan sighed.

29

"*Q*uick, before my father catches us," Sophie whispered.

She jumped up onto his back and reached up as high as her little arms could. She clasped onto the handle of one rapier and handed it down to the boy with dark hair and turquoise swirling eyes. She took another down for herself from the steel rack that all the swords hung on. She jumped off the small boy's back and helped him up from his knees. The two giggled furiously as they tiptoed out of her father's armoury.

Once the armoury door closed behind them, they ran as fast as their little legs could take them. Laughing, giggling, enjoying the sunshine that glinted across their joyous faces and the feel of the grass crunching beneath their boots.

They ran down the grassy hill, towards the river, behind the bridge that would provide them a bit of cover.

"Last one there's a rotten egg!" the boy cawed.

"That's not fair, you're bigger than me!" she shouted in return.

The two ran to the giant rock to the left of the bridge. The boy jumped onto the rock first, turning around to Sophie as she slowly climbed on.

"Ha ha, guess you're the rotten egg!" the boy teased, sticking out his tongue.

"Am not!"

"A duel then." The boy stuck out his rapier, standing tall.

"A duel." Sophie smirked. She'd been practising with the wooden sword her father had carved for her.

The two children bowed to each other and took their stances, one arm behind their backs, ready for a duel.

The boy moved first. Advance. Strike.

Sophie blocked the move perfectly. Parry. Dodge. Strike.

The boy dodged, meeting Sophie's rapier halfway with his. Steel on steel clanged through the air.

Sophie pushed harder. Strike. Strike. Duck. Strike. Just like she practised.

The boy wasn't ready for it. He stumbled back.

Sophie used that to her advantage. Sweep. Strike. Point. She had him. The point of her rapier pointed at his neck.

She panted. "Ha! I beat you fair and square."

"Did not."

"Did too!"

"Did not." The boy smirked, bringing his rapier up in one big movement, trying to knock Sophie's own out of her hand. He didn't expect her to push back. The contact knocked him off balance and he slipped. Right into the roaring river below.

He shouted, rapier flying as he plummeted off the rock.

Sophie gasped and watched as the boy disappeared into the whitewash of water. She waited and waited. Nothing. He didn't resurface.

She took a few steps back, allowing herself a running start and leapt off the edge of the rock. Her arms and legs kicked through the air. She hit the ice-cold water. The water was much shallower than she originally thought. She opened her eyes as much as she could against the moving water, her cheeks puffy from all the air she held in.

There he was. Pushed down in the water. Face down.

She swam. She kicked with all her might towards the boy.

When she got to him, she flipped him over. He was bleeding profusely from his head, the water around him turned murky from all the blood.

She panicked at the sight. Hooking his arm around hers, she kicked up to the surface of the water as hard as she could.

With a huge gasp of air, she broke the surface. The unconscious boy was bobbing just behind her. She swam for the grassy shore.

She was so small and the boy so much bigger than her. But with all the strength she could muster, she pushed him onto the shore, her little head pushed underneath the water from his weight. But she couldn't give up.

Push. Kick. Push.

The boy rolled onto the grassy shore, sputtering.

Sophie heaved herself out of the water and rolled onto the shore next to the boy, gasping for air.

The boy sat up, coughing all the water he'd accidentally ingested out onto the grass.

Sophie sat up too and giggled. "Beat you. Fair and square."

The boy turned to her, face bloodied. "Fine." And they laughed, sopping wet from the river water.

"Does it hurt?" Sophie crouched closer to the boy so she could inspect the wound.

"Just a little." He winced as he brought his hands to the wound, touching it gingerly.

"How are we going to explain this to our parents?"

They were strictly not allowed to play close to the river unless supervised, let alone with the rapiers they'd stolen from her father's armoury. Her mother would be furious. His mother would be furious too!

"We have to keep it a secret," the boy whispered.

"But how? You're bleeding!"

"Maybe... maybe if you kiss it, it'll disappear," the boy explained.

"That's silly."

"Is not. Mother kisses my cuts and bruises all the time, and they always heal."

"Are you sure?"

"Very sure." The boy nodded, closing his eyes, waiting for Sophie's kiss.

"Okay, I'll try." Sophie closed her eyes and kissed the boy's bloodied brow. She opened her eyes. Nothing. Except now she had blood all over her face. "Ick! That was gross!"

The boy paled at her reaction.

They heard footsteps approaching them from up the grassy hill.

"You rascals! Get back inside this instant!" a furious female voice rang through the air.

Sophie and the boy looked at each other. The inseparable rascals.

The boy clutched his bleeding face with one hand, took Sophie's hand in the other and did the exact opposite of what they were being told to do. They ran. Hand in hand. Laughing as they did.

Sophie's eyes fluttered open. That was the first dream she had with the boy where there was sound. His voice was a warmth that wrapped around her heart. She recalled the hill they ran down. It looked so much like the grassy hills in Soxis she'd seen earlier. Her brows furrowed at the thought. Why did that dream feel so real?

"Do you always wake up choosing violence?" Camrine popped his face into Sophie's vision.

Sophie rolled her eyes, swatting him away, not ready for the rude awakening. "It was a strange dream. Now leave me be, you demon." She groaned.

"Not a chance, sweet cheeks. Your turn to row." Camrine winked and helped Sophie up onto her feet. She wobbled, still trying to wake up.

Camrine took the place where she'd lain, arms tucked behind his head and started snoring instantly.

Sophie scoffed. "How does he do that?" she asked no one in particular.

Clambering over to Zala, Sophie took over the oars. Zala took a seat in front of her.

Push. Pull. Push. Pull.

It was nice to focus on something else entirely for a moment.

Push. Pull. Push. Pull.

The two sat there in silence for a while admiring the rising sun. The early morning fog flitted across the surface of the river. They were more than halfway to Castle Terrin now.

Zala sat back straight, dark robes covering her form entirely, her two rapiers crossed on her back.

"What do you see when you sleep?" Zala asked, almost a whisper. Her voice was deep and dark much like her appearance. Sophie was almost startled by it. She rarely spoke.

"Many things. Why?"

"They seem very vivid. Your face strains. Like you are living a different life in your sleep." She searched Sophie's eyes. "May I see?" she asked, lifting two fingers to her own head, as if it meant something to Sophie.

Sophie tilted her head, unsure. "What do you mean?"

Zala moved closer to where Sophie sat. One knee down on the ground, crouched. "I can look. Through here." She tapped Sophie's temple.

Sophie hesitated but nodded.

Zala lifted both her hands on either side of Sophie's temples and pressed two cold fingers softly against them. A low green glow appeared in Sophie's peripherals though she kept her focus on rowing. She watched as Zala's eyes flitted violently underneath her closed eyelids. It felt like a dark smoke had entered Sophie's mind. Not smoke, shadows. Zala's unique power. The shadows danced through her mind, turning over stones, memories, dreams – all of it. Sophie marvelled at the feel of mana travelling through her head. Despite its soft grasp on her mind, she could still focus on her rowing. Barely.

Zala's eyes shot open. Wide. "How is it that you have seen the Ephemeral Lights?"

"What do you mean?"

"The green-and-blue swirling sky you see, what you escape to, it is a memory. Not a dream."

"That can't be right. I've got a vivid imagination. The books I read—"

"It is a memory. I can feel the difference." Zala did not budge. She eyed Sophie. Searching her face. Her features. Her ears.

"What are you...?" Zala cautiously pulled back from where she sat.

As she did, one of Sophie's oars hit something rubbery, fleshy. She gasped at the feeling, almost letting the oar go. "Fuck, I just hit something and it felt really gross." Sophie silently gagged. Her other oar spun rapidly in place as if something held onto it. Sophie screamed at the movement.

Zala grasped the side of the boat, searching the water below. "Keep rowing, Sophie. Don't stop." Sophie obeyed, reluctantly.

Elowan and Camrine roused from their slumber.

"What is it?" Elowan groaned, rubbing her eyes as she sat up. Camrine stretched his arms behind her.

"The Scyllen are toying with us." Zala's brow furrowed.

"Do I even want to know what that is?" Sophie paled. She'd had enough of scary creatures. The Dakin spiders still haunted her sleep. Though what did she expect? She was in Faery for fuck's sake.

Elowan jumped up from where she lay, moving swiftly to Sophie. "Let me take over."

Sophie obliged.

Camrine, as calm as ever, stood and stretched some more. "Half female, half sea serpent, four arms, two giant tusks and hundreds of sharp teeth made perfect for shredding." He paused. "Through bodies, just to clarify." He hummed, satisfied with his stretching.

Sophie gagged. "I didn't ask, but thanks for the image." Shivers ran rampant across Sophie's back. This wasn't going to end well. She could feel it.

Bump. Something hit the bottom of the boat. *Bump.*

The boat rocked violently but Elowan kept pushing through.

"How many are there?" Elowan shouted over the ruckus.

"Twenty or thirty, from what I can tell." Zala's bright blue eyes glowed as if she were searching through the water.

"I can block them off." Camrine moved toward the back of the boat. He stood tall, closed his eyes, arms rigid beside him, palms open. An orange glow hummed from each palm. Sophie watched in awe. He slowly lifted his forearms, bending at the elbow. His face strained at the effort. Elowan rowed faster and faster, creating more distance between them and the mass of Scyllen that swiftly pursued.

In the distance, Sophie could see that Camrine had altered the shape of the riverbed entirely. The water was deep. To alter earth to that degree would have taken so much mana, but he didn't even break a sweat. He created a wall of rock, blocking off most of the school of Scyllen – the ones that weren't fast enough for Elowan's rowing, anyway. The trapped Scyllen shrieked and splashed in anger, watching their boat disappear, farther and farther.

Camrine loosed a breath and turned to the rest of them. The orange glow from his palms fading. "Now tell me that was cool, without telling me that was cool." He whooped.

"Nice one, birdbrain, but what about the four nipping at our damn heels!" Elowan shouted over lapping water and violent rowing. They were desperate to get away. Sophie turned to see that Zala had taken over one oar while Elowan took the other.

"Guys... I don't see them any—" Sophie didn't finish.

Their boat catapulted into the air with a vengeance.

The boat had flipped in its entirety. The bottom now faced the sky. Camrine, Sophie, Elowan and Zala were upside down, feet in the air. Limbs stretched in all sorts of directions. Their packs and supplies flew open, aiming for the water beneath them. The oars spun in circles. Sophie looked down into the dark water that was about to engulf them all. She took one last deep breath and braced for contact.

SPLASH.

Water filled her ears immediately.

She kicked and kicked, not really knowing which way was up or which way was down. All she knew was that she didn't want to get caught by one of the sea creatures.

Finally, she broke the surface, gasping for air.

Elowan and Zala had already reached the overturned boat and were trying to flip it over. Their packs floated around them randomly. Elowan barked orders and Zala obeyed. But where was Camrine?

Sophie treaded on the spot, whipping her head around, searching for any signs of Camrine. But nothing. Not even a splash or tuft of red hair. Her stomach dropped.

Ignoring all logic, she took one deep breath and dived under the surface.

It was so dark. The water was murky. She could barely see a few metres in front of her, but she could hear him. He was shouting under the water. Struggling. Much deeper in the water than she was.

Sophie kicked and kicked. Deeper and deeper she went. She pushed her arms through the water. She felt something slimy. A fin. She almost gagged at what whipped around to face her. A Scyllen.

Camrine wasn't joking. The half female, half sea serpent was made of pure nightmares. It's greeny-black scales and yellow eyes glowed in the water. The one that faced Sophie bared its claws on all four scaly arms at her and hissed. Camrine struggled behind it. Three Scyllen had their claws latched into his limbs, holding him down under the water. Rocks from the riverbed flew around them violently and aimlessly. He couldn't see, she realised. His cloak had wrapped entirely around his face.

Sophie raced for Camrine. Her lungs burned violently. The Scyllen cackled at her efforts, the closest one whipping its serpent tail Sophie's way. She dodged but not far enough as sharpened fins sliced her forearms. Blood billowed out. She kept aiming for Camrine. One of the rocks Camrine wielded with his mana struck the largest Scyllen away from him. Sophie torpedoed for Camrine. With a free leg he struck out, kicking one of the Scyllen in the ribs with his fae might. Sophie took a hold of his cloak, unclasping it from his shoulders. Rocks whizzed past her face as she did. Fins and claws of the closest Scyllen scratched into her back and limbs. She pushed his billowing cloak towards the three Scyllen, obscuring their vision of Camrine. They let him go, preoccupied with the cloak wrapping around them.

Sophie noticed Camrine suddenly go limp. He'd passed out.

Grabbing him by the collar, Sophie pulled him away from the sea creatures. He was so heavy. The creatures' shrieks pierced through the water as they tried to claw away the massive cloak obscuring their vision. They were fast. Sophie kicked to the surface, pulling Camrine with her.

She could see the shadow of the now upturned boat. She aimed for it and broke the surface with a violent gasp. She was bleeding all over. Camrine floating behind her on his back.

"This way!" Elowan shouted, waving her arms furiously.

"I can't! He's too heavy!" Sophie shouted over the choppy water. She didn't have the strength left in her legs. They were cut open and so were her arms.

In that moment, Zala nose dived and swam at breakneck speed towards them. Hooking her arm around Camrine's upper body, she beelined for the boat pushing him up into it as Elowan struggled to get his large form over the edge.

"Quick, Sophie!" Zala shouted from where she pushed Camrine's legs into the boat.

Sophie obeyed. Grunting at the effort, she focused, aiming for the boat.

She was about five metres away when a bony, slimy hand wrapped around her ankle, dragging her into the darkness of the river. She didn't even have time to steal a breath as one of the Scyllen pulled her into a death roll.

The spinning made Sophie dizzy. She'd lost all her bearings within seconds. All she knew was that she had to keep kicking. Faery depended on her. She couldn't give up.

With her free leg, she kicked against the bony hand. The Scyllen shrieked. It let go of Sophie at the brutal contact, only to start cackling. Its voice was croaky. Watery. The sound elicited a deep fear in Sophie that roiled in her stomach, making her sick. She was shark bait. Scyllen bait, to be exact.

The four Scyllen circled her. Dark limbs snapped. Clawed. Fins thrashed in the water, promising violence. Sophie couldn't out swim them. Not a chance. But maybe, maybe she could use Elowan's mana. The tiny drop of power that lived inside her.

Sophie focused. She reached into her mind, her soul, her gut to locate the power. Her power. And like in the books she'd read dozens of times, she pulled at the power. Willing it. Wielding it. Grasping it. She stretched her arm out in front of her, palm facing the circling Scyllen, ready to blast them.

Sophie's blood trailed toward them and wafted around the larger female; the leader Sophie assumed.

The leader sniffed in the blood. Again. And again.

With a piercing shriek, she held up a scaly hand, pausing her sisters immediately.

They all looked at her, confused.

She shook her head and clattered something in their language.

All four Scyllen stared at Sophie. Unmoving.

Still, the leader held her hand up. An order. To stop.

Sophie didn't hesitate. She took that as her sign to leave and kicked up as fast as she could to the surface. The water grew lighter the faster she went.

A familiar hand grabbed hers. Zala.

Breaking the surface, Sophie let in a giant breath of air, quelling the burn in her lungs. Zala swam for her life, Sophie in tow. They'd finally reached the boat when Elowan grabbed Sophie by the collar of her shirt and all but threw her in. Zala followed shortly.

Elowan rowed faster than Sophie had ever seen.

Sophie and Zala breathed heavily. Savouring the air. Panting. Camrine, still unconscious, lay at Ellie's feet on his side.

Sophie whipped her head around only to see, in the distance, four heads watching them leave. Curious.

Sophie couldn't make sense of it. They let her go... but why?

30

"I believe thanks are in order." Camrine plopped down next to Sophie, while Zala rowed and Elowan kept watch.

Camrine and Sophie sat next to each other, towards the back of the boat, watching the bright blue sky and the clouds floating by. Elowan had pulled them hundreds of metres farther down the river before Zala finally gave them the all clear. They'd manage to escape the Scyllen but their supplies were left behind, floating.

"Don't even worry about it." Sophie scoffed. She was tired. She was hungry. And she was still trying to understand why the Scyllen had stopped in their tracks. It was something to do with her blood.

Camrine looked Sophie in her eyes. "I am indebted to you. Truly." He quickly grabbed her right hand, not giving her a chance to object. A faint orange glow began to appear from his hands.

"You don't have to—"

"I want to." Camrine closed his eyes gently and the orange glow intensified. Sophie watched as his favour appeared just above Elowan's, in a dark ink. It was the same shape, Faery's moon encased in a three-sided square. Though unlike Ellie's, it was rotated a quarter way. A dark line connected the two favours. Sophie marvelled at the sight. "Thank you for not leaving me behind." He leaned closer to Sophie and planted a kiss of gratitude on her cheek. Sophie closed her eyes. She wouldn't have played it out any other way. There was no way she was leaving her friend behind in the Southern River. Not a chance. Camrine moved to Sophie's ear to whisper, "You owe me a nice cloak though." He smirked.

Sophie slapped his arm. "Of course all you care about is the cloak, you materialistic fae bastard!"

At that moment, Sophie was glad to have found Camrine, Elowan and Zala. They were the friends she never knew she needed. Her friends. Her people.

"We'll need to make a stop at Soxis," Elowan stated to the group. Their supplies were left behind after the Scyllen attack, and with a full day's journey until they reached Castle Terrin, they'd need sustenance and clean water.

Camrine nodded, turning the boat left, closer to the shores of Soxis.

As they approached the pier, Zala lassoed a thick rope to secure the boat. Camrine stretched while Elowan jumped onto the pier with fae grace.

"Zala, Sophie, stay here. Guard the boat. Cam and I will resup," Elowan ordered. She waited for Camrine as he jumped on the pier just beside her. They looked so much alike. On the way here, Sophie learned that they were distant cousins.

As Sophie watched the two leave, she felt Zala's stare. A question.

Deep down, Sophie knew what the wraith was asking her. "They just let me go," Sophie admitted.

"Why?" Zala bluntly replied.

"I can't explain it." The moment the Scyllen stopped their onslaught, Sophie couldn't stop thinking about why. The Scyllen. Her memories of Faery. Real. Not a dream. Memories. Her inclination to the Faery realm even as a child. Her ending up in Faery of all places. Somehow, it was all connected. The threads of fate were at work, pulling things together but each time she tried to think back to days surrounding her time in Faery, it felt like a thick wall encased them. She could see bits and pieces through the cracks – the various dreams she started having the moment she stepped foot in Faery. Then she tried to think back to her life in Sotera. When her family had just moved to Melbourne. She was about five or so. Back when her father and mother fought a lot. She tried to see things with a different lens. A lens not of her five-year-old self, but her now. As someone who stumbled upon the truth. That Faery was indeed real. But every time she tried, a veiled wall stood in the way, making everything feel murky. Unclear. If anything, it gave her a mild headache. It was only when she stopped trying to pry for the memories that the dull ache in her head dissipated.

Sophie continued, "The leader inhaled my blood. She ordered them to stop, and they did." It didn't make sense to her at all. At least not yet. If Zala had any idea what that meant, she didn't say anything. She sat with her shadows, staring into the distance, arms crossed. "Maybe they don't like eating humans?" Sophie pondered.

"That is their preferred delicacy. We learnt that the hard way," Zala countered. Sophie knew what she meant. They'd most likely tried to smuggle the humans from Southern Helm to Northern Helm using the river ways. They learned the hard way that the underground tunnels were their safest bet, despite being made of iron.

"You are a mystery, girl. And there is nothing I do not know." Zala held her chin high, searching Sophie, as if an answer was written somewhere on her body.

Sophie had no response. She didn't know what to say. She just sat, staring into the water. Her blood. It was most definitely human. Her mother was human. Her dad, plainly human too. Sure, her mother loved to tell stories of Faery, but that was completely fictional, based on books she'd found at Dymocks. Then why did her blood stop them? What did they recognise?

A small splash in the river drew Zala and Sophie's attention away.

About twenty metres from the pier, a head popped out of the water, facing them. It was the Scyllen leader. Her dark blue hair clung to her head. Her tusks peeked out of the water and her scaly shoulders sparkled in the sun. She did not move any closer.

Zala stood swiftly, unsheathing both her rapiers.

Sophie stood with her. Cautious.

"I don't think she means any harm," Sophie said lowly. She stretched an arm out before Zala, silently motioning her to stand down. Zala hesitated but obeyed, slowly returning her rapiers to her back.

Sophie did not break eye contact with the sea creature. Its glowing yellow eyes seemed more sincere.

The Scyllen swam a few metres closer to them then halted. Slowly, she lifted a scaly arm in the air. She held something in her hand. She nodded.

Sophie nodded in return. The energy in her gut told her that it was okay to trust this creature.

With that acknowledgement, the sea creature lobbed the item she held in her hand to their boat. Sophie watched it as it flew, its pearlescent surface glinting against the sun.

It softly landed at Sophie's boots.

A knife.

A knife that was carved from a purple-and-white marbled, pearlescent shell. Sophie picked it up. The blade itself was as long as her hand, curved like a boomerang and culminated in a sharp point. The handle was shaped into a sea-serpent's tail ending in a circle she could loop her finger through. It was light. Perfectly balanced. It was extraordinary. A beautiful display of craftmanship.

It was a gift, Sophie realised.

Sophie, looked back up at the Scyllen. She crossed all four arms across her chest, closed her eyes and bowed her head deeply. For Sophie.

Sophie stood still. Surprised. Confused.

Without warning the Scyllen dived back in the murky water, disappearing completely.

Sophie whipped her head to Zala who just stared at the knife, then back at Sophie.

31

They were about an hour away from reaching the docks by the front gates of Castle Terrin. After her encounter with the sea creature, Sophie strapped the pearlescent knife to her thigh. She wouldn't be heading into the castle unarmed, a lamb to the slaughter. She was smarter than that.

"Game plan. We get to Castle Terrin. We keep our wits about us. We trust no one but each other." Sophie stared down the group. Elowan and Camrine bickered for almost an hour before Sophie had to step in. Zala returned to her shadows and did not speak another word since their encounter with the Scyllen.

"Zala, you're our getaway. You'll remain outside the gates." Zala nodded in acknowledgment. "Cam, you're second line defence. You're just outside the door, down the hall should things go awry," Sophie continued. Ellie had detailed the layout of the main castle and mentioned that they were to meet the queen in the throne room. "Ellie, you're with me, obviously."

Elowan grinned.

When they stopped for supplies earlier, Ellie and Cam had duked it out on their way to the market. Ellie had apologised for not thinking clearly and Cam had apologised for being too harsh. Though it didn't stop them from bickering over their plan.

"We go in thinking the worst. And hopefully, things will turn out in our favour," Sophie stated.

"Was that your attempt at a motivational speech?" Elowan laughed.

Sophie sighed. "Come on, Ellie. Read the room." Sophie glared at her red-headed fae friend.

Elowan just laughed, shaking her head.

Castle Terrin was hideous. Monstrous. Its soot-covered bricks and the two spires that towered over them were covered in black, dead vines. Between the spires stood a large steel gate. Two large lion-like statues stood beside each door, and in their mouths a large flame illuminated the surrounding dark.

The moon had reached its peak when they'd tied off the rowboat by the smaller pier that was a short walk to the castle gates.

"Perhaps I should also negotiate some decorators as part of this alliance. It's giving 'come inside so we can feast on your innards' energy." Sophie muttered, looking up at the castle. It stood out like a sore thumb against the lush greenery of Terrin – the main island of Faery where the castle was located. They had to squeeze through a small canal before entering the moat that surrounded the castle. All around it lay the main town of Terrin. Houses, buildings and market stalls were packed up against each other.

The four friends stood side by side, watching the castle.

"You never really get used to it..." Elowan sighed.

They all turned to Zala and gave her a curt nod. No goodbyes. Not yet. She'd stay behind guarding the boat and listening out for Cam's signals should they need a speedy escape.

Together they strode to the castle entrance.

Camrine peeled off first. Quietly. Secretly. He scanned the open, arched hallways that lined the outer rim of the courtyard before disappearing out of Sophie's sight.

Inside the dark steel gates, the court was quiet. Grey gravel lined the walkways and in the centre a gargoyle fountain gurgled away. White rose bushes lined the main path, leading to the throne room. Large floor-to-ceiling oak doors painted blood red with golden doorknobs in the shape of knotted snakes greeted them.

Elowan and Sophie announced their arrival to the guards stationed outside the main throne room.

Sophie swallowed. Nervous. Her mother's necklace warmed in warning.

Noticing the movement, Elowan placed a firm hand behind Sophie's elbow, grounding her.

Act natural, Sophie. Act natural, she repeated to herself.

She was nervous. On one hand she hoped the queen was innocent, and that they'd form a Faery-Sotera alliance that would see Faery prosper, free from the clutches of the Shadow Realm king. On the other hand, she was terrified of what the queen had in mind for them, if she wasn't as innocent as she claimed.

The two royal guards standing beside the throne room doors stomped their spears on the ground twice, signalling for the doors to open.

The red oak doors groaned and slowly opened as Sophie and Elowan stood side by side.

On the dais, fifty or so metres ahead, sat the notorious Queen Calliea. Queen of Faery in the flesh. Sophie couldn't peel her eyes away.

The queen was an enigma, wearing a bright red gown, its trail pooling over the dais steps. She sat politely, hands over the arms of her large red velvet throne. A silver crown, interlaced like elk-horns, lined with purple gems lay on top of her head of dark red hair. With her chin held high, she looked down on Sophie and Elowan. Peasants compared to her grandeur. She was a vision, Sophie admitted. And younger than she'd imagined.

The royal guards who had opened the throne room doors from the inside struck their spears against the ground, twice.

In a loud clear voice, one of the guards announced, "Introducing Sophie of So—" He was cut short. He gurgled a violent disgusting noise.

A wet scream sounded as Sophie and Elowan whirled around where they stood. The guard was on the floor, grasping his neck that spurted blood in all directions. The other three guards lay limp on the ground, blood pooling from their necks like flowing rivers.

Between them all, stood a tall dark figure, his arms outstretched with knives in each hand, dripping blood. The figure was death incarnate. His long dark hair billowed on a phantom wind and his turquoise eyes narrowed, promising death.

Kaine.

"It looks like the true heir of Faery has come to claim his throne at last." Completely unphased by her slaughtered guards, the queen laughed maniacally.

Elowan and Sophie's jaws dropped.

The true heir of Faery was Kaine.

32

S ophie's heart squeezed at the sight of him. He was alive.

His eyes snapped to Sophie's. Wide. Surprised to see her in Faery again.

"Seize him," the queen huffed nonchalantly. She was arrogant, Sophie would give her that.

In an instant, Kaine threw his two knives into the eyes of the guards that charged for him, knocking them down immediately.

Elowan pulled Sophie to the side, shielding her from the onslaught.

Kaine grabbed for another two throwing knives when *SLING*.

Two iron arrows, whirled through the air from the upper viewing platforms of the throne room, aiming for his arms and shot true.

The sound was horrible.

Iron pierced through flesh in a symphony of crunches and tears.

Kaine grunted from the pain and fell to his knees.

Iron arrows. Muting his powers. Rendering him helpless.

Sophie screamed for him from behind Elowan who was stunned into silence.

"Elowan, be a darling and take that human filth to the dungeons. I need to deal with this thorn in my side." She gestured to Kaine who knelt on the ground, panting, blood dripping down his forearms from where the iron arrows struck.

Ellie did not move. She wasn't even breathing. "No," she gritted through her teeth. She stepped farther back, shielding Sophie from the queen.

"No?" The queen smirked.

"I will not." Elowan's eyes darted from Kaine's kneeling form to the queen and back.

"I do wonder what that delicious blond male might have to say about your disobedience... Regin, that's his name isn't it?" The queen drawled, smiling sweetly at Ellie.

Elowan's body stilled at the queen's words. A silence so painful filled the room.

She lifted her hand, no doubt pulling her mana, ready to strike the queen.

"Ah, ah, ah. My guards are outside his workshop right now. One word from me and I'll make sure you never see him again."

"You so much as hurt a hair on his head and I'll—"

"You'll what?" the queen laughed. "Save your energy. Guards, take her away."

With a swish of her pale spindly hands, the queen wrapped her mana around Elowan binding her movements completely. Four guards moved to whisk her away. Despite being restrained she put up a fight, squirming in the grasps of the four guards. Elowan turned to Sophie. "Sophie. I didn't know. I'm so sorry. Please believe me. I didn't know!" she shouted. Crying. The sounds of her struggles faded away down the hallway where Sophie hoped to all the gods that Camrine would intercept them and run to safety.

Sophie felt unprotected. She felt small. She didn't have any mana, not enough to overbear the queen or even make a run for it. She had the skills she'd learnt in jiujitsu, but the queen would most likely combust her before she could even step forward. She couldn't leave Kaine either. She was just a few metres from him. If she could just run and pull those arrows out, he could use his powers and get them both out.

"You two." The queen motioned towards two guards standing closest to Sophie. "See to it that this bug is sent to the dungeons. I'll deal with her later." With a wave of her hand, the queen wrapped Sophie in her mana, rendering her motionless. The feeling of the queen's mana was hot, threatening to burn Sophie if she tried to put up a fight.

Tears welled in Sophie's eyes, threatening to fall. She felt stuck. She felt helpless. She felt stupid for walking into this trap unprepared. Her heart clenched, knowing her friends were hurting and that perhaps, she would truly never see her mother again. For real, this time.

The two guards hooked their arms around Sophie's and dragged her out of the throne room.

Sophie screamed. She screamed for Kaine. She screamed for Elowan. She screamed at the conniving queen who had outmanoeuvred them.

If this was her end, if this was the last time she was going to see him again, she had to let him know.

"Kaine, I remember you. I always will." Sophie shouted at his kneeled form. Tears fell down her cheeks. Her throat ached with anger.

At those words Kaine lifted his heavy head and turned to helplessly watch Sophie being dragged away.

His turquoise eyes hit her like a storm.

Turquoise eyes.

Like the boy she always dreamed about.

Zala's voice echoed through Sophie's mind... It is a memory. Not a dream.

33

Sophie didn't give up the fight. They'd made it down the entire length of the hall. Camrine, despite her pleas, did not intercept them. Maybe he'd been too busy getting Elowan out? Sophie hoped to the gods her friends were safe.

The queen's suffocating mana was still wrapped around her entire body, and the two guards overpowered her with ease. It was a lost cause. Despite knowing this, Sophie kept kicking and uttering profanities their way, making sure they knew full well how she felt about them and their queen.

"You're a bunch of sheep," Sophie muttered under her breath. The two guards paid her no attention. If the insults she threw their way hit their target, they didn't show it.

Tightening their grip, the guards whisked her down a dark and narrow spiralling staircase. Few sconces marked their descent to the dungeons. It was dark, dingy and mouldy. They were headed straight for the dungeons.

On and on, the staircase spiralled for what must have been several levels, Sophie lost count. In the books she loved, the heroines had the ability to mark every level, analyse every exit but for Sophie, all she could think about was Elowan's face, Kaine's blood dripping down his arms and the echoing of words... the true heir had come to claim his throne.

She remembered the prophecy that Elowan had mentioned when she first arrived in Faery. That one day, Faery's true heir would return from where they'd been hidden. And with their return, the full power and might of Faery.

The queen was going to slaughter Kaine. That's the only reason she'd hold him back. He was the true heir of Faery. He was the only thing standing between her and her endless reign as queen. Yet, if Kaine was the true heir who had returned... where did he return from? Maybe the prophecy meant a literal return to the throne. That he had to physically sit on the throne. But he'd been captain of the Elite for years now. He would have had plenty of opportunity to do so unless... he didn't know. Through all the times they'd spoken, he'd never once mentioned anything about his father, just that his mother was from Summeira and died when he was young.

And where did Sophie belong in the equation? The queen knew something she didn't, that was certain. She ordered for Sophie to be sent to the dungeons to be dealt with later. Perhaps it would answer the questions she had about herself, the questions that Zala asked. Her real identity.

The dungeons were exactly as she imagined – dark, cold and damp. Several iron-clad cells lined the walls on each side with various lengths of shackles, chains, a small blanket and a bucket inside.

Giant beams of iron marked every corner of the room.

To mute mana, Sophie noted. To weaken its magic-wielding prisoners.

At the other end of the dungeon, bright moonlight illuminated a giant round pit perhaps forty metres in diameter. How deep it went, Sophie could not tell.

Large, heavy chains clanked around in time with what only could be described as large footsteps. Dragging. Scraping. Sophie's entire body went rigid with the sound. She'd had enough of Faery and its nightmare creatures at this point. She didn't want to know what sort of beast prowled in that pit. Whatever it was, it sounded big and deadly.

At the thought, Sophie dug her heels into the ground – one last act of defiance.

The guards only laughed at her attempt, throwing her into her cell without any effort. She landed on her arse, fell back and cracked her head against the cold ground from the force.

Fuck, that hurt.

The two guards towered over her as she cradled her head.

One guard knelt. "I don't think a sheep can do this." He sneered, uppercutting her right in the diaphragm. The force of it stole her breath and left her gasping for air. She braced her abdomen, trying to right herself.

"You're still a cunt though," Sophie bit out, bracing herself on the floor, one hand clutching her middle.

The guard stood swiftly, lifted his knee and round-housed her right in the temple, straight into oblivion.

34

"Your ruse is over. I know you killed the king," Kaine said. His arms poured with blood, but he was angry enough to stay awake. Nothing could stop him when he felt this calibre of blinding rage. He slowly lifted himself onto his feet, boots squelching against the blood that pooled beneath him.

He stared Queen Calliea down. The game would end here. She was the culprit. She was the one ordering the death of Faery children. She was the evil force, letting Faery rot in its blight.

"You're right. I killed him. And I enjoyed it too." She smiled sweetly. "You've always been clever, Kaine. It's such a shame..." The queen tsked, examining her nails.

"What? That I would be the one to end you? Your deadliest weapon, turning to kill its master. It's rather poetic, isn't it?" Kaine laughed. His anger seemed to pull at his mana. Slowly, ever so slowly, the wounds around the iron arrows started to heal. Knitting together. Bit by bit. He had to pull them out before they closed completely. But he couldn't make any sudden movements. There were archers stationed around the red throne room, arrows nocked, pointing directly at him, ready to aim true.

"What's poetic is that after twenty years, the missing piece of the prophecy I've upended this entire realm for, stumbled in by accident." The queen laughed, lifting herself from her red velvet throne. She stood tall. "Elowan, ever the obedient lass, brought her right to me. I didn't even have to lift a finger," she mused, a triumphant smile painting itself across her face.

"Leave her out of it," Kaine bit out.

Sophie wasn't a part of this. She couldn't be.

Queen Calliea sauntered slowly over to Kaine, her red gown brushing against the throne room floor. "What, you don't recognise her? Your soulmate? Have all the years of training under my banner robbed you of all your memory?" The queen smirked. Kaine's eyes widened at the word. Soulmate. Sophie was his soul-bonded. Fated. Could it be true? Or was it a pin in the haystack of lies the queen had created? If it were true, it explained the natural pull he felt towards her.

The queen circled his kneeled form, picking at her talons as she sauntered. "Or perhaps it was the death of your mother. Such a traumatic thing to see as a child, wouldn't you agree?" The queen laughed. The cruel words that would normally send him into a rage almost didn't register. Sophie was his fated. It meant that, finally, he belonged to someone and, in turn, someone belonged to him. Kaine's heartbeat quickened at the realisation. His fated was outside somewhere. Unsafe. She'd just been dragged out to the dungeons. He had to get to her, but he couldn't move. He couldn't let his panic get the better of him either. He would get to her. He'd destroy the entire realm to get there.

Kaine shook his head to clear his thoughts. "What does that have to do with anything? The king is dead and by your hands. I've sent a message to all the courts stating as much. The people will revolt." Kaine said. Checkmate.

The queen paused. In a flash she stood before Kaine, an inch away from his face. A hand twisted one of the arrows impaled in Kaine's arm. He gritted his teeth. He wouldn't scream. No matter how much it hurt, he wouldn't let the queen win. Innocent lives had been lost and Faery continued to die. And for what? He would fight her. To the death. For Faery.

"The people will not revolt. They *need* me. They need my power. Once I solidify our alliance with the Shadow Realm, they'll come to realise that I am their last resort. After all, there is no heir left to claim the throne, at least there won't be when I am done with you." She let go of the iron arrow that she white-knuckled in her fist. His body jerked at the movement. Fresh blood ran down his arm.

Kaine laughed darkly. "You are mistaken. I am not the heir." For he would know it if he were. He'd feel it. He'd remember it.

The queen seethed at his tone. With fae speed she gripped his neck, squeezing, restricting his airflow.

"You are the spitting image of that bastard Gydeon." She spat on the ground at the mention of her former husband, the former king. She squeezed her hand tighter. "And I should have let you rot twenty years ago with that bar wench he loved so much. Oh, how I loved to hear her helpless screams." The queen lifted him off his feet, her mana now dangling him in an invisible chokehold. He clawed at it, fighting it.

The death of the king. The death of his mother. Queen Calliea had a part in it all. The truth hit Kaine right in his stomach. His pit of mana filled with a new blinding rage, much darker than he'd ever felt before. He'd have her damned head for what she did to his mother. And supposedly, his father.

The grip around his neck seemed to loosen, distracted.

"...but I needed time to draw out that filthy mutt. I knew that one day, the Fates would bring her to me. To you. I just had to be patient enough. I felt the moment she entered this world, you know. It sent a shock wave through the entirety of Faery..."

Kaine remembered that moment. That fateful night when Sophie landed on top of him. Faery groaned and glittered. An unknown power surged through the entire land. The queen wanted to snuff it out.

"And when I spied you two together, I knew. She was your fated." The queen looked at Kaine right in his eyes and said, "Together with their fated, the blood reign will end, the Fates said. But I will defy the Fates, until my last dying breath. My reign will never end." The queen let go of Kaine's neck. He fell to the ground with a deafening thud. The arrows lodged in his arms rebounded off the floor, bending in all sorts of angles and ripped the wounds anew.

She turned swiftly on her heels. "I've changed my mind," the queen huffed, nose in the air, returning to the dais. "I want to savour this moment. I want to watch the Fates squirm as I rewrite destiny. I want you, the promised warrior," she spat, "to watch your fated die. Just like how you watched your mother beg for her life. Now wouldn't that be entertaining?" She laughed maniacally, perching herself on her throne again as if it were a normal day at court. "Guards," she ordered.

Two more iron arrows sliced through the air, lodging themselves into Kaine's thighs. He went down. His mana sputtered out completely. He screamed, damning the queen. Damning the world that came crashing down around him. His father was the late King Gydeon. His mother's death was orchestrated by Queen Calliea. Sophie was his fated. And he was the rightful heir to Faery. He'd been so close to the throne this whole time and he hadn't a single clue as to what was rightfully his. He had the answer to Faery's blight all along. It was him. All he had to do was take it.

Queen Calliea's smile was all venom. "Keep your friends close and your enemies closer."

After his mother's death, the queen had offered him refuge. A place with the Elite. A place to belong, but it was all part of a bigger game.

His vision danced in and out. The iron arrows drew every ounce of energy out of him, numbing him entirely.

"Take him to the dungeons," the queen ordered with a bored swish of her hand.

Kaine couldn't see who was left in the throne room.

His vision swam. His world muddied. From the very oldest of memories the prophecy Faery folk often muttered, fluttered through his mind...

The return of the strongest warrior that Faery will ever come to know, will bring the full might of Faery, but only with the love they sow.
Together with their fated, the blood reign will end. A life of peace and prosperity, more than one can comprehend.

Kaine wasn't worthy of saving Faery. He'd been fighting for the wrong team this whole time. He'd been focusing on training and following the queen's orders, thinking she had the power to free Faery when he should've spent more time uncovering the truth. *His* truth. He was the prophesised warrior and Sophie was his fated. He would be the end of Faery's blight. If only he survived what was going to happen next.

Rough hands heaved him off the ground and darkness consumed him completely.

35

S ophie jerked awake.

The sound of an iron cell door clanged through her throbbing head, followed by the sound of a body being dragged.

How the fuck am I going to get out of this mess?

She smelled him before she saw him, his sweet and spicy scent coated in blood. Lots of it. She sat up quickly, instantly regretting the motion. The four guards tossed Kaine's giant form into the cell beside hers, to her right. Their purple uniforms were smeared with his blood.

Kaine was barely lucid. He groaned in pain with four arrows embedded in him in a sickening show of angles, an iron arrow in each leg and each arm. Bile rose in her throat.

The guards surrounded him, two holding one leg each. The other holding down both of Kaine's hands. The fourth snickered. "This is for slaughtering our friends at sea." The tree-fae bent low, systematically snapping the arrows, at the front and at the back. Over and over, for each arrow in each limb, so that the remnants of the arrow would remain inside him. It would ensure he stayed powerless against them, Sophie realised.

Kaine groaned with every movement. He barely had any strength to fight the torture.

The noises that left his throat sent her into another dimension of rage.

This isn't happening. Not on my watch.

"You fucking cowards, beating a male while he's already down! Do you have any integrity?!" She stood, shouting and shaking the iron bars with all her might. They laughed at the ruckus she made. A growl left her throat as she bared her teeth.

They'll fucking pay for this.

Content with their handiwork, the guards dusted off their hands and slammed the cell door behind them.

"Traitor." The guards spat at him before assuming their posts down the hall. Two stationed themselves closer to the pit while the other two assumed positions at the entrance of the dungeons.

The moment they were far enough, Sophie scrambled for Kaine. He lay on his back, eyes hooded, barely blinking, confused and completely depleted of energy. She couldn't let him die. There was so much more she wanted to uncover and discover with him. There was more to them than met the eye. They'd shared memories together. They'd known each other before all of this, but why didn't either of them remember?

"Kaine. Stay awake. I'm here. I've got you." Sophie was trying her hardest not to panic as he grew paler and paler. His skin slowly knitted over the shards of iron still buried inside him.

Think Sophie, think. What would a badass fae queen do?

She needed him to heal. She needed him to get his power and energy back. The thought struck her. Her blood. Her blood would be able to heal him. In some of her books, fae would feed on human blood not only for pleasure, but to heal themselves. That was it!

"Kaine. Listen to me, I need you to come to me." She was blubbering at this point. She looked around hoping the guards didn't hear her. "Please. I need you to come here." She knelt by the bars. She could just fit an arm through but was too far to reach his hand that lay outstretched on the floor. Almost popping her arm out its socket, she pushed harder, enough to graze his fingers.

He stirred at the contact, eyes fluttering open to meet Sophie's. His turquoise eyes seemed dull. She whimpered. Her throat ached at the sight of him hurt. "Come on, you beautiful fae bastard, don't fucking die on me." She sniffled, wiping her cheek with her free sleeve. "I've got so many questions to ask you." She laughed, remembering the time she made a fool of herself asking him her incessant human questions. *Sir Kaine*, she'd said. *Idiot.*

Kaine coughed. Gathering the tiny morsel of energy he had left, he rolled onto his side. The movement made blood ooze from each limb. He panted at the feeling, moving closer to Sophie despite the pain.

She grabbed a firm hold of his rough hand and stared into his eyes, silently apologising for what she was about to do.

You can tell me off later.

With both hands, she grabbed onto his wrist and hooked her feet into the bottom of the cell bars. In one swift motion, she hauled his body closer to her, enough so she could reach her wrist to his mouth. He groaned at the motion, a smeared pool of blood lay in his wake.

She scrambled to his face. She was crying. She couldn't stop.

His head lulled against the iron bars. His eyes closed.

Lifting her sleeve, she pushed her wrist against his lips. He wasn't taking to it.

She ran her other hand through his hair, coaxing him to drink. "You're okay. Drink. You're going to be okay," she repeated, running her hand through his hair again.

A deep rumble sounded from his chest.

Kaine's hand flew to the wrist before his mouth. The sudden movement almost made her jump. Still, she held her wrist firm.

He looked up to her with those turquoise eyes. For permission, she realised.

"Drink." She smiled. Encouraging him.

His fae fangs peeked through behind his sinful lips. He kissed her wrist softly, sweetly. With the gentleness that no immortal should ever have, he clamped down on her wrist. His lips fit right around her.

The sensation was sharp but was instantly replaced with warmth and the feel of her blood being dragged out.

Pull. Pull.

Heat pooled in her core.

He didn't break eye contact. Not even for a second.

He pulled and pulled.

She moaned softly.

Colour returned to his cheeks. His turquoise eyes were bright again. And his wounds were almost healed over, the iron still trapped inside his flesh. They'd have to deal with that later.

With the same gentleness, he released her wrist, kissing the two small bite marks until they clotted.

Sophie watched him the entire time. And he watched her back.

They said nothing as he sat up from where he lay, no longer bleeding. Battered, but no longer bleeding.

Holding her hand gently, he pulled her closer to him. His seated form still dwarfed her. He lifted her hand, kissing the back of it. "Thank you," he rasped.

Sophie didn't know what overcame her, maybe it was watching him almost die, maybe it was the rank cell she was wallowing in, but she crashed her lips into his through the iron bars.

The kiss had caught him off guard, he paused for only a moment and he kissed her right back. The kiss was a claiming kiss. They breathed each other in entirely.

In this realm, nothing could compare to Kaine. Sophie knew that much.

They pulled away, hesitantly, remembering where they were.

"Are you hurt?" His gaze searched her body.

She shook her head, still reeling from the kiss that left her speechless and the roundhouse kick to the temple she'd been dealt earlier.

"Did you learn about feeding from one of those books you read?" he whispered, smiling despite the setting they were in.

She laughed and nodded. It was a stab in the dark but one that paid off. Tears threatened to run down her face again. It was so good to see him alive. Talking. Moving. She moved to touch the lines of his face again.

As she reached through, the cell bars clanged. Something like a stick had hit it. Kaine and Sophie whipped their heads to find the source. It was one of the royal guards, a plain fae, neither buff or skinny, but in the middle, standing tall and proud with a short spear in his hand.

"You." He pointed at Sophie. "Get up."

She hesitated, looking at Kaine, her eyes wide, not wanting to leave his side.

Kaine only nodded as if telling her to play along.

Just play along, you'll be okay, he seemed to say.

Sophie nodded.

As she stood, she found the iron bars in front of her had warped. No, melted out of shape from her hands. Two Sophie-sized imprints scorched the iron bars. Impossible. Somehow in that blind rage she felt, she'd melted it. It didn't make sense.

Sophie stilled herself, trying her best to not show the surprise and confusion she most definitely felt inside.

"Face me," the guard commanded.

She obeyed, turning swiftly on her heels.

"Hands out."

She stuck her hands out quickly.

Before she knew it, cold thick shackles found themselves closed around her wrists.

Panic.

Fuck. I can't believe this happening right now. Are they killing me now or later? Sophie's eyes grew wide, her feet wanting to plant themselves in the ground with defiance. The guard moved to her back, pushing her forward with unnecessary force. She looked back at him, snarling.

She wasn't going down without a fight.

36

What in the actual fuck is this?

The guard had shoved a steel bucket full of what Sophie was hoping were animal innards and not human innards. The bucket wreaked; a few days old she assumed.

With another insolent nudge, the fae guard pushed her forward.

To the pit.

The thought sobered her. The clanking of giant chains never seemed louder. The steps that echoed with the chains brought chills down her spine.

Please don't let it be something scary.

As they proceeded closer to the end of the hall where the pit was located, the guard picked up a longer spear from the wall.

Moonlight washed the dark pit in a light luminescence, painting a peaceful serene scene despite the nightmarish creature that lived down there.

When they reached about two metres from the edge of the pit, the guard stopped in his tracks.

Sophie stopped too, but as she did, a sharp prod lanced through her shoulder. The spear.

"Keep moving, filth," the guard sneered, poking her on the shoulder again. The force of it jerked her forward. Wetness started to coat her upper back. "Throw the contents of the bucket in the pit and try not to get eaten while you're at it. The queen doesn't want you dead... just yet." He laughed.

Sophie baulked, turning white at the giant steps that echoed below. The ground reverberated with each impact.

She was only half a metre from the edge when a piercing roar sounded through the entire dungeon. Sophie hit the ground at the sound, knees cracking, trying to shield her ears with her shoulders since her hands were bound and heaving a bucket full of carrion.

Another sharp push pierced into her other shoulder. It told her to keep moving.

She stood, moving slowly, bucket in hand and dared to peer over the edge.

At first it was darkness but then...

Bright yellow reptilian eyes followed her movements beneath the shadows. Curious.

Sophie gulped. The eyes were huge.

The hypnotic sound of its heavy breathing sounded in her ears. With predatorily slow movements, it poked its head from out of the shadows.

What Sophie witnessed before her was otherworldly. Nervousness racked her entire body, and her hands and knees went numb.

From the shadows, bright yellow eyes between purply-pink scales that glittered across a massive dragon-like face, watched Sophie. The creature blinked slowly. Not with violence but something like recognition. The creature moved its nostrils closer to her, sniffing. The moonlight moved across its entrancing face as it moved closer and closer to Sophie. It's two giant horns curled back into a fierce looking crown and its pink-purple scales danced in the moonlight.

Whether it was instinct or lack of self-preservation, Sophie stuck one of her chained hands out towards the creature, intending to place her palm on its nose – a greeting.

You're a dragon. Sophie realised what the majestic creature before her was.

Mother, a deep female voice echoed in Sophie's head.

"HOLY SHIT!" Sophie jumped out of her skin at the voice, flinging the contents of the bucket in the air. Half of it landed on her shoulders and the other half dropped unceremoniously into the dark pit that seemed to have no bottom.

"You incompetent human! Pick up the innards and throw it in the pit!" the guard shouted from where he stood, the spear still stretched out between himself and Sophie.

Without hesitation, Sophie picked up what was left of the intestines and livers, tossing them into the pit before scrambling back a good measure from the edge.

The creature did not seem to pay its food any mind. Its chains rattled, as if they were being lifted slightly from the ground. The beat of giant wings echoed through the chamber. But the chains stopped the dragon from flying up any farther with a huge groan. It was trapped.

Despite the chains, the bright yellow eyes peeked just above the edge of the pit. Dust and dirt particles scattered in the moonlight from the movement of wings that Sophie could not see.

It watched her.

And Sophie watched it back, wondering if the voice came from the creature or if she'd completely lost her marbles.

It cocked its head. *You came back.* That same deep female voice echoed through Sophie's head.

Gasping, Sophie scrambled back to where the guard stood, her chain clanging against her legs.

"Draekins. Nasty creatures," the guard muttered before shoving Sophie down the hall, back to her cell.

Draekin. That's what that creature was.

She'd never heard of them before.

This draekin looked like a Chinese dragon, though much thicker and deadly looking.

Sophie didn't look back to the pit. Though she couldn't help but feel those giant reptile eyes boring into her back.

Sophie's brows furrowed at the words the draekin had whispered. The voice that rang clear in her head. It recognised her. Called her mother and acknowledged that she had come back. Her past never seemed so elusive. She had memories of Kaine. Memories of running around the hills of Soxis with him. They were all memories, Zala had said. Snippets of a past she couldn't quite reach. A part of Sophie still didn't believe it was true. Even the creatures of Faery seemed to recognise her, but the blatant fact that Sophie could not reconcile were her parents. They were utterly and plainly human. And so was she. She tried to dig deeper into her mind again, to uncover her past, but in an instant, that familiar haze washed through her mind. Like a veil, it stopped her from seeing whatever answers she'd find.

37

"Are you okay?" Kaine whispered from his cell.

No. I've just had a giant lizard creature thing whisper in my damned head!

Upon her return, she'd found him sitting with his back against the bars they shared between their cells, eyes closed, meditating.

She thought about the voice that echoed through her head. No, *talked* to her. She'd heard of fae communicating with each other through their minds, but she didn't realise it sounded like someone talking to you. They'd certainly get used to it right? She thought the sound would be muted, as if they were speaking through a phone but no, it was as clear as day. It was as if the creature spoke it aloud. The only thing proving that it was only in her head was that the creature's mouth hadn't moved, and no one else reacted to it speaking.

"It was a draekin," Sophie whispered. Her face drained of colour, not so much about the creature but the fact that it had spoken to her. It called her "mother"!

If Kaine was surprised, he didn't show it.

"I heard. It seems the queen will be feeding us to her favoured pet." Kaine's face was grim from where he sat. "We need to get out of here before she even attempts it."

"Can you use your mana?"

"I tried. I can't use my powers, so we'll have to find our way out the old-fashioned way." As he spoke, he stood up and surveyed the cell. The rattling of the cell bars as Kaine shook them echoed down the hall.

"Quiet down there!" one of the guards shouted in warning.

He was searching for a way out, Sophie realised. Quietly, she hopped to her feet, keen to help him out on the search. The dirt beneath her kicked up with the motion, but then she remembered… the bars.

"I think I can use my mana," she whispered when Kaine was close enough. It was the only logical explanation for what she did to the cell bars. Maybe it was Elowan's and Camrine's favours at play.

Kaine tilted his head. As strong as he was, the iron lodged in his flesh and the mana-muting iron rods placed around the room snuffed out his power entirely.

Instead of telling him how, should unwanted fae ears be listening, she showed him what she meant. Pointing to where the bars that were bent out of shape, moulded to the shape of her hands.

Kaine's eyes widened.

How on earth did you do that? he seemed to say.

Sophie shrugged her shoulders. She wasn't sure. She was just so angry, and it wasn't like she consciously bent the bars.

It could be their only ticket out of here.

Kaine seemed to reach the same conclusion. He pulled her down to the ground, until they were both sitting cross-legged, facing each other through the bars of their cell. He looked around quickly to check if the coast was clear.

Staying as quiet as possible, he motioned to his diaphragm, hovering his palm just above it.

He inclined his head, signalling her to do the same.

Sophie scrunched her features, wondering what he was trying to do.

Trust me, his eyes seemed to say.

Using his hands, he signalled. *Three deep breaths. Think. Bars. Three deep breaths. Think. Bars.*

Sophie didn't quite understand what he meant by "bars", but she obeyed his silent commands. Letting her hands rest on her knees, she let her eyes close and repeated…

Three deep breaths.

Focus. Think.

The bars.

She focused on the raw emotions she felt when she saw Kaine on the ground. His pain. Her pain as a result. She didn't want him to die. The emotion hit her in the gut. It made her senseless. It made her numb.

Three deep breaths. Focus. Bars.

Three deep breaths. Focus. Emotion.

She imagined that her mana was the fire that Elowan had lent her, the earth that Camrine gifted her, like a melting pot of colourful energy, rising through her chest and out through her arms, manifesting in her palms.

She felt it then, the instant warmth of her hands. The dirt around her grazed her skin as it moved passed her, lifting from the ground. And slowly, not breaking the focus on the raw emotion, the focus on the shape she wanted her mana to form... she opened her eyes.

All around her, and in parts of Kaine's cell, small rocks and dirt particles were suspended in the air. In her palms were two small flames, threatening to burn bigger, brighter.

Sophie was in awe.

It felt like she'd unlocked something in her mind, in her chest. For some reason, it didn't surprise her at all that she could do this. It felt familiar. It felt like she'd always had this ability, but she just hadn't flexed it in a while.

Sophie smirked at her show of power.

Despite the irons cells they squatted in and the mana-muters surrounding the dungeons, she could use her fucking mana. It wasn't a giant wall of fire or a gravity-defying boulder, but it was something. And something was their best bet out of here.

Kaine's eyes shone with a mixture of awe, pride and something like envy. Sophie couldn't place it. He motioned her to let go of the suspended earth, and to quiet her flame, just in case one of the guards walked by and saw.

Sophie didn't quite have a grasp on controlling her mana, so she imagined cutting her mana off.

Big mistake.

Sophie gulped and Kaine's eyes widened as the particles of dirt and debris came rushing down creating a whooshing noise that echoed across the dungeons while her flames licked in different directions trying to put itself out, casting shadows in their cells.

Shit.

One of the guards rushed down the hall to investigate the noise. With hands on the short spear that hung from his belt, he eyed them both but Sophie and Kaine made a show of not knowing what noise he was referring to. Sophie lay against the other side of her cell picking at her fingernails, while Kaine sat up, away from their communal bars, eyeing off the guard, promising death with his eyes alone.

The guard seemed wary of the two. Eyeing Kaine up and down, the guard surveyed the dried blood that covered Kaine's clothes and the wounds that had magically healed. He cleared his throat. "You two are on thin ice. No more noises." He huffed, eyeing Kaine's wounds one more time. For some reason, he chose to ignore what he saw and proceeded to his post, near the entrance of the dungeons.

Letting out a breath, Sophie moved closer to Kaine's cell.

They couldn't scheme without the guards knowing. The dungeon echoed as if they were in a giant seashell, and they couldn't risk anyone overhearing their plans of escape.

Sign and body language was all they could depend on.

Kaine beckoned her close. *Use. Mana. Break. Cell.*

If Sophie didn't value her life and Kaine's, she would've laughed out loud. Perhaps she would've added in a knee slap for good measure.

Really? That is the most basic plan I've ever heard in my life. Her eyes almost watered trying not to laugh. Immortal fae warrior, captain of the Elite and THAT'S his big plan?

Do you have a better plan? Kaine seemed to say. She definitely didn't.

They had mana on their side. The guards didn't and that was a good start. Sure, they could break out of this cell but what would happen next? On one end of the dungeon, they had an endless pit currently occupied by a giant dragon lizard creature. On the other end, there could be a ridiculous number of guards stationed outside, waiting to slice and dice them should they even attempt to escape. Kaine's power was as good as gone. Sophie's mana was there but still infantile. Maybe if they had weapons... Sophie moved to feel for the throwing knife the Scyllen leader had gifted her. *Fuck.* She let out a frustrated breath. It wasn't there. The guards must have taken it when she was out cold.

They needed a solid plan before breaking out of the dungeon.

Fine. Which way? Sophie signalled, pointing to the end where the pit lay and the dungeon entrance.

He pointed to the dungeon entrance, pointed at himself and threw a jab in the air. *I can take them down,* he seemed to say.

Sophie didn't doubt it and she'd be able to hold her own, but what if that too was a trap? What if the queen had already planned for them to try to escape that way?

Sophie didn't know why, maybe it was because the draekin recognised her, but her gut, no, her *mana* pointed her towards the pit. Her mana was a force she couldn't argue with. Like a stubborn little girl, it dug its feet into the ground and said *TO THE PIT.*

Sophie shook her head and pointed down the other end of the hall, towards the draekin.

Are you mad?! Kaine's eyes widened. It looked like he wanted to shake her for such an idiotic suggestion, and he was just about to, when the sound of keys jangling echoed down the hall, growing louder and louder.

"There you go, gents," the chirpy old voice said. "Supper for two." The guards muttered their thanks. The small plump figure moved swiftly down the hall, draped in a cloak, holding two more trays for the guards down the other end of the hall.

Kaine's eyes widened in recognition and a small smile appeared across his face.

The smell of warm bread stifled Sophie. She hadn't realised how terribly hungry she was. Between leaving the boat with Camrine and Ellie, she couldn't recall the last time she had a substantial meal. The thought of Cam, Ellie and Zala punched her in the gut too. Were they safe? Were they okay?

The guards stationed closer to the pit muttered their thanks the moment the female figure reached them. While the guards were distracted with their meals, the cloaked figure rushed down the hall but faltered in front of Kaine's cell, pretending to drop her set of heavy keys.

Using the jarring sound to mask the extra movements, she pushed a small wad of cloth into Kaine's cell, quickly and quietly. Picking up the keys she'd just dropped, she left the dungeon as fast as she came, not daring to look back at Kaine or Sophie as she did.

Kaine snatched the package and moved towards the back of the cell where it was slightly darker, silently beckoning Sophie to come with.

He unravelled the black cloth, inside were two freshly baked bread rolls. He handed one to Sophie who inhaled the roll without even chewing.

Beneath the rolls, was a tiny piece of parchment. Kaine quietly unfurled it and leaned closer to Sophie so she could read it with him.

The queen has spelled the entrance with your blood and the young woman's. Step outside and you both will die immediately. I am working to get the spells taken down. I do not know how long this will take but you are smart, Captain Aaryn. There are old passages down in the pit. Find the flaming heart and you'll find the way out. – Felipina.

Incredible. Sophie had no idea who Felipina was, but she was now Sophie's favourite person. Felipina had somehow found out what happened and had planned to aid them in their escape. If Sophie could, she would go and hug the female herself.

Kaine took the second roll of bread and scoffed it within the second. Sophie doubted it was enough to sustain him, but it was better than nothing.

Sophie scanned the tiny scroll again quickly as Kaine ate. *There are old passages down in the pit. Find the flaming heart and you'll find the way out.* Sophie was right after all. She knew it! Well, her mana knew it. Sophie pointed out the words for Kaine to see. *I told you so.*

Something like pride shone in his eyes. He watched her as if she were the most precious being he'd ever laid eyes on. Shaking his head at her, he held her hand, closing it into a fist around the small parchment.

Three deep breaths. Focus. Burn. He motioned like he did earlier.

Sophie nodded, wary of the fact that she hadn't quite mastered her mana, but she trusted herself. She wasn't scared. It was a part of her, an extension of her.

Closing her eyes, she took in three deep breaths and focused on the heightened state of raw emotion that awakened her mana. Pulling up from the mana in her gut, she willed it through her arm and down to the palm that enclosed the telling parchment. The smell of burning paper wafted up to her nostrils, though she kept her eyes closed. Instead of cutting off her mana like she did last time, she willed it to quiet, like turning down the volume dial. She imagined the mana, the flame she manifested, disappearing back into her arm and back into the pool of power. Her palm turned cold in the absence of flame. It worked. She looked up at Kaine, proud of herself that she'd managed to master the flame as opposed to letting it dance about uncontrollably. She'd done it.

Kaine was proud of her. She could tell. He smiled sweetly and nodded.

Sophie smiled too. It was all thanks to her precious books.

Turns out the pen is mightier than the sword, in more ways than one, she thought to herself.

Sophie peered up at the small slit of window they both shared. She could only see a sliver of the Faery moon, high up in the sky. Judging by its position, they'd need to rest at some point. Despite how hungry and weak Sophie felt, she knew it would be sleep and lack of energy that would kill them first.

You rest first. Kaine motioned to the small scrap of blanket that each cell had.

Picking up the blanket, Sophie positioned it towards the back of the cell, next to the set of bars they shared. She needed comfort tonight. She was in the damn Faery realm, in Castle Terrin's dungeon. The queen wanted her dead and she didn't know why. Kaine would have some of the answers, but they needed to get out of here first before anything.

Kaine moved to retrieve his blanket from where it lay. He set it beside Sophie's, sitting down on top of it, back up against the wall so he could take the first watch. They needed to gather intel at all hours – how many guards would be present throughout the night, how many changeovers occurred – the whole lot, so they could time their escape, whether that be through the dungeon entrance or the pit, past the draekin.

Sophie's thin breeches and blouse did nothing to keep her human body temperature regulated. She bunched up close to the bars, stealing any heat she could from Kaine. Lying in a fetal position, she rested her hand on Kaine's thigh while he idly brushed his hand through her hair, keeping watch. He was soothing her. Grounding her. Keeping her alive in this damned hellhole, and she couldn't ask for anything else.

She didn't want anyone else.

"She's so cute!" young Sophie shrilled. She sat in a barn, the young boy she loved so dearly, her best friend, sat right beside her. They were joined at the hip. The hay that they sat on stuck to their legs and hands, and the smell of animals wafted around them.

Before her and her best friend, finding its feet on the table, was a new draekin hatchling. It was just bigger than her little hand. The baby draekin had pink-and-purple scales, and two swirling horns that would certainly grow large and beautiful. Its bright yellow eyes were happy to see sunshine.

Sophie and her best friend oohed and aahed at the newborn draekin. They were rare creatures, only a handful would be born in a century. They were majestic, fierce protectors of the realm and were often paired with members of the royal family. This was a gift from the king himself, she remembered the silver-haired male saying.

"What are you going to name her?" The older silver-haired male asked, face smiling, brimming with excitement. He was tall, strong. A soldier.

The baby draekin ran about the top of the table, playing with the remains of its shell, bouncing with each happy step.

"You should name her something like Fire!" the boy howled in excitement.

"I am NOT naming her Fire, that's not even a name!" Sophie laughed, nudging the boy with her elbow.

"Come on, boy," the older male said, scruffing the boy's hair. "You've already named yours. Let Sophie name hers." The male laughed. Loose strands of silver hair fanned against his face.

The boy beside her crossed his arms. He'd named his black-and-blue draekin Orion and it was clear he wanted to name this draekin too.

"I'll name her... Astraea." Sophie clasped her hands together, testing out the name so the draekin could hear. The little draekin breathed a steady stream of fire, burning up the eggshells it once called home and danced happily. Its little claws tapped blissfully on the table. Sophie laughed with a newfound brightness.

"Well chosen, my dear." The silver-haired male smiled down at Sophie, doing her little happy dance.

She loved the name. It meant "starry night". The way the little draekin's scales shined and glittered reminded her of Faery's beautiful night sky.

"Let's get her flying, shall we?" the male asked the two children. They howled, jumping for joy. Sophie picked up her baby draekin and ran out of the barn, holding the hatchling up in the air so the wind caught beneath its wings. The black-haired boy trailed just behind her.

The baby draekin shrilled with happiness.

38

Astraea. The beautiful draekin's name was Astraea. It was her draekin. The one from her memories, not her dreams. That's why it had called her mother. Which meant, maybe the draekin wouldn't kill them after all?

Sophie's eyes fluttered open.

The ground of the cell bit into her back but the strong hands running through her hair comforted her. Daylight spilled through the small slits of their cells.

He'd let her sleep through the entire night. She sat up quickly at the realisation. He didn't have to. If anything, he was the one that needed more sleep so he could recover.

He watched her the entire time. The sunlight hit his turquoise eyes, making them shimmer. He was painfully beautiful, she thought. His gaze seared into her, and a blush rose from her cheeks.

"You didn't wake me," she whispered.

"You need it more than I do. Fae can go for longer without rest," he explained quietly. She forgot that one tidbit. Fae could go longer without food and without rest – after all, they were magical creatures. "You didn't miss out on much. Just one changeover. Same number of guards."

Footsteps started down the hallway.

"Wake up, scum, the queen is arriving." One of the guards taunted them, running the tip of his short spear across the bars.

Sophie baulked at the news. No. The queen was arriving now? Did this spell the end for them? She whipped her head towards Kaine, hoping he had something to say about their predicament.

His only answer was a death-promising growl at the guard.

Despite the near-silent threat, the guard didn't falter. Funny how confident these guards got when all that was between them and one of the strongest fae males known were a few inches of iron bars.

Sophie and Kaine hadn't even had the chance to plan out their escape. It seemed the queen was ready to get this over and done with, ending their lives, and therefore sealing in her endless reign.

Sophie wouldn't let it happen and she knew Kaine wouldn't let it happen either, but how on earth were they going to get out of here? For what felt like the umpteenth time in her life, Sophie was completely stumped. Each exit lay a trap. Time wasn't on their side. In fact, nothing was turning in their favour.

The guard continued taunting them, running his short spear across the bars, smiling at them conspiratorially like they were caged animals.

Like the predator he was, Kaine didn't let his eyes off the guard.

"Clear the observation deck! The queen is heading down now!" another guard shouted down the hall.

The guard in front of them heeded the command. Leaving them alone, he padded towards the pit, clearing the way for the nefarious Queen Calliea.

The moment he left their sights, Sophie scrambled toward Kaine who looked troubled. No doubt he was racking every corner of his brain to find a solution. It didn't look like he was doing too well.

It was such a risk. A HUGE risk, but Sophie's mana told her it was the right decision. It was trying to tell her it was the right decision since she'd landed in the damn dungeon. They needed to head down the pit. They needed to find the flaming heart and get the fuck out of Dodge.

Sophie pointed towards the pit. "That is where we need to go," she said firmly.

"The draekin will devour us!" he hushed.

"It will not. That is our way out." Sophie's tone was final. It felt weird ordering an immortal fae warrior around, but the fact was that his power was gone and he didn't have any solutions. If the books she'd read taught her anything, it was to follow her gut. Fuck what anyone else said. Her mana was telling her that the pit was their salvation and her memories that played in her dreams were confirmation. All signs nudged them towards the pit. It had to be the right decision. They were going to jump down that pit and whether they got devoured or if the draekin would aid them would be a risk they'd have to take. They had no other choice.

Hesitation danced in his eyes, but he nodded. He needed to trust her. All signs were pointing in that direction, from Felipina's note to Sophie's persistence.

"Make way for Her Majesty!" a guard announced from the entrance of the dungeon.

Fuck. Already? Can't we ever catch a break?

A team of guards marched their way down the dungeon hall in two neat files. Left. Right. Left. Right. Left. Right. Left.

With them they carried their short spears on their belts and a larger spear in their hands. Their armour clanked with their movements, the sound echoing and crashing back into itself throughout the dungeon. The sound was drowning, like drums that marked the beginnings of a war.

In the distance, Sophie could hear a wave of about thirty or forty guards taking their knees as the queen moved by them. They were bowing. Just how many were making their way down here? And for what purpose?

The sight of her was sickening. The queen was impossibly white and the red she wore was menacing - like fresh blood had spilled on white paper. Her blood-red hair was slicked back off her face and she sat ramrod straight on a portable throne.

This bitch had a fucking portable throne? She couldn't be serious. Sophie rolled her eyes. Around her, four guards carried Queen Calliea on her throne. As she passed their cells, she didn't pay them any mind. If anything, she stuck her nose in the air just a little bit higher.

Sophie scoffed. Oh how she would enjoy making the queen pay. She could tell Kaine would too, given how he lunged at the queen as she passed their cells.

The crowd was obnoxious. Roughly eighty guards teemed through the dungeons, making their way towards the observation deck, as one of the guards had called it earlier. Just before the lip of the pit.

As they passed through the hall and the cells, they threw insults at Kaine and Sophie. Some even spat on them. Sophie wasn't afraid to throw colourful insults their way either.

The bustle of the crowd died down.

Sophie and Kaine's cells were too far down the hall to see what was happening, though they knew the crowd congregated around the lip of the pit. To watch them get eaten alive, Sophie realised. They were going to feed them both to the draekin! Unless... Sophie's plan went her way.

Sophie pulled Kaine closer to her through the bars, whispering in his ear the plan she just unhatched.

His eyes widened then softened. He nodded. He trusted her.

Two guards approached their cells, one opening Kaine's and the other opening Sophie's.

"You can trust me," Sophie whispered, planting a soft kiss on his cheek before squeezing his hand. A small goodbye. One last moment of reassurance. She didn't know whether she needed it more or if he did. They needed to get out of this place alive. Together.

Two guards rushed into their cells, clasping their wrists with iron shackles.

This was it. Make or break.

The guards forced them both into the hallway. Sophie turned, facing towards the pit, and Kaine followed, his tall figure just behind her. Their final walk.

On each side of the hallway, guards stood sneering, spitting, shouting at them. Traitor. Scum. Filth. They all repeated. What kind of lies had the queen fed them to have them act so fervently? The queen was the viper, feeding venom and lies into their bloodstreams and they all acted none the wiser. Poor souls, Sophie thought. The queen would be the end of them all. She'd be the end of Faery and they were unknowingly handing their only salvation to death. Kaine was the answer to Faery's freedom. He was the heir, and she played some sort of role in it all.

As they neared the end of the cell blocks, a pearlescent shine caught Sophie's eye.

Her knife.

The curved, purple pearlescent blade sung out to her. It hung above one of the guard stations on a hook, but a row of angry guards stood in Sophie's way. An idea struck her then.

It's time to get another Oscar, Sophie smirked.

The light in the dungeon grew brighter as they made their way towards the pit. The queen, from what Sophie could see, was perched a safe distance from the edge of it. Heavy chains echoed up from the pit, that familiar stomping reverberating through the ground.

The guards continued their onslaught, with much of the anger pointed towards Kaine behind her. The captain of the Elite who betrayed the throne.

A racoon-like fae guard spat right in Sophie's face as she passed the guard post. Perfect. His spittle ran down her cheek. Sophie paused, groaning at the disgusting feel. She stopped right in her tracks, turned to the guard who dared spit at her and puffed her chest.

"You'll fucking pay for that," Sophie said lowly, moving closer and closer to his face, promising death if he asked for it nicely.

The guard that escorted her attempted to pull her along but she twisted out of his arm, moving closer and closer to the fae that had spat on her.

"Hate to break it to you, sweet, you're the one in chains," the racoon guard snickered.

Moving with blinding speed she never knew she had, Sophie jumped up, swiped and wrapped the chain between her shackles around his furry neck. As she did, she swiped for the hook that was just behind him, letting the pearlescent knife slide down her sleeve.

With a violent tug she dragged him onto the floor, pulling him into a tight headlock. She squeezed and squeezed as the guard thrashed beneath her. He sputtered and clawed at her arms as they stole the breath out of him.

Several guards, stunned for a moment by her speed, sprang into action, intending to pry Sophie off the racoon guard. As they approached, she let go immediately before they could cause her any damage. As she stood swiftly, she spat in the racoon guard's face. He still lay on the floor clutching his neck and gasping for air.

"Consider yourself lucky." She smirked. She felt so badass. Is this how all the female protagonists felt when they downed a full-grown fae male? She could definitely get used to it.

Sophie quickly looked back at Kaine. His eyes shone with pride and a layer of worry for what was about to ensue.

The remaining guards pushed her forward and kept a tight grip on her arms as she and Kaine were presented before the queen.

The guards forced them down onto their knees.

Sophie looked over to Kaine. And he looked right back at her. Those turquoise eyes. She hoped this wasn't their end. She hoped her plan would work.

As if sensing her worry, Kaine nodded. *I trust you,* he seemed to say.

She nodded back. *And I trust you.*

The queen raised one of her hands, silencing the room entirely. "Now, let's get this over and done with. I don't want my lunch to get cold." She clicked her fingers; one of the guards pulled Sophie off the ground and shoved her towards the edge of the pit with a spear pointed to her back.

She dared look into the never-ending dark pit.

Astraea? Sophie projected her thoughts towards the darkness. A pregnant pause filled her ears.

Bright yellow eyes opened in response.

Mother, the low gravelly female voice hissed.

Sophie had to make this quick.

She made a show of being nervous, allowing her knees to wobble and her lips to tremble. An act. She wasn't afraid of the draekin. Not anymore. The draekin was hers.

There are passages below. Will you let us pass? Sophie blinked.

Us? The draekin questioned.

The chained male behind me.

Astraea cocked her head, moving out of the shadows to peer behind Sophie. Her purply-pink horns glittered in the daylight. Sophie didn't think she could ever get used to seeing such a giant mythical creature.

A slight hiss sounded from the draekin's lips.

Will you let us pass? Sophie repeated. She was desperate now.

Jump high. I will guide you both down. With that the draekin pulled back into the shadows, giving a loud roar. The sound almost burst Sophie's eardrums.

"It seems my pet is hungry," Queen Calliea laughed.

Sophie turned to face the queen, utterly annoyed by her obnoxiousness. "Hurry along then, love, it's almost Christmas." With the comment, several guards nudged their spears, pushing her a tad closer to the edge.

Another piercing roar sounded. Astraea wasn't too happy about that, Sophie thought.

The queen cocked her head at the confidence exuding from Sophie. Oh Sophie was definitely getting under the queen's skin. Checkmate.

The queen narrowed her eyes on Sophie. "If my mana could work here, I'd rip that blasted tongue out of your filthy mouth." She sneered.

Kaine, still kneeling on the ground, looked at her incredulously. He whipped his head back to Sophie, eyes wide. *Don't push your luck*, he seemed to say.

The queen stood from her throne. "For treason of the highest order, an attempt to assassinate myself, the rightful queen of Faery, I order you, Kaine Dormarth Aaryn, to death," the queen howled.

The crowd cheered.

It looked like the words themselves stung Kaine a little. He winced. Sophie knew why. That was his rightful throne. And Queen Calliea manipulated her entire force and perhaps all of Faery into thinking that she was the rightful queen.

"But not before you watch your soulmate die!" the queen shrieked from her throne. The crowd burst out in another cheer.

Sophie snapped her attention to Kaine, eyes wide at the word. Soulmate. Could that be the cause of her unravelling memories and attraction towards him? Could that be her role in all of this... his fated?

Kaine's eyes widened in response. He wanted to say something but couldn't form the words.

The entire dungeon was a spectacle. The gaggle of guards surrounding Sophie and Kaine, rhythmically hit their spears against the ground, some chanting, others whooping... sending the rightful heir of Faery to his death as well as his fated.

Between the fanfare, several guards moved to pull Kaine off his knees, bringing him to stand right in front of Sophie. First-row seats to watch her fall to her death. As they did, the guards latched a collar around his neck and two more iron cuffs around his wrists, all of them attached to a chain held by several guards. To hold him back, Sophie realised.

Fuck.

That wasn't in her plan at all. She was hoping she'd be able to grab him and jump into the pit.

What should I do? Come on, Sophie, think!

She needed to free him of his chains. She'd need to make sure the guards were far back enough that they couldn't reach her or Kaine before they jumped in. She needed a distraction.

An answer heated in her sleeve.

Astraea.

Mother?

How far can you reach onto the observation deck?

Not very far, mother.

I need you to clear a few rows of these guards. Can you do that?

I can try.

That was all Sophie could hope for. That her draekin would try.

In a show of two lovers being torn apart for the rest of their lives, Sophie pretended to sob with fear and heartache. She lunged for Kaine, screaming.

"I'll never let you go! You'll always be in my heart!" She sobbed, her cheeks slamming into his hard chest.

Kaine caught on. He lowered his head, resting it on top of hers as much as he could anyway, given the chains they were both in. "And you will always be in mine," he said into her ears, only for her to hear. Her heart tightened, unsure if that was part of the ruse or if he meant it.

Queen Calliea laughed, absolutely beside herself. "Star-crossed lovers. What absolute fools! Push her in!" she cawed from her throne. The crowd cheered. The queen had completely lost her mind. She was a maniac.

Astraea let out a warning roar, quieting some of the guards that stood closer to the edge of the pit. The sound of her chains lifting echoed through the hall.

Another piercing roar sounded and her giant draekin head lifted to peer from the pit. Several guards scampered back from the edge not wanting to get snapped up. Her bright yellow eyes watched them all with predatory stillness.

"Hold onto me," Sophie whispered into Kaine's ear as she peeled herself from his broad form. The guards restraining him pulled him back with a violent jerk. He fought the restraints, growling as he did.

Sophie turned to face the queen and fell to her knees, begging.

"Please let us go. I'll do anything. Please." Sophie clasped her hands together as tears spilled down her cheeks. She'd definitely be winning an academy award with this performance.

"Pathetic human," the queen scoffed.

Another roar pierced the room and then...

HISS. CRACK.

Screams from the guards sounded through the room, bouncing off the walls. Astraea's claws reached for the guards that stood closest to the lip of the pit. Fae guards plummeted, some scrambled and some fought against the draekin's grip.

Using the distraction to her advantage, Sophie crouched low and let the throwing knife she held against her body slide down her sleeve and straight into her palm. She hooked a finger into its handle.

It fit perfectly.

Sliding on her knees to Kaine's right side, she threw the knife with a deft flick of the wrist. The pearlescent knife spun towards the four guards restraining Kaine with unnerving precision. As it flew, it sliced open each guard's throat in a violent wave of sputtering blood. The impact made all four drop to their knees, hands flying to their throats, dropping Kaine's restraints entirely.

Like a boomerang, the knife sliced through the air and landed back in Sophie's hand with a *SLING.* In its wake, a fine glitter mist followed as if it were carried on a phantom wind.

Sophie's eyes widened. She wasn't expecting that to happen.

Screams sounded throughout the dungeon as the guards fell to the ground entirely lifeless.

Jumping up, Sophie pocketed her magical knife and pulled Kaine's giant form to the edge of the pit with her.

Grabbing Sophie around the waist, they jumped together, into the dark, dark, never-ending depths. Past the snapping jaws of the draekin.

Sophie held on tight and wrapped her arms around him. She buried her face into his neck where the cold iron collar still sat.

Down.

Down.

Down.

The screams and shouts of the guards above grew distant. The ruckus and chaos dialled down as they plummeted into the darkness. They held each other close. Loose chains whipped around them.

Sophie's stomach flipped uncontrollably, and bile caught in her throat as the feeling of weightlessness hit her right in the gut. She couldn't see Kaine. She only felt him as he held onto her for dear life.

The sound of giant, heavy chains rattling grew louder.

They were reaching the ground at an alarming rate.

Astraea! Sophie shouted telepathically.

With the command, a leathery-feeling vine or rope wrapped around the two, catching them mid fall. Not a rope or vine, Astraea's tail!

The draekin flipped the two onto her back, lowering herself slightly so they could slide down safely to the ground. Sophie held onto Kaine tightly, not ever wanting to let go.

With a harrumph, they both rolled onto dirt ground. Their descent would have been a hundred metres at the very least.

Coughing at the impact, Sophie pushed herself off the ground.

Small eternal flames dotted against the walls of the circular pit. It was enough for them to see through. Several archways lined the walls. The two giant chains restraining Astraea were bolted against the walls. How long had she been chained? What a twisted fate, Sophie thought, a draekin unable to spread its wings.

The draekin continued her distraction above, snapping at any guards that dared near the lip of the pit.

Scrambling to Kaine, Sophie channelled her mana, focusing on the raw emotions as Kaine taught her. She pulled and pulled. Wrapping her hand around the chain restraining Kaine's wrists, she melted them with just a thought. She made quick work of the various chains that wrapped themselves around him. Once done, she quickly moved to her own, wrapping her hand around the points closest to her wrist. The chain dropped to the floor with a rattle.

"Go find the flaming heart," she ordered Kaine, pointing towards the archways that lay around them. "I need to free her." Sophie pointed back at Astraea and the chains that bound her. Kaine obeyed and ran to each archway, looking for a sign of the flaming heart. They had to move quickly.

Sophie sprinted to the giant bolt on her left. The feeling became more natural to her the more she used it. She pulled at the pool of power in her gut again. Flames danced through her veins and through to her palms. They were a good distance away from the giant mana-muters in the dungeon which meant it felt much easier to will her mana the way she wanted to.

She manifested her flame into two giant fiery blades – extensions of her arms. With all her might, she jumped up and sliced through the giant chain in one smooth movement. The chain dropped unceremoniously on the ground. Astraea whipped her head at the sudden freedom, moving lower to the ground, realising what Sophie was doing.

Sophie sprinted to the other side of the pit, and again jumped up high, slicing down on the chain in one swift movement.

Astraea roared. Her loudest roar yet. It shook the ground entirely. Sophie and Kaine almost lost their footing from its sheer force.

She was free.

"Sophie, I've got it!" Kaine shouted through the noise, waving a muscled arm as he stood by one of the archways. Sophie whipped her head towards Kaine, making for a sprint when the full weight of the draekin pushed against the ground. Sophie turned around to find the draekin swooping low. Her giant form barely fit into the pit, yet she craned her neck low towards Sophie. She was beautiful. Glittering purple and pink. Her horns scraped the walls as she pulled her head down, bringing along bits of dirt and debris that added to the chaos of the distant screams.

Sophie stood in awe of the majestic creature before her.

Bright yellow eyes locked onto her.

Astraea's face moved closer and closer to Sophie's.

But Sophie did not falter. She did not baulk in fear.

"Sophie!" Kaine shouted in warning.

Sophie did not pay him any mind as the draekin sniffed her.

This was her draekin.

Sophie closed her eyes and leaned her forehead onto Astraea's muzzle.

Thank you, Sophie breathed.

You freed me. It's been twenty years since I've flown and stretched my wings. It is I who should be thanking you, Astraea acknowledged.

Twenty years without flying. Sophie couldn't imagine what kind of hell that was for a creature born to fly across the realm.

Sophie opened her eyes, planting a kiss onto the draekin.

May the gods guide you. Sophie's eyes began to well as she watched Astraea's beautiful bright yellow eyes.

To wherever I'm destined to be, Astraea responded with a giant shriek.

With that, she launched herself into the air, spiralling into the sky and out of the pit that had kept her prisoner for years. The ground rumbled with power.

She roared. She shrieked. She smashed through the glass pane above that served as her torture. For twenty years she was taunted and teased, doomed to watch the skies above her but never could she fly through them. The queen would fucking pay for that too.

Astraea flew higher and higher above the castle. She stretched out her wings and roared triumphantly. A roar filled with pain and promise.

Sophie and Kaine watched above them in wonder and shielded their eyes as shards of glass slowly sprinkled down in the distance.

In the corner of her vision, Sophie spotted a red smear peering over the edge of the pit. The queen. Sophie could barely make her out, but she knew it was the queen.

Chills ran down Sophie's spine as she spied the queen watching them, no doubt with a promise of death on her mind.

"Sophie, we've got to go. The queen has most likely ordered her guards to watch every exit," Kaine called out from behind her.

Sophie ran towards his outstretched hand.

The archway he stood by was marked by a tiny flaming heart, the size of a fifty-cent piece. It was etched deep into the stone, on the right-hand side.

The path ahead was pitch black.

They would be going in blind.

She intertwined her fingers with Kaine's as he pulled her through the dark archway.

Together, hand in hand, they ran into the unknown.

39

I t was a maze.

A dark-filled, cold stone maze. Dead ends and all.

Sophie and Kaine had been running for a good part of an hour, and it felt like they'd been running in circles.

With a smack, Sophie ran right into the back of Kaine's steel back. *Shit.* Sophie cupped her nose in the dark. She was as good as blind in these dark passages. Luckily, Kaine with his fae sight was able to see through the dark, though not very clearly. He led them through the dark, towards wherever the passage would eventually spit them out.

"Shit," he grunted.

"What is it?" Sophie breathed. Her lungs slightly burned from the pace they were maintaining.

"The path splits out into four."

"Give us a fucking break, you damning gods!" Sophie shouted into the air. She was beyond frustrated. Tired. They'd already been through enough. And her stomach had already started eating itself. If she could have a word with all her favourite authors, she'd request that they detail where to hide snacks, when to strategically take a nap and how to navigate secret ancient tunnels while you're visually impaired. The advice would have been immensely helpful at this point in her life.

"Do you feel anything with your mana?" Kaine asked Sophie, hand brushing a stray hair out of her face. The touch startled her. She could barely see.

Sophie paused, tapping her mana awake. She shot out glittery tendrils, washing her mana over each archway, hoping to feel or hear something.

She scanned the first three archways.

Nothing.

It felt like no life existed beyond the first three doors.

Her gut dropped. *Come on, give me anything. A sign. Please.*

As she moved the tendrils of her mana over the last door... her chest warmed. No, her mother's necklace warmed her chest.

"You've got to be kidding me." Sophie was astounded. Of course, the only thing that would help guide them through the passage marked with a flaming heart, was a flaming-heart necklace. Her worlds were colliding in the most poetic way. She inching closer and closer to her truth. She was sure of it.

Sophie grasped the necklace firmly in her hand before reassessing each archway with her mana. Lo and behold, all archways yielded no reaction barring the final door.

Bingo.

From all the memories that cropped up as dreams, to the necklace that her mum gifted her as an early birthday present not too long after she returned from Faery for the first time... it was all too perfectly planned to be a coincidence.

Oh. Danna Taliesin, you've got some SERIOUS explaining to do if I ever get out of this mess. Sophie scoffed.

"What do you feel, Sophie?" Kaine's hand moved to her lower back, supporting her.

"I feel like it's time I take the reins of this great escape." Sophie turned to Kaine, holding up the necklace. "This is getting us out of here." She beamed.

Kaine held the flaming-heart necklace in his hand, inspecting it. "It's the flaming heart etched in the archway," he admired. "Who—"

Sophie cut him off. "Escape now. Questions later."

With a swift nod, he grabbed her hand and pulled her into the fourth archway.

They spent another half hour running through the dark tunnels. The flaming-heart necklace directing them through the ordeal. Each pulse grew hotter and hotter as they neared what they assumed was the end.

"Left or right?" Kaine breathed.

The necklace pulsed. "Left."

They ran a few steps when Kaine pulled Sophie to a stop.

"It's a dead end, Sophie. We'll need to go right." Kaine started pulling her in the opposite direction. The necklace grew colder the farther she stepped away.

"No. It's telling us to go left." Sophie planted her feet. The necklace had served them well so far. It felt like they were making distance as opposed to running in circles.

"It's a dead end, Sophie. We need to keep moving." Kaine pulled her with him.

She pulled her arms out of his grasp. "Let me see about that." She padded up to the dead end. It was wall full of stone. She brushed her hands across its surface, feeling for a loose brick or maybe a secret lever. Her eyes had finally adjusted to the dark so she could make faint outlines. Pushing, prodding, scanning. Nothing. She reached out with her mana instead but there was nothing of note.

Determined, she moved to the sides of the wall. To the right, she felt a small hole. Tracing the shape with her fingers... It was the perfect fit for her necklace.

Yes! I am going to kiss the beejesus out of you, Mum! She laughed. Lifting the necklace off her chest, and bending over slightly, she placed it into the small socket.

The dead-end wall groaned to life, and slowly the wall peeled open. Behind it, a faint glow seeped out. It was a hidden room.

Sophie stood, taking a fighting stance should anything decide to pop out from behind the wall.

"What in the world is that?" Sophie suddenly felt Kaine's presence just behind her.

The room before them was circular and was completely made of stone like the rest of the tunnel. On the other side was an illuminated archway, stretching into the distance. In the centre of the room, atop a stone plinth surrounded by flames that illuminated the room, was a multi-coloured stone suspended midair. The flames reflected against the smooth, shiny surface of the gem. Streaks of emerald, ruby, amethyst and citrine swirled through the kite-shaped stone. The stone was cut perfectly barring the small part of it that had been broken off. It was roughly the size of a small plum.

Kaine moved ahead of Sophie, checking the room for any traps or spells. It was all clear. At his signal, Sophie moved slowly towards the suspended stone. Her necklace hummed with ferocity.

"My mother's necklace calls to it," Sophie explained. It was telling her to take the stone. She knew it, deep down in her mana – that had to be it.

Kaine nodded, needing no further explanation.

Slowly, Sophie raised herself onto her tiptoes, careful not to burn her sleeves or arms against the flames. The stone was beautiful, spinning slowly in the air.

Softly, she grabbed hold of it, pulling it out of the air it was suspended in.

Sophie stood, cupping the gem between her palms, entranced by its craftsmanship. She'd never seen anything like it before.

Kaine stood carefully on the other side of the plinth, watching her the entire time. She looked up to him, his turquoise eyes dancing with the flames, ready to show him the gem.

The ground beneath them shook violently and cracks formed across the ceiling.

FUCK.

The room started to collapse.

Sophie quickly pocketed the gem and sprinted toward Kaine and to the illuminated archway on the other side of the room. They were just a few metres away when the secret room they uncovered came crashing down with the violence of several angered gods.

Her human legs weren't as fast as Kaine's, despite him being significantly drained of power with the iron rods completely healed inside him.

Kaine slowed enough to grab her hand and dragged her with him as they sprinted for their damn lives. The tunnel came crashing down behind them. Rocks and rubble nipped at their heels. They were in a Faery version of Crash Bandicoot.

"There's a door above!" Kaine shouted above the rumbling that threatened to crush them.

There at the end. The tunnel completely stopped and above was a wooden door.

Sophie pumped her legs harder and harder to keep up. They were almost free.

Kaine ran ahead, sliding across the ground to avoid hurling himself into the wall. He jumped up, unlatched the door and punched it open. Moonlight illuminated the way. Just how long had they been traversing the tunnels for?

Kaine bent low, lacing his fingers together – to boost her up, Sophie realised.

She pumped her legs harder, gritted her teeth and launched herself at Kaine, stepping her foot into his hands as he launched her up, out into the open air. She was airborne for just a moment.

Grabbing the edge, she pulled herself up onto the warm grass. Just behind her, she felt Kaine jump up and grab the edge of the door, grunting as he pulled himself up too.

They both rolled onto the grass onto their backs, completely breathless, the ground trembling beneath them.

Sophie reached for his hand across the grass, and they allowed themselves a moment to catch their breath. A moment to savour the Faery night sky that shined brightly above them.

They were alive. They were *free*.

40

"We need to spell the house should anyone pick up our scents," Kaine whispered.

The tunnels had spit them out on the edge of Summeira. Under the cover of night, Sophie and Kaine snuck through the village to find Kaine's cottage. He'd stay there when the queen permitted or when he was on leave from working with the Elite. It was small, but it would serve their purpose until they could figure out their next steps.

"Show me," Sophie whispered.

They stood in the dark shadows of Kaine's front door. Swiftly, he crouched down just in front of the door, drawing a symbol in a language Sophie did not recognise. He drew three lines with various swirls around it.

"It's ancient Fae. It'll shield the house and our scents," he explained. "You'll need to write it in our blood." He looked up at her, waiting for her answer.

Sophie had read about ancient Faery spells before. It was a different magic to the mana that lived inside her. It was much older. It was blood magic. It only came to life through written spells. Each symbol had a different meaning, and when strung together correctly they would create a spell.

"Very well." Sophie swallowed. She pulled the Scyllen throwing knife from her pocket and made to slice her palm open. Kaine stopped her before she could, with a firm grip on her wrist.

"A shallow cut here"—he rolled up her sleeve and pointed to the soft underside of her arm—"would be a much better place." A trail of goosebumps followed where Kaine traced his fingers. "We use our hands all the time. Having a deep cut there wouldn't be too pleasant," he explained.

Sophie nodded and held her arm out. Slowly, she cut a shallow line across her arm. Blood began to form on her skin. She let a few drops fall to the floor where Kaine had told her to mark. She quickly leaned over to grab Kaine's arm, repeating the motion. His blood dripped down on top of hers, mixing. With her index finger, she traced the outlines of the ancient Fae symbols Kaine had shown her. As she finished the last swirl, their blood glowed an intense dark red before evaporating. Sophie hoped to the gods that it worked.

"Let's get inside." Kaine quickly rose on his feet. Grabbing Sophie by the hand, he pulled her into the cottage.

The small cottage was simple and homey. They were greeted by a warm living room with a couch and fireplace to the left. To the right sat a two-seater dining table and in front of them a quaint kitchen. Beyond the dining table were two doors, one for the bathroom and one for the bedroom. The walls were empty save for a small painting of a young woman with long dark black hair and silver swirling eyes. The captain of the Elite didn't need much. It had everything he needed. It was cosy.

As soon as they passed the threshold, Kaine pulled her into a hug. There was nothing sexual about it. It grounded them. The two stood in absolute silence, numb from the onslaught of adrenalin. From being struck with the truth of the queen and her evil scheming, to escaping the dungeons off the back of a draekin. They finally had a moment to stop and breathe.

Silent tears found their way down Sophie's face.

Fighting and running her way through the dungeons was tough. There was no amount of reading or physical training that would have prepared her for that. Not only was it physically draining, but she was also famished and her eyes felt like they were about to pop out of her face from the amount of focus required to stay alive.

Sophie pressed her cheeks into Kaine's broad chest, weeping. She missed her mother. She missed her world. She missed her Faery friends and still, she had so many questions that no one seemed to know the answer to. Why was she here? Why was the queen trying to kill her and Kaine? Was it just for power or was there something else? Why did her mana work on iron and not Kaine's? It was all a mystery, and she barely had any fuel left in the tank to solve it.

Kaine rocked her gently in his arms until the tears stopped. He was a calming presence she never knew she needed.

"Come on, let's get those rods out of you. It must hurt." She sniffled, pulling away from his embrace, rubbing her face as she did. She couldn't get the image out of her head. The sounds and the sight of the guards torturing him made her sick with rage. Over and over it played in her head.

On silent feet, Kaine moved to the kitchen, grabbing himself a knife, tongs, a few pieces of rope, rags and a bowl of water. Setting each item down by the fireplace he motioned for Sophie to join him. He'd need her help. His skin had completely healed over the iron.

Kaine instructed Sophie on what to do, and with each step she did not baulk in fear or disgust. With every step, he watched her with amazement in his eyes.

They worked quickly, blocking blood flow when they needed to, carefully cutting through skin and easing out the pieces of iron. With each hiss of pain, Sophie soothed him with her warm touch. By the last iron piece in his leg, Sophie swore he was hissing just so he could feel her soothing touch against his skin. She smiled at that. He was a fae warrior, but he became weak for the touch of a human. She was his weakness. She was his *soulmate*, the queen said. Sophie didn't know what to do with that information.

With the iron removed from his body, Kaine's body knitted itself together with supernatural speed but still, the larger incisions they'd made lagged. Sophie hovered her hands over the wounds, calling to her mana. She imagined his skin knitting together, cell by cell. A faint purple glow illuminated her hands and danced around his wounds. Magic.

"You're a natural." Kaine watched her the entire time, as if wanting to say something more.

Sophie smiled from where she knelt beside Kaine, not pulling her entire attention away from the healing work she was doing. "So, soulmates huh?" She laughed lightly.

"I didn't want you to find out from the queen," Kaine hurriedly said.

Sophie continued her healing, avoiding his gaze.

"I... don't know how I feel about it." It was the truth. Sophie knew her feelings for Kaine were real but still, she had a whole other life in Sotera. Her mum was most likely waiting for her, and she had friends. She couldn't just up and leave them to stay here with Kaine. They were two worlds apart.

Kaine stiffened at the words. "Am I not to your liking?"

Sophie whipped her head to his handsome face. His black hair was tied roughly behind his head and his turquoise eyes shone with a vulnerability she hadn't seen before.

"Gods, don't get me wrong. You are perfect. You are everything a mortal could dream of..." She took his hand in hers. "But I am a mortal. I have a life in Sotera that awaits me. A limited life at that. Whatever we have, whatever we will have, will end in heartbreak for the both of us." She smiled sadly, brushing one of his locks behind his pointed ear. She remembered the promise she made to herself long ago. She wouldn't let anyone break her heart again. She'd been through enough and even though Kaine was literally carved out of stone by the very gods themselves, she couldn't bear to give her heart over, not that easily. Soulmate bonds be damned.

Hurt washed over his face. He stood up quickly.

"I... excuse me." Kaine hesitated. It looked like he wanted to say something but opted to escape into his room. To breathe. To think. Sophie was certain that he wasn't expecting her to say those words.

The sudden emptiness of the room left her heart aching. Perhaps she could have worded it better, but was she not right in protecting her heart? Or was she damning his soul? Either way, she was a fool. A fool to have entertained the idea of a whisking romance with a fae. A fool for letting her heart flutter this far over the edge.

Sophie felt terrible. She hadn't intended on hurting him at all. She wanted to voice how she felt but instead drove him into the darkness of his room.

She busied herself with cleaning the rags and bowls they'd used to extract the iron and once that was done, she moved around the living space, examining the only picture Kaine had hung up in his cottage. *Riviera, loved by all* was engraved on the frame. Her nose and the shape of her eyes were identical to Kaine's. They had the same inky black hair but where she had silver swirling eyes, he had turquoise. On her breast lay the sun-shaped necklace Kaine always kept on him.

His mother, Sophie realised. She was beautiful. She looked kind, like she had love for everyone who walked into her life and judging by the engraving, everyone loved her back.

Not being able to stand the awkward rift between them, Sophie moved quietly to the bedroom door and knocked twice. Nothing.

Defying all logic, she slowly opened the door to find Kaine staring blankly into the ceiling, hands clasped across his stomach.

"You're right," he said as she approached the bed.

"Ah, the immortal fae warrior speaks," Sophie teased. Smiling, she propped herself on the edge of the bed.

"You're mortal. I'm immortal. There are no two ways about it." He frowned at her, sitting himself up. "I guess I imagined it going differently."

"What, you imagined that your fated would jump into your arms without any questions?" Sophie laughed.

"Well, yes. The soulmate bond is ancient. It dates back to the Fates. It's meant to hit you in the gut like nothing else. Death itself would be a much better fate than being apart from your soulmate," Kaine explained, moving closer to Sophie.

Something about those words caught in Sophie's mind. She never felt that so-called punch to the gut. While her attraction to him was painfully clear, she still had her doubts about their compatibility. Perhaps it wasn't a one soulmate bond fits all? What Sophie knew was that all signs pointed to her being his fated. The queen. Her memories. Her mother's necklace. Everything pointed to her being here with him at this moment. That was undeniable.

"I think they oversold it to you..." Sophie whispered, catching the hunger in his turquoise eyes.

"Be that as it may, the way I feel is undeniable." He ran his finger across her delicate cheek. The moonlight from his bedroom window cast sinful shadows across his face. Slowly he traced his fingers, all the way down to her neck where he stopped, placing his entire hand along her chest, stopping where her heart stammered. "And I hope to the gods you feel the same way."

Sophie didn't know if it was the build-up of adrenaline that left her mind numb and void of common sense or if the bond had completely overwritten any promises she made to herself. She didn't care anymore. In this moment alone, all she wanted was Kaine.

Crashing into his lips, they united in a passionate kiss.

His large hands roamed all over her, grabbing a hold of her breasts and down to her waist, pulling her over him.

In a frenzy, she straddled him, already feeling how turned on he was. She was instantly wet at the feel.

Breaking the kiss, he moved to pull her blouse over her head. An animalistic hunger washed over him. It was like he'd switched gears. Gone was the noble fae warrior and in his place was a hungry wolf.

He moved to cup one of her bare breasts, using his other hand to pull her down back to his lips. With every movement, Sophie could feel where they were joined. She was desperate to feel him on her skin, to feel him inside of her.

In one swift movement, Kaine flipped them over, not breaking the kiss in the slightest. In a frenzy of kisses, he moved down her neck, nibbling and pulling at her as he did. She moaned at the feel of his perfect lips on her skin. With an impatient growl, he unbuttoned her pants and pulled them off in one swift motion.

Sophie lifted herself onto her elbows and splayed her knees exposing her centre before his kneeled form. An invitation.

"You will be the end of me," Kaine breathed, raking a hungry stare over every inch of her body. Never had she felt more wanted than she did in this moment before Kaine. He stepped off the bed for a moment to pull his shirt and breaches off.

His body was shaped by the gods themselves. Tall, athletic, tan. His black hair unbound, spilled across his broad shoulders and travelled down his broad chest. A happy trail of dark curls led down to his cock. Sophie swallowed at the size of it.

With the prowess of an age-old predator, he moved back to Sophie, settling himself between her thighs. His tip just rubbed at her entrance. She wanted him inside so badly.

Sophie gasped at the skin-to-skin contact. This felt right. In this moment, she wanted Kaine and no one else.

"Tell me you want me," Kaine whispered as he showered kisses all over breasts.

Sophie's breath hitched at the feeling. Distracted, she couldn't move her mouth.

Slowly, he trailed his fingers down her stomach to cup the bundle of nerves at her centre.

She moaned as his fingers swirled, dipping in and out of her as she panted.

"Tell me you feel it too, deep down in your heart." Kaine growled, creating more frantic swirls around her clitoris as he did. A new wave of wetness found itself on his palm.

She needed him now. "I do," Sophie panted.

At those words he drove himself in all the way to his hilt, slowing just enough for her body to adjust to his size. They moaned together.

He thrust slowly, reclaiming her lips with his. They held each other tightly as he repeatedly buried himself in her. In, out. In, out.

With every thrust, the intense feeling built inside her. Her breathing grew frantic. He showered her in kisses as he continued thrusting, increasing his speed until she was about to spill over. She was a hair's breadth away from peaking when he sunk his fangs into her neck. The mixture of pleasure and pain sent her into another dimension. She came so hard. The feeling of her pulsing around him sent Kaine into his own ecstasy. He breathed her name as he did.

As soon as his quivers stopped, he pulled himself out and rested between her legs with his head on her chest. She held him tightly. And in that moment, she swore the ice that barricaded her heart slowly started to melt.

What had she just done?

41

They spent the rest of the night talking about how they both came to be in Faery, connected someway, somehow by the Fates. It wasn't even a question anymore.

Kaine spoke of the Fallen Seas as he held Sophie close to his chest. How a few royal guards had attempted his assassination on behalf of Queen Calliea and how he overpowered them, forcing the sailors onboard to turn the boat around. Before they even docked, one of the sailors had betrayed him. The hurried flapping of the messenger raven's wings spelled the sailors' instant death. Not long after, the wanted posters were up. Plastered all over Terrin. He was wanted for the attempted assassination of the queen. How could he have attempted her murder when he only just returned to Terrin soil? He lived in the shadows for a few days before making his way to the queen with the intent to do exactly as she had so eloquently claimed.

"And that's when I found out who my father was. While I can't trust the queen and any word that comes out of her mouth, the words ring true for me." Kaine breathed, looking distantly at the ceiling, trying to piece together the parts that made him, him.

The late King Gydeon was his father.

Sophie turned out of his arms and sat up, turning towards Kaine. He wished he could spend every waking moment like this. With her in his arms. His soulmate.

"Well, it makes sense, doesn't it? You don't remember who your real father is. The queen herself literally confessed that she killed your mother, but not before she called out King Gydeon for being a simp. If King Gydeon is indeed your father, that makes *you* the rightful heir." Sophie clasped her hands around her mouth. Slowly, she continued, "You are also insanely strong. The strongest of all the Elite. You're the best of the best. You have just returned from the Fallen Seas. And it turns out that I am your fated." Sophie stared at Kaine with her eyes and mouth wide open. He could see her mind working. Whirling. The pieces that long ago did not make sense, the pieces that felt ill-fitted slowly started to fall into place.

And finishing the chaotic train of thoughts for her, Kaine spoke of the prophecy that the people of Faery clung to. "The return of the strongest warrior that Faery will ever come to know, will bring the full might of Faery, but only with the love they sow." He took her hands in his. "Together with their fated, the blood reign will end. A life of peace and prosperity, more than one can comprehend."

"But what does that even mean? The love we sow? I don't understand."

"The love we sow. The love we create with our union."

"Like marriage?" Sophie gulped.

"In a way, yes. When two souls are bonded, or fated, there's a special connection that exists between them. A bond. A tether of sorts. One that transcends realms and lifetimes. And if the pair so choose to unite not just themselves physically, but their essence and mana, they can. Only a high priestess can cast such a strong spell. Though this union comes at a cost. If one soul were to die, the other would too. Their lives are one and the same. Tethered for eternity."

Eternity. Kaine wondered what that word meant for Sophie. Eternity was expected for fae... but for a human? What Kaine would give to know what she was feeling and thinking right now.

"So you're saying, when two souls bind themselves together, they can essentially double up on power. Join forces and mana, right?"

"Correct."

A pregnant pause filled the room.

"We're going to stop the blood reign together, aren't we? We're going to stop Queen Calliea." Kaine watched as the weight of the words dawned on her like a house of bricks. Her shoulders stiffened. Her hands became unsteady. And her eyes were distant, no doubt imagining her future the way she never imagined it. She wasn't ready for this. What human could possibly be? Saving a realm. Being bonded for all eternity. She was once but a speck in the world and now she was the key to saving it. As much as Kaine wanted her to be by his side, he couldn't help but sense hesitation in her. He wouldn't force her into it. As much as it meant to him... and the people of Faery.

Kaine nodded. "Correct."

42

"You don't remember at all?" Sophie asked softly.

They'd moved to the fireplace, letting the weight of the prophecy sink in while the licking flames warmed them. They didn't want to let go of this tiny peace they'd found amid chaos. As a way of distraction, Sophie told Kaine of the memories she'd dreamed of. Of her and Kaine as children sword fighting, spending every waking moment together and of them playing with their draekins.

With every memory she divulged, Kaine shook his head. Sophie couldn't help but be disappointed. With every shake of his head, her heart sank. He did not remember at all.

They narrowed the block in his memories down to the trauma of watching his mother die in front of his eyes. He could barely remember anything before and even directly after the matter.

"While I cannot remember, your memories only cement my belief in our destiny." He lifted her hand and brushed his lips gently across her knuckles. "I know that you are human and that you'll live a mortal life span, but in this moment"—he wrapped his arms around her so her back was flush against his chest and he rested his chin on her neck—"with my arms wrapped around you, I know that I'd fight tooth and nail for you. I will never let you go. I would start a damn war over you."

Sophie's heart squeezed to the point she thought it was going to burst. If she wasn't convinced of their destiny before, she was most definitely convinced now. Her heart sung for this fae warrior. Perhaps opening herself up to him and giving into their Fates wouldn't be such a bad idea.

It felt like they were stuck in a gruesome fairytale with queens, kings, draekins, true heirs and *soulmates*. Despite the chaos, Sophie shifted in his arms, twisting to face him. To face herself. Was this the love she'd long been searching for? It had to be. All roads led to Kaine. She was sure of it.

Tired of her inner turmoil, Sophie gave in. Promises be damned. She answered his sweet serenade with a passionate, fate-sealing kiss.

"Sophie, look my darling!" The long-silver-haired female scooped young Sophie off the ground, holding her tightly on her hip. The kind older female placed a shining flaming-heart-shaped necklace in Sophie's little hands. It shined so brightly in the sunlight of their cosy home.

"Is it for me, Mama?" Sophie smiled brightly, wanting to keep the beautiful necklace for herself.

"Not yet, honey. One day, when you're big and strong like Daddy, it will be yours and you must guard it fiercely with all your might," Sophie's mother smiled down lovingly at her, moving the hair from out of her face. Sophie oohed and aahed at the necklace that was still warm. "For now, mama will need to hold onto it."

Sophie reluctantly handed the necklace back to her mother who fastened it effortlessly around her neck.

A dark-haired female with swirling silver eyes waltzed through the room with the young dark-haired boy in tow. Her face beamed with beauty, and the young boy's turquoise swirling eyes were filled with energy as he jumped up and down with excitement.

The female had such a joyful aura about her. It felt like, wherever she walked, flowers would bloom and the sun itself would come down from where it sat in the sky to kiss your cheek. She was kind. She was warm.

"My loves, come sit." The silver-eyed female beckoned Sophie and her mother to sit on the couch with her and the boy.

They all huddled together like they were in a secret club.

The silver-eyed female held out her hand. Without a word, Sophie's mother unlatched the necklace from her neck and placed it firmly in the female's expecting hand.

The silver-eyed female nodded quietly.

Sophie's mother stood quickly, unsheathing a hidden knife from her boot and made a small cut against the inside of her arm. She quickly sketched intricate symbols on the floor next to them. The symbols sizzled with red glowing light before sputtering out and evaporating. Only then, did the silver-eyed female speak.

"Listen carefully, my darlings. You must protect these with your lives. As a family, it is a rule that we do not keep secrets but these..." She lifted the flaming-heart necklace in her left hand and in the other she lifted a matching gold necklace in the shape of a sleeping sun. "You must keep them a secret. You must protect these with your lives. You are not to tell or show anyone these necklaces. Do you understand?"

The black-haired boy nodded fervently with a determined look on his face. The female looked to Sophie. She nodded, matching the determination the boy showed.

"These are keys to unlocking a very strong power, one that you will one day share together." Sophie didn't quite understand what she meant, but she nodded anyway. The woman pointed the longest sunray into the centre of the flaming heart, and a small click sounded. "They belong to one another, these necklaces. As you two do." The female looked to the two children with such love in her eyes. "Shall the flaming heart need to be opened, just look to the sun. Can you remember that for me?"

The two children looked at one another. Best friends forever. Two sides of the same coin. They reached out to hold each other's hands and nodded in unison.

43

Sophie woke to the feeling of light swirling patterns being made along her back. The feeling sent shivers down her spine, lighting a fire in her core. Her eyes fluttered open to see bright turquoise eyes watching her.

"Good morning," Kaine breathed, a smile splaying across his handsome features.

"Now this is an alarm I'd willingly wake up to." Sophie laughed, stretching in his arms. She turned to face him.

"As much as I'd like to stay in bed watching you sleep, I'm afraid we've got a realm to save." Kaine smirked, reaching around to cup her bottom.

"But where would we even start?"

At the words, Kaine stopped his fondling, much to Sophie's dismay. "Last night had me thinking." He lifted himself onto his elbows as Sophie readjusted herself on his chest. "I'll send word to my trusted Elite. They'll have contacts throughout the courts. I've already sent word to my own contacts about the queen's attempt to assassinate me. We'll start pulling together forces and a game plan on how we can stop the queen." Kaine turned to Sophie then. "And you. You said that when you were younger, your mother would tell you stories about Faery all the time. You have memories. Her necklace guided you. Your mother must have answers. There's got to be something there. She could be the missing link. You've just got to dig for it. You need to go back to Sotera."

"Are you joking? Back to Sotera now? While I've got a bounty over my head? We barely made it through last time. What's to say we will make it this time?" Sophie scrunched her brows.

"We're outnumbered and outmanned. Anything will help us, Sophie. I promise that I will get you to Sotera safely. And that's an oath."

Sophie gulped. A promise. Like he did last time. "How would we be out-numbered? The queen's got a few hundred royal guards but that's nothing against your Elite, right?"

Kaine said nothing.

"You know something I don't, don't you?" Sophie tried to look into his eyes, but he kept avoiding her.

"It's a theory. The queen was wrapped up in a rage when she mentioned that she had an alliance in the works."

"With Sotera?"

"No. With the Shadow Realm."

Sophie tried hard not to gasp. "The proverbial hell that Terr, the Shadow King rules?"

"Precisely. The queen flaunts her youth when she is hundreds if not thousands of years old." Kaine jumped from the bed and began to pace.

"Okay? I'm not following." While that was true, Sophie also wasn't following because Kaine had just jumped out of bed, without any clothes on. It was distracting.

"The hellhounds that seemed to have just appeared out of nowhere. And disappear, just like that, without a trace."

At the words, all distraction melted away. "As if they came from a portal." Sophie's eyes widened as she began to cotton on.

"A portal so strong that could rip through not only time and space, but realms."

"A portal that requires a great sacrifice..." Sophie almost vomited at the realisation. "A sacrifice like the blood of children. The promised children."

"And if my theory is correct, then we are, how you say, in deep shit."

"No fucking shit." Sophie's soul left her body at the revelation they'd just landed on. "Unless, unless we had more power on our side." Sophie jumped out of bed, joining in on Kaine's pacing. They looked like two mad men, pacing around completely naked. "I had a dream last night... A memory."

Kaine didn't say anything.

"Your mother was in it."

Kaine stopped in place. "That was definitely not what I was expecting to hear." He cleared his throat as sadness filled his eyes.

"She showed me your necklace." It was Sophie's turn to stop in place. "It was made with mine." She rushed over to the stand beside the bed where she'd placed the flaming-heart necklace. Holding it out with one hand, she showed it to Kaine. The gold was bright, and the flames seemed to burn brighter today.

Kaine walked over to his own nightstand where he'd left his sleeping-sun necklace. He offered it to Sophie.

She held each in her hand. The gold tones had matched each other perfectly, and it looked like they were made by the same jeweller.

Shall the flaming heart need to be opened, just look to the sun.

She brushed her fingers across the sleeping sun's face and noted the longest sunray protruding from the top. It was carved into a point.

She then lifted her flaming-heart necklace, brushing her finger across the diamond-shaped keyhole. And like how Kaine's mother showed them in her memories, Sophie pierced the flaming-heart locket with the sun's ray. A small click sounded.

Sophie opened the locket slowly. Kaine watched every move.

In the centre of the heart was a rough-cut gemstone with streaks of emerald, ruby, amethyst and citrine swirled through its entirety.

Sophie gasped, almost dropping the necklace and gemstone from her hand. It was the missing piece to the gem they'd found in the secret tunnel under Castle Terrin.

"Mother of Faery..." Kaine gaped, moving himself closer to Sophie's hands, just to take a closer look.

"I think I know..." Sophie didn't finish her sentence. She was completely dumbfounded by how fate itself had led her down this path. She stumbled back into Faery not by accident but by the will of the Fates. Her memories had returned to her for a reason and now she was here, with the two necklaces that were made together. Two necklaces that would be the key to unlocking a very strong power.

They needed to make the gemstone whole again. And perhaps by doing so, they'd unlock the power that Riviera spoke of, or at least, it would lead them to the next stage of their journey.

Sophie jumped up from the bed to fish out the gemstone from where she'd hid it last night – in her boot. She clasped her flaming-heart necklace around her neck again, holding the fragmented gemstone piece in her other hand.

She took a deep breath, slotting the two pieces that had been apart for so long, together. It was a perfect fit.

The stone was whole again.

Nothing happened.

Sophie thought the stone would come to life or make some sort of show, but nothing happened.

Sophie shrugged her shoulders at Kaine who sat on the bed on the other side of the room. She lifted the plum-sized gemstone in her hand. "Well that was disap— OW FUCK!" Sophie hissed in pain, dropping the gemstone onto the wooden floor. It bounced a few steps ahead of her. The stone had burned her hand. "It burned me!" She waved her hand in the air trying to cool it.

Kaine threw his legs off the edge of the bed, making his way over to soothe her but before he reached her, the gemstone began to levitate off the ground between them.

That stopped him in his tracks.

Sophie stopped her fussing too.

The gemstone swirled, suspended in the air on a phantom wind. Its shining, now complete surface, sparkled in the sunlight.

It called to Sophie.

A soft, harp-filled melody echoed through the room.

Slowly, she reached out her hand; the gemstone seemed to float its way closer to her.

"Sophie, don't," Kaine warned, eyes wide, posed in a fighting position.

She heard him. But she didn't obey him. She couldn't. Her mind had gone completely numb, tunnel visioned on this one floating stone.

As soon as Sophie's fingertip brushed its surface, a white blinding light cast itself from the stone across the entire room.

The room spun with the light.

It grew brighter and brighter.

Sophie could see Kaine shouting. An invisible force had pushed him to his knees. He was trying to fight against it. To get to her.

She felt her feet leave the floor.

Together with the stone, she levitated, her breath leaving her completely.

The bright light dimmed and turned dark, murky, then a black glittery colour.

Dark tendrils of magic reached out to Sophie as she spun in the air.

A wind so violent washed through the entire room, sending books flying, whipping her hair all around her.

She could barely see, barely breathe.

The dark tendrils from the stone latched onto her chest and the pain Sophie felt as it did was one she had never felt before. She swung her head back, shrieking from the feel of it. It felt like she'd been stabbed with a burning blade.

The stone closed the distance between itself and Sophie, clinging onto the centre of her sternum.

It burned so badly but Sophie couldn't move. She was suspended in the air. She was helpless.

It buried itself into her skin, making its way through bone to the centre of her chest.

As soon as the stone had completely burrowed itself inside her, a blinding glow shot out from Sophie's eyes and mouth, spilling out in the dark glittery chaos around her.

Sophie screamed and screamed at the pain.

Tears ran freely down her face.

The wind whipped violently around her and the room.

Electricity ran through every single fibre of her body.

Then fire.

Then earth.

Then air.

Sophie shrieked until her throat was raw.

Then the feel of a tranquil stream of water washed through her entire body and quieted the chaos.

The light from within and around her dimmed.

And slowly, the phantom wind eased her down to the floor.

She fell softly on her knees, panting from the otherworldly pain she'd just experienced.

The wind eased to a light breeze.

The harp-filled melody faded.

Then it was quiet.

Panting, Sophie looked up to where Kaine sat on the floor, his eyes wide open as if he'd just seen a ghost.

44

"Sophie... your hair," Kaine whispered. He moved closer to where she was heaped on the floor. His hands reached out to touch her hair, completely awestruck.

Sophie groaned, slowly coming back to her senses after the strange ordeal. She stared into his eyes, the only anchor to reality. It felt like her head had been pushed under water.

Kaine's eyes were wide, watching her, studying her as if she were an art installation in a museum.

"My hair...?" Sophie managed to groan. She furrowed her brows in confusion. Her head spun with viciousness as she tried to right herself. She patted her head, wondering what Kaine was referring to. What she found surprised her. Her hair was much longer now, flowing down to her waist in luscious waves. She grabbed a tendril, her eyes struggling to adjust to the brightness of the room. She studied the colour of her hair in her hand.

Silver and purple.

Grabbing all the hair around her, she examined it with her hands. Panic set in. Her hair was silver and purple. Sophie let out a small squeak of surprise and fear. "My hair!"

Sophie ran to the mirror just above Kaine's dresser. She screamed. This couldn't be right.

In a flurry, she ran to the bathroom, fumbling as she did. It felt like her body was moving faster than her mind intended. The imbalance of it all made her tummy turn.

She ran into the bathroom, and looked at herself in the mirror, white knuckling the sink in front of her, panting.

"Holy mother of Faer—" Sophie dropped to the floor like a wet noodle.

Sophie woke to the feel of strong arms cradling her. She was still in Kaine's bathroom.

"Please tell me that I was just dreaming?" Sophie wrung her eyes from the exhaustion she felt.

Kaine laughed as he pulled her closer. "I'm afraid you weren't."

What Sophie saw in the mirror was something she was not expecting at all. She was fae. She was outrageously and undoubtedly fae.

Her hair had grown longer, luscious and turned various shades of purple and silver. It reminded her of nebulae. Her ears were delicately pointed, and her skin was a perfect, glassy texture. Her eyes found everything brighter, sharper and she could hear everything going on outside of the cottage, like tiny insects making burrows and the whispers of wind across the grass. She felt taller, faster and more agile.

Sophie ran her fingers across her teeth. Fangs. She had two. Protruding from the rest of her normal teeth. *So this is what being fae feels like? Holy shit!* Sophie marvelled at her hands and skin. She felt clearer. Awake. Like her true self.

Sophie looked down to her chest where the stone had entered her body. Right in the centre of her sternum, between her breasts was a tattoo of what seemed like Faery's version of a celtic shield knot. Patterns danced all around the swirls, and underneath, black inky lines like veins faded around it. It was beautiful. It felt powerful.

"I've never seen a mana marking so large and dark before." Kaine marvelled, tracing the outline of the marking on Sophie's sternum. The feeling of his fingers on her skin lit her up, sending goosebumps all over her.

Sophie peered down at the marking. It started in the middle of her chest and ended at the edge of her rib cage. "What does it mean?"

"A mana marking is similar to the favours you have on your wrist but instead of having a slice of someone's power, it's their entire mana. It looks like someone went to great lengths to hide theirs in that gemstone. Considering you held its missing piece, they wanted you and only you to find it," he said matter-of-factly.

Sophie's mind flew back to the dream she'd had last night.

"Our mothers had a part to play in it…" Sophie's brows furrowed. That answered one part of the story, but the rest of the story was still a mystery. Whose power were they trying to hide and why?

Kaine's eyebrows raised at her words, so she explained to him the memory that came forth in her dreams. *These are keys to unlocking a very strong power, one that you will one day share together.*

"Now more than ever, I need answers, Kaine. *We* need answers. I need to find my mum. That's even if she is my mother given I'm…" Sophie gulped, looking down at her hands again. She was fae but her mum was human, or maybe she wasn't. She had flashbacks, memories buried deep down that proved that her mum had known about Faery and in fact lived in it. Though none of her dreams had shown her mother's ears. It never gave her true heritage away. She needed answers and she needed them now.

Kaine held one of her hands gently, tugging at them, wanting her to look into his eyes as she sat in his lap.

"You know what this means?" Kaine looked deep into her soul then. He held her hand tighter.

"What…?" Sophie breathed, completely hypnotised by their closeness.

"It means we can be together." Kaine smiled sweetly.

"I guess… it does." Sophie smiled back, but something deep down did not feel right to her. There was an evil queen and the beasts of the Shadow Realm still kicking around raising hell. It felt remiss of her to be so selfish in finding solace and love with Kaine. Plus, she had an entire life outside of Faery. But in saying that, Kaine was right. She was undoubtedly fae which meant she was an immortal, and that changed everything.

Stop self-sabotaging, Sophie. You deserve to be loved. Everyone does. Don't push him away. He's the only good thing that has happened to you. She battled with herself internally. Sophie had been hurt, deeply. It was difficult to open up, but love and all things worth having weren't always easy to obtain. It would hurt, it would be difficult, but being with Kaine, body and soul, would be worth it, so she thought.

"We can think about it later. We've got a world to save." Kaine grinned brightly, holding her arms in his hands.

Despite turning fae by some sort of miracle, Sophie's focus still ran strong. She'd need to find the answers from her mother, then she needed to return to Faery to help Kaine overthrow the queen.

Together, they'd save Faery.

The Fates had commanded as much.

45

"I can't believe we're here again..." Sophie whispered as she and Kaine stood by the gate that fed into Northern Helm station. It felt like so long ago that they were here, hugging each other goodbye. Back when the only concern they had was getting Sophie back to Sotera. Now they had an evil queen hellbent on killing them and an unknown enemy size waiting in the Shadow Realm.

After her surprise transformation into an immortal fae, Kaine had helped Sophie cut her hair off to the original bob-length she had and pinned various strands strategically so that it covered her pointed ears. She was about an inch taller, but she hoped no one would really notice.

She couldn't believe it. Every book she'd read about the Faery world had drawn her in and hypnotised her. To think all of it had to do with her heritage and that it wasn't just some random interest. Faery was real. Who knew what else could be real?

"I guess there's no turning back." Kaine crashed his lips into Sophie's, hot and passionate, as if it were the last time he was going to see her.

The sound of the train's horn echoed through the tunnel. With a quick, tight hug, he nudged Sophie towards the train.

Quickly, Sophie leopard crawled towards the train and silently climbed on like she had many weeks ago. She sat silently in the engine room all by herself. She wondered about the humans she'd made her first trip to Faery with. She wondered how they fared.

The train jerked into motion, chugging, faster and faster towards the portal to Sotera.

Sophie waited a moment before lifting her head enough to spot Kaine.

Her stomach dropped.

In the distance, she saw Kaine. Utterly outnumbered. Surrounded by a swarm of royal guards. She could see his power, flinging guards around but they'd had him by surprise.

She whipped her head towards the portal ahead of the train.

Then back to Kaine.

If she jumped out right now, she could make it to him before the portal zapped her into Sotera. But she had to jump out now.

Kaine was then dragged away, back into the tunnels, completely limp.

Sophie's body flew into action, out of instinct or who knew what, she rolled off the back of the train and pushed herself into a sprint.

By the time she reached the gate to the tunnels, they were gone.

Crippling anxiety laid itself deep in her chest.

Not a trace of the guards or Kaine was left behind.

Fuck.

46

It'd been almost three weeks since Sophie had been trailing various groups of royal guards and their movements around Castle Terrin. None of them led her any closer to finding Kaine's whereabouts nor did they reveal any of the queen's plans.

Sophie had kept a low profile, using her newfound mana to mask herself. It was bad enough that the queen had captured Kaine, Sophie didn't need to get captured as well. As for Elowan, Camrine and Zala, she found no trace of them. Sophie often reached out using her mana, attempting to track Cam and Ellie through the favours they'd given her. Nothing.

As each day rolled by, her patience grew thin. She needed to infiltrate the castle somehow. A smidgen of information about Kaine was all she needed. Anything. Hopelessness ate away at her stomach and so did her hunger. Where she could, she'd hunt small game in the surrounding bushlands with her Scyllen throwing knife as her only weapon.

Sophie stood in the shadows of a tree line, watching a small group of royal guards enter a stone passage that surely led to the castle. She'd been monitoring the movements of this particular group for two days now – they were the only ones who didn't use the main entrance to the castle.

The sun was beginning to set.

Sophie sent out a tendril of her mana to the group, feeling their intentions. Trying to decipher where they were headed and why they'd use this secret passage.

A snap of a twig sounded behind her.

If she were human, she wouldn't have heard it, but her fae ears heard everything. It surprised her how none of the fae complained about headaches. It was difficult to filter out all the sounds she heard, from the rustling of leaves to the sound of moving water off in the distance.

Silently, she pressed herself up against the tree she leant against, trying to make herself one with the shadows.

She felt it then, a different power, not hers but someone else's.

"Steady there," a low, muffled voice said. Female.

Sophie stilled every fibre in her body.

On silent footsteps, the voice came closer.

"Pull your hood down," the voice demanded.

Sophie did not obey. She stood still. Gripping her throwing knife in the palm of her hand, Sophie was ready for a fight.

As the presence moved closer, Sophie ducked and kicked out her foot in a wide sweep. The presence immediately landed flat on their back. Long red hair swept out from underneath their hood and piercing green eyes stared up at Sophie in surprise.

"Ellie!" Sophie gasped. She hadn't seen her friend since that treacherous day in the throne room. Without a second thought, Sophie threw herself on top of Elowan, pulling her into the tightest hug she could muster. Since escaping the dungeons, she had no clue how to get in touch with her fae friends. It didn't help that she couldn't get too close to the castle because of the amount of mana she now possessed. Scared that the energy would set off some sort of trap the queen had laid out for her, Sophie remained cautious. "I can't believe it! You're alive!" Sophie pulled her friend closer and closer.

Ellie let out a soft chuckle. "I should be the one saying that." She pulled away from Sophie, surveying her friend for any injuries.

Sophie pulled down her hood.

Elowan stilled immediately. She stared at Sophie's now silver and purple hair, and what peeked through all the layers. Her pointed ears.

Sophie shot her hands to her ears, noticing Ellie's stare.

"There's a lot to explain," Sophie whispered.

"I can see that... No wonder why I couldn't find you. I'd been searching for your human scent and an inkling of my power this whole time. It seems like both have been overwritten." Elowan marvelled at Sophie's now perfect fae form.

"Listen, Ellie, we don't have time. The queen has captured Kaine. I can't feel anything through our bond. It's like his powers have been cut off or something," Sophie said frantically, helping Ellie back on her feet. It was so good to see a familiar face again. It had been weeks since Sophie had spoken to anyone. She'd been keeping to the shadows, watching and listening for any clues.

"I know. We just confirmed his location. He's in the queen's personal quarters," Ellie said grimly.

Sophie's stomach lurched. What did that mean? Why was the queen keeping him in her personal quarters? What kind of torture was she subjecting him to?

"We don't know the extent of the damage she's caused. Our contacts in the castle have told us of his haunting screams that echo through the halls, but she hasn't let anyone close. Not even servants," Ellie continued.

Sophie paled at the thought. Her soulmate wasn't just captured, he was being tortured too. The queen had Kaine in her possession for weeks now and she hadn't killed him. It must be a trap then, to lure Sophie out, so she could finish the job with the two of them.

"Then let's bring him home," Sophie said, a wash of determination flooding her senses. They'd finally figured out where he was being kept and with her newfound powers, who knew what she could achieve. She grabbed Ellie's hand, dragging her closer to the stone passage the royal guards had just disappeared into.

Ellie stopped her, pulling back. "Sophie. I just need you to know that I had no idea..."

Sophie knew exactly what she meant. Ellie had no clue that the queen would turn on them like that, at least not to that degree. She didn't know what she was unwittingly leading her friend to her death. "I know. You can make it up to me by saving my soulmate." Sophie smirked.

"I KNEW IT!" Elowan screamed a little too loud.

47

E lowan had convinced Sophie that running into the castle with no weapons or armour, or a foolproof plan was a bad idea. They squabbled for all but five minutes until Elowan pulled Sophie in the direction of her safe house.

They stood outside a quaint cottage in Fyllera with worn wooden doors. Maple leaves scattered all around it in vibrant shades of orange. The maple trees themselves stood tall against the cottage which was situated far enough from the centre of town. It was a private home. In the distance, towards the back of the home, the clanging sound of metal being forged echoed towards Sophie.

The front door flew open. A familiar tall, red-haired figure sprinted towards her.

Cam.

He opened his arms, laughing as he beheld Sophie. Lifting her up from her feet, he swung her around in a firm hug. "Gained a few pounds, have we, human?" Cam laughed as he set Sophie down on her feet. She punched his arm for the absurd comment. "And some new ears too it seems!" Cam marvelled, flicking her pointed ears. She swatted his hands away from her. Oh how she missed his cheerfulness.

And surely enough, Zala appeared from the cottage. A soft smile appeared across her face despite the shadows that danced around her. Sophie nodded an acknowledgment in her direction.

Sophie hadn't realised how much she missed her fae friends until this very moment. She was so happy to see them safe, alive and smiling.

"C'mon, supper is almost ready." Cam pulled Sophie towards the front door but Elowan placed a firm grip on her shoulder, stopping her.

"Actually, there's someone I want you to meet," Ellie said shyly.

Cam gave up pulling Sophie and just inclined his head towards Ellie. He went ahead, making his way back into the front door where Zala stood. "Don't keep us waiting. You know how annoying I get when I'm hungry," Cam shouted.

Sophie laughed, following Ellie towards the back of the cottage where the sound of forging metal rang through the air.

They approached a work shed, with various pokers, mallets and pliers hung up all over the walls. Pieces of armour were strewn haphazardly across work-tables and various weapons from swords to bows were neatly placed in display racks. In the centre, a tall, fair-skinned fae male was welding what looked like a silver chest plate. His long blond hair was tied neatly in a battle braid behind his head. Sweat glistened over his shirtless torso as sparks flew all around him. Sophie watched in awe as he beat the armour into shape with a decently sized mallet.

Elowan cleared her throat.

The male whipped his head towards them; clearly engrossed in his work, he was startled by the sound. Within a heartbeat he dropped his equipment, wiped his soot-stained hands on the apron that hung sinfully around his hips.

He padded towards Elowan, gripped her face between his two worn hands and kissed her passionately.

Something like envy roiled in Sophie's stomach, not of Elowan, but more so for the fact that they could kiss so passionately. Sophie had longed for the feel of Kaine's lips. It felt like they were together for only a brief moment before being ripped apart. It was torture.

Sophie cleared her throat.

Elowan pulled away from the kiss, bashful. "This is Sophie." Ellie waved her hand.

"Lovely to meet you." Sophie lifted her hand for him to shake.

"Ah, my love's favourite human!" he exclaimed, completely dismissing her hand, he pulled her into a tight hug.

Gee the fae really love hugs, don't they?

The male pulled away from the hug that had Sophie stunned in place. "The name is Regin..." He stopped his words as he beheld her eyes, and she beheld his.

Regin's eyes were purple. Much like Sophie's but lighter, more diluted. But still, they were purple.

Sophie's breathing hitched. Never had she met anyone else with similar coloured eyes as hers. It was no wonder that the only other person or being that came close was fae.

Judging by his stunned face, Regin was caught off guard by it too. Shaking his head, Regin returned to Elowan's side and he interlaced his fingers with hers. Matching tattoos mirrored one another on their wrists. *Fated,* Sophie realised. In that moment, a small pang of pain shot through Sophie's heart. Would she ever be able to hold her soulmate again?

"Let's head in for some supper." Regin smiled at the two of them, leading them into the cottage's back entrance. The smell of roasted meats, topped with various spices and vegetables wafted through the air. Sophie's mouth watered furiously, and her stomach flipped with excitement. She hadn't had proper food in weeks, let alone a home-cooked meal.

The only way to describe the insides of the cottage was homey. Across the walls were pictures of family, friends and pets. The furniture was worn and well loved. Lots of memories were made here, from first steps to first jobs. It was a family home. Sophie's heart melted at the sight.

The back entrance they came through led into an open-plan living room with a small fireplace, several couches and by its side a large wooden dining table that sat about eight people. Sophie could only imagine the number of family feasts that were held here.

All around the wooden table, plates, cutlery and a few smaller dishes had already been laid out. Cam and Zala both sat in front of the fireplace discussing what sounded like their infiltration plan to get Kaine out of the sticky situation he was in.

Sophie placed her cloak onto the coathanger by the door that teemed with everyone else's articles of clothing. Her heart ached at the sudden rush of emotions she felt. This felt like a home and oh how she missed her mother in that very instant.

"All right, you gremlins, get into your seats! Your father's hungry and he'll have your heads if you get between him and his roast!" a deep, warm female voice rang from the kitchen down the hall.

Cam and Ellie raced each other to the table, aiming for the end where the main course was surely going to be laid. Zala glided across the space, taking a graceful seat. Regin sat close to Ellie as soon as she decided which seat she would take. Sophie took a seat closest to the door, at the other end of the table, facing down the hall towards the kitchen.

The smell of roast became more intense. Careful, heavy footsteps followed.

A tall, older fae male surfaced from the kitchen. His mid-length blond hair was neatly tied back from his face. He focused solely on the piping hot roast dish he held in his hands.

"Papa, do you need a hand?" Regin screeched back his chair, making to help the older fae male. *Regin's father. Noted,* Sophie thought to herself. Of course that was his father. Regin was the spitting image of him. They even had the same shade of blond hair.

Regin's father swiftly shook his head.

He peered up to the table of misfits Regin had decided to house for the night. Cam already had his knife and fork in his hands, tongue licking his lips in anticipation. Elowan scowled at him, whispering something about not having manners.

Zala sat with her shadows, rolling her eyes at Cam.

Regin watched his father carefully.

Regin's father was a few steps away from the dining table, ready to set the dish down when he noticed Sophie sitting at the end.

He stopped dead in his tracks.

Sophie almost fell out of her seat.

Regin's father had her eyes.

Where Regin's eyes were lighter and fairer, his father's eyes were the exact same tone as Sophie's. His eyes felt familiar too. And that's what unsettled her.

Regin's father froze, dropping the entire roast across the floor. The dish shattered on impact, sending bits of oil and shards of ceramic across the room. He stared at Sophie as if she were a ghost.

All heads at the table turned to watch Sophie, in utter silence.

"Dearest, are you okay?" the lovely older female voice sang from the kitchen.

The entire room was silent. Tension filled the spaces between them all.

Sophie quickly moved to help Regin's father clean up the mess. She didn't know what else to do. She bent low, picking up the broken ceramic shards before nabbing a plate from where Cam sat, shovelling the roast back onto it.

The older female moved swiftly from the kitchen, towelling off her hands. She froze as soon as she beheld Sophie, crouched on the floor.

She let out an audible gasp.

Regin's father was still frozen in place, staring wide eyed at Sophie.

"Sofreya..." the woman whispered, recognition plastered across her face.

Sophie gulped.

48

"How can this be, child?" Regin's mother gasped, moving closer to Sophie, reaching out a hand as if she were a mirage. Regin's mother was petite, just a touch taller than Sophie and her energy, it felt strong. She had silver hair with piercing blue eyes and the pale blue dress she wore only complimented her features further.

"How do you mean?" Sophie stood up from her crouch, confused.

Sophie looked back at Regin's father who had tears in his eyes.

Regin's mother's voice caught, as if she were on the verge of tears as well. "We thought we'd never see you again, and yet you are here, in the flesh at our table." She moved to her husband whose tears now flowed freely. She consoled him by holding him close as he cried. He watched Sophie as if she were his most prized possession, like something he never thought he'd see again. "You must excuse Alston, he gets rather emotional. He cannot speak, you see." Regin's mother chided.

Alston, as Sophie just learned, pulled her into the biggest hug she ever had, sobbing. Sophie's mana brushed against his. *Family*, it seemed to say. Sophie gasped. The feel of crying stuck right in her throat.

Alston pulled away from the hug, grabbing Sophie's cheeks between his hands. He shook his head in disbelief. Smiling and crying, he looked up to the heavens as if they'd just answered his long-unanswered prayers. Sophie couldn't help it then. Tears flowed freely from her eyes, running down her cheeks. She hugged Alston tighter.

"You may call me Aunt Alfre. This is your Uncle Alston. And that"—she pointed with tears still in her eyes straight to Regin who sat with his mouth open like a fish—"is your cousin Regin. Welcome home." The older female laughed.

Sophie swung her head back to the crew she'd forgotten were sitting at the dining table behind her. Colour had drained from all their faces. Cam had a piece of roast hanging halfway out of his mouth – a piece he'd surely just picked up from the floor. Elowan looked like she was going to be sick, and Zala just sat there with her brows furrowed, as if she were solving a difficult math equation.

"Come, my child. Let's eat. You can tell us of your journey." Alfre guided Sophie back to her seat, resting a comforting hand on her upper back.

Zala stood up with such swiftness she almost knocked her seat over. The sudden jerking movement was so unlike the wraith that it caught everyone's attention. Zala's eyes were wide as the beheld Sophie in her full fae form. In a shaky, low voice "Sofreya Brighid Taliesin..." Zala gasped, taking a step closer to Sophie. "Daughter to the former right hand of King Gydeon. The princess who never was." The wraith placed a hand across her heart and dipped her head low. A sign of respect.

Sophie was lost for words.

The combination of words and underlying tone of realisation that layered Zala's words made absolutely no sense. Princess? Former right hand?

Cam had completely choked on his food while Elowan dropped the cutlery she had ready in her hands. Sophie thought it would be impossible but somehow, Regin paled even further.

The dinner was awkward at first.

Alston ebbed and flowed between sobbing and signing stories. Aunt Alfre interpreted all his signs for the room to hear. They spoke animatedly about Sophie's father. It turned out that Sophie's father was Alston's younger brother. They grew up right here in Faery, in Soxis. Her father was the right-hand man of the king and his best friend was King Gydeon Taranis. It made sense that Kaine and Sophie were the best of friends as kids. Their fathers were best friends.

Alston continued doting on his younger brother. With a wide smile, Alston mentioned how her father was loved and cherished by the people of Faery, and because of how the prince and Sophie were attached at the hip, the people of

Faery coined her the princess. Sophie was no princess by birthright, but the people of Faery adored her as such.

Alston spoke of Sophie's mother, Danna. Of how she one day appeared as if from a portal – no doubt the portal in Melbourne, Sophie thought – and how she turned Sophie's father, an elite fae warrior, into putty. She teared up at the mention of her mother. She missed her so much.

Alston then spoke of his time in service to Queen Calliea. An act of treason had resulted in his tongue being cut off. The queen had deemed his mana too valuable to be thwarted, so she cut off his tongue so he could never speak again. When Sophie asked what degree of treason he committed to warrant such a punishment, he hesitated.

Alfre looked down at her empty plate sadly. Tears shining in her eyes again as she looked up at Sophie.

"It's quite a heavy subject to have over dinner. Perhaps you can ask your mother the next time you see her. She will tell you the full story," Alfre said quietly, gripping her husband's arm in comfort. Sophie felt such a melting pot of emotions. She felt hurt that her mother and father had hidden this whole life from her. Perhaps it was out of protection but that still didn't excuse the lies. On top of the hurt was relief. Relief and happiness in finding her family. It finally felt like she belonged somewhere. In Sotera, she felt so alone. Sure, she had her mother, but she didn't have an extended family. She was so envious of all the kids that talked about their loving cousins, aunties and uncles. She never had that and now she knew why – they were in a completely different realm.

Sophie pondered on that. Her mother had always been inclined to Faery stories and always had a magical air about her. It made sense that she'd lived and thrived in Faery but her father, Jim the computer sales guy? Really? He didn't give brooding warrior energy at all. If anything, all he gave was a distant-parent-with-an-avoidant-attachment-style kind of energy. Sophie struggled to put two and two together.

"I guess I'll have to interrogate my parents when I finish saving this realm." Sophie laughed, a little nervously.

Alston and Alfre looked at one another confused. Alfre tightened her grip on Alston's arm again.

"Child, we are a little confused. You said parents," Alfre said quietly, leaning in a little closer to Sophie, a wash of concern plastered across her face.

"Oh, yes sorry, my mother and father," Sophie clarified, thinking they'd misunderstood or had never heard the term 'parents' before.

Alston and Alfre shared the same concerned look again. They were like each other's mirror and sure enough, Sophie spotted the matching tattoos that splayed across their upper arms.

"Okay, now I'm confused." Sophie looked between the two.

Alfre responded. "Just hang on a second, my dear. We've something to show you." The female excused herself from the dining table.

Sophie surveyed the room. A thin layer of sadness had washed over everyone. It felt like they all knew something that Sophie didn't. The feeling made her uneasy as she waited for Aunt Alfre to return.

Not a moment later, the older female returned. In her hands was a small wooden box, roughly the size of her palm. Carved on the lid was a flaming heart and next to it, a sleeping sun. All the elements of mana danced around the two symbols in various swirls. Sophie appreciated the craftsmanship.

Alfre gently placed the box in Sophie's hands. Sophie was unsure if she wanted to open the box at all. Something like dread and anticipation sat heavy in her chest.

Slowly, Sophie opened it to find faded pictures. She almost choked as tears began to spill uncontrollably.

It was a picture of her mother, heavily pregnant. Her silver hair spilled like a waterfall all around her. Her golden eyes were bright and a silly grin was plastered across her face. Her pointed ears were decorated with various gold earrings. She sat in the middle of a colourful flowerbed and her hand was outstretched as if asking the person behind the camera to come join her.

Sophie trailed her fingers across the picture. Her mother was breathtaking, and most certainly she was fae. While that answered her heritage and explained away Sophie's transformation, it didn't explain the secrecy that shrouded her life.

Sophie pulled out the second photo from behind the first. Stunned. Sophie just stared and stared at the photo.

Who she saw was not her father. It was the silver-haired male that watched her name her draekin. He was the male that taught Astraea how to fly. Sophie's stomach lurched.

The tall fae male soldier with silver hair smiled brightly. His arms were wrapped around Danna's and his large hands rested on her swollen belly. His chin rested neatly in the space between her mother's shoulder and neck. They looked so happy. They looked so in love. She stared at the silver-haired male that she'd once dreamt of. Purple eyes stared right back.

This male right here, was her true father. She knew it. She felt it deep in her heart. They even shared the same face shape. Tears streamed down Sophie's face. She mourned the father she never knew and the mortal father she had known. Her heart ached terribly. Silently and painfully, she cried.

Sophie peered up through her tears at her Uncle Alston, whose tears started up again. The sadness that showed on his face only meant one thing.

"How did he...?" Sophie couldn't finish her question.

"He died protecting you." Alfre began to cry. Sophie remembered then. The silent dream she had when she first arrived here in Faery. The dream that left her throat raw. It was of a silver-haired guard, her father, holding back Kaine while she was taken away by a female with silver hair... her mother. They were escaping, Sophie realised.

"From what?" Sophie sniffled. She looked back down at the two pocket-sized photos.

"From Queen Calliea," Regin interjected rather grimly from the other side of the table. It seemed like he unravelled the mystery while he quietly listened to the stories his mother and father told. The entire room turned their attention to Regin.

"The prophecy," Sophie finished off. Her hands shook violently. The queen had tried to kill her and Kaine when they were children, but they'd managed to escape, well at least Sophie did. And the queen had been waiting patiently, like the viper that she was, for almost twenty years to finish the job.

For more than twenty years, the queen had been scheming, making sacrifices to Terr, King of the Shadow Realm, to fortify her empire while waiting for Sophie to return. She would have built enough power to kill both Kaine and Sophie, circumventing the very fabric of the Fates, rendering the prophecy moot. The realisation sickened Sophie to the core. She'd unwittingly played into the queen's game. And right now, the queen was winning.

It was all too much.

Sophie threw the photos back in the wooden box, slammed it shut and ran out the back door.

49

S ophie practised deep breaths.

The catastrophe of emotions she felt in this given time was difficult to control. She felt angry at her mother most of all for spinning this cobweb of lies or omission of truth. Sophie already had enough trouble trusting people, she didn't expect lies to come from the one person she depended upon – her mother.

By that same token, she knew her mother. Her mother was always kind, always loving and she was always there for Sophie. For whatever reason, her mother thought it best that she did not know her true heritage and what role she played in the fate of another realm. To be honest, had Sophie known, she would've been more prepared. The omission of truth did not do her any favours, it only placated her mother's guilt or warped thinking of "what was best".

Perhaps shielding the truth from a younger child would make sense to some degree. Perhaps her not knowing would tie up any loose ends that her mother was trying to hide. But not telling your fully grown daughter who her real father was and where she came from... It felt like a huge blow to her identity. She didn't know who she was anymore. She didn't know what was real and what was a lie. Most of all, she felt disappointed in herself, for not knowing and not picking any clues up. But how could she have known? The façade her mother painted was the only truth she'd known.

Sophie wiped a tear from her cheeks as her chest ached painfully. How could she ever trust again?

Sophie sat at the back of the property, on a log watching fireflies go about their business. The scene was enchanting and provided her respite from the turmoil she felt within. The cool refreshing night air that washed over her skin helped too.

She heard soft footsteps approach her.

"Do you mind if I sit with you?" Aunt Alfre softly asked.

Sophie shook her head, sniffling and wiping the tears from her face. Gods, she probably looked like an outright mess.

Sophie avoided eye contact. She felt so raw and vulnerable.

"I understand that you are upset. Elowan told me of your other father." Alfre rested her delicate hand on Sophie's arm in comfort. Sophie appreciated it but it didn't stop the pain in her heart. She smiled softly in thanks. "People tell lies for all sorts of reasons, child. To protect themselves or, seemingly, the people that they love – mostly out of fear for what that person may feel as a consequence of knowing the truth." Alfre let go of her hand and joined Sophie in watching the fireflies dance. "Parents especially are guilty of it. I know I am." Alfre laughed.

Sophie scoffed. A tear spilled down her cheek. Her aunt was beautiful. It was as if she glowed with the fireflies.

"Your mother is a kind female. She always gave and expected nothing back. During her time here, she was fierce and most of all she loved you and your father, Lou. There was nothing that could stand between her and her family, even the gods themselves," Alfre said distantly as if recalling events from the past. She smiled sweetly. "I could swear it upon my life that she would never purposefully hurt you."

Sophie sniffed through the tears again. "I know…" Sophie cleared her throat. "But it doesn't dull the pain I feel here." She pointed to her heart. "My mother has always played the strong female lead in my life but sometimes I forget that heroes have weaknesses. They're just like you and me, they're human – figuratively anyway. People make mistakes and despite what everyone thinks, everyone is still trying to figure it out for themselves. So I understand her intentions, even if my heart aches from the thought of her unintended betrayal." Sophie smiled softly to herself.

Alfre pulled Sophie into her side, squeezing her shoulders as she did.

"You are definitely your father's daughter. Full of wisdom beyond your years." Alfre laughed.

The words singed all the softest parts of Sophie's heart.

Together, Ellie, Cam, Zala and Sophie sat by the fire with spiced hot cocoa in their hands, discussing the plan they'd pulled together to free Kaine. Ellie sourced random rocks, sticks and pieces of string to create a makeshift map representing the layout of Castle Terrin and the queen's quarters. She ran them through the plan twice. Cam for once stayed silent, listening intently. By to-morrow evening they'd have infiltrated the walls of Castle Terrin with the help of an inside contact and would come out unscathed with one more member in their midst: Kaine. Until then, they needed to rest, and Sophie needed to learn a few tricks from the shadow master herself, Zala.

As the night grew to an end, everyone had peeled off to their rooms to sleep except for Sophie. Her eyes were raw from crying and anxiety lay in her belly like a crazed cat. The last thing she wanted right now was to be asleep. Who knows what kind of nightmares she'd dream up in this state? Sophie helped herself to another serve of spiced cocoa before sitting herself in front of the fireplace again. It was deliciously warm and the smell of burning wood soothed her soul.

Soft footfalls approached her from the hallway.

"Apologies, Sofreya. We'd wanted to speak to you in private." Alfre's tender voice warmed the room. Next to her stood Alston, with a slight sheepish smile on his face.

Sophie nodded to the space beside her on the couch.

They sat beside her, cautious, as if not truly comprehending how Alston's younger brother's daughter was here and alive, when for twenty years they'd lost all hope.

Alston placed a small, weighted item wrapped in black cloth into Sophie's hands. The weight of it felt familiar.

He nodded, urging her to unwrap it.

And so she did. She let out a small gasp.

"It was your father's," Alfre explained.

Tears threatened to well in Sophie's eyes again. It was the twin blade to the one she currently had strapped to her thigh. The handle was shaped like a sea-serpent's tail ending in a circle she could loop her finger through. It was light and perfectly balanced. It wasn't a Scyllen knife at all, they were her father's knives.

But why did the Scyllen have one of his knives?

At the thought, Sophie pulled out the twin blade that was strapped to her thigh, showing Alston how they matched. "This was gifted to me by the Scyllen," Sophie offered.

Surprise shone across his face. He signed as Alfre interpreted.

"He thought he'd never see the matching blade to his brother's most favoured one. It's been more than twenty years since he has seen it." Alston laughed with fondness in his eyes. Alfre smiled with him. "It is a story that Faery would remember for a long while," she continued.

Alston told Sophie the story of how his younger brother, Lou Taliesin, had a death wish. They'd gone on a fishing weekend when Lou spotted a Scyllen caught in an iron net. The Scyllen back then were less picky and more blood-thirsty. Lou felt sorry for the creature and did what no sane immortal would do. He dived in the deep dark waters of Faery, headfirst to free the shrieking Scyllen with his favourite throwing knives. The Scyllen he saved coincidentally was the leader of the sea creatures. He had gifted one of his knives to them, so that if they ever found themselves in the situation again, they'd be able to free themselves. From that day onwards, the Scyllen had sworn off harmless fae who travelled the waters of Faery. Though with Lou's death, the Scyllen had resumed their normal bloodthirsty habits. It was a momentous time of harmony between the sea-fae and land-fae.

Sophie marvelled at the blades and the story her uncle Alston had told her of her father.

"Thank you." Sophie smiled. She was grateful, not just for the blades but the stories that helped her know her father, who he was and what he stood for. She'd been carrying around a piece of her father this whole time. The realisation warmed her heart. It was like he was protecting her. Even in death, he was there. Sophie pulled her uncle into a hug, the closest thing to her real father she'd ever known. This was her family. Her blood. And slowly, the emptiness she'd felt throughout her life started to fill. Her heart started to heal.

50

"You might want to try a little harder," Zala teased.

Sophie scoffed, sweat dripped down her back and furiously across her forehead. They'd been up since dawn, practising portal creation while Cam and Ellie prepped their weapons for their rescue mission tonight.

"You don't think I'm trying?" Sophie gritted through her teeth. The autumn sun beat down on her cheeks. Zala had coached her on how to create portals. It wasn't as simple as going from point A to point B. Opening portals required you to go through layers of time and space. Despite it looking like a straight line, it involved a lot of twists and turns, most of which weren't too harmful but if you didn't get the maths quite right you could end up somewhere that meant your death. It required skill, finesse and mental agility and at this moment, time wasn't on their side.

"Visualise point A. Visualise point B. Traverse the between with your mana. Once the path is confirmed, lock in point A then point B." Zala explained it as if it were the alphabet. Inclined to shadow use, Zala was the master of creating portals.

They'd learned from one of Elowan's contacts that the queen had spelled all entrances with the group's blood and essence, including Sophie's from when she was a human. They would have been stuck out of options if Sophie didn't point out that she was now fae, in blood and in essence. It meant Sophie was their in.

Sophie delved deep into her new mana. It felt so much larger than the mana she had while being utterly human. It was like a beast that had finally woken from a century-long sleep. Her mana now felt ancient and unruly.

Sophie got as far as traversing the between with her mana, similarly to how she used her mana to feel things in the distance, but as soon as she tried to lock point A and point B with a shot of her mana, she'd accidentally send a fireball down range. Despite having a bit of control of her mana in the dungeons, it felt like she'd regressed entirely. It felt like her mana was too much. That it was completely off balance.

Of course it was. It was a *strong power, one that you will one day share together.* Sophie's newfound power was meant to be shared with Kaine. And right now, it overwhelmed her.

Despite the overwhelming feeling, Sophie kept trying to lock in her points of contact. She was certain that Regin and his family wouldn't appreciate the random holes that had burned through the fencing around their property.

"I don't get it. I can FEEL the path. I KNOW which path to take but each time I reach down to my mana, I keep pulling up fire." Sophie waved her hands in the air dramatically. Time wasn't on their side at all. It made her all the more frustrated.

Zala however, was as calm as ever. "Keep trying. You're too slow."

Sophie grinded her teeth. *Slow?! I'll show you slow.* Sophie groaned out loud, letting Zala know exactly how she felt about her rather unhelpful advice.

Sophie closed her eyes and breathed in deeply. She pinpointed point A. *Faster.* She sprinted through the between with her mana. *Faster, Sophie.* She then jumped through point B. *You've got this, Sophie.* With a swirl of her hand, she viciously locked both points in.

A slow clap sounded from where Zala stood. "Well done." The wraith smiled.

Sophie opened her eyes. In front of her, two large black portals swirled, bright and fiery.

"Now test it," Zala ordered.

"What?" Sophie stuttered.

"You made it. Now see if you've done it correctly." Zala motioned to the two portals. What could go wrong, right?

"Okay, well, let everyone know that I love them, will you?" Sophie shrugged her shoulders and sprinted through the portal on the left. The ground felt soft and gritty like the portals she'd gone through the first time she arrived in Faery.

She saw a patch of light seep through the glittery matter of the portal. She gunned for it, landing gracefully on her feet in front of the second portal. "Fuck yes!" Sophie whooped, doing a little happy dance. She'd finally done it. It took her several hours, but she'd done it! It wasn't a massive portal jump, but it was something. She understood the basics, now all she had to do was push her mana to the next level. She needed to get it down to a precise magic before they set off for their rescue mission.

"I'm impressed." Zala smiled. "It took me weeks to get as far as you did in two hours."

Sophie blushed, unsure how to take the compliment. Then she paused. "Hang on, if I hadn't set that up correctly, what would've happened?" Sophie was unsure if she actually wanted to know.

"You would have been lost in the Between and your soul would have perished," Zala said a little too seriously as she made her way towards the water pitcher they'd set up for their training.

"Zala, you heathen!" Sophie's sputtered.

"You would've been fine. I knew you were close to getting it right." Zala laughed.

"Gee, well that makes me feel a thousand times better. Thanks!" Sophie drawled sarcastically, reaching for a cup of water.

They stayed in the paddock until Sophie had her portal manifesting down pat with little effort. Each time she tried, she became faster and more agile. The distance between each portal grew even larger. By the end of their fourth hour, Sophie had built her portals strong enough to travel with Zala. It would be enough for their plans tonight. Sophie just hoped she didn't get performance anxiety.

"You ready to rock'n'roll, Princess?" Cam swung his arm around Sophie's shoulders.

Sophie let out a disgusted noise. "Ugh, please don't call me that." She softly pushed him off her.

"Whatever you say, Princess." Cam smirked at her. If they weren't about to step off for a rescue mission, Sophie would've started a brawl with the red-haired pain in her behind. Cam was like a brother she never had or rather... the brother she never asked for.

Their light pack of supplies were prepped, and their weapons had been sharpened and oiled with the help of Regin and his family.

Elowan, Zala and Cam had all donned their dark fighting leathers which made Sophie feel so out of place in her peasant blouse and breaches.

"You can't go on a mission dressed like that, cousin." Regin laughed from behind where Sophie secured their horses.

"Well I don't have a choice, do I?"

"You do. Come with me." Regin smiled. Ellie nodded at her soulmate as they walked by the crew, towards the shed at the back of the cottage. Regin led her towards the back of the work shed. The furnace near the centre burned hot. "It's not my finest work nor will it fit well, but it'll help in any case." Regin gestured to a bust that donned a small breastplate, roughly the size of Sophie. Engraved in the centre of it was a flaming heart, and underneath, the face of a sleeping sun, just like how it was etched on top of the keepsake box Uncle Alston had.

"How did you even make this? I've only been here for what... twenty-four hours." Sophie gasped. The breastplate was remarkable display of craftsmanship. It was entirely dark black. Small gold flaming-heart-shaped clasps were emblazoned on each shoulder, and the neckline was high enough to protect the softer bits of her throat. It was stunning.

"It was an old set that my mother had. I made a few quick tweaks, so it didn't take me long at all." Regin smiled.

"Oh, I can't."

"You can and you will." Regin moved to grab a fighting suit like the one Elowan had on. "Put this on." Sophie obeyed. Walking to the other side of the shed, she quickly donned the suit. Moulding against her body, the material was soft, supple and flexible, perfect for fighting. It felt like a second skin, though the sleeves and legs were a little too long. Sophie quickly rolled the extra material up. "It might be a little long on you," Regin explained in the distance while putting away tools, "but it should suffice."

I guess my assassin queen dreams are coming true with this kind of suit. Hot damn! Sophie marvelled at the feel of it. She definitely felt like a badass in it.

Regin removed the small breastplate he'd made from the bust. "My father is a proud man and to this day he still holds much guilt." Sophie listened carefully as she slipped on the breastplate, sliding her arms through the arm holes and fastening it against her chest with the clips on her shoulders and sides. "He warned your father and mother of the queen's plans to kill you and the heir. It cost him his tongue and a life of guilt knowing that his dearest brother died while he lived." Sadness washed over his words. "I've tried to convince him many a time that the queen would have had her way regardless. If it wasn't then, it would have been later. Still, he thinks he is the cause of my uncle's death..." Regin trailed off.

Sophie's heart ached for her uncle. Imagine warning your brother then to have his death thrown back into your face? Regin was right. The queen would have had her way in any case. Her father's death was as much her uncle's fault as it was her own. That was the plain truth.

Regin walked up to Sophie who'd just secured the breastplate across her torso. He placed his large hands on her shoulders and bent down to her level. "So give that bitch hell." Tears welled in his light purple eyes. "For our family."

"I will, cousin." Sophie smiled. "And thank you for this." She motioned to her beautifully crafted breastplate. Sophie gave her cousin a tight hug before padding back to the group.

"May the gods guide you!" Regin called from behind her.

"To where I'm destined to be!" Sophie smiled brightly.

A new sense of purpose filled her entire being. She'd kill the queen all right. She'd stop the blood reign with her bare hands, not just for herself and her friends, but for her family. Her uncle. Her father. Everyone.

The queen would fucking pay.

51

*K*aine heard Sophie's sweet giggling emanating from their cottage home. He smiled at the sound. He'd just been at the markets where he picked up a bouquet of vibrant sunflowers that reminded him so much of her. Eager to see Sophie's bright smile, he burst through the front door with the bouquet hidden behind his back.

"My sweet, I'm home!" he called out, knocking off his boots by the door. He quickly padded to the bedroom where Sophie was most likely resting after a long day in the gardens.

Soft whispers sounded from the bedroom.

She wasn't alone.

Kaine's heart stopped.

He twisted the door open to find Sophie laying on her back, knees bent and Cam's muscular body lying in between, surely buried deep inside her.

The pair gasped in surprise.

Kaine saw red and charged for the fae male that lay between his beloved's thighs, dropping the bouquet of sunflowers entirely.

Before he reached the wretched red-headed male a sharp burning pain lanced across his pectoral...

Kaine came awake with a start, panting and filled entirely with rage.

It was just a dream. It was not real. Sophie would never. He continued to repeat to himself until his heart calmed.

He had been held captive in the queen's personal quarters for weeks now. Meals were served irregularly and only when he pleased the queen in whatever game she wanted to play for the day. There were no windows, so he couldn't tell when the sun rose or set. Despite the queen's ministrations and the hunger and thirst that derailed his entire being, Kaine did not lose hope. Hope that his love and light had made it home to Sotera where she was safe, and that somehow, someone would help free him.

The queen's personal quarters were dark, lit by varying candles and decorated with red regal furniture. Kaine couldn't see much from where he was restrained, up against the wall, opposite the queen's bed so she could watch him while she lay. His wrists and ankles were shackled tight up against the wall, his entire body forming the shape of an X.

The queen laughed as she pulled her red spindly nails out of Kaine's chest. Blood trickled down in small rivulets.

"Your soulmate is nothing but a whore, isn't she?" The queen laughed.

If Kaine's mouth wasn't stuffed with cloth, he would've told the queen to shove her silly efforts where the sun didn't shine. He'd already tried it, and it didn't end well for him. He'd spent several days without food and water while the queen fed him hallucination after hallucination. As each day passed, he struggled to differentiate between reality and illusion. His only way out was compliance.

His head heavy with sweat and body itching with scabs, he nodded weakly.

Queen Calliea ripped out the cloth from his mouth.

"I want you to say it." She sneered, her yellow-gold eyes bore into his. Waiting.

He wouldn't. He couldn't say it out loud. It would make it real if he did. He wouldn't give in. He'd nod and shake his head as the queen needed, but he would never say it all out loud.

Queen Calliea bared her teeth with the viciousness of a hellhound. Reeling back her hand she gave Kaine a violent backhand, knocking some of his teeth loose.

"It seems like you don't agree with your queen today." She smiled when he did not answer or move. She stuck her blood-red nails in his chest again to get his attention.

Slowly and begrudgingly, he obeyed. He learned that command within a few days. It was the queen's way of getting him to look at her if he didn't obey.

"Then go to sleep." The queen cackled, retracting her nails to place her hands by Kaine's temples.

No, no, no, anything but sleep! Kaine wanted to scream but he couldn't. He thrashed against his restraints. His throat was painfully raw, and the cloth that the queen had stuffed back in his mouth made it difficult to breathe.

Upon his capture, Kaine quickly learned that there was something worse than physical, brutal torture. There was sleep. Nightmarish events unfolded and he could never tell if they were real or fake. He could never control them. He was completely helpless. He'd rather be castrated several times over before falling asleep to the queen's hallucinations.

Dark glitter danced in his vision.

"Sleep, my pretty prince," the queen whispered.

An Atarangi demon from the Shadow Realm hissed at the sight of Kaine's mutilated body hanging on the wall. The bright red portal it stood in front of was such a contrast to its blue scaled skin and fluorescent yellow eyes. Standing at eight feet tall, it towered over Queen Calliea, especially with the dark blue horns sticking out from its forehead.

"To what do I owe the pleasure? Perhaps my elixirs are ready? My crows feet are starting to set in..." Queen Calliea smiled sweetly, smoothing out her dress, then sinfully at Kaine's body noticing the demon's line of sight. Kaine thrashed about as he faced his worst nightmares in a state of limbo. There was something so satisfying about watching what the Fates had deemed as your end, losing his mind. There was such clarity and control that she gained from watching Kaine suffer by her hands.

The demon sniffed in the direction of Kaine's brutalised body, crossing its arms in disgust. "Master requires more blood each time he creates them for you." The Atarangi demon spat on the floor. "The quality of blood you've provided has been poor. Master has communicated as such. Much younger it needs to be." The demon ground its jaw as if it already had this conversation a thousand times with the queen.

"Well, if he wants my throne... he'd better hurry up. Am I not right?" Queen Calliea glided over to the Shadow Realm demon, daring to rake a finger over its blue skin.

The demon bared its teeth at the touch. Swiftly, it swatted the queen's curious fingers away. Motioning towards Kaine's barely lucid form, it grumbled, "Have you found his wench yet?"

"Not yet, but I've laid the necessary traps. She will be here in due course," the queen quickly responded. "And if my plans go accordingly, he will kill her himself." She smiled, proud of the leagues she'd gained over the past few weeks. Queen Calliea tried to turn his love into hate but when his willpower proved too strong, she realised she needed to pivot. The idea came to her in the middle of the night. She would let them love each other. Let them think they were reunited by the Fates and while the wench slept peacefully, she would be none the wiser of the viper that lay in her bed. She'd die by the hands of her mate and that was a bloody poetic justice Queen Calliea thrived on. There was one thing she loved more than watching her enemies die, it was watching her enemies fall for the traps she'd meticulously laid out, suffering for all eternity by their own actions. Feeding on their entrails came a close second. It was what they truly deserved.

The demon nodded swiftly, it's face scrunched in utter disgust. "Master awaits his Faery throne. Nothing is to stand in his way." The demon snarled.

"*Our* way," Queen Calliea corrected the demon.

The demon's hand twitched as if it were about to backhand her into the Shadow Realm. "Our way," the demon agreed.

A soft, triumphant smirk appeared across Queen Calliea's face.

"What have I done?!" Kaine bellowed.

His beautiful mother's body lay in a giant pool of blood. Her eyes turned milky white and stared blankly into the sky above. He held her tightly as the knife in his hand glistened with her still-warm blood.

He began to blubber. Was he the reason his mother died? Was he the cause? Where were the hellhounds? This was not how his mother died, or was it? There was no denying the truth that lay in front of him. He'd killed his mother, if not by the dagger in his hand, then by his inaction.

Her blood turned the forest floor grey, sucking the life out of the trees it touched.

Kaine dropped the knife and stood quickly, watching Faery, his beloved home and land, turn black with rapid decay.

No, no, no. Not Faery. He needed to stop the blight. How was he going to do that?

Kaine ran through the forest, looking for the answers. Panting. He knew it was here somewhere. He'd searched this forest a million times. He felt like he'd killed his mother a million times. And Sophie. And Elowan. And Zala. And Cam. He'd lived this dream over and over, for what felt like centuries. Each day it would be someone different. Someone he loved. After he killed them, he would run into the endless forest for an answer he could never find. An answer that would stop the endless killing. An answer to stop him feeling altogether. Where is it? Where's the answer?

"One life for many..." a soft feminine voice echoed through the forest.

Darting his head around, Kaine ran towards the source of the voice. Deeper into the forest.

"MAKE IT STOP!" Kaine's head hurt so much. His heart had bled like it had never bled before and he'd had enough. He would do anything to get out of this personal hell. Anything. He clutched his head and screamed until his throat was raw. He bent over, punching his own head violently to make it all go away.

When self-harm proved futile, he sank to his knees. "Please... make it stop..." he sobbed.

A ghostly wind caressed his cheek in triumph.

52

Z ala moved quickly and quietly towards a small building beside Castle Terrin. Sophie stuck closely behind the wraith, steeling her body, conscious
of making any sounds.

Zala knocked quietly. Two quick knocks. A pause. Then a final knock.

On bated breath, they waited.

The door before them, heavy, groaned awake to reveal an older fae female,
whose full form almost filled the frame.

It was Sophie who broke first. "You're..." Sophie couldn't finish the words
that formed in her mouth. She knew the woman who stood before her. She was
the cloaked figure in the dungeon. The one that slid that life-saving parchment
and warm rolls of bread into Kaine's cell. If it wasn't for her...

Sophie threw herself onto Felipina, embracing the woman who had saved her
and Kaine's lives. Felipina let out a small chuckle. "It's lovely to finally meet you,
Sophie." She braced two firm hands on Sophie's arms. "Come inside. We've got
to get you moving."

Zala waltzed into Felipina's office first, scanning the room for anything amiss.

Sophie didn't even have a moment to think for herself as Felipina dragged her
across the scroll-filled office. A vase of wilting blue hydrangeas sat sadly on her
desk.

"Put this on." She handed Sophie a dark purple cloak. "And pull your hair
back as much as you can." Sophie obeyed. "All my assistants wear these cloaks.
Dark purple. For staff," Felipina explained. She was calm. Focused. Determined
even.

Sophie paused as she pulled her hair back, fastening it with a hair tie Zala had
given her. "Why are you helping us?"

Felipina paused. Taking in a deep breath, she took a step closer to Sophie and held her stare. The lines of Felipina's face showed wisdom and grace. Her eyes shone with something like guilt, but pulling everything together was kindness and sorrow.

Sophie gulped.

"Some call it redemption. Others, desperation." She took Sophie's hand in hers. "I call it revenge."

Sophie wondered what those words meant. She wanted to ask, but simply put, they did not have the time.

Felipina gave Sophie an approving once-over and pulled the dark hood over Sophie's head. "I've one thing to handle before I meet you in there." With grace, Felipina moved to the desk to retrieve a small golden brooch. It was a bouquet of hydrangeas with tiny blue gemstones. She moved to fasten it on Sophie's dark purple cloak and in a low, hope-filled voice, Felipina bid Sophie and Zala luck – the fae way. "May the gods guide you."

"To where I'm destined to be," Sophie and Zala responded quietly.

With a curt nod, Zala moved across the room, opening the door just enough for them to pass through. Sophie moved quickly, tightening the hood of her cloak to cover more of her face.

They moved swiftly as two shadows to another side entrance, the one they marked as the closest to the queen's quarters. Under her breath Zala explained, "Felipina lost her son many years ago. He was one of the first promised children."

An ache started in Sophie's throat. She knew exactly what that meant.

"Remind me to wallop Kaine's ass when we get out of here," Ellie whispered, back to back with Cam. Both were poised for a fight with their short spears in hand.

"Remind me to join you. I'll bring my favourite throwing knives." Cam laughed, focused on the twenty guards that circled them in Castle Terrin's main courtyard. The stench of white roses filled their nostrils to a dizzying degree.

The moment the pair stepped onto Castle Terrin soil, the queen's royal guards had descended upon them, confirming their suspicions. The queen had somehow obtained their essence or blood, binding it with an ancient fae spell that would notify the queen of their presence. Ellie and Cam waited patiently for the courtyard to fill with more and more royal guards looking to capture or kill them. Despite being stupidly outnumbered, Ellie and Cam did not quake in fear. In fact, this was just an appetiser, a distraction.

"Just a few more..." Ellie smirked.

"Oh, this is the most fun I've had in a while." Cam laughed lowly.

There was one distinguishing feature that separated the Elite from the royal guards. Their mana.

Elowan jumped into action, sending out a wall of fire blinding and burning the circle of guards that surrounded them. The yin to Ellie's yang, Cam's sent rocks catapulting down on the guards that writhed in pain. They both launched themselves into a thrall of writhing and screaming guards – slicing, kicking, punching and ducking with fae swagger.

A royal guard threw his short spear, aiming true for the back of Cam's neck. Ellie round-housed it away before it got any closer and flamed the guard in the face where he stood.

Cam ducked swiftly, sending a guard right on his back.

The majority of the guards had fallen with their initial mana attack and only the stronger ones remained.

Ellie gulped as she was cornered by three giant fae males. Cam had his hands full fighting off another team of royal guards. Despite the number of guards already downed, the group kept replenishing. How were the royal guards still sending in back up? Surely the queen didn't have that many in her ranks.

"Clear the way!" the guards screamed as they ran through the hallways of Castle Terrin. Sophie had just left Zala at their rendezvous point beside the castle. Should anything go wrong, it was where she needed to run back to. It was where Zala would portal them back to Fyllera.

Sophie pulled herself hard up against the wall, dressed as Felipina's assistant. She wore the dark purple cloak with the hood fastened around her head, the golden brooch sparkling in the dim hallway lights.

"There you are. Come with me," Felipina said confidently, like a head of staff should. Quickly, the female pulled Sophie with her as they sped down the hall. The queen's quarters was just a turn away.

Last night, when Sophie asked why they couldn't just portal into the queen's chambers, grab Kaine and pop back out, they'd collectively laughed at her. It turned out that with portalling, you had to have visited the place or at least know in detail what the place you were portalling to looked like. It made sense. If you forged the incorrect pathway between point A and point B, you'd end up a ghost in the Between. Sophie couldn't imagine what that torturous consequence would feel like, let alone the consequence of getting point B wrong. It was why they needed an insider, in this case Felipina, to guide Sophie there. Zala couldn't step foot in the castle itself unless they wanted the queen's eyes on Sophie. Zala's blood was bound along with Ellie's and Cam's into the ancient fae triggers Queen Calliea had laid down. And given the rescue mission they were on, they needed the queen's focus to be elsewhere. Thankfully, Elowan and Cam volunteered to be that distraction.

Grinding to a halt and with centuries worth of grace, Felipina pulled out her ring of keys and knew exactly which one she was after. With a click, the door to the queen's private quarters slowly swung open.

"Quickly, my dear." Felipina all but shoved Sophie inside. "Captain Aaryn needs you. I'll keep watch."

With that, the door slammed shut.

The antechamber was lined with red velvet chaises and various-sized portraits of the queen.

Gees, talk about being full of yourself. Sophie scoffed at the outright vainness. The queen literally had a whole room filled with art... of herself.

Moving quickly, Sophie worked through each room searching for any sign of her beloved. Panic set in when she approached the last door. She couldn't hear anything or feel anything.

Quickly she opened the room to the queen's bedroom chamber.

Please be okay. Sophie repeated to herself.

No amount of time, patience or exposure could have prepared Sophie for what she saw in front of her.

Kaine was chained up and elevated off the floor in an X shape. He was much thinner than the last time she saw him. His skin was pale and sweaty. Scabs of various sizes, that hadn't quite healed, oozing infection, scoured every part of his body. His body wasn't repairing. The queen must have injected something into his blood to stop him from healing. Iron, perhaps. His head hung limp between his shoulders, but his eyes moved rapidly beneath his closed eyelids.

Alive. He was alive.

Sophie let out a sob as she rushed to her soulmate and brushed his long inky hair out of his face. "Kaine. Wake up. Please." She shook him, but he did not respond.

Fuck. How am I going to carry him?

She had to keep moving. She surveyed the chains he was in. She could melt them, but they were awfully snug around his joints. There was no way that she'd be able to free him without burning him a little.

"I'm so sorry." Sophie whispered. She didn't really have a choice at this point. Making quick work of it, she freed his feet first, propping them solidly on the ground. She hissed at the scabs and wounds that reopened with the movement.

She then made way to one of his wrists, but they were way above her head. She needed a boost to get up there. Quickly pulling a chair from across the room, she lifted herself up and slowly melted the chain that left his wrist raw. She tried her best not to touch his skin with her flames, but the pressure of time made her mana sloppy.

"Please forgive me," she repeated while she worked quickly.

The moment his wrist was free, Kaine's giant form dropped closer to the ground, hanging limp from one wrist.

One more chain to go.

Sophie tried not to sob at the state that her soulmate's body was in. How was he even alive?

Pulling the chair up for assistance again, she melted the last chain that held his wrist. Kaine slumped to the ground in a heavy heap.

And as he hit the floor, a giant ancient Fae symbol burned bright red against the wall he'd just been freed from.

"That can't be good." Sophie gulped.

Zala launched herself into the air and off the castle walls, like the lethal assassin she was. She flipped into the centre of the onslaught where her friends were slowly being outnumbered. She landed in a superhero crouch, shadows dancing all around her.

"Glad you could join us!" Cam panted as he plunged his short spear deep into the guts of a guard that charged at him.

Zala blasted the remaining guards down with a shot of her shadows and that silenced them completely.

A slow clap sounded through the courtyard.

"Well done, my Elite." The shrill voice of the queen never failed to give them shivers. The blood-red queen waltzed across the courtyard, over bodies, limbs and groaning men, as if she were out for a morning stroll. "You've proven yourselves." She smiled.

"We have nothing to prove to you." Elowan gritted through her teeth, Cam and Zala steady by her side.

"Be that as it may, you have still proven yourselves"—she kicked and stomped down the hand of one of the guards that reached for her—"fools." The queen smiled brightly at her Elite. She was a cruel, twisted beast.

Ellie stilled. They'd downed most of the queen's forces and maintained a distraction, causing the queen to reveal herself here while Sophie made way with Kaine. They'd won.

"You forget I have decades and centuries on you all. I can smell a distraction from a mile away." The queen laughed, swishing the skirts of her gown on the blood pooling at her feet for fun.

They stood their ground. She was bluffing. Surely.

"I'd hurry, if I were you." The queen waltzed with an imaginary dance partner over the bodies of her fallen men, humming a haunted tune. It was a twisted sight.

Ellie didn't hesitate.

Together they ran for Sophie and Kaine, hoping to the almighty gods that they weren't too late.

"I am centuries old, boy. Do not take that tone with me!" Felipina's voice echoed. The guards had made it into the antechamber of the queen's suite. They only had to bust through the last door to the queen's room to find Sophie, but Felipina stood in their way.

Fuck. The spell must have triggered the guards. Come on, Sophie, focus. Point A. Point B. Traverse the Between and go.

She needed to portal herself and Kaine to the edge of Fyllera. From there they'd need to ride back to the safe house. Regin and his family had left horses for them in the forest to use. When Alston was banished from the castle, he'd fortified his home with his mana so that the queen could not seek him out and hurt his family again. The boundary he created was strong enough to stop anyone from portalling in and out. You could portal within the mana bubble all you wanted, but if you wanted to portal elsewhere, you needed to step outside the boundary. It was why they needed to travel out far enough from the property to portal to Castle Terrin.

Gathering Kaine's limp body in her arms, she tried to open a portal just like how she practised with Zala.

Make it fast, Sophie. But she couldn't. Her heart was racing and the sight of Kaine's battered body left her mind in a complete jumble.

Focus.

"You shall not pass!" Felipina bellowed. It sounded like she'd launched herself at the group of guards. A few groans and shouts sounded from the men.

Focus, Sophie, come on. Felipina is centuries old, she can handle herself.

Sophie took three deep breaths and reached into the mana that she was still trying to learn. It felt slippery between her fingers, unstable.

Felipina's battle cry sent Sophie's adrenalin into another dimension she never knew existed.

The sounds of fighting seized. Silence.

"Take that, old bitch," a male voice sneered.

No. Felipina. Sophie sobbed as she tried gathering Kaine in her arms.

The sound of angry guards grew louder and louder. They were gaining on the room where Sophie held Kaine.

Pull your head in, Sophie.

The guards rammed the bedroom door open.

Shards of wood spun through the air having chipped away on impact.

The approaching guards should have scared her.

But all Sophie could do was look past them.

To the floor.

Where Sophie caught a glimpse of Felipina's form laying still on the ground, covered in blood.

The royal guards ran at Sophie, shouting and screaming something. She couldn't hear them through all the adrenaline pumping through her ears. It felt like her head was dunked in water. A high-pitched tone rang through her entire being.

With an anger so pure and bright, Sophie portalled herself and Kaine out of the queen's quarters without so much as a thought.

"Felipina." Elowan gasped at the older fae female whose still form lay on the ground, covered violently in blood. She'd cared for the Elite like they were her own children. Ellie didn't need to feel her pulse to know that she'd died – a painful death at that. She crouched down low, softly closing Felipina's eyes that were still furrowed in anger. "May the gods guide you to your eternal rest and happiness in the Elysian Fields," Ellie whispered, kissing Felipina's eyelids.

"Sophie's not here. Neither is Kaine. She must've made it out in time." Cam surveyed.

"Let's hope to the fucking gods she did. The Fates would have a damned hissy fit otherwise," Ellie said grimly.

"Let's not waste any more time." Zala quickly opened a portal to the edge of Fyllera, motioning Elowan and Cam to get in.

Sophie crashed through her portal and dived straight into the safe house's dining room. She cradled Kaine's head in her lap.

"Help!" Sophie sobbed.

Regin came bursting in through the back door, looking between Sophie and Kaine like they'd just appeared out of nowhere. Well, technically they did.

Uncle Alston and Aunt Alfre came rushing from the kitchen to see what the commotion was about.

"Mother of Faery!" Alfre gasped at the sight of Kaine's limp body and ran around the cottage to gather supplies.

Regin quickly cleared the dining table and helped Sophie lift Kaine's form onto it.

Alfre came back with supplies. As if she'd done this a million times before, she placed a bucket beside the table, placing Kaine's left hand above it. She sliced his wrist.

"What are you doing?!" Sophie screamed. Regin held Sophie back.

"Cousin, it is okay. We must drain his blood of the iron so we can quickly heal him with our mana," he assured her.

Sophie nodded through her tears in understanding. She stepped out of Regin's hold to hold Kaine's hand. Oh, how she missed the feel of his skin on hers.

Uncle Alston raked his hands through his hair, his face screwed in worry. Alston signed to Sophie. Hurriedly. Urgently.

Sophie looked to Regin for an interpretation. Before he spoke, he tensed his jaw. "Sophie, how did you get through his mana boundary?" Concern laced his words like poison.

Sophie's eyes widened. The mana boundary. No one was supposed to be able to portal in or out of the safe house.

"I... I..." Sophie stuttered through her tears. She was unsure how she managed to override its power.

Her uncle took a knee before her, bracing her arms with his hands and signed. A little more animatedly this time.

"Father, please, she's upset." Regin came in, placing a hand on his father's shoulder and helped him up from the floor. Regin took a deep breath. "He wants to know if you at least covered your tracks. You did, right?"

A sense of fear shook Sophie to her core. She wasn't even thinking. She felt such hot rage and anguish that she just portalled straight to the safe house. She didn't think it would be possible considering the mana boundary Alston had fortified over decades but somehow...

Alston nodded in understanding, placing a firm hand on Regin's shoulder, and his other hand on Sophie's. Regin smiled, nodding to his father then turned to Sophie with a sad smile. "It is okay, dear cousin. Whatever arrives on our doorstep, we shall face together. As a family." He was attempting to make her feel better, but Sophie could tell a morsel of fear had nestled its way into their hearts.

Anxiety clawed through her chest as Sophie realised what she'd done. In her blinding fear and anger of what had been done to Kaine, along with Felipina's sacrifice, she was barely even thinking. She'd portalled straight for the safe house instead of the edge of Fyllera where they had horses waiting. She didn't think it was possible, but by the Fates she did and in doing so, she'd damned her entire family. She'd accidentally lead the queen straight to their doorstep. The queen they'd been hiding from for years.

Sadness, anger and guilt punched her right in the gut. *I'm such a fucking idiot.* Sophie closed her eyes in frustration as hot tears rolled down her face.

They didn't deserve this. None of them did.

53

Kaine woke with a violent start, gasping for free-flowing air he hadn't felt in a long time. His mouth was no longer stuffed with cotton and he didn't feel like his chest was taut from being hung up against the wall.

A soft hand tucked his hair behind his ears. He hadn't felt such soft hands in so long, he instinctively leaned into the familiar touch.

Sophie. Kaine growled.

"Woah, down boy." Sophie laughed.

Kaine opened his eyes to see Sophie in one piece. His Sophie. She wasn't in Sotera, she was here with him. His heart soared right out of his chest at the thought. Everything felt clearer. His body was no longer sore or itching from scabs and his wrists and ankles were no longer restricted. He pulled her into the tightest hug he could muster, burying his face into her hair. He would never let go. Never. This was real, right?

The thought pulled him to a stop. He quickly pulled back as if he'd been burned. He looked at his hands, then back at Sophie. Was this one of the queen's illusions?

"It's okay, I'm here. I'm real. See?" Sophie pulled his hand to cup her cheek. She felt real. She smelled real, but the dreams felt real too.

Kaine nodded, slowly. This was real. It had to be.

Cam burst into the dining room, arms outstretched. "It's good to see you, boss!" He embraced Kaine like a long-lost brother. Elowan and Zala followed closely behind, embracing him, sharing smiles as they beheld Kaine in one piece.

Kaine cleared his throat. "It's good to be back." He allowed himself to smile. He had no idea how long he'd been held captive for. He had no way of knowing if he had truly escaped or if his friends before him were real. He had no other choice but to give in to it.

"Now that you're awake, we need to move," Elowan announced. "The queen could be hot on our tails and we'll need to lay low while we gather forces and recoup your mana." She pointed at Kaine. "Let's knock the bitch off her throne once and for all," Elowan declared with determination.

"You can't," Kaine groaned. The group instantly whipped their heads towards him. "Not yet. I can confirm that the queen has allied with Terr. They're planning to take over Faery. Together," Kaine said, squeezing Sophie's hand.

"You're certain? I'm assuming it's a takeover of the hostile kind?" Elowan hissed.

"Indeed. They're planning to wipe out any fae who denies their union," Kaine said grimly.

"No one would support that. He's killed thousands of fae with his hellhounds. And once news of the queen and her betrayal hits the courts, there will be an outright war in our lands. The people will revolt," Elowan thought aloud, raking her hands through her hair.

Cam seemed to pale.

"It's why we need to gather forces immediately. They're calling it The Purge. I don't know when it'll happen, but I can only imagine it will be soon. Terr wants Faery and no one's going to be strong enough to stop him..." Kaine looked at Sophie, squeezing her hand. "Except us."

Sophie nodded meekly.

They would need to officiate their soulmate bond and share the strong power currently housed inside her, so that they could kill the queen and Terr. And they'd need to do it soon. Time was not on their side.

54

It was their third night in Wrenntia. The lack of fae citizens made it a good place for them to lay low while they schemed and recouped their energy.

During the day they'd send letters, calling in favours from the royals of every court and every notable citizen, warning as many as they could about the looming attack by Queen Calliea and Terr.

By night, they'd discuss schemes and manoeuvres. While they had enough mana to overthrow the queen herself, they didn't know Terr's true power nor the size of his forces. They were going in blind. But for Faery, they had no other choice but to fight with their heads held high.

Sophie lay next to Kaine on the rooftop. A thin layer of snow dusted across the streets below and the warm yellow lamps glowed, reminding Sophie of a Swedish town in winter. They'd spend most nights watching the stars, holding each other. Since his time under the queen's torture, Kaine had an aversion to sleeping – Sophie understood why.

When they arrived in Wrenntia, he explained what happened, how he was tortured and the hallucinations he'd been fed. Sophie marvelled at his strength. If she were in his position, she'd have a mental breakdown every minute. But here he was, calm and focused on what needed to be done.

"Have you given it another thought?" Kaine asked, circling swirls on her open palm. He'd asked her every day if she were ready to go before a high priestess to officiate their soulmate bond and each day she said she'd think about it. The truth was, Sophie was torn. She had a life back in Sotera, a life she hadn't had the opportunity to mourn over now that she was fae. And as much as she wanted to love Kaine wholeheartedly, she felt like she was still healing from her past trauma. She wasn't ready to commit, despite what their mating bond symbolised.

Despite all this, she felt an obligation to a realm she'd only just learnt existed. While memories of Faery cropped up, it was Sotera she grew up in, but by some twisted fate it was Faery's people that she'd be turning her back on if she didn't oblige the Fates. She felt trapped. It was either choose the fate of an entire realm and lose herself, or it was choose herself and damn an entire realm.

Kaine paused at her silent response. "Faery needs you. I need you, Sophie."

"I know." Sophie swallowed as a pain started to rise in her throat. She hated this feeling. Like she was being cornered. Now more than ever she wanted to see her mother. Danna had always been wise – a calming presence that always knew what to do in the hardest of situations.

"Come on, we can go to the temple tonight. The priestess will bless us and merge our powers." Kaine sat up, pulling Sophie up with him by her wrists.

"I'm not ready, you know that." Sophie tried to smile through the panic that rose in her chest.

"I know that, but Faery depends on you. Faery and all its people are hinging on this one decision of yours."

"How can you put that pressure on me?"

"It's not pressure, Sophie. It's common sense. It's for the greater good." He held her wrist tighter. "I know you're hesitant now, but the truth is that we're soulmates. We're already bound together by the Fates. Why are you fighting it?" His unexpected anger rose, tightening his grip around her wrist even further.

The truth was that Sophie didn't know why she was fighting it. All roads led to Kaine but a small voice in her head told her that he wasn't her destiny. She couldn't shake the hesitation no matter how hard she tried.

"I'm fighting it because I'll lose all that I am. All that I know!" Sophie's eyes pricked with tears.

Since their arrival in Wrenntia this was how they spent their nights. Kaine had developed an obsession and unreasonable urgency in getting their bond officiated. It was nonsensical. They hadn't even gathered all their forces or developed a concrete plan of attack, yet this was all Kaine pushed for.

"You won't. You have me! You'll save Faery. How can you not see that?" Kaine gripped her wrist tighter. "How can you be so selfish?"

Sophie wrenched her wrist from his grip.

"How can I be so selfish? Are you kidding me? I am ALLOWED to be selfish because the prophecy involves ME and funnily enough, I didn't ask for it to be me." Sophie fumed, matching his fire with hers.

Sophie stomped off towards the rooftop door. She didn't want to argue with Kaine any further.

"Get back here, Sophie, I'm not done talking to you!" Kaine threatened.

Sophie stopped, pausing mid step. "I'm over it, Kaine. I don't want to argue anymore," she said softly, defeated.

"You are my soulmate. You are MY fated. We are doing this no matter how you feel. The Fates have decided as much," Kaine said, a touch calmer than he'd been just a moment ago.

His words rubbed her the wrong way. They were fated, fine. But in all the books she'd read this was not how she imagined the soulmate bond to be. She imagined it being a force that lay her bare, a love so strong that she'd give up her entire life for. But that was not how she felt at all.

She wanted to love him, but deep in her heart it didn't feel right. It didn't feel whole. And given his blatant disregard of her feelings over the past few nights, Sophie couldn't help but feel that this was all wrong. She felt insane. Everyone pushed her towards this union, arguing logic, but when she pushed back they condemned her selfishness. That wasn't the case at all. She was trying to just figure it all out. She was just a girl from Melbourne, she had no experience in being fated to someone, a princess that never was, or a key part of any prophecy.

"Damn the Fates. For all I know, you're not even my soulmate!" Sophie really shouldn't have said it, but she did. They didn't have matching tattoos like every other couple had and she couldn't hear his thoughts. When Sophie expressed her concerns, Kaine had argued that it would snap in place at some point. And as their arguments escalated with each night, she couldn't help but feel like the tell-tale signs of their soulmate bond simply wouldn't snap into place at all.

She felt unbelievably angry with him. With the world. With her mother. With everyone.

Sophie made to storm off, but Kaine quickly seized her arm, pulling her back to him. He kissed her, angrily, forcefully. Sophie pushed him away.

"How dare you say those words? You are my mine. I don't care what anyone says," he panted, letting go of her.

Sophie walked away, tears streaming down her face.

55

"That's all we know." Kaine poured over the makeshift map of Faery he had made and the skeleton crew that sat around it.

Sophie, Cam, Ellie and Zala stared blankly at the map.

Despite various hallucinations and ministrations, Kaine was certain that the queen had formed a partnership with the Shadow Realm king. He'd heard whispers of conversations between the queen and Terr's demons, whispers that confirmed the queen had long been providing Terr the blood of Faery youth for various reasons – one being the elixirs for her eternal youth.

Despite her righteous fight for Faery, the queen in all her selfishness and wickedness was giving Faery up to Terr himself. She was going to let him sit on the throne but what Kaine failed to grasp was her end game. What did she want to achieve out of this all? The people of Faery were going to wither and the land with it.

They understood Terr's thirst for power, but what did he offer the queen? Perhaps he offered her a piece of the Shadow Realm? There were so many questions left to be answered and zero ways to find the answers to them. The crew were stumped with no resources and pending alliances.

"We're fucked." Cam harrumphed from where he sat, elbows braced on his knees.

Silence.

In an irrational rage so sudden, Kaine flipped the table, breathing heavily as if he were possessed. He made a beeline to Camrine, the promise of death etched across his face. Camrine leaned precariously back in his chair with Kaine's face within inches of his, his hand wrapped tightly around Camrine's neck.

The entire room shot to their feet with lightning fae speed.

Sophie was the first to reach Kaine. "You're not hallucinating. Come back to me," she said firmly, repeatedly, trying to wedge herself between the two males.

Since his return, Kaine had moments where he couldn't decipher what was real and what was a hallucination. There'd be moments where he'd be within inches of killing one of his friends and sometimes Sophie. And it was only the sound of Sophie's voice that could ground him. Only her.

The sound of her soft lilting voice echoed through his mind, a calm to the roaring rage inside of him. His vision started to clear and before him, he saw the face of his red-headed brethren – stern but calm. Understanding even. Pitying, perhaps.

Kaine loosened his grip, realising that Sophie was right. This was real. It wasn't a hallucination that the queen orchestrated to manipulate his mind.

Shame, sorrow and helplessness washed over him.

Kaine shook his head, trying to dispel the haze that had just washed over him. "I'm-I'm so sorry..." He quickly turned on his feet and rushed out of the war room.

Sophie watched as he left, worry etched over her face. She looked apologetically towards Cam who sat silently, soothing his neck. Ellie and Zala sat alert, hands ready to launch their short spears as if Kaine were going to rush back.

"I'll go check on him," Sophie said to no one in particular. Her heart ached for Kaine. He was broken, no matter how much he denied it. He was severely broken. And even though she was still trying to figure herself out, a part of her soul she never quite understood promised to pick up the pieces for him. However many pieces there were.

56

"You seem distant. Are you okay?" Elowan asked.

Sophie, Cam and Ellie sat together by the town river, breathing in the much-needed fresh air. They'd spent the morning writing correspondences to the royals that had accepted their call for aid and discussed more war tactics. It was a heavy topic for the morning, but they needed to keep their plan moving.

"I'm fine," Sophie wasn't. Kaine had given her the cold shoulder all morning after their heated debate on the rooftop. She already felt sick given the looming war they were prepping for, but Kaine's avoidance made her even more sick to the stomach.

"Well that's the biggest lie I've heard all day. I can see the steam coming out of your damn ears!" Cam pointed at Sophie. It made her smile. Just a little. "Ah there she is, our beloved Sophie." Sophie grabbed a handful of muddy snow and slapped it in Cam's face. For all his centuries of training, nothing had prepared him for that.

"Oh, you did not. You've just unleashed the snowball kraken." Cam hefted a snowball back in her face.

Sophie stood from where she sat. "Game on, mole."

Grabbing another hand full of snow, she pretended to throw it at Cam but launched it right in Ellie's face instead.

Ellie gasped dramatically.

An all-out snowball fight ensued.

Sophie ducked and weaved.

They all laughed and laughed as they threw snowball after snowball. It was a nice respite from the gloom they'd carried since Kaine's rescue.

Cam had taken cover behind a bench, while Ellie and Sophie ganged up on him. He held his hands up in surrender. "I yield! I yield!" Cam shouted from behind the bench. He slowly rose from the ground. "NOT!" He belt-fed the snowballs he'd been hoarding right into Ellie and Sophie.

"Take cover!" Sophie yelled, laughing all the while. They both slid behind the bench across from Cam's, piling up snow to block his onslaught.

"Surrender before it's too late, you honourless bastard!" Ellie shouted from their fort. They made hundreds of snowballs with their fae speed, readying their attack on Cam. Sophie pushed her sleeves up her arms so she could work a touch faster.

Elowan paused her snowball making suddenly.

"Come on, Ellie, we need to make more!" Sophie laughed.

But Elowan did not make more.

"Who did this to you?" Elowan stopped Sophie's hands, holding them in hers.

Bruises wrapped around Sophie's wrist and on her forearm, a giant bruise in the shape of a hand marred her skin.

Instantly ashamed, Sophie pulled her hands from Ellie's grip and pushed her damp sleeves down to where they were. Sophie swallowed hard.

"What happened, Sophie? You can tell me. I will never judge you," Elowan said comfortingly, moving closer to Sophie to embrace her.

As soon as Ellie embraced her, Sophie bawled her eyes out. She felt an immense pressure from her chest release as she leaned into Ellie's comforting embrace. This was what she needed right now. Someone to just hold her and tell her it would all be okay, even if it wasn't going to be. The truth was that she felt ashamed. She felt embarrassed that she allowed herself to be hurt by the one person who wasn't meant to hurt her. She felt embarrassed that she didn't have the strength in herself to walk away.

Cam ran to Sophie's side at the sound of her crying. "What's the matter?" Cam knelt beside her, resting a hand on her back as she sobbed.

Sophie bowed her head in her hands, defeated. "I can't take the pressure anymore." She cried into her hands.

Ellie and Cam looked at each other with concern.

"Honey, what do you mean by pressure?" Ellie urged, rubbing Sophie's upper arm.

"Everything. This oncoming war. Me being Kaine's fated. I'm not cut out for this at all, I'm just a girl from Melbourne who's still trying to figure out who she is!" Sophie sobbed uncontrollably now, her feelings compounded from last night's argument with Kaine and his avoidance this morning.

"Sophie, we are here for you. You came into Faery guns blazing and you've learnt the basics of mana as if it were the ABCs. No one's ever done that in the amount of time you have. We believe in you, and you don't have to do anything you don't want to," Cam assured her.

Sophie cried even harder at Cam's admission. She didn't feel worthy of their belief or support at all. Deep down she knew she couldn't do this. She'd gone through so much in her past relationships to know when something wasn't right. She owed it to herself to put herself first... even if it meant damning an entire realm.

Sophie pulled Cam and Ellie into a hug. Sniffling. "You mean so much to me. Thanks guys..." Sophie cleared her throat, wiping her tears away. She stood up slowly from where she sat. "I... just need to go for a walk. Alone," Sophie clarified.

"Are you sure you don't want us to come with you?" Ellie asked, pulling herself up from the ground as well.

Sophie nodded through the tears. Turning, she slowly walked away from Ellie and Cam - into Wrenntia's town centre.

Ellie and Cam watched as she walked away.

"She had bruises," Ellie admitted.

"What do you mean?" Cam's brows furrowed.

"Dark, painful ones, all over her wrist and arm. I can only imagine it's to do with their nightly arguments," Ellie explained.

"That fucking bastard... you can't do that to your fated." Cam sneered, visible anger rising in his chest. He moved to confront Kaine back at their quarters.

Ellie grabbed him before he could move any farther. "Leave it Cam. He's been through enough. Let them sort it out themselves." She met his eyes, so much like hers.

He gave her an incredulous look. Shaking his head, he walked after Sophie instead.

57

It had been several days since Kaine had spoken to her. Sophie felt like no matter what she did, it was wrong. Every tactic she offered in their scheming, he argued. It was so unlike the Kaine she knew prior to capture. He was cold, cruel and he lacked the vulnerability she fell in love with. He was an entirely different person. Despite this change, their fate remained the same.

Sophie found him in the war room by himself, poring over the map they'd made of Faery. Since they'd camped up in Wrenntia, they had no updates from their contacts on the queen's movements. Everything seemed normal, which made them even more antsy.

Slowly, she padded across the room to him. Without a word, she wrapped her arms around his waist and leaned into his back. "I'm sorry," she whispered.

He tensed at the words, paused, then relaxed into her embrace. "No, I'm sorry. I shouldn't have laid a hand on you." He turned in her embrace, wrapping his arms around her shoulders. They stood like that for a moment. Leaning into the touch they'd deprived each other of the last few days. "Sophie, you are my fated and I understand that you've grown up in a completely different realm where that concept doesn't exist, but to me, it means everything," he said, brushing her hair away from her face. "I said it before and I'll say it again, I would start a war for you." Kaine kissed her with a possessive fierceness Sophie had never felt before. She breathed him in, surrendering her entire being to him.

"And I you," she breathed. As the words left her mouth, she didn't know if she meant them. She just didn't want to say the wrong thing anymore.

"Come, I've a surprise for you." Kaine smiled brightly. Grabbing her hand, he pulled her out of the warmth of their quarters and onto the cold streets of Wrenntia. Sophie's heart melted at the sight of his smile. Since he'd come back to them, he barely smiled, if at all.

He pulled her through the streets of Wrenntia, remarking every building and their history, all the while holding her hand tightly. As if at any moment, she'd disappear into another realm.

They stopped in front of the temple where fae citizens would have gone to worship all the gods of Faery. Everything was made of marble, from the high pillars that lined the walls to the statues of all the gods. They were carved into different fighting positions and poses. Her favourite was the goddess of Faery who was carved holding a faceless child, her arm braced in front of her to stop her unseen enemies. It was a fierce statue.

Kaine pulled her to the other end of the temple where there was an open-air viewing platform.

She marvelled at the sight before her. The perfect juxtaposition of enchantment and sorrow. Faery was beautiful, more beautiful than she could ever imagine it to be. Below them was the winding river that sprawled through the entirety of Wrenntia. The empty river that spliced the entire Winter Court itself in half. The only living entity in a dark, decaying court. It served as a reminder that all was not well in Faery.

In the distance, she could make out the small lights in Fyllera. The double rings of the Faery moon cast a warm blanket of light all over the town. The stars danced with wild abandon. How could she damn an entire realm this beautiful? How could she put herself before all of this? She couldn't. She didn't have the heart to. She couldn't abandon Faery, even if it meant her soul would never quite feel at peace.

"I used to look at the night sky and think its beauty was unmatched..." Kaine whispered against her ear. He held her around the waist as they watched Faery before them. "And then you fell on top of me," he purred into her ear.

Sophie laughed at the memory. She remembered how stunned she was when she first met him and how drawn to him she was. It felt like it had been years since they'd first met.

"Take us back to simpler days I say..." Sophie leaned her head back into Kaine's large chest.

He pulled her around to face him. He grasped her face between his hands and something like pain or regret washed over his face. "I love you Sophie, with all my heart. So please understand why I brought you here today." He smiled softly.

Confused, Sophie furrowed her brows. She was about to ask why when a high priestess entered her line of sight.

The high priestess's skin was alabaster, her silver hair pulled back in a tight braid. She wore a silver chiton and a small veil that shaded her eyes.

Shocked, Sophie snapped an accusing stare at Kaine.

He held her in place with his strong arms as the priestess moved closer to them.

"It is my understanding that you two would like to officiate your soulmate bond," the priestess said happily.

Sophie saw red.

Kaine hissed as Sophie set her entire body aflame.

She whirled to face him with the anger of a thousand suns. "How dare you force me into this?" She pointed an angry finger at him.

"You are my fated, Sophie. Don't you understand? How DARE you deny me?!" he rebutted, meeting her with unmatched fervour.

That angered Sophie even more. If he truly loved her, he wouldn't force her into a situation she didn't feel comfortable in. He wouldn't be yelling at her. He wouldn't have ignored her for several days. That was not what love was. It was the opposite. It was torture, manipulation, it was anything but what love was supposed to be. Utterly broken-hearted by the realisation, Sophie ran from the temple, tears spilling from her eyes.

It was poetic really. This was how she came to Faery, crying and in despair. She thought she was made whole again after meeting Kaine but here she was, broken again. How many times would it take for her to fall apart before she was permanently damaged? She couldn't take this anymore. This was her rock bottom. This was no way to live. She deserved more. She deserved to be treated like a human being – one with needs, thoughts and feelings that were valued and valid.

Sophie ran through the streets of Wrenntia, the cold ripping against her tear-slicked cheeks. She burst into the apartment they were all staying in, hyperventilating and sobbing.

Elowan and Zala had gone to Fyllera to gather more food, so Cam stayed behind to mind their quarters and pore over tactics.

Cam shot up from where he sat and ran to Sophie. "Dear gods, what happened?" He grabbed Sophie by the shoulders. She was so hysterical she couldn't even string a sentence together. Her heart and throat ached deeply as she tried to calm herself down.

Sophie took three deep breaths before she attempted to speak again. "He"–sniffle–"tried to force"–sniffle–"to officiate our bond." Sophie managed to blurt out between tears.

Camrine looked like he needed to flip a godsdamn table. "Listen to me, Sophie. No one can treat my friend like this. In all my two-hundred years of life, I've never heard soulmates hurting each other the way Kaine does you. If anything, it's outright impossible to hurt your mate emotionally or physically. The queen must have royally fucked up his brain if he thinks this is acceptable." His voice shook with anger. Cam grabbed his short spear from where it rested on the table and stormed out of their apartment.

Sophie chased after him. "Where are you going?!"

"To have a strong word the bastard that dared hurt my friend," Cam shouted in response. Sophie tried to stop him but he portalled himself to the temple with unnerving speed.

Sophie tried to get to the temple to stop him through a portal of her own making before Cam did. She wasn't fast enough.

Jumping out of the portal ahead of her, Cam prowled towards Kaine who stood along the viewing platform of the temple.

Kaine swirled at the sudden presence behind him.

"How fucking dare you lay a hand on her." Cam sneered, pushing Kaine back into the railing. Cam's short spear pressed dangerously close to Kaine's throat.

"Cam, don't. Please," Sophie urged. She didn't want this to happen. As much as her heart was broken, she didn't want anyone getting hurt.

Kaine looked from Sophie then back to Cam. A fury so rabid and rancid snarled across his face. He pushed Cam violently off him. "You're fucking her, aren't you?" Kaine pointed at Cam with an accusing finger, his face screwed up with a frightening amount of disgust. His eyes glazed over as if he saw some sort of flashback or hallucination. "You've been fucking her behind my back. I knew it wasn't a hallucination!"

"What the fuck is wrong with you? No, you bastard!" Cam shouted, whacking Kaine's finger away from his face.

Kaine turned to Sophie with murder in his eyes. "That's why you don't want to officiate our bond isn't it? You've been fucking this Fylleran filth this whole time." He prowled towards Sophie like a predator, promising death. "Admit it, you fucking whore!" he bellowed into her face.

Anger pierced through her so violently. The accusations he flung her way were a backhand to her very existence. It couldn't have been farther from the truth.

"Why would I admit to something that is blatantly not true! You've lost your fucking mind!" she shouted back in his face.

"You lie!" Kaine struck her across the face with such brutal force that Sophie fell to the floor. Sophie froze, looking up at Kaine who seethed with such anger. Pain rippled across her face as her heart broke into a thousand irreparable pieces.

Cam ran at Kaine, spearing him to the ground, punching him with all his might as they crashed onto the floor.

Kaine pushed him off with his mana, flinging Cam into the air. Cam fell to floor with a crunch but to his credit, pushed himself up immediately, taking on a fierce fighting position.

"We settle this like real men." Cam breathed while wiping the blood off his face.

A bright light appeared in the middle of the temple. A portal appeared with Elowan and Zala jumping out. "We heard shout— STOP!" Ellie shouted. She quickly moved to put herself between Cam and Kaine. "We are all friends. We need not argue." It was at that moment that Ellie noticed Sophie on the ground, cupping her swollen cheek. Ellie pierced an accusatory glare towards Kaine. "What did you do?!" she shouted.

"Get out of my way, Ellie. This is between Cam and I," Kaine commanded.

"I will not." Elowan stood her ground, chest puffed, raising her hands between the two males wanting to duke it out.

Without a word, Kaine backhanded her and flung her across the room with a show of his mana. Elowan shrieked in pain as she crunched to the floor.

Zala ran to her aid.

"You fucking asshole! We should have let you rot with the queen!" Cam slammed his fist into Kaine's face. They fell to the floor grappling each other, pounding each other with unearthly violence.

Sobbing, Sophie ran to them to pull the two apart but as she came close enough, she was flung back by an invisible force. She slammed her fists on the forcefield that Kaine had created around him and Cam, to stop anyone from getting any closer.

"Please! Stop!" Sophie pounded against the forcefield of air.

They didn't. They kept beating each other. Blood sprayed in all sorts of directions and the sound of bone crunching rang through the temple.

Kaine managed to get an upper hand on Cam, straddling him and rained down punches like his life depended on it.

Sophie's pleas were futile.

Elowan had been knocked unconscious and Zala was busy healing her.

"Please. Stop. I don't want anyone hurt." Sophie cried, sinking to the floor, blocked out by Kaine's forcefield.

Sophie's breath caught.

The air around her stilled.

A ringing sounded in her ears.

Her entire body froze.

Kaine's hands lifted in the air, and what lay between his palms glinted in the moonlight.

With a rage so violent, Kaine wedged his short spear into Cam's immortal heart with a brutal crunch.

"NO!" Sophie shrieked with such force that temple windows shattered. The voice was not hers. It was layered. Unearthly. Powerful.

Sophie watched through tears as Cam sputtered out blood, trying his best to claw Kaine's hand from where he continued to push all his weight into the short spear.

The sight was sickening.

Sophie slammed and slammed her hands against the forcefield. Screaming. Wanting more than anything to turn back time.

"Fuck... you..." Cam breathed his final breath, snarling at his so-called brother in arms. His body went limp.

Sophie cried with such fierceness as her friend's body turned a ghastly grey and his beautiful green eyes turned milky white.

Kaine leaned down closer to Cam's face. "You stopped being a real man the moment you fucked her," he breathed into Cam's ears. Then, and only then, did Kaine bring down his invisible shield.

Sophie ran to push Kaine off her dearest friend's body. She cried and cried. This couldn't be real. Her friend was dead and for what? Standing up for her, when really she should have stood up for herself? Guilt racked her entire body as she sobbed over Cam.

Kaine dared to grab her wrist, attempting to pull her away.

"Don't fucking touch me, you piece of shit!" Sophie screamed with all her might, wrenching her wrist from his grip. A force field of mana enveloped her entire body and Cam's. Light glowed from her eyes and fists as she pinned her death stare towards Kaine. She blasted him with unfettered power, pinning him to the ground. Winds so violent pushed through the temple, forcing everyone down to the ground as well. Zala shielded Elowan who stirred from where she lay on the floor.

"It's over. He's gone. All you have left is me!" Kaine strained, trying to shout over the wind.

Sophie's hair glowed and levitated all around her while she faced Kaine. A crown of fire formed atop her head. In that same layered voice so powerful, she said, "I will never be with someone like you." She lifted her hand in front of her to blast him again.

Kaine cowered where he was on the ground as a giant ball of light grew in her hands.

Her vision began to blur, and the light all around her began to dim.

No. Not now.

She felt it. Her mana was guttering out. She'd used too much, too quickly. Her body wasn't used to it and now it was shutting down.

Not now.

Sophie wailed in absolute agony. Over the friends who'd been hurt and killed. She wept for herself. For her love lost. For the Kaine she once knew and the male he was now. For the realm she'd just damned to hell. She looked up at the sleeping sun that was carved into the temple ceiling and prayed to all the gods that they'd take her out of this place. She didn't want to be here anymore.

The forceful winds that held everyone down to the ground eased.

Kaine took that moment to move towards Sophie.

Thunder rumbled violently outside the temple. The sound echoed and bounced across the walls.

Sophie collapsed on Cam's body, completely burnt out in mana and mind.

Before Kaine could reach her a lightning bolt so bright flung him back into a wall.

Her vision began to fuzz, and her ears started to ring.

Sophie felt an unearthly, powerful presence enter the room.

Kaine's voice sounded so distant now, like she'd been placed in a glass room. He shouted colourful profanities that Sophie couldn't decipher over the ringing that pierced her ears.

Darkness beckoned her to come closer.

She felt strong arms pick her up with ease from where she lay, a familiar scent of sandalwood washed over her. She leaned into the arms that felt like home.

Lighting and thunder struck as she felt herself being lifted into the air.

A gentle masculine voice sounded in her ear like a lullaby she longed to hear. "You are safe now, my queen. No one will hurt you again," the male said.

THIS STORY WILL CONTINUE...

BEYOND TWO REALMS.

Want to sneak peek of book two?

I left you on a cliffhanger. I know, I'm sorry (sort of).

Sign up to download the first chapter of book two for FREE.

Enjoy this book?

Or better yet, want to make me cry?

Leave a review.
I'll cry happy tears knowing that someone's taken their time to read my work.
Every review helps.

Amazon

Goodreads

ACKNOWLEDGMENTS

Well, colour me pink and consider me speechless. You made it! We made it!

Writing *Between Two Realms* was an epic adventure within itself. All of which I could not have done without you, my readers. Thanks for jumping onto this rollercoaster of emotions with me. I've poured some personal experiences into this story and I hope you enjoyed the ride.

To my editor Kat Betts who has unmeasured patience and skill. I am still amazed by your tenacity and did I mention patience? This book would not be what it is without you. Heck, I wouldn't be either.

A huge thank you to Beck from WHIMSY Book Cover Graphics, who designed the cover of this novel. The ability to express my work and dreams into a stunning cover is a wondrous super power.

To my Spicy Book Club, thank you for your support and words of encouragement. I can't wait to write more ridiculous cliffhangers so you can be angry at me again. It's truly an honour to be living in the world of fantasy with you.

To my husband and my two hellhounds, thanks for listening to my incessant, dramatic retellings of scenes that you never asked for. I appreciate it.

Lastly, to me. Well done mate.

ABOUT AUTHOR

Mazrine L Amaris is the Vietnamese-Australian author of the epic fantasy series *Between Two Realms*.

Based in Melbourne, Australia, she's only here to have fun. She's a creative at heart who enjoys writing stories she wants to read and making music she wants to escape to.

The pandemic catapulted her desire to dream up a story worth reading. Weaved with her lived experiences, a bit of magic and a pinch of spice, *Between Two Realms* is her debut novel that she hopes will be a world worth escaping to.

Keep in touch:
Instagram: @mazrinelamaris
Facebook: @mazrinelamaris
TikTok: @mazrinelamaris
Website: www.mazrinelamaris.com